ROSIE THOMAS is the a........ novels, including the best............... and Ruby. Once she was established as a writer, she discovered a love of travelling and mountaineering. She has climbed in the Alps and the Himalayas, competed in the Peking to Paris car rally, spent time on a tiny Bulgarian research station in Antarctica and travelled the Silk Road through Asia. She lives in London.

For more information on Rosie Thomas, please visit www.rosiethomas.co.uk.

PRAISE FOR ROSIE THOMAS

'Her evocation . . . touches on the variances and nuances of love between men and women, and the power of family relationships to destroy lives'   ELIZABETH BUCHAN, *Daily Mail*

'Thomas can write with ravishing sensuality'
KATE SAUNDERS, *The Times*

'Rosie Thomas writes so beautifully about the feelings of people in war, the imminence of death and the importance of passionate and romantic love'

DAME TANNI GREY-THOMPSON

'Honest and absorbing, Rosie Thomas mixes the bitter and the hopeful with the knowledge that the human heart is far more complicated than any rule suggests'
Mail on Sunday

'Rosie Thomas writes with beautiful, effortless prose, and shows a rare compassion and a real understanding of the nature of love'   *The Times*

ROSIE THOMAS

Constance

McArthur & Company
Toronto

First published in Canada in 2007 by
McArthur & Company
322 King St. West, Suite 402
Toronto, ON
M5V 1J2
www.mcarthur-co.com

Copyright © 2007 Rosie Thomas

This paperback edition published in 2008.

Library and Archives Canada Cataloguing in Publication

Thomas, Rosie   Constance / Rosie Thomas.

ISBN 978-1-55278-712-0

I. Title.
PR6070.H655C65 2008   823'.914   C2008-901250-X

Printed in Canada by Webcom

10 9 8 7 6 5 4 3 2 1

For Cameron Mitchelson

Bali

London, June 1963

The boy and the girl were both just sixteen. It was nearly ten o'clock, which meant they would soon have to separate for a night and a whole day.

They crept down the empty street with their arms twined, he shortening his step to match hers and she resting her head on his shoulder. The overhanging plane trees made a tunnel of the pavement. The gardens on either side were dark recesses of rustling leaves, the territory of prowling cats and maybe a rat invading a dustbin. Under one of the trees the boy stopped walking. He hooked his arms round the girl's shoulders and kissed her for the hundredth time. Her mouth felt bruised, but she kissed him back. His hands moved down to cover her breasts.

'Mikey.'

'I love you,' he protested. His knee rubbed between her thighs and he heard the soft, enticing rasp her nylons made against his jeans.

'*Mikey*. My dad said ten o'clock. You heard him.'

'We've got ten minutes, then.'

He raised his head and glanced about. There was no one to be seen. This was a quiet road with only a few parked cars, and tall hedges screening the bay windows of the houses. Turn left at the end, and he reckoned it was a couple of minutes' walk to Kathy's house. If you ran.

He steered her towards the nearest gate. It stood open and a tiled path of coloured triangles and diamonds

1

gleamed faintly in the darkness. No light showed behind the glass door panels, or in any of the windows.

'Mike, we can't,' she murmured, but she came with him anyway.

Behind the hedge she pressed her mouth against his, teasing him with the sly curve of her smile. He answered by stroking his hand upwards from her knee. High up, his fingers met the smooth bulge of soft bare flesh above the stocking-top. They pressed into the vertical mattress of leaves, breathing into each other's mouths, their tongues busy. The powerful, coarsely sweet smell of privet blossom flooded around them.

At first he thought the sound was a cat among the dustbins. It was a high-pitched cry, somewhere between a bleat and a howl. It stopped and then started again.

Kathy moved her head sideways. Her sweet spit smeared his lips.

'What's that?' she breathed.

'Some old cat.'

The cry came again.

'It's not. Listen, it sounds just like a baby.'

'Don't be soft. Come back here.'

'Leave off. Where *is* it?'

She stooped down, her oval face and her pale cardigan a conjoined blur against the blackness. She pushed aside the lowest branches of the hedge and felt along the margin of dead leaves and blown litter underneath.

'My God.' Her voice turned high and sharp.

'Shhh,' he warned.

Kathy rocked back, almost tipping over her heels. She was lifting a bag in her two hands, a bag like the one his mother took to go to the shops, made of brown plastic that was supposed to be leather, with a zip and two upright looped handles. The mouth of the bag gaped open and the cat's cry was much louder.

'Look at this.'

He knelt beside her as she dipped her hands inside. He could smell dusty earth as well as privet.

'Look,' she breathed.

She was holding a small bundle of blanket. Between them they turned the folds aside and touched the baby's tiny head. It was streaked with dark patches and waxy white stuff. Its mouth was open and its eyes screwed shut. Now that they saw it really was a baby, its crying sounded weak and nearly hopeless.

Mike was amazed. 'What's someone's baby doing out here?'

With the baby cradled against her, Kathy glanced up at him. She looked serious, and wise, suddenly much older than a mere minute ago.

'It's abandoned. The mother's left it because she can't keep it. Probably no one knows she's even had it. The poor thing.'

With the tip of her finger, Kathy stroked the baby's cheek. Mike wasn't sure whether *poor thing* meant the baby or its mother.

'What'll we do?' He was deferring to her now, slightly in awe of her because she knew more than he did. She even knew how to lift and hold the baby close against her shoulder, with one hand cupping its head.

Businesslike, Kathy answered as she knelt and rocked the bundle, 'We'll have to call the police. And an ambulance.'

'Well. Yeah. There's a phone box up on Weir Road.'

'We can't go all the way up there. It's an emergency. We'll have to knock on someone's door. Big houses like these, they've probably all got phones.' She glanced up at the house, but there were still no lights. 'Next door, there's someone in. Go *on*, then.'

'Just ring their bell, you mean, and say we've found a baby?'

'Yes,' she shouted at him.

A displeased man came to the door in his slippers, and behind him a woman in a nylon housecoat peered into the street. Mike had hardly finished his sentence before the woman brushed past both of them and ran round to the other garden. She reappeared with the brown bag in her hands, and with Kathy still cradling the baby. Kathy's eyes were very bright and wide and there were ladders at both of her knees from where she had knelt in the gravel.

'Graham, ring the police and say what's happened. Come in here, love. Let's have a look at the poor mite.'

The two women went into the front room and bent down together. They laid the baby on the cushions of the settee and unwrapped the blanket. The crying had stopped; now it just lay still. Underneath it was dressed in nothing but a tiny yellow cardigan and a dingy piece of towel secured with a safety pin. Its limbs were mottled and drawn up close to its body. The woman unpinned the improvised nappy.

'It's a little girl,' Kathy whispered. Mike caught a glimpse of a thick purple-grey stump where its belly-button should be, and quickly looked away. There was an upright piano against the opposite wall, with framed photographs arranged on the lid. A picture of the Queen in a tiara and a blue sash and the Duke of Edinburgh in naval uniform hung above it.

'What's this?' the woman said. She pointed, and Kathy saw the glint of something pinned to the blanket.

It was a little pendant of marcasites with a rod and a tiny screw fastening for a pierced ear.

'It's an earring.'

As she lifted it, Kathy's eyes filled up with sudden hot tears.

Before she said goodbye, before she pushed the bag into the hedge, the baby's mother must have fixed her earring to the blanket as a memento. Perhaps at this very minute she was holding its pair, and crying for her lost daughter.

It was the saddest thing Kathy had ever imagined.

The woman touched her shoulder.

'You just don't know, do you? About people's lives?'

She hurried away and came back with a folded terry nappy and a white shawl.

'I keep these here for when my Sandra brings her little one round. Mind you, she's out of nappies now.' Her tongue clicked. 'Baby's cold, isn't she? Out in the night like that. Let's get her wrapped up. I'm going to put the kettle on for a hot-water bottle, try to warm her up.'

'I'll hold her while you do it.' Kathy was using a voice Mike hadn't heard before. It didn't allow for contradiction.

'Slip her inside your cardie and hold her against your skin. You know, for body warmth.'

Her husband cleared his throat and looked away, and Mike studied the royal photograph more intently.

'Police ought to be here any minute now,' the man muttered. He went to the window and looped back the curtain so he could see into the street. Before the woman came back with the hot-water bottle, the blue light of a police car was flashing beyond the privet hedge. They heard the shrilling of an ambulance bell and then the room filled up with men in glinting uniforms. One of them took the baby out of Kathy's arms and there was nothing left for her to do but watch as they prepared to take the baby away.

'Well done, love,' the ambulance man said to her. 'The nurses will give her a bottle and warm her up and she'll be as right as rain.'

A few minutes later, the ambulance had driven the baby away.

Kathy sat on the sofa with her knees and her ankles pressed very close together. She was shivering a little. Mike sat beside her and held her hand, but she didn't seem to notice him.

The woman told her, 'She'll be fine, dear. You heard what the ambulance men said.'

Kathy nodded and stared at the floor. The brown bag along with the yellow cardigan, the blanket, the damp towel and the single earring lay at the policeman's feet. With a cup of tea balanced on the arm of his chair, he was waiting to take their statements. His partner sat opposite them and their two caps were placed side by side on the piano stool.

'We were just walking home from the pictures,' Mike said.

'You were walking past and you heard a cry?'

'We weren't walking. We'd stopped.'

'On the pavement?'

'Well, no. We'd gone into next-door's garden. Just for a minute. Didn't seem as though there was anyone in.'

The policeman looked at him. 'Let's see. You'd slipped behind the hedge for a kiss and a cuddle?'

Kathy blushed crimson.

Mike said, 'No. Um, yes . . .'

'It's all right, son. It's not against the law, David, is it?'

'Wasn't in my day.' The other constable winked.

'Did you see anyone?'

Kathy and Mike shook their heads. The street had been deserted, they were both sure of that. It had been so quiet, it was as if they were the only two people in the world.

'Then we heard this crying. I thought it was a cat.'

'I didn't,' Kathy said. 'I knew what it was straight off.' She chewed at the corner of her thumbnail. 'Will you find her mother?'

'We'll do our best to get her to come forward. She'll be needing medical attention, for one thing. That baby's no more than a few hours old. But she'll be running the risk of prosecution if she does, and that could mean up to five years in prison, depending on the circumstances. So they don't often change their minds, in my experience.'

'They? Not *often*?' Kathy repeated.

'It's not quite the first time I've seen an abandoned newborn, let's say.' He put his pen away and looked at his watch. 'That's it, then. Back to work, Dave. Thanks for the cuppa.'

When Kathy heard it was ten past eleven her hands flew up to her mouth.

'Oh no. My dad'll kill me,' she gasped. 'My mum will be all right about it, though, when I tell her what's happened.'

'I'll be there. I'll make sure you don't get into trouble,' Mike said. But as Kathy turned her head to him he saw that there was a different look in her eyes. Something had changed tonight; she had seen something to do with the baby that he didn't quite understand.

7

In a small, clear voice she said to him, 'I'll be fine. You just go back to your place.'

The policemen gave them a lift home. Kathy's house was nearer and Mike waited in the back of the patrol car as she walked up to her front door with one of the policemen at her shoulder. Even in the dim light of the porch Mike could see how angry her dad was when he opened the door, but the sight of the policeman changed that. After a few words Kathy's dad put his arm round her and led her inside.

She didn't look back, and the door closed behind her.

*   *   *

At the Royal London Hospital, a paediatrician and a nurse finished their examination of the baby. The doctor filled in a form and signed it, then looked up at the nurse.

'We'll be needing a name.'

The nurse glanced at the reports that had come in with the ambulance crew.

'A young couple found her, in a bag under a hedge. In Constance Crescent. I think that's pretty.'

'You can't call a baby Constance Crescent.'

'Constance, I mean.'

The doctor scribbled it down. 'And the surname?'

The nurse glanced at the paperwork again. 'The name of the young girl is Kathleen Merriwether.'

'Constance Merriwether? That's a bit of a mouthful.' But he had already written it in the vacant space on the form.

'If the mother doesn't come forward in the next twenty-four hours, it'll be a "Baby Constance" picture and story for the local rag,' the nurse said.

The doctor sighed and took off his glasses.

Fed and washed, and dressed in clean clothes, the baby slept in her hospital crib.

ONE

Nights on the island were rarely silent.

The guttural scraping and grunting and booming that was the frog chorus could rise into a din sufficient to drown out all the other wildlife before fading away into a single disconsolate bleat. The many dogs who ranged the village streets barked incessantly, and in the small hours the roosters started up a brassy call and answer that lasted well into daylight. But towards dawn the world suddenly fell silent.

On this day the sky lightened from pitch black to a vast grey touched at the eastern rim with green, against which the coconut palms on the crown of the ridge stood out like paper silhouettes. In the waiting hush the light strengthened and the horizon flushed with pink and orange.

In a beautiful place, another lovely day was breaking.

Wayan Tupereme yawned at the door of his house and then shoved his feet into the brown plastic sandals that he had left neatly paired on the step. He made a brief circuit of his garden, nipping off a flower here and there and cupping the blooms in his left hand. By the time he was back at his door again, it was daylight. A little later he trod quietly down the dusty path beside the swathe of leathery leaves and twined stems that separated his garden from the Englishwoman's, and strolled up to the next-door house. Even though the sun was rising there was no visible sign of life. He stooped to place something on the lower step of the deep veranda that ran all the way round the little single-storey house. It was a tiny basket woven from palm fronds and containing some squares of coarse leaf on which were laid an orange flower like a miniature sun, a scatter of scarlet petals, and a few grains of rice. Wayan touched his hands to his forehead, then stood up straight again and made his way back to his own house. He was getting old, and he walked slowly.

Ten minutes later, Connie's alarm clock went off. She wasn't used to waking to its shrill beep, and her arm thrashed as she tried to find the button to silence it. She extricated herself from the tangle of thin sheet and blinked at the time. It was six thirty. The car would be here to pick her up in half an hour but she lay still for a moment, letting the familiar outlines of the room and its furnishings reassemble themselves in the dim light. She had been dreaming, a thick coil of a dream that still clung to her although she couldn't remember what it had been about.

'Come on. Get going,' she advised herself, once the chair and cupboard and the horizontal slits of pale light marking the shutter louvres were properly distinguished. She felt apprehensive, although not unpleasantly so, but there wasn't time to dwell on any of that. The car was coming. There was a seven-thirty call.

The bedroom doors opened onto the veranda at the back of the house. As she did every morning, Connie opened them to let the light flood in, and stepped out into the air. It was still cool, with a faint breeze stirring the leaves of the banana palms. There was no pool, she had deliberately chosen not to have one, although the other Europeans who lived in the area all did. There was only the liquid music of water trickling down the rocks a little way off, and the view itself. It took her by surprise and then engrossed her, even after six years.

The house clung to the upper rim of a steep valley. From beneath her feet the ground fell away into the gorge and rose again on the opposite side, densely clothed in a tangle of trees, feathery leaves against broad blades against sharp spikes, a lush billow of textured greenery. The crowns of the highest coconut palms spread against the sky, three-dimensional in the brightening light. At the bottom of the cleft lay the river, a wide silver sweep with the morning mist rising from it. The cocks were still crowing, and as the warmth of the sun filtered through the leaves the first cricket started up its dry rasp. From the road on the other side of the house came the distant buzz of motorbikes as people headed for work.

Connie smiled at her view, thinking how lucky she was to have all this. She rocked on her bare feet, spreading her toes to connect with the warm, varnished boards. On an ordinary day she would have made tea and sat out here, gazing at the green wave until it was time to do something else. But today was not ordinary. The outside world had arrived.

She had laid out the shooting script the night before, her tape-recorder and her laptop and the sheets of music, even her clothes. All she had to do was shower and dress, make a last check and pack her bag.

At 7 a.m., still with a persistent flutter beneath her ribcage, Connie carried her bag out of the house. The offering placed by Wayan lay in front of the house temple, a little shrine sited at the appropriate corner of the veranda. She nodded her head to acknowledge it and then stepped past. The car was already waiting for her, pulled off the road into the grass and bare-earth space where the way to her house joined up with the path to Wayan's. It was a big silver-grey Toyota 4x4, with tinted windows and enough room to seat seven people.

The driver leapt out as she emerged, and hurried to open the rear door for her.

'*Selamat pagi*, ma'am,' he said. 'Good morning. All set now?'

Connie knew him quite well. His name was Kadek Daging and he was Wayan's relative by marriage. Usually he worked in his small general store up in the main street of the village and was famous as a source of local gossip, but today he would have left one of his several sons in charge of the shop in order to undertake this important driving assignment for 'the movie company', as he put it. Actually it was less a movie than a trio of expensive thirty-second commercials for an online bank that were being shot on the island. But Connie didn't want to diminish his sense of importance by making the distinction.

She would have shaken his hand, or even lightly touched his shoulder, but she took her cue from him and put the palms of her hands together to make a polite bow.

'Good morning, Kadek. Thank you for coming.'

To preserve the formality of the occasion she climbed into the back of the car, even though she would have preferred to sit up front. Kadek jumped smartly into the driver's seat and eased the Toyota out into the stream of scooters and motorcycles. One young man on

13

a motorbike tried to race them, his blue shirt ballooning and his black hair raked back in the wind, but Kadek hooted and they sailed majestically past him.

Once they were established as the kings of the village traffic he asked over his shoulder, 'Ma'am, would you care for a cold drink? A cool towel?'

Normally he would address her as '*Ibu*', as he called all the other European women customers and neighbours, or '*Ibu* Con' when he remembered, although Connie tried to persuade him to make it just 'Con'. Today, however, they were in a different relationship.

'Thank you,' she said gravely.

'In the box,' he reminded her.

There was a cool-box in the foot-well, in which were bottles of water and soft drinks and a couple of rolled hand towels. Connie took out a towel and patted her hands and face with it, although she wasn't hot. Kadek nodded with satisfaction at having done the right thing.

'Busy day for you,' he observed.

'Yes.'

It was going to be.

After half an hour's driving, away from the village and following the course of the river to where the valley spread in a series of pale ledges planted with rice, they reached the location.

There were several Toyotas parked in a line, three bigger trucks standing with their doors open, two motor caravans, a trailer-mounted diesel-powered generator, a couple of pick-ups from which heavy boxes were being unloaded by local labour under the direction of one of the key crew, green awnings set up for shade, groups of people converging on a larger tent, and a general air of purposeful activity. Con looked at her watch. It was seven thirty precisely. The sun was gathering strength,

14

promising a hot day ahead. On the horizon, across the shimmering paddy, the sacred Mount Agung was a pale-blue pyramid.

'Thanks, Kadek.'

He opened the door for her to step out. 'Welcome, ma'am. Anything more for you? I have to collect other film people. The young girls, you know, who take part.'

'Of course you do. Off you go. Thanks for getting me here so punctually.'

As he prepared to reverse away, Kadek permitted himself a wink and a grin that revealed his filed teeth.

Connie shouldered her bags and walked towards the set.

'Hi,' Angela called out, and waved her arm in welcome. Angela was Connie's old friend from London, a producer with the company that was making the commercials.

Connie gave her friend a hug. 'You all right?' she murmured in her ear.

Angela had an unusually expressive set of features. With her back to the location, she made her wasps-invade-the-picnic face. 'Couple of the crew complaining about their hotel. Ran out of beer last night is what it amounts to.'

'That all?'

Angela shrugged. 'More or less.'

Connie was relieved to hear it. Usually she worked alone in her studio, either here in Bali or in London, and she rarely came face to face with the agency who commissioned her work, let alone travelled to commercial shoots. But she knew enough about the ad business to be certain that worse things could go wrong on location than the booze being in temporarily short supply. Could, and probably would.

She was anxious, and in Bali that was most unusual.

Her life here was calm, pared-down and minimal like the interior of her little house, and in its own uneventful way it was satisfying.

Now, disorientatingly, London had come to her.

She put her arm through Angela's. She said cheerfully, 'So let them drink green tea. Or vodka. Or fresh mango and papaya juice. Be different. This is Bali, isn't it? Come on, Ange, let's get ourselves some breakfast. How's Himself this morning, by the way?'

There was no doubt who she was referring to.

'Fine. In a pretty good mood. Really keen to get rolling.'

Rayner Ingram, the director, was a tall, saturnine man who said little, but when he did speak he made his remarks count. He and Angela worked regularly together as a director– producer team.

Connie had tried to joke mildly, privately, about him to Angela.

'*Rayner?* What's that about? Is his real name Raymond? Do you call him Ray?'

Angela had reproved her, without a glint of a smile. 'No, of course not. Why d'you say that? His name's his name.'

It hadn't taken even this exchange for Connie to conclude that Angela was in love with Rayner Ingram. Producer–director relationships weren't exactly uncommon in the business. It was just uncommon for them to have happy endings.

Connie half-listened to Angela, but the other half of her attention was on the stacks of metal boxes and lights and cables being unloaded from the trucks, and the way people were rushing about, and the British and Australian colloquialisms shooting across the set.

It was bizarre to contemplate this other world, this self-important capsule of schedules and shots and scripts, given birth to by a line of trucks drawn up beside a half-ruined temple in a rice paddy under the blue cone of a volcano. A few yards away, behind a loose cordon of local men who had been recruited to keep spectators off the set, Connie could see two women squatting at the edge of a green thicket of rice. They had been harvesting, and their hand-scythes lay at their feet. They looked as though they might be mother and daughter. The younger one, perhaps sixteen years old, wore a bright red sarong that made a brilliant slash against the green and the dark earth. She carried a baby bound against her chest. The two women watched the activity on the set with wide eyes and motionless attention.

Connie tried fleetingly to establish which of these places was the more real to her: the silent women and the rice paddy or the ring of people within which a hairy man in shorts and a khaki waistcoat with a dozen pockets across the front was yelling for someone to bring over the genny cables. Both were familiar, she decided, and she could feel at home in either. Whatever home meant. It was the juxtaposition that was disconcerting.

The two women reached the open flap of the tent, which had a fine netting screen across it to keep out the insects. As Angela gathered the netting in one hand she whispered, 'You haven't met the clients yet, have you?'

'No, I haven't.'

'Now's your chance.'

Two men were sitting in canvas chairs at a folding table, surrounded by three others and a woman and a circle of cups and plates and cafetières. Both of them looked up at Connie. She had time to see that they were the kind of men who naturally wore grey worsted, and that now they were dressed in what Angela, using her primitive-tribe-found-in-Papua-jungle face, called 'clients' shoot clothes'.

Angela said warmly, 'Simon, Marcus? This is Constance Thorne. Our musical director, of course.'

The older one half got to his feet and held out a big hand. There were croissant crumbs on his safari jacket.

'Ah, Boom Girl,' he shouted. 'We're honoured. Simon Sheringham.'

'Hello,' she smiled at him.

She hated being called Boom Girl. If it had ever been welcome, it had stopped being so a very long time ago. She had written the Boom music when she was barely twenty. A fluke. A day's work.

'Boom, boom, baboom ba ba, bababa *ba*.' The younger client sang the few bars as he also stood up. '*And* it was long before my time,' he asserted, intending a compliment. 'Hi. Marcus Atkins.'

'Hello.' Connie shook hands with him, and smiled some more. From further along the table the ad-agency copywriter and art director nodded at her, too cool for introductions. The agency producer was very pretty, Connie noted.

Angela and Rayner were conferring over the schedule of the day's shots.

'I'll just get some breakfast,' Connie murmured.

Two Balinese men in white jackets were clearing plates. Connie followed them out of the back of the tent. Behind the scenes, enclosed by canvas screens, Kadek Wuruk, who was moonlighting from Le Gong Restaurant ('Don't Go Before You Come'), was frying

18

eggs on a two-ring gas burner. He beamed at Connie and waved his spatula at her.

'Hello! Welcome, *Ibu*. Egg for you? Very good, you know. My own chickens.'

'Yes, but no thanks. It's a bit early for me. I'll have some coffee, though. Everything okay, Kadek?' There was quite a limited range of Balinese first names.

'Everything fine, great.'

His assistant was chopping onions, three women were peeling vegetables, two young girls were washing up, and a line of boys processed by with cases of bottled water. Connie was reluctant to pass back through the canvas flap that separated kitchen from tent. It was more comfortable out here, with the women laughing and chattering and the shy girls with their bare lovely feet planted in front of the portable sink unit. She poured coffee into a Styrofoam cup, and watched Kadek Wuruk and his assistants at work as she drank. There would be *nasi goreng* for lunch.

She heard a crackle of walkie-talkies.

'We're in,' the first assistant called to the crew. It was the signal for work to begin on the other side of the canvas. People began shifting towards the set, but there would be several hours of waiting and watching while the rest of the gear was brought in and lights and cameras were set up. If everything went really well the camera would be turning over before the lunch break was called. Connie's *gamelan* orchestra was listed as the first shot.

When she had first arrived in Bali, Connie had been intending to make a short stopover on her way to London from Sydney. The plan had been to keep still, to take stock of what was left of her life, and let her bewilderment subside a little. It was only a few weeks since Seb had told her that he was in love with a Chinese violinist, and intended to marry her.

At that time Sébastian Bourret was becoming a sought-after conductor. When he made the announcement, sitting on the balcony of their rented flat overlooking Sydney Harbour, Connie had been his lover and partner for more than six years. Their home was nominally in London but Seb travelled so much that they were away more than they were there, and this had suited Connie well. Their peripatetic life together had been comfortable and civilised, and she had been sure that it was what they both wanted and needed. She had her own work, composing music for television and commercials, and as technology developed it was becoming increasingly easy to do that work anywhere in the world.

She wasn't under the illusion that Seb was wildly in love with her, at least after their first year together, any more than she was with him. But they had much in common, and they were considerate and mutually respectful and deeply fond of one another.

Then Sebastian really had fallen in love, with the gifted Sung Mae Lin who was no bigger and looked hardly older than a child, even though she was almost thirty. Unwittingly Mae Lin made Connie feel too big and the wrong age, and unwanted, and unhappy in a way that was too familiar, however hard she fought against that and the memories that were stirred by it.

None of it was Mae Lin's fault, or Seb's, really, or her own for that matter. It was just one of those things that happened. There had been no alternative for Connie but to withdraw from her own life, as quickly and as gracefully as she could manage it.

Seb and Connie had said goodbye to each other gently, and with regret, but there had been no question that he might change his mind. Connie had seen him only once since then, when he was conducting a Beethoven Festival concert series in London. He and Mae Lin had two children now. Twin girls.

Connie's London home was still the apartment that she had shared with Seb. He had made his share of it over to her and she had kept the place, although it was bare of most of the furniture they had chosen and there were few of her possessions set out in it. She liked it better that way; it was easier to slip in and out of an almost empty space. Minimalism was closer to invisibility.

When she'd arrived in Bali, she had had no plans and no expectations of the place. It had simply been somewhere to put herself that felt like nowhere in particular.

In her raw state she had fled from the big hotels and beaches and cocktail bars of the coastal strip close to Denpasar and headed inland. It was here in the village that she first heard *gamelan* music played live, by solemn musicians, not for tourists but for the musicians themselves and their knowledgeable friends. This was temple music, and music for festivals and processions and weddings. She had loved the sonorous gongs, and the shimmering notes of metal that fell through the air like drops of clear water.

Angela peered from between the flaps of canvas.

'I'm here,' Connie said, rapidly gathering her thoughts. She drank the last mouthful of her coffee and stood upright.

'I'll be on set.'

The day's set was the temple at the edge of the rice paddy – permit to use for filming applied for and finally

21

granted by the authorities in the nick of time – over which the set dressers were swarming.

Constance consulted her watch, having already looked at it more times this morning than she would normally do in a week. 'The musicians will be here in fifteen minutes or so.'

'Right. Straight to costume and make-up, then.'

The bus carrying the musicians arrived punctually and Connie hurried forward to meet them. Battling with their instruments, a line of six men spilled down the steps. They were not much bigger than their metallophones, big xylophones with keys made of bronze, and considerably smaller than the great gong. They were her friends.

'I am very, very nervous,' Ketut called as soon as he saw her.

Connie held out her hands to him. 'Don't tell me you don't want to do it?'

There were beads of sweat on his forehead and above his long-lipped mouth. Ketut had smooth skin and it gleamed in the bright sunlight like oiled wood. 'Oh, no. We are film stars already in Seminugul, let me make clear. There is no going back. But I am afraid of letting you down, Connie.'

Ketut was one of the most talented musicians she had ever worked with. She had been recording some of his performances with the big ensemble of fifty musicians called the *gamelan gong*, and she counted herself lucky to be able to play percussion with this smaller, less perfectionist group. Connie knew that she was not the best drummer in the world, but she loved the sessions when they played together. Sometimes, during the rainy season, they could make music for hours under a roof of palm thatch while water dripped from soaking leaves.

The musicians clustered around her.

'You won't, Ketut. You don't even have to play if you don't want to, just look as though you are for the camera.'

The actual music track would be laid down in post-production. This was the music that Connie had been commissioned to produce. She found herself blushing in retrospect at the memory of the demo disc she had supplied.

'Light and poppy, but unmistakeably tropical-island exotic,' was the agency's brief.

Confronted by Ketut and the others, combed and dressed in their best clothes, and versed as they were in the classical traditions of their native music, she felt embarrassed.

Behind her she could hear the Australian gaffer routinely cursing into his walkie-talkie because someone hadn't brought over a camera dolly. All the musicians were staring into the snake-pit of cables, and at the little temple caught under the brilliant ultra-sunshine of the lights.

'Don't worry, really, don't worry,' she reassured them all. She asked if they wanted anything to eat or drink and they shook their heads. So she led them over to the caravan that was being used for male costume and make-up and left them there.

The script called for a Balinese wedding.

The temple was dressed up with flowers and baskets of fruit. Over the pop-eyed stone statues props people had fixed parasols of bright yellow silk with lavish fringes, and there were rakish garlands of scarlet and orange blossoms draped around the necks of stone dragons and snakes. The hot colours seemed to vibrate under the lights.

Eleven o'clock came and went. Connie supervised the unpacking and setting up of the instruments, on the exact spot that the crew indicated. The musicians emerged from make-up, giggling among themselves. They had been costumed in sarongs of black and white checks with broad saffron-yellow or vermilion satin sashes tied round their middles. They wore flowers around their necks, their eyes had been painted and their lips reddened. Their ordinary haircuts, as worn by waiters and teachers and shopkeepers, which is what they were, had been combed and gelled into slick quiffs. Every time Ketut or one of the others caught a fresh glimpse of a fellow musician there was another explosion of laughter. Trying not to laugh herself, Connie shepherded them onto the set.

Another long interval of adjusting lights and equipment followed. It was hot, and hotter still under the lights, and a Balinese make-up girl kept darting forward to powder a shiny face.

Connie positioned her recording equipment and ran the players through an approximation of the twenty-two seconds of music that would accompany the finished commercial.

'This is really not Balinese wedding music,' Ketut protested.

'I know. Forgive me?'

Angela came across and reassured the musicians that they wouldn't have long to wait. Connie could read the anxiety in her rigid shoulders. The schedule listed the bridal-attendants shot for completion before the lunch break as well as the *gamelan* orchestra, and that called for ten little Balinese girls wearing complicated head-dresses who were at present corralled in the female

24

wardrobe caravan. Connie began to sweat in sympathy with Angela, who had reckoned up and costed every minute of a week on location. Rayner Ingram was still frowning and shaking his head as he looked into the monitor.

But then, suddenly, there was a flurry of action.

'We're going,' the first assistant called. 'Camera rolling.'

Connie gave the signal to Ketut. As if there were no lights, microphones, cables or cameras, as if they were doing it for their own pleasure under a bamboo shelter in a rainy village forsaken by tourists, the little orchestra played her makeshift music.

Their faces lit up. The camera rolled towards them.

After twenty-two seconds, she gave them the cut signal. Reluctantly the metallophones and kettle gongs pattered into silence.

Rayner and Angela conferred. Then Angela and the first assistant crossed to the agency people and consulted with them. The musicians waited, their eyes fixed on Connie.

'Going again,' came the call.

They did three more takes. The agency indicated to Angela that they would like yet one more, but she shook her head and tapped a fingernail on her watch face.

The first assistant told the musicians, 'That's fine with the orchestra. Director's happy. We're done with you.'

It was Connie they looked to for confirmation. She beamed and applauded.

'Ketut, you were brilliant. All of you. Thank you.'

'I don't know. There were some things,' Ketut began, but the crew were hurrying them and their instruments off the set. Time was money.

Connie and the file of musicians heading back to the caravan passed another procession coming the other way. The bridal attendants were overawed eight-year-old girls cast from the nearby school. Their faces had been painted to resemble dancers' masks, with eyes outlined in thick lines of kohl that swept up at the corners, rouged cheekbones and brilliant crimson lips. With tall gilt crowns on their heads and tunic dresses of pale gold tissue, they looked exquisite. Their role was to scatter flower petals in the path of the as-yet-unseen bride as the bridegroom and his supporters waited for her at the temple steps.

Behind the children came their mothers in a swaying group, chattering and exclaiming. Some of the mothers knew some of the musicians and there was a slow-moving bottleneck as everyone stopped to talk and laugh and exchange views on the filming. Crew immediately hurried them apart. The children were needed on set.

Once they had changed into their own clothes the musicians settled into the service tent, eyeing the swooningly handsome Indonesian actor, cast as the bridegroom, who was busy with his mobile phone. Connie quietly handed Ketut the fee, in cash, for the orchestra's work. At least, she thought, they had been well paid.

On the set five pairs of beautiful Balinese girls scattered flower petals on a strip of crimson carpet. Out of shot, set dressers sprayed the temple garlands with water in an attempt to stop them wilting under the hot sun. Miraculously, the attendants were wrapped after just two takes.

'Okay, people, let's have lunch,' called the first assistant.

Within three minutes the service tent was full of ravenous crew. Ketut and the others politely took this influx as a signal to leave. Connie went with them to the bus.

'We play again on Tuesday? You can come?' Ketut asked her.

Tuesday was their regular evening for music.

'Yes, please,' Connie said. It was one of the best times of her week.

She stood and waved as the bus bumped down the rice-paddy track. The mother and daughter who were working in the paddy straightened their backs to watch too. They had been joined by several more women.

In the service tent Angela was asking Tara, the pretty agency producer, what she thought they might do about the British actress who was playing the bride. She had spent the morning confined to her bathroom at the hotel. She must have eaten something that disagreed with her, Marcus Atkins remarked. The creative team sniggered.

'I've absolutely *no* idea,' Tara sighed.

On their way out later, Angela said to Connie through clenched teeth, 'If that damned woman says she has *no idea* once more about what is supposed to be her bloody *job*, I'm going to hit her.'

'She's getting a great tan, though,' Connie laughed.

In the absence of any bride, the afternoon was given over to the bridegroom and his friends. They marched out of wardrobe splendid in starched white jackets with red headcloths knotted over their foreheads. Tara sat up in her chair at the sight of them and slipped her sunglasses down over her nose.

It was a complicated reaction shot. The men were supposed to be waiting in profile in a proud, anticipatory little group for the big moment, the first sight of the bride following behind her petal-strewing attendants.

Then, as they caught sight of her, the men were to register a sequence of surprise, disbelief and then dismay.

Once the camera had captured all this the view then shifted to the other perspective.

The bride's father – an approximate Prince Charles look-alike – was to be kitted out in full morning dress. On his arm would come the bride, dressed in white meringue wedding dress with a bouquet of pink rosebuds and a dangling silver horseshoe, blonde ringlets framing her face within a froth of veil.

With the establishing shot Connie's music was to segue into a suggestion of 'Here Comes the Bride', then dip into a minor key to match the surprise and dismay, and end in a clatter of discordant notes. Then, on the screen would appear the bank's logo and the words 'The Right Time and the Right Place. Every Time. Always.' To the accompaniment of a long, reverberating gong-note.

'It's advertising,' Angela said drily.

The day wore on. After five or six takes, Rayner Ingram declared that he was satisfied with the shot. The tropical dusk was beginning to collect at the margins of the paddy, and Mount Agung was a conical smudge of shadow on the far horizon.

'That's it for today, folks,' announced the first assistant.

The crew began dismantling the lights, and Simon Sheringham stood up and yawned. 'Time for a drink, boys and girls,' he said.

'You are so completely right,' Tara drawled.

Angela murmured to Connie, 'Are you joining us for dinner?'

Angela's duties would now shift to hostess and

leisure facilitator for agency and clients, but her eyes were on Rayner Ingram who was stalking away towards the waiting Toyotas.

'Do you need me?'

Connie was thinking of tomorrow's music – a reprise of the main theme for the closing shot of the bride's father, the worse for wear, smoochily clinking his champagne coupe with a second glass crooked in the elbow of a grinning stone dragon.

And she was also thinking of her secluded veranda and the frog chorus, which would sound like a lullaby tonight.

'Well . . . not really,' Angela said.

'Then I think I might just quietly go home.'

'Doesn't anyone else *want* a drink?' Simon bellowed.

An hour later, Connie sat on the veranda in her rattan chair and watched the darkness. It came with dramatic speed, filling up the gorge and flooding over the palms on the ridge. Packs of dogs barked at the occasional motorbike out on the road, and sometimes she could hear a squeak of voices from Wayan Tupereme's house, but mostly there were only the close, intimate rustlings of wildlife in the vegetation and the conversation of frogs. Damp, warm air pressed on her bare skin. Connie was never afraid to be alone in this house.

She ticked off a mental list.

After tomorrow, there were two more linked commercials to shoot.

It was going to be a hard week's work, but now it was under way her apprehension had faded and she felt stimulated. It was good to have a surge of adrenalin. And then when it was all over the agency people and the crew and Angela would disperse, back to the cities, and she would still be here quietly making *gamelan* music with Ketut and his friends and looking out at her view.

At the same time the Boom music started running through her head, and obstinately stayed there.

Damn Simon Sheringham and Marcus Atkins.

It wasn't just the bank clients, though. It was the disorientating effect of finding London in Bali. It was being made to feel alive, and the way that that stirred her memories and brought them freely floating to the surface of her mind.

Connie's thoughts tracked backwards, all the way down the years to when she was a little girl, to the day after they moved into the new house in Echo Street, London.

She was six, and her sister Jeanette was almost twelve.

On their first night she had had a terrible nightmare. A faceless man came gliding out of the wardrobe in her unfamiliar bedroom and tried to suffocate her. Her mother rushed in wearing her nightdress, with her hair wound on spiny mesh rollers. Connie was shouting for her father but Hilda told her that her dad needed his sleep, he had to open the shop at eight o'clock in the morning, like he did every day.

'I don't like this bedroom. It's frightening,' Connie sobbed.

'I've heard quite enough about that.'

Connie had had a fight with Jeanette over who was to get which bedroom. Jeanette had won, as she always did.

Hilda scolded her. 'It's a lovely room, you're a lucky little girl. Now go to sleep and let's have no more of this nonsense.'

In the morning, Connie had decided to put the spectres

of the night behind her. She would impress herself on Echo Street, somehow or other.

She marched through the house, past Hilda who was clattering the breakfast dishes, out into the garden and past the puffy blooms of hydrangeas and hazy billows of catmint, all the way to the garden shed at the far end.

She climbed the garden wall and made the daring leap to the shed roof, and then perched on the sooty ridge. From that vantage point, with its view of the neighbouring gardens, she had launched into a long, loud song that she had made up herself. She stood on the shed roof and bawled out her song to the backs of the houses and the railway line beyond the fence until Hilda shouted through the kitchen window that she was disturbing the whole neighbourhood.

Almost forty years later, what Connie recollected most clearly about that day was the singing itself, and the complicated song, and the importance that both had assumed – like a reef in the turbulent currents of daily life. Music was already becoming her resort, in a family with a mother and father who would have had difficulty in distinguishing between Handel and Cliff Richard, and a sister who could not hear a note of music. Or any other sound.

In the new front room at Echo Street there was the upright piano that had come with them from their old flat. No one else in the family ever played it and it was badly out of tune, but the instrument had belonged to Connie's father's mother and Tony always insisted that it was a good one, worth a bit of money. Hilda kept it well dusted and used the top as a display shelf for the wedding photograph (Tony Brylcreemed in a wide-shouldered suit, Hilda in a ruched bodice, a hat like the top off a mince pie, and very dark lipstick), a photograph of Jeanette as a newborn asleep in layers of pink knitwear, and one of Connie as an older baby, propped up in Jeanette's lap.

As soon as she was old enough to lift the gleaming curved lid for herself, Connie had claimed the piano for her own. When she perched on the stool her legs were too short to reach the pedals, but she loved the commanding position and the way the ivory and black notes extended invitingly on either side. She splayed her hands over the keys, linking sequences of notes or hammering out crashing discords. She could sit for an hour at a time, absorbed in her own compositions or in picking out the tunes she heard on the radio. To Connie's ear these first musical experiments sounded festive in the quiet house.

In time, music and musical composition became Connie's profession.

Success came early, almost by accident, with the theme music she wrote for a confectionery commercial.

The Boom chocolate-bar tune turned into one of those rare hits that passed out of the realm of mere advertising and drilled straight into the collective consciousness. For a time the few bars turned into a shorthand trill for anything that was new and saucy and self-indulgent. Builders whistled it from scaffolding, children drummed it out on cans in city playgrounds, comedians referenced it in their acts. The confectionery company used it not only for Boom, but in a variety of mixes for their other products so that it became their worldwide aural signature. The royalties poured in and Connie's small musical world acknowledged her as Boom Girl.

Nowadays the money from her early work had slowed to a trickle, but Connie still earned enough to live on. When she needed more it was possible to make a rapid sortie from Bali to London and put in some calls to old friends like Angela. Quite often, she could bring the bacon of commissions home to Bali and work on them there.

She had no idea how long this arrangement would remain possible, but Connie didn't think about the future very much.

The past was much more difficult to evade: it was there in her dreams, and the long bones and ridged tendons of it lay always just under the skin of consciousness, but in her quiet daily life among the villagers and the *gamelan* musicians she could easily contain it.

Now Angela and all the people with her had landed like a spaceship on Connie's remote planet, and they brought London and memories leaking out of the airlocks and into this untainted atmosphere.

Not that her old friend was a taint, Connie hastily corrected herself, nor were her colleagues, or the business that had provided her with a living for more than twenty-five years. But their company, the banter and the jostling for position and the surge of adrenalin that came with them, caused her to examine her life more critically than she would otherwise have done. As she sat in the warm, scented night she was asking herself unaccustomed questions.

Is this a useful way to live?

Is this what I want?

These questions seemed unanswerable.

She shifted in her rattan chair and it creaked accommodatingly beneath her weight. She let her head fall back against the cushions and listened to the rustling of leaves and the throaty frogs.

And am I happy?

That was the hardest question of all. In this beautiful place, living comfortably among friends and making music with them, she had no reason for unhappiness.

Except that this island life – for all its sunshine and scent and richness – did not have Bill in it.

Connie had learned to live without him, because there was no alternative. But happiness – that simple resonance with the world that came from being with the man she loved – she didn't have that, and never would.

The thought of him, as always, sent an electric shock deep into the core of her being.

Connie leapt from the chair and paced to the edge of the veranda. The invisible wave of leaves and branches rolled away beneath her feet, all the way down to the curve of the river.

By concentrating hard she cut off the flow of thoughts and brought them back to the present. She had work to do, and that was a diversion and a solace as well. She had learned that long ago.

She would do the work and maybe the questions would answer themselves, or at least stop ringing in her ears.

There was a seven-thirty call in the morning.

TWO

Noah headed downriver, towards the battlements of
Tower Bridge and the pale shard of Canary Wharf tower
in the hazy distance. It was the beginning of June, a
warm and sunny early evening. The Embankment was
crowded with people leaving work and heading home,
or making for bars and cinemas. The girls who passed
him were bare-legged, the skin above the line of their
tops showing a pink flush from a lunchtime's sun-
bathing.

Noah had sat with his mother for over an hour. He
linked his fingers with hers, not talking very much, rubbing his thumb over the thin skin on the back of her
hand. Sometimes she drifted into a doze, then a minute
or two later she would be fully awake again, looking
into his eyes and smiling.

'Do you want anything, Mum?' he asked, leaning
close to her so she could see his face.

She shook her head.

At the end of an hour, she had fallen into a deeper
sleep. He sat beside the bed for a few more minutes, then
slid his hand from beneath hers. He stood up carefully,
bent down and kissed her forehead where the faint lines
showed between her eyebrows.

'I'll be in tomorrow, same time,' he murmured, for his
own benefit rather than hers.

Noah hadn't worked out where he was going; he just wanted to be outside in the fresh air. Even though there was a thick waft of grease and fried onions from a hot-dog stand and a blast of beer and cigarette smoke rising from the crowded outdoor tables of a pub, it still smelled better out here than inside the hospital. He stuck his hands in his pockets and walked more slowly, threading through the crowds, his head turned towards the khaki river. A sightseeing boat slid by, trailing a noisy wake of commentary and the smell of Thames water.

Under a plane tree, just where the shade from the branches dulled the glitter of dusty cobbles, one of the performance artists who regularly worked there was setting up his pitch. He was wearing a boxy robot costume sprayed a dull silver colour, and all the exposed skin of his body was painted to match. As Noah idly stood watching, the performer laid out a blanket and placed a silver-painted box on it, and positioned a small matching plinth behind the blanket. He made the arrangements with mechanical precision, his head stiffly tilted in concentration. Then he tapped a silver metal helmet over his silver-sprayed hair and took a step up onto the plinth. His arms rotated through a few degrees and froze in midair. A few of the passers-by glanced at him, probably wondering why an able-bodied individual should choose to spend an evening locked into immobility on a plinth instead of heading for the pub. Losing interest, Noah was about to walk on when he noticed the girl standing on the opposite side.

She was watching the performance with surprise and delight, as if it was completely new to her. After a moment she took a step closer, then cautiously skirted the blanket to stand directly in front of the robot. She waved her hand in front of his face. The man gave a reasonably convincing impression of being made of metal and Noah remembered how tourists used to make similar attempts to distract the Guardsmen frigidly mounted on horses in front of the sentry boxes in Whitehall.

The girl was laughing now. She reached out a hand with the index finger extended and gently prodded the robot in his metallic middle.

The girl was very pretty, Noah noticed. Her head had the poise of a marble sculpture, and her mouth had a chiselled margin to it that made her lips unusually prominent. She really did have an amazing mouth. He considered the rest of her. Her hair was short and spiky, blonde with a greenish tinge that suggested it was dyed. She was quite tall, thin, with long thighs and calves. Her clothes were similar to those worn by all the girls in the passing tide, but at the same time there was something very slightly wrong with them. Her top was flimsy and gathered from a sort of yoke and her jeans were an odd pale colour. Her open-toed shoes were thick-soled and dusty and their heaviness made her protruding toes look small and as fragile as a child's.

Noah experienced a moment's dislocation, as if he were drunk or had just stepped off a theme-park ride that had been whirling too fast for him. His body felt very light and insubstantial, and the plane tree and the metallic man and Tower Bridge seemed to spin around him and the girl. He rocked on his feet, establishing a firmer connection with the ground beneath.

The girl drew back her hand, still laughing.

Noah took a breath. The world steadied itself.

He said to her, 'You won't be able to make him move. It's more than his job's worth.'

She gave no sign of having heard him.

Disbelief flooded through Noah. It wasn't possible. Maybe it *was* possible, maybe that's why he had noticed her in the first place.

Then she slowly turned her head. It wasn't that she hadn't heard, he realised, rather that she hadn't understood what he was saying.

'Do you speak English?' he smiled.

'Of course. Why not?' she shot back. She did have an accent. It sounded Slavic, or Russian.

'I thought you were, you know, perhaps a tourist.'

'No,' she said flatly.

'Ah. Right.' She was making Noah feel a bit of a fool. As if she sensed this and regretted it, she jerked her chin at the robot man.

'This is clever. Not moving one muscle.'

'Yeah. Sometimes there's a Victorian couple, and there's a gold man who does it as well. Usually you see them at weekends in Covent Garden. It always looks to me like a really hard way of earning money.'

The girl's eyes turned to him. She looked disappointed, and at once Noah felt sorry that he had diminished the originality of the spectacle for her. 'But it is clever, you're right.'

'I was not trying to tease him, you know? I was thinking he cannot be a real man because he is so still, even though I saw him walk up on his step.'

'He won't move, though. That's the point.' Noah was beginning to feel that it was time to steer this conversation forwards. 'Um. Are you on your way somewhere? Would you like to have a drink? There's a bar just here. Bit crowded, but we can sit outside . . .'

Suddenly an empty table to one side of the open space looked intensely inviting.

'I have the bicycle with me.' The girl pointed to a bright yellow mountain bike propped against the river wall.

'Nice bike. We can lock it up . . .'

'I do not have a lock.'

'Really? You should have one, someone'll nick a bike like that in five seconds. Look, we'll just park it beside us so we can keep an eye on it.'

They were walking towards the table, the girl wheeling her bicycle, when she suddenly stopped.

'We did not give him money.'

Noah was pleased with the *we*. He grinned at her. 'You can, if you want.'

She didn't smile back. 'I don't have any. Not today.'

He sighed. 'All right.' He made a little detour and dropped a pound coin into the robot's box. The man's head gave a sudden jerk and his hands rotated. 'Thank you,' a robot's voice mechanically grated. The girl beamed and clapped, and Noah judged that that was easily worth a pound of anyone's money. He touched her elbow. 'Let's be quick, before someone grabs the table.'

He left her sitting with the bicycle, fought his way to the bar for two beers, and was pleased and relieved when he got back to find that she was still waiting for him.

'Cheers,' he said as they drank. 'My name's Noah, by the way.'

'I am Roxana.'

'Hello Roxana.' He put out his hand. I am acting like a *total* prat, he was thinking, but he couldn't stop staring at her mouth. He wondered what it would take to make her laugh again, the way she had done when she prodded the robot. Roxana took his fingers, very cautiously, and allowed an infinitesimal squeeze before drawing back again.

'Where are you from? Are you Russian?'

She looked levelly at him. 'I am from Uzbekistan.'

'Are you? Uh, I don't think I even know where that is.' He sighed inwardly. That's right, go on, let her know you're thick as well as a prat.

'It is in Central Asia. We have been independent country since 1991. Our capital is Tashkent. We have borders with Afghanistan, Kazakhstan, Kyrgyzstan, Tajikistan and Turkmenistan.'

Noah raised an eyebrow. 'Thank you. Now I do know. What brings you to England? Are you a student? Your English is really good.'

'Thank you very much. I'm not a student. I'm working here, I would like to stay. It's better for me.'

'What do you do?'

Roxana paused. 'I am a dancer.'

Yes, she had the body for it. And that explained the studied poise of her head on the long, pale column of her neck. Noah found that he didn't want to speculate too hard, not here and now, anyway, on the look of her in – what were those things dancers wore? Leotards.

'Ballet?' She was a bit too tall for that, though.

'No. Not ballet. Modern.' She nodded towards the yellow bicycle. 'I have only just been for, um, a test?'

'Audition?'

'Yes. I have the job, they tell me there and then.' She did smile now and Noah blinked.

'Congratulations.'

'Thank you. And I should of course ask now about your job but I have to go soon. It's not my bicycle, I have only borrowed it to come to the place over there for my audition.' She nodded across in the approximate direction of St Paul's. 'But in London for two weeks I haven't yet been to see the river Thames, so I came for one hour.'

She pronounced it with a soft *th*, to rhyme with James.

Noah's stomach did something that he associated with a lift dropping very fast. Jesus, he thought. What's happening? Can you fall in love with someone after ten minutes, just because she says *Thames* instead of *Tems*?

'What is your job?' she asked softly.

'I work in IT. For a small publishing company.'

'Near to here?'

'In the West End. I've just been visiting my mother, in the hospital. She's had an operation. She's got cancer.'

Roxana didn't react in the usual way. Her face didn't contract with distress or sympathy and there was no rush of consoling words, although Noah realised a second later that this was what he had been looking for. Instead she just nodded, quite matter-of-fact.

'Will she recover?'

'Oh yes, I think so.'

'That's good.'

He might have concluded that she was unusually detached. Most people, in his experience, when you told them your mother had cancer, were concerned for you and her, even though they might never have met her. There was a look about Roxana, though, that told him she wasn't unconcerned. He noted the way her incredible mouth drew in at the corners and her neck bent a little, as if it were made of soft wax. He thought she might have heard a lot of stories that were sadder than the illness of a stranger's mother.

Their glasses were empty. 'I have to go, really,' she said.

He said too quickly, 'No time for one more drink?'

'No. Thank you for this one.'

They both stood up, awkwardly negotiating the edges

of the table. Roxana twisted the handlebars of the yellow bike and prepared to wheel it away.

'Which way are you going?' Noah asked. He was thinking, Do you have to sound so desperate, you sad bugger?

'Over there. There is a small bridge.'

'Oh yeah, that's the Millennium Bridge. Known as the Wobbly Bridge, usually. I'll walk that far with you.'

They wove through the crowds together. Noah heard himself giving an overlong and over-animated explanation of why the footbridge had acquired its nickname. She might perhaps have been half-listening, but she was also frowning and biting the corner of her lip. She was anxious to get away, probably to return the borrowed bike to its owner. He wasn't usually quite this hopeless with women. What was it about this one?

They were crossing the bridge. Streams of people poured past them, which meant she had to keep dodging and breaking away from him.

'Would you, um, like to meet up again? As you don't know London, maybe we could, ah, go on a riverboat.' A big white one was passing directly underneath. Roxana briefly glanced at it. 'Or do something. See a film? Or I could come and see you dance.'

'No.' She said that very quickly, and in a firm voice that meant absolutely not.

At the far end of the bridge she bent her head and pushed the bike up the steps, leaning into the job. She looked tired now, and – what? Forlorn. That was it.

'I do have to go.' She gestured at the handlebars. 'There will be trouble.'

'Can I have your phone number?'

'I don't have any phone. Not at the moment.'

'Roxana, I'd like to see you again. Is that all right? Won't you tell me where you live?'

She looked away, in the direction she would be heading as soon as she could get away from him, and Noah knew that she was concealing something.

'I will have a place. In a few days.'

You're getting nowhere, mate, Noah decided. Can't you take a hint? She's probably got a huge Uzbek boyfriend stashed away somewhere.

'Well. I enjoyed talking to you.'

Roxana made to get on the bike, then stopped.

'You have a telephone?'

'Sure. Yes, of course.' He took a work card out of his wallet and scribbled his mobile number on the back. 'Call me.'

'Okay. Goodbye, Noah.'

She tucked the card away, slung her plastic handbag over her shoulder, straddled the mountain bike and forged out into the traffic. She was looking the wrong way and he almost called *Look out*. But she veered away from an oncoming bus and wobbled into the left-hand lane, then pedalled uncertainly away. He watched until she was out of sight.

He was sure he would never see her again and the thought left him entirely disconsolate.

His mobile rang and he tore it out of his pocket, allowing a flare of hope.

'Oh, yeah. Hi, Dad. Yeah, I was there for an hour, maybe a bit more. She was very sleepy. Call me later? Yeah, me too. Bye.'

His father was on his way to the hospital. Noah put his head down and started walking towards the tube.

As soon as she was safely round the corner Roxana peered up at a street sign, then stopped to search in her bag for the street-map book that the man Dylan had loaned her. She found where she was now, after some flipping back and forth through the small grey pages, and also where she had come from. It didn't look so far, in terms of map centimetres, but remembering the difficulty she had had in getting to the place Dylan had sent her to for the audition, she suspected the return journey was going to cause problems.

Still, she'd find it in the end, wouldn't she?

She tried to memorise the names and the sequence of the four or five big roads she needed to follow, but before she had even reached the first junction they had jumbled themselves up in her head.

London was a big place. She couldn't even imagine how far it spread. All these rooms stacked on top of each other, all these tall buildings and streets and glassy shops. All these people. She felt very small in the thick of it, as if she were no more than a speck of dust, a little glinting mineral fragment that the wind might suck away. She kept on determinedly pedalling, bracing herself against a gust of fear as well as the buffeting of the traffic. Buses and trucks hooted at her as they roared past.

It would turn out fine, she kept telling herself, why not? She had a job now, at least.

She had got talking to Dylan on her first morning in London, in the café near King's Cross Station where she had looked out at the rain and the crowds of people all walking heads down with somewhere to go. She had spent the previous night in a nearby hotel, in a room that was noisy and dirty and had still cost far more than she budgeted. Her savings and the money her mother's old friend Yakov had loaned her wouldn't go far at this rate.

The young man, thin as a bamboo pole, asked her for a light and then slid closer along the red plastic bench. He offered her one of his cigarettes and bought her another cup of coffee. It was nice to talk to someone.

It turned out that Dylan lived in a house where there were cheap rooms to rent. When he asked if she wanted him to find out if the room next to his was free, she said yes, because she had no other ideas. Once she saw the place she didn't want to stay there, not even for one night. But she did stay, because she had no alternative. She promised herself that it was just until she found some work.

The house was a catacomb of rooms, the doors leading off the dim staircase all padlocked and the grey walls daubed with slogans. Apart from Dylan, Roxana didn't know who else lived there. She rarely met anyone on the stairs, and when she did they hastily drew back into the shadows. It was only at night that they came out. The nights were constantly disturbed by running feet, thunderous crashes and outbursts of wild shouting. A door would be wrenched open to set a jagged burst of music throbbing in the stairwell before the door slammed again. After a few nights she learned to pull her pillow over her ears and not to speculate about who was murdering or being murdered on the other side of her door. She bought her own padlocks, two big heavy ones, and kept the door locked day and night.

Dylan had tried to get inside the room with her, of course he had, but she told him what he could do with himself. He hadn't taken it all that badly. He was lonely, too. When he wasn't at work and didn't have any money for drugs, they sometimes went for a walk or a bus ride together.

She told Dylan that she needed a job and that she was a dancer, not necessarily expecting the two statements to connect. It was true that in Bokhara, where she grew up, Roxana had sometimes gone to classes and then for a whole wonderful term Yakov had helped her and she had studied dance in Tashkent. She had clung to this tenuous historical link to her maternal grandmother, who had died before Roxana was born and who as a young woman had been a professional dancer. The wife of Tamerlane the Great himself had also been renowned for her grace and skill as a dancer. Both these women had been called Roxana.

But it was not easy to live in Uzbekistan. After her brother was killed in the uprising she made up her mind that she would find a way to leave it behind, every broken street and Russian soldier, all the memories, everything her native country stood for and everything that had happened to her there, and live in America, or England. She would become an American girl by sheer force of will.

Or an English one, that would do.

It had taken a long time to get the money for a holiday flight from Tashkent to Luton, but she had managed it.

Yakov had wished her good luck, knowing that he would never leave Uzbekistan himself.

Roxana didn't plan to be on the return flight.

In London her intention was to find work looking after children, pink and white cherubs who would be dressed in little coats with velvet collars, that would be nice. Or if not that, maybe she could be a chambermaid in a big hotel. She saw herself in a maid's uniform, plumping up pillows and setting out white towels and crystal glasses.

But she had soon found out that without references and papers there was no work with English children. The hotels she walked into had all told her that they weren't taking on casuals at the moment. It was Dylan who had come to her rescue again.

'Ye said ye can dance.' His accent was so strange. He told her he came from Ireland. When she first met him in the café she could hardly decipher a word, but by now she could understand him better. 'There's a feller ye can go to see.'

He wrote down a name and an address for her, lent her the map book, told her which bus to catch and what time to be there, and advised her not to be late. To make sure she knew where she was going, Roxana traced the route from the house to the place. And on her way out of the house, on a sudden impulse, she borrowed the yellow bike.

It had been in the hallway ever since she had come to live there, leaning in the same place among the litter of envelopes that no one picked up. She had not seen anyone touch it, let alone ride it. There was no lock. Maybe someone had just left it at the house and forgotten all about it.

And she had already worked out that to take it would save her the bus fares. Buses and tube trains in London cost a lot of money.

She had bumped the bicycle down the steps of the house and boldly set off. At first it was exhilarating to be so free. She flew along in the glittering traffic, the wind of her own speed whistling in her ears and pinning a smile to her face. It was a shame that she ended up getting lost. It meant that she was late for her meeting with Mr Shane at The Cosmos. He was a small, elderly man with quick cold eyes. He looked Roxana up and down as if he was pricing her for sale.

'This is a quality venue, do you understand me?' was the second thing Mr Shane said to her, after telling her that if she was ever late again she could forget working for him.

'I understand, yes,' Roxana answered, glancing around her at the tables and the shuttered bar. Before the club opened for the night it looked sordid, but she supposed that it would be different when the lights came up and it was full of people.

'Right. Where are you from and how long have you been here?'

She told him.

'Legal?'

'Yes,' she lied.

Mr Shane sniffed. 'Let's see what you can do, then.'

There wasn't any music and the only audience was Mr Shane sprawled in a front-row armchair with his mobile phone pressed to his ear. It wasn't difficult to envisage what he wanted, but making her body perform the right sequences wasn't easy at all. Roxana concentrated very hard on making it look as though what she was doing came naturally. The performance seemed to go on for a very long time.

At last he held up his hand. 'All right. That'll do.'

'I could do some more, something different if . . .'

'You can start on Friday,' he said impatiently.

Roxana could hardly believe her luck. 'Yes? Friday. Thank you. Thank you, I . . .'

'Seven o'clock sharp. Five minutes late and you can go straight home.' He didn't have time for her gratitude.

He was already on the phone again, and gesturing for her to get dressed and leave.

She came out of the cavernous dimness of The Cosmos and into the fluttering air, breathing deeply with relief. She had a job. She was on her way.

She did get lost on the way back from the river, but not quite as badly as the first time. She had the first inkling that instead of being fragments of a puzzle, the few pieces of the city that she was beginning to recognise might even be logically and manageably connected to each other. She was whistling as she pedalled into the street and even the sight of the house, with peeling paint and torn curtains and the rubbish sodden in the basement area where the windows were boarded over, didn't depress her spirits too much. She hauled the bike up the short flight of stone steps and leaned it against the broken teeth of the railings while she groped for the key to the front door. Before she pushed it open, she had a brief premonition that there was something waiting for her on the other side.

The flurry of violence was so sudden that she didn't even have time to scream.

The bicycle was seized and hauled inside, dragging her with it. One of the pedals bit deep into her shin at the same time as the man grabbed her wrists and forced her up against the wall. The door slammed shut, cutting off her escape route.

'Did I miss something? Did you buy that bike off me? Or did you say to me, "Mr Kemal, I need to borrow a piece of your property"? Or did you just nick it out of here without a word to no one, like you own the world?'

She tried not to inhale the smell of cigarettes and unwashed skin.

'No,' she said. Her teeth rattled in her head as he shook her.

'No what?'

'I didn't buy it. I didn't ask. I thought it wasn't anyone's.'

'That was a mistake, Russia.'

Roxana lifted her head. The man was plump, black-haired, unshaven. He was wearing a grey singlet and there were thick tufts of glistening hair under his arms and curling all the way up to his throat. 'I am from Uzbekistan,' she said. 'Not Russia.'

'Like I give a shit.' He twisted her arm and she winced. 'You're not hurt, Russia, not yet. If you take things that don't belong to you, then you'll find out about being hurt. Do you understand what I'm saying to you?'

'Yes.'

'What do you say now?'

'I am sorry,' she whispered.

Mr Kemal let go of her arms. 'Upstairs,' he ordered. He followed her up through the breathless house, made her unlock her padlocks and kicked open the door of her room so he could take a good look inside.

There wasn't much to see.

She had sellotaped a picture postcard of a tropical beach to the wall beside her bed. She had bought the postcard from a street vendor in Tashkent, when she was out shopping with her friend Fatima. She had fallen in love at first sight with the image of silver sand and blue sea. Apart from that there were her few clothes hanging behind a curtain mounted across one corner, a two-ring gas burner and some tins and packets, a transistor radio in a turquoise plastic case, and her Russian–English dictionary lying open beside her plate and cup on the small table.

As he flicked through her belongings the man made a dismissive *tssshhh* through his teeth.

'Didn't you say to me you're not Russian?'

'My father, he came from Novosibirsk. That's Russia, okay. But my mother was Uzbeki and I was born in Bokhara.' Roxana was recovering herself. She said quickly, in Uzbek, 'I think you are Turkish, yes?'

To her relief, she understood that he was finished with her. From the doorway he said, 'Born in Stoke Newington, if that's any of your fucking business. Now, keep your thieving hands off my stuff, all right?'

Roxana nodded. She would make every effort never again to come into contact with Mr Kemal, or any of his belongings, until such time as she could move out of this house for ever.

After he had gone she quietly closed the door and secured it from the inside. Then she sat down on the bed, her head bent and her hands loosely hanging between her knees. She could feel blood congealing on her shin and her arm throbbed, but she didn't make the effort to examine her injuries. Once the initial shock and fear had subsided, what Roxana was left with was a feeling of dreary familiarity. Life had a way of repeating itself. To stop the cycle it wasn't enough to be in a different place, even a different continent. You had to be a different person. You had to become a person like, say, the English boy. Noah. Big, and crumpled in a way that meant you were not worried about what anyone thought of you, always smiling, and completely certain that you had your rights and that justice was on your side. Roxana wasn't so sure, after all, that she could make this much of a difference in herself.

Half an hour went by and someone tapped at the

door. She ignored it for a while, then heard Dylan's voice. It came out as a breathy hiss, which meant he must have his mouth pressed right up against the splintery panels.

'Roxy, I know ye're there.'

'I'm busy.'

'What in the name of feck were ye doin' with Kemal's bike?'

'I borrowed it.'

'What was it, a death-wish?'

'Go away.'

'Listen, all right. I'm just askin' about the job.'

'I got the job.'

He whistled. 'Did you so? It's good work, that. There's good money in it. Easy work too, lap dancing. Waftin' yerself around in front of a few boozed-up City boys.' She heard his chuckle through the door.

'Dylan, I'll see you tomorrow, maybe.'

'Yeah, right enough. See yer, Roxy.'

Dylan needed to make himself different too, she thought. He didn't know it, though. That was the difference between the two of them.

'That's it, people. We're all through. Good work. Thanks very much everyone.'

The first assistant scissored his arms in the air and Tara flopped back in her seat with a trill of satisfaction. The last shot for the third of the online-bank commercials was in the bag.

The middle-aged cellist in the string quartet gently put aside her instrument. Connie saw that there was sweat beaded around her hairline, and the bow-ties and starched shirts of the violin and viola players had gone shapeless in the humidity. She thanked them for their hours of work, playing the same few bars of music for the commercial over and over in the afternoon's heat, and paid them their money. The violinist carefully counted it.

'We should be thanking you,' he said formally. He was German. 'If there is any more work of the same type, please be kind enough to think of us.'

'Of course I will,' Connie said warmly as they all shook hands. She couldn't imagine the likely circumstances, though.

She wasn't sorry that the week to come would not be as ripe with crisis as the one that was just past. The main actress had barely recovered from her stomach upset, and her enfeebled state had led to rescheduling and hours of overage costs which Angela had had to negotiate with Tara. Relations had become strained.

Then the agency and client teams had both shown remarkable and competitive stamina when it came to after-hours partying. The mornings-after had been difficult. One of the Australian crew members had entertained a woman in his room and had been outraged to discover the next morning that his wallet, laptop and MP3 player had vanished with her into the night. Connie had been called on to act as go-between with the local police when the stolen property wasn't instantly recovered.

'What did he expect?' Angela sighed to her in private. 'Tarts with hearts of gold only exist in the movies, you'd think he'd know that.'

The musicians hurried with their instruments to the waiting bus. Their evening job was playing light classical pops in the main dining room of the most expensive hotel in Jimbaran, and they would have to go straight there from the set.

Still in his costume, the handsome actor's stunt double strolled ahead of Connie as she made her way to the service tent. She absently admired the smooth, oiled breadth of his shoulders and the way his bare torso tapered to the waist of his breeches, and then laughed at herself. One of the riggers whistled at her as he hoisted a grip stand towards the waiting trucks. In the service tent itself the Balinese catering team were packing away chairs and folding down the tables. Angela was standing there with her knuckles tight around a cup of coffee. She looked as if she hadn't slept for a week.

Probably, Connie reflected, she actually hadn't.

'Well done,' Connie said to her.

Kadek Wuruk stuck his head into the tent. 'Hello, *Ibu*,' he beamed. 'Kitchen closed, end of shooting, but you like drink maybe?'

'Yes please, Kadek.'

'Could you take a beer to Mr Ingram, too?' Angela called after him. Rayner Ingram had been absorbed in his creative cocoon all week long, and had taken no note of the problems besetting the shoot. 'He's pretty exhausted. He's done a great job, you know. The agency and the client are really pleased.'

'Ange.' Connie removed the cup from her hand and took her by the shoulders. 'How are *you*? You look, if you don't mind me saying, knackered.'

'Oh. You know.'

For a moment, Connie thought her friend was going to cry. She told Kadek to take the drink to Rayner and led Angela outside.

The sun had slid behind the cliffs that they had used for the backdrop to the set and the rock was now a wall of darkness crowned with a halo of golden light that no lighting cameraman could ever have created. The first bat of the evening flitted overhead. Set-dressers were rolling up an artificial lawn, the cast were changing in the caravans. The self-important world of the shoot was folding up on itself, shrinking back into the waiting trucks and Toyotas. Tomorrow, when the cast and crew were on their planes home, the clearing would be deserted except for the birds and the bats.

'Look at this,' Angela sighed, as if she was seeing it for the first time. The trees were heavy with dusk.

'Why don't you stay on with me for a few days? Have a holiday. You've earned one.'

'I'm fine,' Angela said. She laughed. 'Completely fine. I've got to start next week on pre-production for a yoghurt commercial. It's really, really busy at the moment and that's good, isn't it? Can't turn the work down while it's there.'

'Angie?' It was Rayner Ingram's voice. Her head turned at once.

'Coming,' she called. 'Con, you'll definitely be there tonight, won't you?'

Tonight was the wrap party, traditionally hosted by the production company. Connie knew about last-night parties more by reputation than recent direct experience.

'Yes. Course I will.'

'See you later, then. You've been an absolute star all this week. I couldn't have got through it without you.'

Left alone, Connie sat down on an upturned box. There were more bats now, dipping for insects against the blackness of the trees. She could almost feel the week's edgy camaraderie being stripped away from her, rolled up like the fake turf and tossed into the back of a truck. She would feel lonely here next week, when Angela and the others had gone. She had her work, of course. She had planned to make some more recordings of the *gamelan gong* for her orchestral library. There was Tuesday night's music to look forward to, and she should think about asking some people to the house, fill it up with talk and lights once in a while. The string quartet, for example. She should find out which was their night off and make dinner for them and their partners.

This time tomorrow, Angela and Rayner and Tara and all the others would be halfway back to London.

Connie found that she was thinking about London as she rarely did, remembering the way that lights reflected in the river on winter's evenings, the catty smell of privet after summer rain, the glittering masses of traffic and the stale, utterly specific whiff of the Underground. She kept the focus deliberately general, excluding places and people for as long as she could.

'I'm going to need that box.' The voice made her jump. She saw it was the rigger who had whistled at her.

'All yours,' Connie smiled at him as she got to her feet. She wasn't sorry to have her train of thought interrupted. In any case it was time to head home to change for the wrap party.

There were more than forty people for dinner. They ate in the garden of the better hotel, under the lanterns slung in the branches of the trees.

'This place is a bit of all right,' one of the Australians shouted up the table. 'You guys did well.'

'Next time,' Angela called back.

'Holding you to that, ma'am. They've even got beer here.' In the last-night surge of goodwill, the disagreements of the week morphed into jokes.

The actress emerged from her room to join the crew

for dinner. Draped in a pashmina against a non-existent breeze she was telling everyone who would listen that she had lost nearly a stone and wouldn't be coming back to Bali in a hurry.

Tara was wearing a dress that measured about twenty centimetres from neckline to hem. Simon Sheringham's arm rested heavily along the back of her chair, and he regularly clicked his fingers at the waiters to ensure that their two glasses were kept filled. Marcus Atkins and the agency's creative duo sat with their heads close together, planning how to make the best of the rest of the evening.

Rayner Ingram naturally took the head of the table. After a successful shoot everyone wanted their piece of the director, and there had been a scramble for the seats closest to him. Connie was relieved to see that he beckoned Angela to the place on his right. She was surprised, as she took her own seat near the other end, by the rigger darting into the next chair. He extended a large hand.

'Hi. My name's Ed.'

'Connie Thorne.'

'Boom Girl, somebody called you. What's that about?'

She was entirely happy that he didn't know. 'Nothing. History. Let's have a drink.'

'Let's make that our motto.'

The food came and they ate and drank under the lanterns.

Connie learned from Ed that he owned a ski lodge in Thredbo and only took on film work when he needed a cash injection.

'You should come out. I'm heading back for the best of the ski season now.'

'I can't ski.'

He grinned. 'No worries. I'll teach you.'

You could go, Connie told herself. Ed's blue shirt cuffs were rolled back and she noted that he had nice wrists. He seemed a good, dependable, practical sort of man.

Damn, she thought. Why can't it happen?

That question did have an answer, but it wasn't one she was prepared to listen to at this moment.

Glancing up the table she saw Angela's and Rayner's heads close together. They were deep in conversation. That was all right, then. For tonight at least.

People were already swaying off in search of further diversions. There were loud splashes and a lot of shouting and laughter from the swimming pool.

'Think about it,' Ed murmured. He took out a marker pen and wrote his email address on her bare arm. 'It's indelible ink, by the way.'

'I will think about it,' she promised, untruthfully.

Tara asked for the music to be turned up and began dancing, stretching out her hands to whoever came within reach. Simon Sheringham had a cigar and a balloon glass; Rayner was talking about the big feature he was soon to start work on. Someone had unwound a volleyball net on the lawn and several men were leaping and punching at the ball. Connie slipped away from the table and walked over the grass. She was hot and she had drunk more than she was used to, and it was soothing to drift in the dusk under the trees.

Someone rustled over the grass behind her.

'There you are. I've been hunting for you.' To her partial relief it was not Ed but Angela, and she was carrying a bottle and two glasses. 'Shall we sit here?'

There was a secluded bench with a low light beside it

that hollowed an egg-shape of lush greenery out of the darkness. They sat down and Connie obediently took the glass that Angela gave her. Angela kicked off her shoes and rested her head against the back of the bench.

'I meant it, you know. About not surviving this week without you.'

'You would have done,' Connie laughed.

'I don't think so. Christ. Tara? Sheringham? And that other woman, you'd think no one in the history of the world has ever had the shits before this week. Sorry. Listen to me. I just needed a quick moan.'

'It's over now.'

'Until the next one.' They clinked their glasses and drank.

'How is it with you and Rayner?'

Angela exhaled. 'Oh. You noticed?'

'Well. Yes. Probably no one else did, though.'

Angela's smile was a sudden flash in the gloaming. 'He's amazing. We've been working together quite a lot, and we started seeing each other . . . it's difficult because he's still officially married to Rose and he's very close to his kids, so we're keeping the lid on it, especially on shoots, but in time I think we'll be really good together. You know, he's so special, such a talented director; that has to come first a lot of the time.'

Connie did her best to receive this information optimistically. Angela was elated now, probably because Rayner had given her a sign for later. She was revelling in the anticipation of him slipping into her room, locking the door behind him. Connie could remember what all that felt like, more or less. But the provisos sounded too ready, and they were ominous.

Not that I'm the one to judge, she thought.

Maybe Rayner Ingram will turn out to be loyal, tender, considerate and generous. And maybe he will be all of those things for Angela and no one else. And her friend was enviably happy tonight, Connie could feel the pulse of it in her. Somehow everything had turned round since the tense ending of the afternoon, and she should be able to bask in the moment without anyone spoiling it for her with sage advice. Angela wasn't a child, or any kind of innocent.

'Don't put his happiness before your own,' was all Connie advised.

'They're the same thing,' Angela breathed.

They sat in silence for a moment.

'Anyway, I wanted to talk about you, not me,' Angela began again.

'Why's that?'

Angela waved her glass. 'About here. And why you stay, and what . . . Are you hiding from something, maybe? Out here. On your own, you know what I'm saying, ever since you split from Seb. Why don't you come back to London? Be with your friends, everyone you know. Don't your family miss you, apart from anything else? You've got a . . . sister, haven't you? And that amazing flat. And it's not as though you don't get plenty of work. Honestly. You can't stay out here for ever, you need to come back and . . . connect. Think about it, at least, won't you? Aren't you lonely? Don't you ever think, is this what I really want?'

Angela was warming to her subject. She was happy, and in her benign daze she wished the same for everyone. They had both had quite a lot to drink, Connie allowed. She tilted her glass, then gazed around at the glimmering garden. The frogs were loud, but the noise of the party was eclipsing them. Soon, probably, the other guests in the hotel would start complaining. That would be something else that Angela would have to deal with.

'Connie, are you listening?'

'Yep.'

She was wondering which end to pull out of the tangle of Angela's speech. She didn't say that she only asked herself what she really, really wanted when her solitude was compromised.

'I do come back to London. Quite often.'

'You slip in and out of town like a . . . like a . . .'

'Mouse into its hole?'

'I was trying to think of something polite.'

'I like my life.' It was true, she did.

'But – don't you want – love, marriage? A family?'

'I'm forty-three.'

'That's not an answer.'

'No, then.'

That silenced Angela for a moment. Eight years younger and uncomfortably in love, she couldn't imagine any woman not wanting those things.

Love, marriage, family?

Love Connie did have, and she had come to the conclusion that she always would. Love could exist in a vacuum, without being returned, with nothing to nourish it, without even a sight of the person involved. It was always there, embedded beneath her skin like an electronic tag, probably sending out its warning signals to everyone who came within range.

Yes but no. Available but not.

The truth was that Connie had loved Bill Bunting since she was fifteen, and Seb hadn't been the first or even the last attempt she had made to convince herself otherwise. She wasn't going to marry Bill, or even see him, because he was another woman's husband. He wouldn't abandon his wife, and if he had been willing to do so Connie would have had to stop loving him. That was the impossibility of it.

And family . . .

It was significant that even Angela, who had been a friend for more than ten years, had to think twice about whether Connie had a family or not, and what it consisted of.

That was the way Connie preferred it to be.

She turned to look at Angela and started laughing.

'What's funny?'

'Your expression. Angie, I know what you're saying to me, and thank you for being concerned. Your advice is probably good. But I'm happy here, you know. I'm not hiding. And it's very beautiful.'

'Do you feel that you belong here?'

'Do we have to feel that we belong?'

There was a sharp scream and a splash followed by some confused shouting.

'What now?' Angela groaned.

'It sounded like Tara.'

'Will you think about what I'm saying, though?'

'Yes, I will.'

'It's mostly selfish. I want you to come home so we can see more of each other.'

Connie smiled. 'I'd like that too. But I *am* home.'

The evening was finally over. Connie walked the empty side-roads back to her house, the way ahead a pale thread between black walls of dense greenery. It was a still night, and she brushed the trailing filaments of spiders' webs from her face.

When she reached home, she saw that there was a small, motionless figure sitting on a stone at the point where her path diverged from her neighbours'. The figure took on the shape of Wayan Tupereme.

'Wayan? Good evening.'

He got to his feet and shuffled to her in his plastic flip-flops.

'I have a grandson,' he said. 'Dewi had a son tonight.'

Connie put her hands on his shoulders. The top of his head was level with her nose.

'That's wonderful news. Congratulations.'

Dewi was his youngest daughter, who had married and gone to live with her husband's family. Wayan and his wife missed her badly.

He nodded. 'I wanted you to know.'

'I'm so pleased. Dewi and Pema must be very happy.'

'We all are,' the old man said. 'We all are. A new baby. And a boy.'

THREE

'Nearly there,' Bill said unnecessarily, but in any case Jeanette's head was turned away from him. She seemed to be admiring the bitter green of the hawthorn hedge and the froth of cow parsley standing up from the verge. It had rained earlier in the day but now the sky was washed clear, and bars of sunshine striped the tarmac where field gates broke the line of the hedge. 'Nearly there,' he repeated. Conscious of the bumps in the road, he tried to drive as smoothly as he could so she wouldn't be jarred with pain.

Their house was at the end of a lane, behind a coppice of tall trees. Jeanette had found it, two years after Noah was born, and insisted that they buy it. Bill would have preferred to be closer to town but in the end he had given way to her, and he had to concede that she had been right. They had lived there for more than twenty years. Noah had grown up in the house, had finally left for university and then gone to live in London; Jeanette and he were still there. It would be their last home together. Lately they had talked about moving, maybe into town, to a minimalist apartment with a view of the river, but it had been just talk.

He swung the car past the gateposts and stopped as close as he could to the front door. Jeanette did turn her head now, staring past him and up at the house. It had a steep tiled roof with mansard windows that had always made him think of eyes under heavy lids. A purple-flowered clematis and a cream climbing rose grew beside the front door, the colours harmonising with the dusty red brick of the house. Bill didn't know the names of the varieties, but Jeanette would. She was a passionate gardener.

He turned off the ignition and the silence enveloped them. He took his wife's hand and held it. He wanted to crush it, to rub his mouth against the thin skin, somehow revitalising her with his own heat, but he didn't. He just let her fingers rest in his.

Jeanette's eyes were on him now.

'Are you ready to go inside?' he asked.

She nodded.

He helped her out of the car and she leaned on his arm as they made their way. Once they were in the hallway she indicated that she wanted to stop. The parquet floor was warmed by the late sun, the long-case barometer indicated *Fair*, there was a pile of unopened post on the oak table next to the big pot of African violets.

'Good to be home?' Bill asked.

– *Yes*, Jeanette said. – *Thank you.*

But he could feel the rigidity of her arm, and her neck and her spine. Her fingers dug into his wrist. Gently he urged her forwards, thinking that he would establish her in her chair beside the French windows so that she could look out into the garden while he made her a cup of tea. She let him lead her but instead of sinking into her chair she stood and gazed at the room. It looked as it always did.

Her sudden movement startled him.

Jeanette broke away and snatched up a stone paper-weight that stood on the glass-topped table. She raised her thin arm above her head and brought it down. There was a crack like a rifle-shot as the glass shattered. She lifted the paperweight once more and smashed it down again, this time catching the rim of a porcelain bowl and sending it spinning to the floor. Jeanette swung the paperweight a third and a fourth time and the tabletop shivered into a crystalline sheet. She kept on and on, her arm pumping in a series of diminishing arcs until she had no strength left.

Appalled, and with a shaft of pain in his own chest that left him breathless, Bill tried to catch her wrists. She threw the paperweight away from her and it thudded and then rolled harmlessly on the rug. She clenched her fists instead and pounded them against Bill's chest. Her mouth gaped and her head wagged and gusts of ragged sobbing shook her body.

Jeanette had been deaf since birth. The sounds she was making now were shapeless bellows of anguish.

He managed to catch her flailing arms and pin them to her sides.

'I know,' he crooned. 'I know, I know.'

She was gasping for breath, tears pouring down her face and dripping from her chin. She was too weak to sustain the paroxysm of rage. It subsided as quickly as it had come, leaving her shuddering in his arms. Bill stood still and held her, smoothing the tufts of her pale hair. When he thought she could bear it he took out his hand-kerchief and dried her cheeks. At length he was able to steer her towards the chair and she sank down. He brought up the footstool and sat close against her knees.

Her wrists and fingers were limp now. It cost her a huge effort to speak.

– *I don't want to die.*

Her words came as loose, blurted outbursts. Bill was the

only person she trusted to decipher what she said. Even with her son, she preferred to use sign language for almost everything.

'I know,' he told her. 'You aren't going to die yet.'

Jeanette gazed into his face, searching for the truth.

She had always told him, from when they first knew one another, that he was easy to lip-read because he had a generous face. Some people were costive, keeping their lips pinched in and biting their words in half as if they were coins they were unwilling to spend, but not Bill Bunting.

– *No?*

'No, you are not,' he said firmly.

The oncologist had told them that she might have six months. It could be rather less, just conceivably more, but six months was what he thought they should allow.

Her head drooped.

– *I'm sorry*, she said.

'It doesn't matter. It's a table.' He smiled at her. If he could have changed places with her, he would have done it gladly.

– *For being ill. Leaving you and Noah*.

'You haven't left us,' he said. His hands cupped her knees.

The first time he saw Jeanette Thorne was at a student union party. She was with someone else, a mathematician he knew only slightly. The room was crowded and there was barely enough space for leaping up and down to the punk band. Through a thicket of legs he caught a flicker of her red shoes, platform-soled with a strap across the instep. Then she jumped in the air and the hem of her skirt flipped up to reveal the tender pallor of her bare thighs. He had elbowed his way through the sweaty crowd so he could stand behind her to watch, and ever since that moment he had loved the long blade of her shins and the bluish hollow behind her knees.

That was when they were both twenty-one.

Later that evening he had found himself next to her, packed in a wedge of people between the wall and an angle of the bar. He had studied her pale, abstracted profile against the surging crowd. She looked as if she was deep in thought and he had longed to talk to her. In the end he had positioned himself at her shoulder and had murmured something into the bell of blonde hair that swung to her shoulders, some banal question about what she thought of the band. She ignored him, and he had been about to creep away, abashed. Then a girl he knew pressed her elbow into his ribs.

'That's Jeanette Thorne. She's in Biological Sciences. She's completely deaf, you know. She does everything, just the same. Amazing, really.'

At that moment Jeanette turned her head and for the first time looked straight into his eyes. It was as if she could see into his head, and read the sexual stirring in him before he had even registered it properly himself. Words would have been entirely superfluous. Jeanette's mouth merely curved in a smile that transformed the dingy bar into some antechamber to Paradise.

'I am Bill,' he said.

She placed the flat of her right hand over her breast-bone and gently inclined her head. A lock of hair fell forwards and revealed the thick plastic aid that curved behind her ear. Bill wanted nothing more than to lean forward and kiss that faulty ear and tuck her hair back into place.

It was only when he came to know Jeanette much

better that he understood that her voluptuous body and her mass of blonde hair were at odds with her personality. Jeanette looked wanton, but she was not. She was too determined to be more than just a deaf girl to let even sex distract her for long.

He fell in love with that contradiction.

– *When's Noah coming?*
'He'll be here for dinner.'
– *Will you tell him?*
'I don't exactly know yet.'
Noah would have to be told that his mother's cancer was terminal.

It was a terrible word, that.

They sat with the overturned bowl and the hurled paperweight on the rug beside them, holding on to each other and looking out into the garden as the sun drifted behind the trees. Permanence had turned into fragility. What had been certain was now a series of questions, neither spoken nor answered.

Later, after Jeanette had gone to bed, Bill and Noah sat in the small, cluttered downstairs room that Bill used as his study. They had eaten dinner together, or rather the two men had eaten and Jeanette had made a flattened mound of her food and then placed her knife and fork on top of it.

– *I'm tired*, she had confessed. Noah made the slow journey upstairs with her, and then came down again to join his father.

Bill poured himself a whisky. 'The news about Mum isn't good,' he began tentatively.

'What? What do you mean?' The aggressive edge to

Noah's voice suggested that on some level he had feared this and was now intending to contest the information.

'The surgeon who did the operation told us this morning. They found when they reached the tumour site that there was only a part of it they could remove.'

The television in the corner was on with the sound muted. Familiar newscaster faces floated between footage of soldiers in Afghanistan and the highlights of a football match. Bill kept his eyes on the screen as he talked because he was as yet unable to look at Noah without the risk of weeping.

'So there was another part of it that they couldn't remove? What does that mean? Is she going to *die*? Is that what you're trying to say?' Noah's voice rose.

With an effort, Bill kept his steady.

'They think it's likely to be about six months.'

Noah had a bottle of beer. He rotated it on the arm of his chair, staring as if he hoped each time the label came into sight it might read differently.

'I don't understand. Wait a minute. Are they sure? They can't be certain, can they? I mean, you hear of people who've been given a certain amount of time to live and who get better against all the odds?'

The surgeon had been quite precise. Bill did not think he would ever forget the way the man's hands had rested on the buff folder of Jeanette's notes, the neutral odour of the room that seemed to have had all the air sucked out of it, and Jeanette sitting upright in her chair intently lip-reading as the doctor delivered his news. She had turned only once or twice to Bill for confirmation.

Bill said, 'You do hear of that. I don't want to give you false grounds for optimism, but if you can believe that she will get better, maybe that's how it will turn out. I don't know. All I do know is what the specialist told us today. He didn't leave any room for doubt in my mind. I wish he had done. I wish I could say something different to you.'

There was no rejecting this, after all. Noah was beginning to take in what his father's words really meant.

He said at length, 'It doesn't seem right. Poor Mum.'

The weather man materialised in front of his bands of cloud and clear sunny intervals. They watched the sweep of his arm as he indicated the movement of a front. Weather seemed just as irrelevant as politics or football. Bill drank some of his whisky and the rim of his glass slipped and clinked against his teeth.

'I can't get my head round it,' Noah muttered. 'It's not fair, is it?'

Life had a tendency not to be strictly fair, Bill reflected, although Noah was still too young to appreciate precisely how unfair, how meticulously and even poetically unjust it could be.

Noah said after a while, 'Dad? I'm glad you didn't decide, you know, that you were going to try and keep it from me. Thanks for telling me straight away. I'd much rather hear than have to guess.'

'It was your mother who asked me to tell you tonight,' Bill scrupulously pointed out. He didn't believe he should take the credit for courageous honesty when most of his instincts had been to keep the truth from his child for as long as possible.

He was used to being the speaking intermediary between Jeanette and Noah, but he had long been aware that he was only valuable on the median level. The simple exchanges, relating to mealtimes or rooms to be tidied or homework to be completed before television was to be watched, those they had easily and naturally dealt with between themselves through a mixture of sign language and lip-reading and a range of facial expressions. It had fallen to Bill to put into words for Noah the more mundane but complex facts – timetables, instructions and information connected with day-to-day living. This responsibility had occasionally, he thought, made him appear duller and more pedestrian in his son's eyes than he really was. On the deepest level, for those communications that involved the most intense emotions, any intervention from him would have been superfluous. Mother and son had always understood each other and conveyed their responses to one another with a level of fluency that Bill didn't feel he possessed.

And now, cruelly, there was this. The relaying of more information, tactfully delivered by a concerned doctor, that was nonetheless savage.

Noah didn't ask about how Jeanette had taken the news, or what her state of mind now appeared to be. This he would find out directly from his mother: Bill understood that.

There was one more piece of information he felt he should convey.

'Mum's afraid that she's letting you down.'

'Me? How come?'

'By dying before you are grown up. Before her job's done, is the way she put it.'

'But I am grown up,' Noah said quietly.

At last, Bill's gaze slid from the television screen to his son's profile. Noah's chin was tipped to his chest. Through the mask of adulthood Bill could quite clearly see the child's underlying features, even the soft curves of babyhood. Was the job ever done? he wondered.

Probably not. Jeanette wasn't quite fifty. No wonder she felt that she was leaving too much undone.

'What happens now?' Noah asked.

'Once she recovers from the hospital and the operation, she won't be too bad for a while. She may feel almost herself. I was thinking, perhaps we could go on a holiday. Somewhere we've never been, so there aren't comparisons and memories waiting round every corner. Jeanette will have to decide about that, though.'

A holiday? It would be hard to plan a trip to the Loire Valley or Turkey, Noah thought, with the prospect of death so close at hand. But he had no real idea; he had hardly ever thought about death.

'That sounds like a good idea. And what about you, Dad?'

Bill hadn't yet had time to put the question to himself. Or perhaps had chosen to evade it.

'I want to try to make it as easy as I can for her. Whatever's coming.'

Noah only nodded.

'I need to ask your advice,' Bill continued.

'Go ahead.'

'Should I tell Constance?'

As soon as he uttered her name it seemed to take on a weight of its own, as if it occupied a physical space between them. Noah shifted a little sideways, away from his father, to make room for it. He rocked the beer bottle on the arm of his chair, still studying it with apparent attention.

'Tell her that Mum's ill, you mean? Doesn't she know?'

'I haven't told her.'

And Jeanette certainly would not have done.

Noah considered further. 'It's going to be a shock for Connie, if she doesn't even know that much. I mean, it's bad enough for us, and we've kind of been in on it all along.'

'The later it's left, then the worse it will be.'

'But it's for Mum to decide. It's their relationship, isn't it?'

'Exactly. It's Connie's as well as Mum's. Don't you think we should – *I* should – let her know? Jeanette, you and I, we're her only family.'

Noah shrugged. Here at last, in this raw new dimension, was a place where he could direct a jet of anger. 'I don't care. I only care about Mum. If she doesn't want Auntie Connie around her, then she doesn't. Simple as.' He grabbed the bottle by the neck and tipped it to his mouth.

'Maybe you're right,' Bill said. Half-truths and evasions and unspoken confessions crowded out of history and squeezed into the room with them. Their shadows cut him off from Noah at the moment when he wanted to feel closest to him. Neither of them spoke until Noah sighed and pushed himself to the edge of his chair.

'Dad, I think I'll go up. Unless you want me to stay with you? I could make a cup of tea, if you like.'

'No. Go on up to bed. Get some sleep, if you can. Do you need anything?'

'No, thanks. I'll see you in the morning.'

They both stood up. They hesitated, up until now not having had the kind of adult relationship that involved conspicuous hugging or shedding of tears. Noah rested his arm awkwardly round his father's shoulders and Bill put his hand to the back of the boy's neck. Noah was the taller by an inch. He inclined his head until their foreheads touched and they shuffled together, a rough two-step of grief. It was Noah who broke away first.

'We'll manage, Dad,' he said.

'Of course we will.'

Noah hugged him briefly then dashed out of the room.

Bill stood for a moment, then took the empty beer bottle off the arm of the chair and looked round for somewhere to put it. In the end he replaced it on the tray of drinks. He picked up his own glass, sloshed whisky into it and drank it down in one.

In his room, his childhood bedroom, Noah took his mobile phone out of his pocket and studied the display for a moment. Then he laid it on the table next to his bed. He unlaced his trainers and placed them side by side on the floor beneath the table, undid his belt and took off his jeans. He had always been tidy, Jeanette had insisted on that and even after he had left home he had somehow been unable to cure himself of the habit. There was a row of his old paperbacks on a shelf, a couple of posters and some club flyers pasted to the wall. Noah clenched his fist and thumped the wall beside his bed, just once, but hard enough to make him wince. The silence of the house was undisturbed.

Noah lay down in the remainder of his clothes and locked his hands behind his head. The geography of the ceiling, laid out like an enigmatic map, reminded him of being a child. He screwed his eyes shut and then opened them wide, stretching the orbits, but the reality was still there. At length, bringing faint relief, tears rolled out of the corners of his eyes and ran down his temples to soak into his hair.

Roxana was on the stage. She had been nervous when she first started at The Cosmos, but she learned quickly. The two Brazilian girls were the best dancers, which meant that they earned the most money from giving private dances, so she had watched very carefully to see what they did. And then she had copied their best tricks into her own routine.

She slid her body up the pole, slowly winding one leg around it, then tipped her head back and arched her spine until only her heel kept her anchored. Then she whipped herself upright again, raised her chin and slid her hands up the pole to stretch further upwards, up on tiptoe, to her full height. This, she knew from having checked it in the mirrors, made her look hard-bodied and imperious. So next she softened all her muscles and sank onto her heels, bending her neck so that her head nodded like a flower on its stalk. From this vulnerable pose she raised her eyes, as if coming out of a dream, and stared straight into the wall of men who lined the bar. Her gaze would connect with one of them, and stay fixed while she rotated around her pole.

She would play a game with herself, to see if she could compel the customer to walk down to the front of the club and take a private dance.

Roxana caught her bottom lip between her teeth and smiled at the man she had chosen. When she looked away from him, unhooking the front of her black bodice with deliberate twists of her fingers, and then flicked her glance back again, he was still grinning at her.

This one was almost too easy.

She rotated on her pole again, then detached herself for long enough to peel off the bodice. She stood with her naked back to the audience, braced on her high heels, swaying gently to the music. Then she crossed her arms across her front before turning back again, her face lit up with a teasing smile. This dance was almost over.

The girls stripped to their pants on the pole and no further, that was the routine. Nakedness was reserved for the private customers. The spot would blink off and come up on one of the other dancers while Roxana slipped off the stage.

It wasn't difficult work. The nights were long and the other girls were bitchy, especially the two Brazilians, but Roxana had done worse jobs. It was quite safe, for one thing. Mr Shane's rule was absolute, customers were never allowed to touch the girls. The law for himself was different, but in the week that she had worked at The Cosmos he had hardly tried anything with her. His preference was for the dark-haired voluptuous girls, not 'skinny-arsed Russian tarts', as one of the English dancers had called her backstage, well within her hearing.

'I am from Uzbekistan,' Roxana told her flatly, but the girl had only stared though a pall of cigarette smoke and then turned away to laugh.

With her clothes on again, a short black top over a lace bra, she worked her way through the crowd to the bar. Her customer was one of a group of men in suits with ties pulled open at the neck. They had flushed faces, hair that was either shaved to the skull or fixed in little spikes, and they drank beer from bottles that they slapped down on the bar.

She went straight up to him and said, 'Hello. I am Roxana.'

The other men jostled, grinning and showing their teeth. Heat seemed to rise off the mass of them.

One said, 'Oi Dave, yer in, mate.'

'Hello darlin'. Give us a special dance, then.'

She took Dave's hand and wound past the tables to the chairs at the front in their partially screened alcoves. Only Mr Shane, up in his room behind the one-way mirrors, could see everything that went on in the booths.

'That will be twenty-five, please,' she murmured in Dave's ear before the dance. Her lips almost touched his skin. He took a note out of his wallet and waved it in the air before tucking it inside her garter. It was fifty pounds. Quite often, the men liked to demonstrate to each other how much money they could spend. Roxana thought that was funny, but it worked to her advantage.

She gave him his dance, a really good one. It brought small beads of sweat out on his crimson forehead. The folded note crackled minutely against her skin.

And after Dave, two of his friends wanted private dances too. It was a successful night. When it finally ended, Roxana had earned over three hundred pounds.

Most of the girls took taxis home, but Roxana preferred to save her money. A small wad of notes had already accumulated, wrapped in an old T-shirt that she kept under her mattress. She walked towards the night-bus stop with the hood of her outdoor coat pulled over her head.

Once she was outside the club, the elation brought on by dancing and making men appear to do what she wanted quickly faded.

Tonight she felt hungry and thirsty, and at the same time faintly sick. She hadn't eaten anything since before work, and then only a banana and some slices of white bread. With a customer she had drunk some of the sweet fizzy wine that passed for champagne, but that had only made her more thirsty. Close to the bus stop there was a twenty-four-hour supermarket so she turned towards it. Through the murky glass the lights showed drained blue or dull orange that made the goods on sale look as if they were coated with a sticky film.

A boy and a girl came out of the shop. They were her age, perhaps younger. The boy was carrying a bag of groceries under one arm and the girl had a round sweet on a stick that she licked and then offered to the boy. They balanced against each other for a second while he closed his mouth on the sweet, making a pop-eyed look at her, and then they danced apart again. They brushed past Roxana and hurried away.

There were few other people in sight, but they all seemed to be couples hurrying home to burrow together in a warm bed.

Loneliness descended like a black bag dropping over her head. Through the shop window she could see shelves stacked with packets and tins but she couldn't imagine what she was going to buy. Not even the thought of the night's money zipped against her ribs offered any comfort. She hesitated, then turned away from the shop and walked heavily towards the bus stop.

The house was silent when she let herself in. It was very late; the running feet and slamming doors, even the music, had all subsided. Roxana pressed the timed switch next to the front door and walked quickly up the stairs because the light only stayed on for a few seconds.

Dylan's door was closed. Then she looked at her own and her breath caught.

The wood was splintered round the lock. There were splits in the panels where someone had kicked them.

She put out her hand and reluctantly pushed, and the door swung open.

Her bed had been tipped over, the mattress now lay beneath the frame and the pillow had been slashed. Her clothes lay scattered and little shards of blue plastic and metal from her transistor radio glinted among them. Her packets of rice and biscuits had been upended and the debris lay on the floor in a swamp of soured milk.

Roxana knelt beside the mattress and felt for the folded T-shirt. She recovered that, but the envelope of money was gone.

She backed out onto the landing. It was hard to work out which felt less safe now: her ripped-apart room, the shadowed stairwell with its stained walls and scrawled graffiti, or the streets outside. Then the light blinked off and left her in darkness.

Roxana shuddered but she made herself keep steady. She felt her way across the landing to Dylan's door and knocked. Softly at first, and then when there was no response she banged with her clenched first. At last he opened the door and a crack of yellow light shone through.

'Did you do this?' Roxana hissed.

She saw at once that he had not. Dylan looked too thin in his holey vest, too scared and fragile himself. His black hair stood up where he had slept on it.

'Jesus, no. I did not. What d'ye take me for?'

'Who did, then?'

Dylan shook his head. 'Dunno.'

She could have gone back into her room and cleared up the mess and found a way to wedge the door shut, but she knew that however much effort she made it wouldn't be enough to keep the house at bay. Not in her head, anyway.

One thing at a time. Get through this night, first of all.

'All right. Can I sleep with you tonight?'

A flash of eagerness lit up Dylan's face. 'Sure ye can.' He was already reaching for her as she stepped back.

'Not like that. Just let me put my stuff on your floor.'

'Eh? Oh. Right. Well, yeah, I suppose.'

'Help me with my mattress.'

They dragged it into his room and squeezed it into the small floor space. Carefully Roxana unstuck the beach postcard from her wall and brought it with her, placing it next to her torn pillow. When Dylan turned the light off she lay in the darkness, her fingers resting on sand and palm trees.

'They stole my money,' she whispered.

'Did they so?'

'Was it Kemal?'

'Dunno,' he repeated. He probably did, but he wasn't going to risk telling her. 'Animals, they are.'

Roxana closed her eyes. Her body buzzed with adrenalin. Sleep, she ordered herself. Sleep now, and tomorrow find somewhere else to live.

Within touching distance, Dylan scratched and fidgeted. 'Don't ye want to come in here with me?'

It would be a comfort to feel the warmth of another body. To concentrate on sex might be to forget everything else.

'No,' Roxana said. She turned her back on him and pulled the blanket over her shoulders.

In his flat in Hammersmith Noah was yawning and making coffee and playing one of Andy's mixes. Normally at this time on a Sunday morning he would be asleep, but today he was planning to go home again to see Jeanette and Bill. He glanced at the number when his mobile rang, but didn't recognise it.

He knew her voice, though, as soon as she spoke.

'Hello. Is this Noah?'

'*Roxana*. How are you? Where are you?' Now it was happening, he realised how often he had imagined this exchange. Mild fantasies had provided an escape route from worrying about his mother.

'I am . . . I am in a telephone box, near to where I used to be living.'

'Used to be?'

'There is some trouble.'

'Tell me about it.'

An hour later, he was waiting for her at the entrance to the tube station.

Roxana came up the escalator and struggled through the ticket barrier with a cheap tartan suitcase. She looked bruised today, not surprisingly after what she had told him about the break-in. There were circles under her eyes and her hair was greasy and flat, but her mouth was lovelier than he remembered.

They walked through mild summer sunshine back to the flat. Noah carried the suitcase. It wasn't heavy.

'Is this everything, or have you got more luggage?'

She looked surprised.

'This is all.'

He was briefly wondering, now that it was too late, whether he had been over-hasty in asking a girl he hardly knew to stay in his flat while she searched for somewhere else to live. Even a girl who looked like Roxana. But his flatmate Andy had just gone to Barcelona for a week. There was plenty of room, for the next few days at least.

Was he really going to say to her, no, I'm afraid I can't help you?

Apparently reading his mind, she said, 'Thank you, Noah. You are kind to do this. I am not going back to that house. It is a really bad place.'

'Are you going to tell the police about your money being stolen?'

'Police? No. I don't like to deal with the police.'

She would have her reasons for that, Noah realised. Probably to do with her immigration status. He glanced at her as they walked. He did have a suspicion that he had just invited into his life someone who would not disappear as quickly as she had materialised, but the thought didn't bother him too much. On the contrary, new beginnings might be just that, and they would be welcome. Elsewhere in his life he was hobbled either by anxiety or routine.

'How's the dance job working out?' he asked cautiously.

'It is okay.'

When they reached the house she followed him up the communal stairs and stood silently while he fumbled with his keys. Once they were inside she glanced round then her shoulders slumped with relief.

He apologised automatically. 'It might look a bit of a mess. You know, two blokes sharing. But it's all right underneath.'

'It is beautiful,' Roxana said.

Noah knew that it wasn't anything of the kind, but the word gave him a dim picture of what she must have left behind.

'Here's the kitchen, and that's the living room. Bathroom there. This is Andy's room, and this one's mine.' He opened the door. 'You can sleep in here. I'll just dig out some clean sheets and stuff.'

He'd better not put her in Andy's room, he thought. She could sleep in his bed, and he'd camp out in Andy's.

'Thank you,' Roxana said again. She dragged her suitcase towards her and sat down on the edge of his chair. 'I am not sure what to have done if you couldn't help me.'

Her accent was thicker than he remembered, and although her English was competent she sometimes constructed her sentences oddly or was at a loss for a word. She seemed less enigmatic than when they had met by the river and more fleshed-out, now she was in his flat, a proper person with a history and problems to solve. He was drawn to her even more strongly.

Noah fetched a clean sheet and a duvet cover. He bundled up his own linen, relieved that it didn't look too bad. She helped him to make up the bed, and this domestic collaboration made him smile and remember Lauren, his most recent girlfriend, who had gone travelling two months ago. Before she went she told him that she thought they should have a year's break from each other, but when she got back, well – you never knew. He had found this degree of uncertainty disconcerting and inhibiting. Until now, at least.

The room was right at the top of the house, under the roof. There were no proper windows, only a skylight over the bed. Roxana looked up into the rectangle of blue.

'I like this. It feels safe here.'

'You're safe. No one's going to break in. There are four giant Kiwis living downstairs, anyone tries to get in the house they'll be kicked straight into touch.'

Roxana's eyes travelled to him.

'Rugby,' he explained lamely. She laughed for the first time that day. For Noah, it was like a firework going off in his chest.

'Now, what are we going to do?' she asked.

'I have to go in a minute. I'm late already.'

Her eyes widened. 'That is a shame. Where are you going?'

'Home, to see my parents. My mother's out of hospital now, but the news isn't very good. She's only got about six months to live.'

'I am sorry for that. But I thought you said before that she would get better?'

'I was wrong. I didn't know, then. Are your parents in Uzbekistan?'

'My father and mother are both dead. I have a stepfather still alive, but I don't care for him. He is a bad man.' Roxana shrugged, dismissing this as a topic.

'Brothers and sisters?'

'No.'

'Nor me.'

'I had one brother but he was killed,' she said without expression.

Noah looked harder at her. He didn't know anything about her and he was becoming aware of how much there was to find out. With Lauren and with other girls, he had been starting from the same place: eighty per cent, he reckoned, of their experiences were comparable with his own even if not strictly in common. Not so with Roxana.

'That's really very sad. I'm sorry. Was it some kind of accident?'

'In my country there was an uprising, in Andijan, and

he was shot by soldiers. Niki came to see me one week before this and told me that there would be violent times, and I told him to be careful because we only had him and me, the two of us, against the whole world. After that I did not see him again.'

As an only child Noah had longed for brothers and sisters. He had envied those of his friends who had the shoehorned-in, day-and-night constant narrative of close siblings, even though they quarrelled and fought with each other. He could barely imagine the pain of having had a brother and then losing him.

He would have liked to offer Roxana some protection, maybe to tell her that he would be her defender from now on, if she would like it, but he couldn't think of a way of saying it that didn't sound either comical or entirely fake, as if he was trying to set himself up as some kind of hero. He was also quite conscious of his own inadequacy. Whatever he offered, he would be unlikely to be able to actually deliver it satisfactorily. He knew this because Lauren had often told him that he meant well, but meaning and doing were two different things as far as she was concerned, right?

Instead of any of this he put his hand awkwardly on her arm, above the elbow, where the short sleeve of her strange top protected her pale skin.

He said as simply as he could, 'I'm very sorry, Roxana. It must have been terrible for you. And you must be lonely without him.'

Noah knew that he had been sheltered. Popular at school and university, good at games, adequate at academic work, he had never been without protection and had never felt significantly lonely in his whole life. Bill and Jeanette had seen to that.

Roxana's eyes had acquired the red-rimmed look that preceded tears.

'Why are you here, in England?' he asked.

She rubbed her nose with the back of her hand and at the same time moved out of his grasp. Noah let his hand fall to his side.

'I am working, earning good money, saving it up when I do not get robbed. I am going to be an English girl.'

She said it with such fervour that he had to laugh.

'Really? Are you sure that's what you want?'

She blinked at him. 'Why not? Where I came from there is no work, people are poor, ignorance is every-where.'

Noah collected his thoughts. He said, 'I suppose, wait a minute – Uzbekistan is your home, the culture is yours, the language and traditions. All that has made you what you are, as well as your family, and everything that's happened to you since you were born. Why do you want to turn your back on it? I mean, by making yourself English you'll only be a replica, whereas what you are already is the real thing.'

Roxana unzipped her suitcase. She took out a few clothes and laid them on the bed, then propped a picture postcard of a beach beside the magazines and piled CDs on Noah's table.

In a tone that denied the possibility of contradiction she said, 'I believe that you can be whatever you want.'

Yes, Noah had to concede, Roxana probably could be. He had the impression there was determination in her, strong as a rib of steel.

He checked his watch.

'I've really got to go,' he sighed. 'I promised my dad

I'd be home for Sunday lunch. But I'll be back here this evening, we could maybe go out for a pizza or a drink, and we can talk some more. Shall we do that?'

'I have to go to work this evening.'

'Really? You do a performance on a Sunday night?'

He was envisaging a contemporary dance ensemble, something very avant-garde with dancers in white face-paint and stylised costumes. The image loosely connected in his mind with Roxana's interest in the robot beside the river.

Roxana frowned and hesitated, obviously trying to come to a decision. Then she said flatly, 'I work in a club, I think I had better tell you. It's called The Cosmos. It opens every night of the week. You live here in this very nice apartment, you have a good job, a nice family I'm sure. Perhaps you don't like to have someone doing this type of work staying with you?'

'Cosmos? I've never heard of it.' Noah believed that he had a good working knowledge of London clubs. 'What do you do there?'

'I am what is called a lap dancer.' Roxana tilted her chin up as she announced this. She looked even more like a primitive carving. 'Do you know what this is?'

'Of course I do.' Noah was assailed by a series of images. For a moment he thought it best not to say anything more.

'You are shocked?'

'No,' he managed to say. Shocked wasn't it at all.

'So?'

'I bet you're really good at it.'

Roxana began to laugh. Soon Noah was laughing as well. They laughed until they were both breathless.

'So I'll definitely be coming to see you.'

She turned serious at once. 'No, please, don't do that. I would find it very embarrassing if you were there.'

'Embarrassing? Would you?'

'Of course. It doesn't matter when I dance for men I don't know, it doesn't mean anything. But with you, because I like you, it would be different.'

Noah was disarmed. There was such a contradiction in the idea of this girl doing a lap-dance routine in a room full of punters, and at the same time being shy enough not to know where to look as she paid him a mild compliment.

He tried to think what Lauren or one or two of her friends might say if they were included in this conversation.

Almost certainly it would be something correct about how places like this Cosmos club were degrading to women. This judgement didn't quite connect, though, with what he had already learned about Roxana. She needed the money, yes, but it was quite likely that she went about getting it in a way that didn't damage her too much. She would probably wield more power in the transaction than the men did.

Noah admired her.

She was also beautiful, she was like no other girl he had ever met, and now they were looking at each other in the equivocal aftermath of her confession and their shared laughter.

'Will you be all right here while I'm out?' he asked. 'I'll give you the spare set of keys.'

She beamed back at him, suddenly full of confidence.

'I am safe here with the men downstairs who play rugby. You told me. All I will do is lie in your bed and go to sleep.'

Noah swallowed hard. 'Good. I'll see you later, then.'

After he had gone, Roxana put her clothes neatly aside. Noah's room was tidy, she liked that. She curled up under the crisp bedcover and fell asleep.

The garden looked to be at its summer peak, to Noah's uncritical eyes. There were the roses, and tall pale-blue spikes of flowers, some other round shaggy pink ones, and metallic clumps of silvery leaves spilling on the mown grass. But Jeanette was shaking her head as they made a slow circuit after lunch.

He told her, 'Mum. It looks beautiful. Don't sweat it.'

– *There is so much to do.*

'Like pruning the effing roses?'

Her hand touched his arm. The skin on the back of her hand looked thin, and as finely crinkled as an old leaf. Noah thought that she was ageing and fading before his eyes. He wanted to reach inside her and tear out the black tumour and crush it in his fists, and the fierceness of the impulse balled up in his chest like terrible anger.

She signed again – *You don't prune this time of year.*

'Whatever.'

– *It's dead-heading. Chopping off dead blooms. Like me.*

'Is that what you are thinking?'

– *I'm still getting used to no next year. But there will be for you and Dad. I think of that. I love you both very much. Do you know?*

They had turned back towards the house. Bill was sitting on a patio chair reading the Sunday newspapers and Jeanette's eyes rested on him. Noah had always been aware that Jeanette loved his father unequivocally and possessively. His friends' mothers didn't do the ironing and suddenly press their faces blindly against a shirt or a pair of gardening trousers, the way he had seen his mother do, for example. His childish suspicion was that Bill didn't know she did things like that.

For himself, Noah knew that Jeanette loved him and he accepted it without question. Mothers always did love their children, didn't they?

'I do know,' he said.

– *Good. Will you remember?*

'I promise. But I don't want to talk like this. We're still here, the three of us. Now is what matters, here, today, this sunshine, not next year or next month.'

Jeanette nodded.

– *You are right. But I can't pretend not to have cancer.*

'I didn't mean that.'

– *I know. Tell me about your week?*

'Let's think. Work's okay. Andy's in Barcelona. Oh, and I met a girl.'

– *Did you?*

Her face flowered in an eager smile. But Noah was wondering what possibility there was of any conversation about anything that wouldn't bring them straight up against a blank wall that had *six months* painted on it in letters higher than a house.

Jeanette wouldn't live to see his wedding. She wasn't going to know her own grandchildren.

Her head was cocked towards him, her eyes on his.

'Her name's Roxana.'

– *Unusual.*

He talked, and they made another slow circuit of the lawn. There were wood pigeons calling in the coppice trees. He told her about Roxana being robbed, and how she was staying with him while she looked for another place. He kept any mention of her job to a minimum, and then said that her brother had been killed in Andijan. He only vaguely remembered the news stories of the time about the brief popular uprising against a virtual dictatorship.

Jeanette nodded. She was interested now and she signed rapidly, occasionally adding a word that came out of her mouth like a bubble bursting.

– *Yes. A massacre. Their government claimed it was only a few. The international human rights organisations accepted that in the end. President Karimov was supported by the West, until he turned the Americans off their bases out there. Bush needs his allies in Central Asia.*

Noah was impressed, but not surprised that his mother knew so much. Jeanette always read everything that came her way, storing up news and comment, fiction and history like bulwarks against her deafness. She had been an early adopter of the internet as a source of yet more information, and her email connections and correspondences were more numerous than his own.

– *Your Roxana's brother was one of the rebels?*

'I think so. She's not "mine". Not yet, anyway, although I'm working on it. Her parents are both dead, she told me. Her brother was all she had. How sad is that, to lose your only sibling? The person you grew up with. It must mean Roxana hasn't got any reference left to the little girl she was.'

Jeanette waited.

– *Go on?*

Noah faltered. 'I wasn't trying to say anything else, Mum. Not consciously. It must be in my mind, though. You and Connie.'

– Yes. I know. Me and Connie.

Here we are again, he thought. Six months.

He faced her. It meant she could lip-read more easily.

'Dad and I were thinking, Connie would want to know that you're ill.'

– You and Dad?

'Well, yes.'

– Please. Don't.

'I'm sorry. It was only a brief mention.'

Jeanette looked towards Bill. Some instinct had made him lower his newspaper and he was watching them over the top of it. She moved close to Noah's side again and they resumed their slow walk. Jeanette's face was suffused with sadness.

– She is my sister.

'Yes.'

– I should decide what to tell her. And when. Shouldn't I?

'Of course, Mum, if that's what you want.'

Bill strolled across the grass towards them.

'What are you two talking about?'

Noah hesitated. Auntie Connie was rarely mentioned in the family. Or never, now he thought about it.

– Uzbekistan, Jeanette indicated.

'Really?'

– Noah has a new girlfriend who comes from there.

'She's not my girlfriend yet. I've only met her twice.'

Bill smiled easily at him. 'I'll look forward to hearing about her. If and when. Now, does anyone want a cup of tea?'

Noah washed up the lunch dishes and Bill made tea. They sat out in the sun until it sank behind the trees and the garden receded into shadow. The pale roses began to glimmer against the depths of green. Noah said that he thought he would head back to town. In his mind was the thought and the hope that maybe Roxana wouldn't have gone off to her club quite this early.

He kissed the top of his mother's head and noted the pink channels of scalp visible through her hair.

'I'll talk to you tomorrow, Mum.' Talk was by email.

Bill walked him to the front door and leaned on the open door of Noah's rusted Golf.

'You haven't told me about the girl.'

'Nothing to tell. Let me know if anything happens here, Dad.'

Bill stood back. 'We're all right.' He waved until Noah pulled out of sight.

Jeanette went upstairs to her study and turned on the computer.

Back at the flat, Noah found nothing but darkness and silence. Roxana had correctly double-locked the flat door and the street door. He looked into his bedroom, and saw that she had smoothed the duvet and plumped up the pillow after her sleep.

He drifted back into the living room and stretched himself out on the sofa. He thought he would wait up for her, to make sure that she came back safely.

FOUR

Suitcases and boxes of film equipment almost filled the hotel lobby. Taxis and 4x4s were waiting to sweep them away, Angela and Rayner and Simon Sheringham, the complaining actress, the creative duo who were hiding their hangovers behind dark glasses, and all the rest of the cast and crew.

'Thanks for coming to see us off,' Angela murmured to Connie in the hubbub of departure. 'Think about what I said, won't you? I mean, it's beautiful here, but it's not *home*, is it?'

'Yes,' Connie said, ambiguously.

Miraculously, the mounds of luggage fitted into the vehicles and people variously scrambled for places in the cars that looked as if they would have the best air-conditioning. Only two minutes ago it had seemed as if the point of departure would never arrive, and now everyone except Connie had piled into a seat.

She stood back and waved. Angela blew her a kiss and Rayner Ingram lifted one hand before adjusting his Ray-Bans. People shouted goodbye to her and then hastily wound up their windows to keep out the flies and the gusts of hot, steamy air. The convoy of cars rolled forwards and Connie saw Ed looking at her through the rear window of the last 4x4. He touched two fingers to his temple in an ironic salute.

Connie stood still as silence descended. There was no clamour of mobile phones, no crackle of walkie-talkies, and no one was shouting. There was only birdsong, and the faint scrape of rough-edged leaves spreading in the sun's glare.

She drew in a long breath and then exhaled.

The week had been like a runaway train ride. She had been right to be apprehensive. She had been very thoroughly shaken out of her equilibrium.

Maybe she should have gone back to Ed's room last night.

She muttered to herself, 'How many more chances d'you think you're going to get?'

Then she saw that the doorman was glancing curiously at her. She gave the man what she hoped was a composed smile, and set off down the hotel drive towards the village street.

Connie didn't have a car. As with her choice not to have a pool, her European neighbours (Kim and Neil who were in property and rentals, the French couple who owned a gallery in the main street, Werner Baum the sculptor, and all the others) regarded this as wilfully eccentric. But Connie liked walking, she had a bicycle for errands, and on the island she was never in a hurry. If she needed to go further afield there were the public bemos, small buses that ran fixed routes all over the island, and taxis were cheap.

The main street was quiet this morning. She passed a couple of dogs lolling in the shade, and a young woman sitting on her step with two smooth, plump toddlers playing at her feet. In front of the Café des Artistes a group of tourists in shorts and Birkenstocks were consulting a map and talking about a visit to the monkey forest.

'They bite,' one of the girls warned the others. 'And then you get rabies.'

'Noooo? They look so cute.'

Connie crossed the road and took her favourite route through the village's central market. She loved the blazing colour and exuberance of the enclosed square. Two-storey buildings with open fronts were hung from ground to roof with dresses and T-shirts, *ikat* weavings and multicoloured sarongs, and the paved space in the centre was jammed with blue and red parasols. In the shade the stall-holders were selling racks of beads and earrings, woven baskets in all shapes and sizes, plastic toys and cheap CDs. It was too early for the tourist crowds to be out in any force and the vendors were quietly gossiping with their neighbours. Connie was heading for the flower stall in the far corner. The blooms made a wall of brilliance beneath a sun-bleached awning.

Recognising Connie, the broad-hipped woman who owned the stall sprang up and began yanking stems of orchids and tuberoses out of buckets and pressing them into her hands. Business wasn't good for any of these traders. Tourists had almost disappeared after the Kuta bombing, and they were still not coming to the island in the same numbers. Connie went through the ritual of praising the flowers for their freshness and the elegance of their blooms and at the same time firmly putting them back in their places.

She saw what she wanted at the back of the stall. They were scarlet cannas, blisteringly bright, offset by ribbed bronze leaves. When she had chosen an armful and told the stallholder what she wanted them for, the woman wrapped them in a swathe of white tissue brought out from a special hiding place, and finished off

the bouquet with a stiff crepe-paper bow. Connie counted out *rupiah* notes, worn as soft and floppy as thin
cloth.

'Thank you,' she said.

She ducked out of the market, waving to two or three
of the shoppers, and walked on towards Kadek Daging's
general store. He was back in his usual place after his
week of driving for the movie people. As soon as he saw
her coming he bustled out from between his sacks of rice
and drums of oil.

'*Selamat siang, Ibu*,' he beamed. 'Glamour all finished
for you and me. Back to ordinary life.'

'*Selamat siang*, Kadek. I don't know about glamour.
We had a busy week, though, didn't we?'

Kadek glanced round and lowered his voice. 'I did not
see her myself, but she was here, wasn't she? Working in
the film?'

'Who?'

He checked again to make sure that there was no one
eavesdropping from behind a tower of detergent packets
and then whispered,

'Penelope Cruz.'

Connie considered this. 'I'm not sure. In a bank commercial? I certainly didn't see her.'

Kadek stood back with a satisfied nod. 'Yes. I knew
that she was. I heard it from the mother of one of the
young girls. Very beautiful. Not as beautiful perhaps as
Angelina Jolie, but still. I expect you didn't get the
chance to work with her?'

'No,' Connie agreed. 'I didn't, unfortunately.'

'Never mind,' he consoled her. 'Films are being made
all the time, here in Bali. Perhaps next time. Those are
very good flowers. Are they a gift, wrapped like that?'

'I'm taking them to Dewi. Wayan Tupereme told me last night that she has a son.'

'Yes, the birth was yesterday. I hear the baby is very small. You will be needing some first-quality rice.'

'That's exactly why I'm here, Kadek.'

They spent five minutes debating a suitable choice, and then Connie made her way onwards with the two-kilo package under her other arm. The quickest way to Dewi's husband's family house, on the far side of the village where the paddy fields opened up, was to cut through the monkey forest. She walked briskly to where the street petered out in a clutch of little shops and open stalls.

The same group of tourists was now at the margin of the forest enclosure, negotiating with a small boy over the price of bunches of finger-sized bananas to feed to the monkeys.

It was cool and shady under the canopy of tall trees and the dirt tracks were easier on the feet than the uneven paving of the village streets. Connie often walked here, enjoying the quiet and the scent of damp leaves and trodden dust. She slowed her pace to a stroll, but she always kept an eye on the monkeys who sat in the branches or knuckle-walked at the edges of the paths. From behind her came a thin scream of alarm and then a chorus of shouts. She smiled; without even turning to look she knew that a troop of monkeys had executed a classic distraction manoeuvre followed by a pincer attack, and had successfully snatched the bunch of bananas from the grasp of the most monkey-friendly of the tourists.

In the middle of the forest was a temple complex. It was a mossy group of red-brick structures, open to the sky, the stone facings fleeced with lichen. A few people were on their way to or from prayer, women with baskets of fruit balanced on padded headpieces and men in the obligatory sarongs and bright sashes. Those who were returning had flowers behind their ears and grains of rice pressed to their cheeks, and their hair was beaded with moisture from splashing with *tirta*, holy water.

Monkeys prowled along the temple walls and sat in rows on the steps, picking fleas from one another's backs. Several of them bit into the hijacked bananas. They were macaques with black-faced babies clinging to their fur. Connie noticed with sudden dismay that instead of a monkey baby, one male had a tiny, bedraggled ginger kitten. He detached the little creature from his chest and flipped it over the back of his hand like a set of worry beads. Then he tossed it in the dust at his feet, yawning as he poked at it with his prehensile fingers. The kitten gave out almost soundless mews of distress when the macaque upended it and delicately scratched its pale-pink belly with black hooked fingernails. But when the monkey withdrew its hand the kitten righted itself and crawled back towards its tormentor, searching for protection.

The temples had colonies of wild cats as well as monkeys. Connie stared around her, wanting to rescue the little creature and restore it to its proper mother. But if she tried to swoop in and snatch it away the monkeys would certainly attack her. The tourists were right about that; they did bite. The monkey picked up the kitten again, perhaps in response to its mewing, and tucked it against his chest. It glared at Connie and the kitten hung on like the other babies, blinking its pale gummed-up eyes at the world.

Connie walked on. Trying to get the little scene out of her mind, she told herself that without its mother's milk the kitten wouldn't have to suffer for very much longer. The back of her neck and her shirt where the packet of rice pressed against it were clammy with sweat.

The path out of the forest crossed a small gorge by way of a plank suspension bridge, the metalwork crusted with decades-worth of wood-pigeon droppings. The planks creaked and swayed under her feet and she broke into a laden dash for the safety of the opposite side, stepping onto solid ground again and then laughing at her moment of panic.

Out here was the real village. Tourists never penetrated this far from the centre and there were no coffee shops or galleries. A sprawl of smallholdings and palm-thatch houses were separated by rank ditches clogged with refuse. Connie ducked under the silver filaments of a spider's web and noted the impressive size of the tortoiseshell-mottled spider gently swaying at the centre. She stepped over another ditch and made her way up to Pema's family house. Today it was distinguished from the others by *penjors*, tall bamboo poles with curled bark and flags to denote a special occasion.

There was no one sitting on the frayed rattan chairs drawn up against the wall, only a line of washing suspended between two palm trunks. Underneath the laundry a row of woven bamboo cages the size and shape of large bell jars each housed a dusty brown hen. The dried mud around the cages was starred with the prints of chickens' feet and speckled with scattered corn.

Connie tapped on the door jamb. After a moment a woman bobbed up out of the dimness of the interior. She was big, wearing a pink blouse and a faded sarong. Connie recognised Pema's mother. She placed the flowers and rice on the nearest chair, pressed the palms of her hands together and bowed over her fingertips before murmuring the expected greeting and congratulations.

Pema's mother returned the salute.

Connie handed over the traditional gifts, flowers for fertility and rice for prosperity.

'Thank you. Please come inside.'

Connie left her sandals in the row beside the door and went in barefoot. A small fan churned the air, but the room was still stuffy and as hot as a furnace. It seemed to be crowded with people, most of whom were pressed between the two weaving looms that occupied two-thirds of the floor space. A very old woman, perhaps Pema's grandmother, sat at the bench in front of one of the looms. Her brown hands rested on the unfinished length of *ikat* cloth, and she was so small that her feet dangled six inches short of the treadles.

Everyone bowed to Connie and she returned the salutes, working from the oldest down to whoever appeared to be the youngest. One of the teenaged girls, a sister, held a baby of a few months, a round-faced infant with the heavy-lidded stare of a miniature deity.

Dewi lay propped up on cushions on a wooden divan. She held a swaddled bundle in her arms. Two or three years back, Connie remembered, she had been hardly more than a little girl, and even now she looked far too young to be a mother. There were purple rings of fatigue around her eyes but her small, even white teeth showed in a broad grin of pride as Connie stooped beside her.

'Well done,' Connie smiled.

Before her marriage Dewi had often come over to Connie's house to drink Cokes or make herself imaginative snacks from the sparse contents of Connie's fridge, and to giggle over Western magazines. She had a good voice, and loved to sing or la-la the lyrics of pop songs while Connie sat at her keyboard playing the melody and joining in the choruses.

Pema's mother asked if Connie would care to drink a glass of green tea, and Connie politely accepted. There was a stir of large bodies in the crowded room.

'Would you like to hold him?' Dewi whispered.

'Yes, please.'

Dewi handed the tiny bundle into Connie's arms. It weighed almost nothing. She looked down into the baby's sleeping face. One purple-grey fist was bunched against his cheek, and two tiny commas of damp black eyelashes punctuated the wrinkled mask. He looked premature, and also prehistorically ancient. Connie's throat tightened.

'What's his name?'

'Wayan.'

Wayan or Putu for the firstborn of Balinese families, depending on caste; Kadek or Madé for the second; Komang or Nyoman for the third and Ketut for number four, then back to Wayan again. That was how it went. No fanciful baby names, even for a girl who pored over second-hand celebrity magazines as eagerly as Dewi did.

'He's beautiful,' Connie told her.

Pema came in with another group of visitors in tow, also carrying flowers and packets of rice. Everyone in the room edged up to make space, and Connie thought that she would certainly melt if it got any hotter. She pressed her lips to baby Wayan's forehead, breathing in the scent of fresh birth. There was an urge inside her to hold the child more closely, feeling his damp skin against her own, but instead she replaced the bundle gently in Dewi's outstretched hands.

'I'll go outside. To make some room,' she mumbled. Through the thickets of flowers and staring faces she made it into the air. She was sitting on one of the rattan chairs and watching a large black pig, tethered by the leg to a sapling, when Pema came out with one of his sisters behind him. The sister poured green tea into glasses and handed one to Connie and one to Pema. Pema sat down and they sipped their tea while the pig rooted in the ditch and contentedly grunted to itself.

'You must be proud, Pema,' Connie said.

He smoothed back his thick hair. He was small but quite good-looking. Before he and Dewi fell in love with each other, Connie had often seen him with a group of his friends, circling on their motorcycles like a flock of two-wheeled birds and eyeing the tourist girls in their shorts and bikini tops.

'I am. But I am also worried about being responsible.'

Pema was an apprentice mechanic at a small garage on the road that led down to the coast. He would be earning very little money, which was why he and Dewi were living with his parents. Until the two of them could save enough money to buy or build their own house, they would have to stay here among the stepped genera-tions of grandparents and brothers and sisters and the various other babies.

'That comes with being a father,' she smiled at him. Pema was a good boy, she thought. He was looking at her in that unspecifically hopeful, speculative way that meant he was wondering if her immense, uncountable Western wealth might somehow be harnessed to his advantage.

'Do you have children, perhaps?'

'No, I don't,' Connie told him.

'That is a shame for you,' Pema said, all sympathetic awareness of the divide that now existed between the two of them. He was probably thinking that piles of her money wouldn't compensate for not having a baby son like day-old Wayan.

There wasn't much else to say, and neither of them felt the need to make further conversation. They drank the rest of their tea and sat looking thoughtfully at Pema's mother's garden of peppers and chillies and coconut palms. Behind a small hedge flies swarmed around the brown haunches of a tethered buffalo.

More people kept arriving. When Connie went to say goodbye, she could only manage to wave to Dewi and blow a kiss from the edge of the crowd. Later in the day, according to custom, the washed placenta would be wrapped in a sacred cloth and the visitors would all witness its burial inside a coconut shell near the gateway to the house.

By the time Connie made it home the afternoon had reached the point where the light was at its ripest. It lay like melted butter over the vast swathe of gently stirring leaves, gilding the fronds of tree ferns and shining on the stippled trunks of palm trees so that they gleamed like beaten silver. Connie went out to her chair on the veranda and sat listening to the trickle of water and the various layers of birdsong.

She let the questions sink slowly to the bottom of her pool of thoughts. In time, as the shoot receded, the sediment of habit would cover up her memories.

Peace lapped round her once again.

She sat for a long time, until the tropical twilight swept up again from the depths of the gorge. As the sudden darkness fell, she wandered back into the house and poured herself a glass of wine. Connie seldom drank alone, but tonight she felt the need for just one drink.

There were no telephone messages. She took a long swallow of wine, and set the glass down on her desk as she switched on her computer. It was days since she had checked her emails. Broadband hadn't yet reached the village and she wandered out to the veranda again while the unread messages slowly descended from the ether and filtered into her inbox. She drank some more wine and then, counter to her intentions, topped up her glass.

At the screen again Connie clicked through the spam and a couple of emails from London to do with work. There was a message from the leader of the string quartet, thanking her for booking them for the commercial. Connie closed that and her eyes flicked to the sender of the next message. *Bunting*. Her brain had hardly taken it in before her heart was hammering. She looked away from the screen and then back again, but it wasn't an illusion. *Bunting*.

It was only then that she saw the sender wasn't *BBunting*, but *JBunting*. Jeanette.

The last time she had seen her sister was four years ago, after Hilda's funeral.

They hadn't spoken since then, nor had they written.

That was the last time she had seen Bill, too.

She shouldn't allow herself to remember their joint history, even to think about him. But what harm did it do to anyone, except perhaps herself?

A message from her sister now could only mean that something was wrong.

With Noah? With *Bill*?

Her mouth was dry and her hands shook as she opened

the message. It took two readings before the news began to sink in.

There was indeed something very badly wrong. Connie read and reread the brief lines.

Dear Connie,

I hope this address still finds you because I want you to hear this news from me, not from anyone else.

I have cancer. I won't go into detail, but after several months of treatment and having our hopes raised and then lowered again, we were told this week that there isn't any more to be done. Six months is the estimate.

I am beginning to work out for myself what this means. What does it mean?

It's very hard for Noah. And for Bill. Both of them are full of love and concern for me, and I feel blessed in that.

There it is. I don't want anything, except to know that you know.

Love (I mean this . . .)

Jeanette

Connie lowered her face into her hands. Her forearms pressed against the keyboard and, unseen, the screen split into layers of files. The immediate shock made her shiver. Jeanette had always been there: in her silence, in her brave focus on doing and being what she wanted, her influence most powerful – partly because of its very absence – in all Connie's past life.

Behind her eyes, images of her sister receded into their remote childhood.

The chair she was sitting in became one of the pine set at the kitchen table in Echo Street. The desk became the knotty old table that had come with them from the flat before, the top half of a house in Barlaston Road, where old Mrs McBride lived downstairs.

Jeanette had planted the idea in Connie that their neighbour was a witch.

– At night, she rides in the sky. If you look, you can see the broomstick in her back kitchen.

Now Jeanette was sitting opposite her, eleven years old, full of hope and strength in spite of her deafness.

Connie lifted her head. She reached for her glass, and drank the wine.

The computer screen was blinking, asking her if she wanted to close down now.

It took an effort to reopen the email programme. Connie's fingers felt uncertain on the keys, like a child's.

She started a new message and typed a single line.

I'll be there as soon as I can get a flight. Connie.

The train from the airport ran past the backs of Victorian terraced houses, irregular and broken like crooked teeth in an overcrowded jaw. There were brief glimpses of clothes lines, cluttered yards, interiors veiled in dingy grey, all pressed beneath a swollen grey sky. Connie watched the terraces sliding past, absorbing the steady flicker of snapshot images from other people's lives. This couldn't be anywhere but England.

In an hour, she would be back in her London flat.

She was glad of this interval between the long flight and whatever would happen next.

The backs of the houses were identical, all of them

108

clinging to the curves of railway lines and arterial roads and abraded by the dirt and noise that rose off them. Their bricks were dark with soot and the wan trees in patches of garden were weighted with layers of grime.

Echo Street was a terrace just like one of these, with a railway line carrying local trains into Liverpool Street, running through a shallow cutting beyond a high fence at the end of the garden.

Connie closed her eyes.

There was lino down the narrow hallway, dark red with paler bluish-pink swirls in it that looked like skimmed milk stirred into stewed plums. The stairs rose steep as a cliff, each tread usually with a sheet of the *Daily Express* folded on it because Hilda had just mopped them yet again. Hilda had a fixation with cleanliness. The smell of bleach always sent Connie hurtling back into her childhood.

In the old flat, Connie and Jeanette had shared a tiny bedroom, the two divan beds separated by a channel only just wide enough for one of them at a time to put their feet to the floor. There was a shelf above each bed. Jeanette's displayed a neat line of books, whereas Connie's was silted up with scribbled drawings and broken toys and crushed wax crayons.

But in Echo Street they were to have their own rooms. Jeanette was delighted with hers. As Tony was downstairs helping the sweating removal men to carry in the piano, she stood in front of her door and held on to the knob to show that her sister wouldn't be admitted. She signed to Connie, folded hands to the side of her head and then clenched her fist to her chest: *my* bedroom, *mine*.

When Connie looked into the room that was to be

hers, she saw a narrow box with a window that faced the brick wall of the next-door back extension. The lino on the floor was the same as in the hallway and the only other feature was a tall cupboard built across one corner. She twisted the handle and saw that the cupboard was empty except for two coat-hangers on a hook. In the dim light the hangers suddenly looked like two pairs of shoulders that had mislaid their heads and bodies, but which might easily clothe themselves on a dark night and come gliding out of the cupboard in search of little girls.

She ran for the safety of the landing. Jeanette's door stood open by a crack, allowing a glimpse of a bigger room where the sun cast a reassuring grid of light and shadow on the bare floorboards. Jeanette was sitting with her back against the wall, her knees drawn up and her books and magazines laid out beside her. Her fair hair was drawn in one thick plait over her shoulder and she was thoughtfully chewing the bunched ends.

It was Connie who started the fight. Overtaken by one of the surges of rage that were her last resort in the unending series of skirmishes against Jeanette, she launched herself through the doorway and fell on her sister. The square box of the bulky hearing-aid battery that Jeanette wore strapped to her chest juddered between them. Magazines slithered and tore under their flying feet.

'It's not fair. I want the big room. It's not fair.'

Connie yelled and pummelled her fists, then tried to haul Jeanette up and out of the room. An earpiece dropped from one ear and the wire tangled between them.

Jeanette shouted back, but no words were distinguishable.

'Listen to me,' Connie screamed.

At the Joseph Barnes School for the Deaf the speech therapist had made little progress with helping Jeanette to talk. When she was upset or angry she gave up the attempt to verbalise and lapsed into shapeless bellowing.

In any case Connie and Jeanette had their own private hostile vocabulary, a shorthand matter of stabbed fingers and sliced-throat gestures that led to full-blown kicks and blows.

'You sound like a cow mooing,' Connie screamed. 'I want this bedroom.'

Jeanette fought harder. Her face swelled close to Connie's as she hooked her fingers in Connie's tangled hair and propelled her backwards until her head smashed against the wall. Connie doubled up like a snake and closed her teeth on Jeanette's upper arm.

The noise brought both parents running, their feet like thunder on the stairs.

Tony caught hold of Connie and hoisted her in the air, her arms pinioned and her feet kicking against nothing. He put his mouth against her ear and his moustache tickled her skin.

'All right, Con. That's enough. Calm down. Leave your sister alone now.'

Connie still wriggled and squawked that it wasn't fair, but the rage was ebbing away. Its departure left her feeling breathless, and confused, and finally soaked in despair. She slumped against Tony's shoulder, letting out little whimpers of grief. He stroked her hair off her hot face and rocked her against him.

Jeanette's arm showed a ring of red puncture marks. Hilda pinched the corners of her mouth inwards and went for the first-aid box. She wrung out a hank of cotton wool in a bowl of water clouded with Dettol, and made a performance of disinfecting the tiny wound in front of Connie.

Jeanette's eyes gleamed with the lustre of martyrdom.

'Let go of her,' Hilda said to Tony. He released Connie and Hilda took hold of her by the ear and marched her to the other bedroom.

'You stay in here, my girl,' she said.

Connie sat down, back against the wall and knees drawn up, instinctively copying Jeanette. She sat there until teatime, staring at the closed cupboard door, willing the ghosts to stay where they were and not come shimmering out through the keyhole.

That evening, the first in the new house, Hilda was still only speaking when she had to, even after the tea had been cleared and the plates washed and put away in the unfamiliar cupboards that had already been lined with fresh paper. She shook aspirin out of a brown bottle and swallowed the pills with sips of water, in front of both girls.

'Your mum's got one of her bad heads,' Tony told them.

Jeanette gave Connie a look that said *See? See what you've done?*

'Look at the state of this place,' Hilda sighed. There were cardboard boxes stacked in the kitchen and along the hallway. Connie could see saucepan handles and the blackened underside of the frying pan sticking out of one of them. Everything ordinary looked strange because it was in a different place.

Tony said, 'We've just moved in. There's plenty of time. Why don't you have a rest, love?' But Hilda went on unpacking, wincing every time she stooped to a box. Jeanette sailed up to her bedroom to arrange her books.

Connie hated the thought of the darkness in her room. She had only been able to keep the ghosts in their cupboard in daylight by sheer effort of will. She knew that at night she would never be able to control them.

'I won't sleep in there.'

Hilda frowned at her. 'Yes, you will.' She massaged her temples and lowered her voice. 'I don't know what's got into you, Constance.' It wasn't the first time Connie had heard her say this, and it always made her wonder whether she had swallowed a wriggling worm by mistake.

'I don't want to go to bed,' Connie murmured. She turned to her father. 'Tell me a story first?'

'You're a big girl,' Hilda said, but Tony had already taken her hand.

'Come and sit on Dad's lap, then.'

Hilda looked at him over Connie's head. 'Don't you think I need any help with all this?'

'Five minutes, love.'

The three-piece suite was in the front room, but put down any old how. They sat down in the old armchair that was wedged up into the bay window, facing out into the new street.

'Why does Jeanette have the best things always?'

'She doesn't, pet.'

'*I* think she does.'

Tony hesitated. 'You know your sister's deaf.'

Connie didn't understand rhetorical questions. She wondered how Tony could imagine that she might not have noticed. Joseph Barnes School had been a long way away from their old flat, and so they had moved here to be nearer to it. One way or another, Jeanette's deafness seemed to steer most of the things that happened to all of them.

One of Connie's earliest and clearest memories was of being in the steamy back kitchen of the old flat, standing on a stool at the sink to splash some dolls' cups in a bowl of soapy water. She had looked out of the window and down into the branches of a stunted tree that grew over the fence in the next garden. There was a moment's silence, the only sound the faint popping of bubbles in the sink. Then a bird began singing in the branches of the tree. It was a pure, flute-like sequence of notes that utterly entranced her.

Even as she listened, the knowledge that one day soon she wouldn't be able to hear this melody fell on her from nowhere. It had the force of a physical blow.

She jumped from her stool and ran to where Hilda was standing at the stove. She wrapped her arms round her mother's knees and hid her face in her apron. Even then, she could feel that Hilda didn't yield to the touch, or offer a comforting pillow of flesh. Her arms bent under pressure and her back formed an angle, but they soon sprang back to their unbent positions.

'I won't hear the birds,' Connie howled through her sobs, folds of apron stuffing her mouth.

'What's the matter? What are you talking about?'

'I won't hear the *birds*. Will I? When I'm deaf?'

Hilda took hold of Connie's shoulders.

'Don't be silly. Jeanette's deaf, not you.'

'Won't I be, when I'm big?'

Hilda shook her head. 'No. You won't. You're just an ordinary little girl.'

This was how Constance learned that deafness wasn't something that happened automatically to children in her family.

From about that time, whenever she looked at her sister

a feeling that seemed bigger than herself had pumped through Connie. It was her first experience of pity and sympathy, and it was mixed with relief that she wasn't going to be like her after all, and with guilt for being relieved.

She didn't confess what she felt even to Tony – how could she explain what she didn't properly understand herself?

It was just that plenty of people, not only Hilda, already made an extra fuss of Jeanette. Mrs Dix in the newsagent's gave her a pink lipstick that came off the front of a magazine, and when Hilda took them to buy new shoes the shop man brought out half the pairs in the back room for her to try on. It took so long for her to choose that Connie had to have the same style as the old ones she had grown out of, which meant nobody could see they were brand-new. It wasn't fair, even though Jeanette was deaf and Connie felt sorry for her.

Tony shifted Connie's weight on his lap and hugged her tighter. 'You know your sister's deaf,' he repeated. 'Yes?'

Connie picked at one of the tiny brown looped threads in the arm of the chair. She tucked her head under Tony's chin and gave the smallest nod.

'It's hard for her. She's going to have difficulties in her life that you never will. We have to make allowances for her. It's hard for your mum, too.'

'Why?'

'Because Jeanette inherited her deafness from Mum's family.'

'How?'

'These things get passed down, from mothers to their babies. Like Martin's hair, which is the same as his mum's hair, isn't it?'

Martin was a boy Connie knew from her old school – the one she wouldn't be going to any more because it was too far from Echo Street. Martin and his mother both had hair the colour of the nasturtiums that grew in the front garden in Barlaston Road.

'How do you get babies?'

'Ask your mum about that. Do you want this story or not?'

'Yes. Tell me about when you were little. About the milkman.'

Tony wasn't good at making things up, but he often told her about what East London had been like when he was growing up. Connie loved these stories.

'Oh, the milkman. In our street he had a little blue cart with a canvas canopy, and an old grey horse to pull the cart. The horse's name was Nerys, and in the summer she'd have a bunch of cornflowers tied to her bridle. The coal used to come in sacks on the back of a wagon, and then the coal man carried the sacks on his back and tipped them into the cellars of the houses through a hole in the pavement. He had a leather coat with studs on the back of it, so it didn't wear out so fast from the heavy sacks rubbing on it all day long. Another man used to come up from Gravesend with fresh fish off the trawlers to sell door to door. He'd say, "Lovely fish, Mrs Thorne. Lovely fresh herring."'

Tony was good at doing the voices. Connie pressed her ear closer against his shirt-front because she liked the way his voice seemed to come from deep inside his chest. She could hear the steady rhythm of his heart, too. She didn't know then how finite was the number of those beats.

Connie opened her eyes. The train crept past Battersea Power Station and made a sighing arrival at Victoria. Announcements washed over her head. She lifted her small bag, dodging the sharp corners and wheels of other people's luggage, and let the surge of passengers carry her off the train and into the thick of London. Only a taxi ride separated her from home. A version of home.

It was three months since she had last been in her apartment.

From the front door she could see that there was dust on all the glass surfaces and dead flies speckling the white floor. The air smelled as if it had been hot too many times; all the moisture it had ever held had been leached out of it. Connie's lips and the backs of her hands smarted with dehydration from the long flight. She walked down the white corridor to her bathroom and turned on the shower and all the taps. She breathed in the steam, stripped off her creased clothes and stood under the spray until she felt clean again. Then, without giving herself time to think, she wrapped herself in a towel and padded back to the main room.

When she and Seb had shared this tall white space, they had given parties for musicians and composers and cooked dinners for the loose network of their shared friends, but nowadays she rarely asked anyone to come here. It was quiet enough, she thought, to hear the dust settle.

She stood for a moment at the window that ran the length of one wall, staring out at the view. The apartment was on the top floor and she could see a broad sweep of the city from Canary Wharf tower all the way west to the dome of St Paul's. There were different cranes positioned like storks over new developments, but everything else was the same. London glinted weakly under a dirty sky.

Connie's desk faced the view. She stared out at the towers and the brown streets, knowing that she was delaying the moment.

She made herself open the address book that lay next to the telephone, and looked up Jeanette's number. She hadn't committed it to memory; she had hardly ever used it.

They never saw each other, but Jeanette's massive presence was always there like a headland jutting out into the sea. Jeanette was the only person left in the world who knew the same things that Connie knew from long ago, and Connie held her sister's memories furled tight within her in just the same way.

It was *unthinkable* that Jeanette was going to die.

Connie realised that she had made the headlong journey from Bali as if she believed she could do something to change that.

She pressed the buttons of the handset. Her heart was thumping as if she were running for her life.

She listened to the ringing tone. Another thought rushed in on her, one she had been keeping at bay by holding Jeanette in the forefront of her mind.

In a second or two I'll hear his voice.

Because Jeanette wouldn't answer. She never went anywhere near the telephone.

If anyone picked up, it would be him.

It was almost fifteen years ago, now.

Connie went to a party in a newly completed glass

tower in Docklands. There had been a view not unlike the one that faced her now.

One of the advertising agencies was moving out there, with a big fanfare to announce to the known world that a building site east of the City was the new Soho.

She looked past a group of chattering account people and clients and with a shock saw Bill watching her from across the room.

She put down her glass and went to him.

'You look very beautiful tonight,' he said.

There were shadows under his eyes, and he had been drinking.

'Hello, Bill.'

'We don't often run into each other, do we? I am here because I have the privilege of handling the PR account for TotalTime TV. What about you?'

'One of the creative heads at the agency is a very close and dear acquaintance of mine.'

'Small world. And are you here with . . .' his eyes scanned the room '. . . Sam?'

Connie and Sam had split up years ago.

'No. I'm not here with anyone.'

They turned to each other, as if there was no one else in the room, as if there was finally no other move they could make but this one.

Bill murmured, 'Connie, can we get out of here?'

'Yes.'

They rode down in the glass-sided lift and walked out into a bulldozer park. Bill blinked at the desolation.

'If I could magic-up a taxi, would you run away with me?'

'We don't need magic, I've got my car,' Connie said. 'Where would you like to go?'

Inside the car, with his face lit by the dashboard lights, Bill said, 'I don't care where we go. As long as you are with me. I don't care what happens.'

'Yes, you do.'

'Don't pretend to be rational, Con. Don't pretend that what there is between us has ever been rational.'

She was driving an unfamiliar route past hoardings and cranes and what would some day be new roads raised on huge concrete stilts over the razed docklands. She had the strongest sense that they were running away, out of an old world and into a new one that hadn't yet been made. He *had* said the words out loud: *between us. What there is*. He had acknowledged the existence of a truth, even though he hadn't defined it, and now it couldn't be unsaid. Alarm and joy and longing hammered in her chest. She had to remind herself how to breathe.

'I don't know where we're going.'

'Stop the car,' he said roughly.

She circled the mire of a half-made roundabout, turned into a contractors' by-way fenced off with tilted sheets of corrugated iron. Her fingers were shaking as she switched off the ignition.

It was almost dark now, and the cloudy sky was coloured orange by the fierce lighting on the new road.

Bill twisted towards her and their mouths met.

This time, as his fingers knotted in her hair and the blood surged in her ears, she knew that there was no way back. Even if she had wanted one.

They were doomed. Lost, and found in one another.

When they drew apart again, they were both gasping as if they had run a distance too fast.

'Connie,' he said wonderingly. She rubbed her bruised mouth, tasting him on her tongue.

'Where shall we go?' he asked.

'Home,' she answered. Her lack of hesitation should have shocked her, but it did not. Nothing about what was happening or about to happen was shocking, because of its inevitability. It was wrong, and it was dangerous because of the hurt it would certainly cause, but it didn't take her aback.

'Where might that be?' he almost laughed.

'*My* home. Where I live, that is.'

'You would take me there?'

Her eyes widened. 'Of course.'

They drove back into town, fast, in almost complete silence. When her hand moved to the gear lever Bill's covered it, as if he wanted to make sure that she was real, that she wouldn't escape.

They stumbled into the flat she had lived in back in those days like a pair of wild fugitives.

Bill had never even been here before. He slammed the front door behind them and at once they were in each other's arms. He undressed her as they crossed the hallway. A trail of shoes and clothes marked their passage to the bedroom door.

'Bill . . .' she said, but his hand covered her mouth.

'We'll talk afterwards. Talk for hours if you like. But first this.'

This.

With the man she had loved since she was fifteen years old. With the only man she had ever truly loved. With her sister's husband.

At home in Surrey, with Jeanette asleep in their bedroom upstairs, Bill picked up the phone.

'Hello?'

She would have known his voice if she had heard him whispering in an earthquake.

'Bill.'

'Connie,' he said.

He spoke her name as if he were holding her hand.

'I am in London,' she said carefully. 'I want to come and see Jeanette.'

'You know?'

'Yes. She sent me an email.'

She heard him taking in a breath.

'Come tomorrow,' Bill said.

'Yes. All right. I'll be there.'

FIVE

Echo Street, February 1974

On Saturday mornings Hilda had started taking Jeanette to a special audiology clinic for extra therapy sessions. Jeanette's teacher at the Joseph Barnes School for the Deaf reported that she was an exceptional academic pupil, but she needed more help with her speech if she was to live up to her potential. Hilda's first instinct was always to shield Jeanette from outside pressure, but she was impressed by Mrs Archer and pleased to have her own faith in Jeanette's abilities so definitely confirmed.

'Well, I really don't know. Do you want to go?' she asked Jeanette.

Jeanette was sixteen. It had become part of her philosophy to deny that she had any limitations.

– *Yes.*

So on Saturday mornings Connie went with Tony to the shop. She would sit in Hilda's place in the front seat of the Austin Maxi and Tony would drive them there, turning to wink at her as they eased out of Echo Street and saying, 'Just you and me, eh?'

Thorne's on the Parade was a hardware shop in a row of similarly sized shops on a busy junction. As they searched for a place to leave the car Tony complained that there was too much traffic for anyone to get anywhere. Where could they all be going? People weren't

123

shopping, were they? The strikes meant there was no money in anyone's pockets. But they were better off than some, he told Connie. He couldn't sell enough candles for people to use during the power cuts, and there was a run on paraffin too because they were lighting up their old stoves and even lamps dragged out from their attics.

'Who'd have thought the unions would take us back to the days of paraffin heaters, eh?' he asked. 'And when was the last time someone asked me for a new glass mantle for a pump-up lamp?'

When Tony had unlocked the shop door and rolled up the heavy shutter that protected the front, Connie helped him to carry out the street stock. Tony shifted the heavy items, the bags of coke, bundles of sticks and metal stepladders, and Connie made a dozen journeys with bunches of galvanised mop buckets, bristly yard brushes and festoons of mop heads like scarecrow wigs. She nudged them into what she judged to be inviting arrangements while Tony put on his brown working coat with biro stains over the top pocket and wound down the old canopy for the day. It usually served more as a partial rain shield than to protect anything from the sun.

The interior of the shop was a cavern of shelves, with a range of goods from mousetraps to boxes of sugar soap and balls of tarry twine mounted on either side of a high wooden counter. Best of all, behind the counter were tiers of wooden drawers containing shiny screws, nails and tacks, and bolts with heads like thick silver threepenny bits. There was a specific, comforting smell of metal polish, paraffin and harsh yellow soap, and Connie had always loved everything about it.

If there were no customers waiting for them at opening-up time Tony would unfold the *Daily Express* that he had bought on the way in, via a carefully judged ritual exchange with the son of the Pakistani newsagent's next-door-but-one, smooth it out on the counter and say to Connie, 'What kind of assistant are you? Is that kettle not on yet?'

Connie would hurry round to the rear of the drawer tiers, into a cramped space where a cracked sink and draining board sagging away from the wall were almost cut off by baled packs of wire wool and bound slabs of abrasive sponges in sickly pastel shades, boil the kettle and make tea the way Tony liked it, in the brown pot with the tannin-enriched interior, two teabags (Tetleys), brewed until dark and then poured into the pair of mugs whose inner surfaces were marked with complex stains like annular rings. She would carry the mugs through and put them on the counter beside a packet of granulated sugar with a dug-in teaspoon, and they drank it accompanied by two fingers of KitKat each. They never discussed it, but they took their mutual pleasure in this sloppy behaviour because Hilda would never have allowed it at Echo Street. Connie would lick up the last crumbs of biscuit and chocolate and massage the silver foil with the side of her thumb until it was a smooth weightless sheet, then fold it into a wedding band.

There was only one stool behind the counter, a high wooden one with the seat polished slippery with use. When she wasn't counting stock against lists in Tony's neat handwriting (*144 pkts Decors wire wool 00*) or tidying shelves, or peering into the wooden drawers and daydreaming that the brass-headed tacks were ancient coins, Connie perched on the stool to read her book or draw pictures. Tony was always on his feet, fetching and wrapping and ringing-up sales. He hated it when a queue of sighing and shuffling customers built up. Every time the door opened to admit another, bringing in a gust of cold wet air and a hiss of traffic noise, his frown would deepen and he would try to work faster. As he searched the shelves he twisted the pencil that lived behind his ear.

'Where's that box of rawlplugs got to? Won't keep you a minute, Des.'

'I see you got your assistant in today,' Des or whoever would remark, before lengthily searching his mind for the last item he needed while the queue grew increasingly restive behind him.

'Can't I serve, Dad?' Connie begged.

'Not really, love. Tell you what, though, I could drink another cup of tea.'

She would immediately slide off the stool to make it, but as often as not the tea would go cold under a strange brown skin while Tony worked. Saturday mornings were always busy, as men glumly equipped themselves for a weekend's odd-jobbing and decorating. If there were no customers, there was always something to be done to maintain the unruly bulwarks of stock.

At two o'clock, Connie would turn the sign that hung in the glass half of the door from Open to Closed and they would reverse the morning's procedure with the outside goods.

'That's it then. Until Monday morning,' Tony always said as the shutter unrolled with a shriek of tortured metal.

Connie remembered these uncomplicated hours in the shop with Tony as the very happiest times of her entire childhood.

Then in the darkest week of that bad winter of 1974, came the opportunity of piano lessons.

Jeanette's inspiring teacher was by that time becoming an advisor to the whole Thorne family in her efforts to help an unusually able deaf child. Hilda despairingly confided to Mrs Archer that Connie was disruptive at home, aggressive towards her sister, a poor sleeper and was becoming a problem at her mainstream school. Mrs Archer mildly suggested that Hilda might try to make Connie feel that she was special in some way as well as Jeanette, and what was she good at? Did she enjoy maths and biology, like her sister?

'Not at all. She likes music and singing,' Hilda eventually acknowledged. 'She's good at making a lot of noise, at any rate.'

'What about channelling that into learning to play an instrument, perhaps?'

'Our family doesn't go in for music lessons,' Hilda said stiffly. After a glance from Mrs Archer she added, 'We've got a piano.'

'Piano? Good idea. I'll see if I can come up with a teacher in your area, shall I?'

Not long afterwards, Hilda answered a telephone call that wasn't from her sister Sadie or Tony's brother in South Wales, who were the only people apart from Jeanette's various therapists who normally rang them. It was Mrs Polanski, the piano teacher. She had one spare weekly slot, on Saturday mornings. Next term, maybe, the little girl could come on a Tuesday or Thursday evening.

Connie had protested at first that she preferred going to the shop with Tony on Saturdays. But in the end, because she liked the idea of learning to play the piano, sheagreed.

'I'll do without my assistant for a few weeks. It'll be difficult, but I'll manage,' Tony told her.

Connie remembered thinking that Tony sometimes spoke to her as if she was younger than ten, turning eleven this summer. She was a thin, small child. Perhaps he simply forgot she was getting older. Or perhaps, she thought shrewdly, he didn't want her to stop being like herself and start being like Jeanette, who wore a bra, and hideous fashionable shoes with thick platforms, and who – with the encouragement of Jackie and Elaine, their cousins who were the daughters of Auntie Sadie and well-off Uncle Geoff – was now experimenting with make-up.

Piano lessons with Mrs Polanski were a success. Connie was allowed to catch the 274 bus to her house and back, the first time she had been trusted to go anywhere except school all by herself, and Hilda even gave her a door key to Echo Street because she and Jeanette had to go quite a long way to the speech therapist's and were not always back before Connie came home. Hilda didn't drive, so they had a Saturday bus journey too.

Mrs Polanski was Polish. Her house smelled strange and there were gloomy religious pictures on the walls and a plaster statue of the Virgin Mary on the mantelpiece, but Mrs Polanski herself was fat and laughed a lot. Connie knew immediately and instinctively that she was a good teacher. She made everything fun, even C major and D major scales and finger exercises.

'And one, two, three, *play*, my girl,' she would trill as Connie launched into her piece, and she sang the notes to keep her in time and slid her ringed fingers over the backs of Connie's hands to show her the proper positions. Connie practised eagerly every afternoon after school, racing through all the exercises that Mrs Polanski gave her in order to win even more of her liberal praise.

'Well done, Constance. We will make a concert artiste of you, wait and see.'

It was early in March. Constance had been learning the piano for two months and she could already play the right-hand part of *Für Elise* with the proper fingering. She would never have believed that a whole hour could pass so quickly.

Mrs Polanski said, 'Very good this week. Maybe I speak to your mother about some more teaching.'

On the way home Connie sat happily in the front seat on the top deck of the bus and peered through sharp rain into bedroom windows and the unmasked upper regions of small shops. The route was familiar now. She flexed her fingers as she had seen Mrs Polanski do and thought about becoming a concert artiste. She was sure that it would involve a glittering dress with perhaps a gathered train that she would sweep aside with a flourish before taking her seat at the grand piano.

She hurried through the rain from the bus stop to Echo Street, checking that the front-door key was securely in its place in the inner pocket of her blue zipper jacket. As she slid the key into the lock she heard the telephone ringing in the front room. This was unusual enough to make her fumble to turn the key more quickly and almost trip over the doormat as she catapulted herself inside, but the ringing stopped just as the door caught in a gust of wind and slammed shut behind her. Connie hung up her jacket on the hall stand and went into the kitchen. She knew that she was clumsy because

Hilda was always telling her so, but she made herself a glass of orange squash without spilling a single drop of sticky concentrate. She shook droplets of water out of her hair and drank her squash. Hilda and Jeanette would be back soon. She rinsed the glass and upturned it on the draining board.

She was sitting at the piano, about to start practising her new scales, when the telephone started to ring again. It made her jump.

She told the woman caller that Mrs Thorne wasn't at home. This was her daughter. Yes, Mrs Thorne would be back soon. Yes, she would get her to call this number as soon as she came in. The woman was very insistent that Connie fetched a pen and wrote it down. She made Connie read it back to her, to make sure that she had noted it correctly. Mrs Thorne was to ask for Sister Evans. As soon as she came home, because it was urgent.

Connie replaced the receiver and went back to the piano.

The front door slammed again.

Hilda and Jeanette bundled down the hallway. Hilda's umbrella rustled into the recess in the hall stand. Connie let her hands fall into her lap, then stood up and followed her mother and sister into the kitchen.

'There was a telephone call,' she began.

Hilda was unpicking the knot in the ties of her plastic rain hood.

'Let me get in the house, Connie.'

'It's urgent.'

Hilda's eyes flicked to her. 'Well, what is it?'

Connie gave her the number she had written on the cover of the *Radio Times*. Ignoring Connie, Jeanette filled the kettle and put out two mugs and a jar of

Nescafé. Hilda went into the front room to make the call, closing the door behind her.

Jeanette poured boiling water, clinked a spoon, unscrewed the lid of the biscuit jar. She sat down at the table and began to read a magazine. Hilda's coffee mug stood on the kitchen counter waiting for her to come back.

Connie stared out of the window into the damp passage that separated their house from the next in the terrace. As the minutes passed she slowly became aware of a silence that drew all the oxygen out of the air. Her lungs felt tight with the change in pressure and she could hear the slow surge of blood in her ears. The only movement in Echo Street was Jeanette turning the pages of *Woman's Own*.

After what seemed a long time, Connie followed Hilda. At the closed door to the front room she cupped her fist over the doorknob and turned it, listening for the familiar click of the metal tongue. She pushed the door open and looked in.

Hilda was sitting in the armchair next to the telephone table. She was white, dry-eyed, frozen. Her eyes moved, settled on Connie as if she had never seen her before.

'Mum?'

Hilda's hands lifted as if to ward her off. Her tongue passed slowly over her lips.

'Tony's gone. He's left us.'

Connie frowned. She knew this wasn't possible. Tony was at the shop, just like always. 'Gone where?'

'Gone,' Hilda repeated.

The telephone began shrilling again. With a shocking, uncoordinated lunge, Hilda launched herself at it. The white mask of her face suddenly split, broke up into teeth and tongue and twisted lips.

'Sadie? Sadie, he's dead.'

She was gripping the receiver with two hands but she was shaking so much that she could hardly hold it in place.

'Tony's *dead*.'

Connie took two steps backwards. She reached behind her with the flat of her hands, pressed herself against the wall and tried to retreat further as fragments and then huge chunks of her world began to rain down around her.

Hilda kept on repeating these two inconceivable words, louder and louder, while her sister on the other end of the line tried to make herself heard.

Suddenly Jeanette was there, in the doorway. Hilda was sobbing and coughing. Connie shrank, knowing instinctively that she couldn't run to her mother. Jeanette's head turned from one to the other. She couldn't hear, even though Hilda's voice was rising to a shriek.

Jeanette's fingers came up to her lips.

– *Speak*, she signed.

Connie stuttered. Her mouth wouldn't form any words.

Isolated in silence and incomprehension, Jeanette turned wild with bewilderment and terror.

– *Speak, speak*.

She dug fingers like claws into Connie's arms and shook her until Connie's head banged against the wall.

'It's Dad,' Connie screamed into her contorted face.

The funeral service was held at the crematorium near Thorne's on the Parade. Tony's brother and his wife came from Newport, Sadie's husband Geoff took the day off from his garage business and drove his wife and daughters in from their detached house in Loughton, Mrs McBride came from Barlaston Road, and some of Tony's old friends and shop owners and customers from the Parade gathered in the colourless room. Hilda and Jeanette and Connie sat in the front row of chairs and listened to a stranger telling the mourners what a devoted husband and loving father Anthony Thorne had been. Connie gazed at the plain coffin under its purple cloth and tried to believe that her father was lying inside it.

She was cold. She had felt either cold or hot ever since last Saturday when Auntie Sadie and Uncle Geoff had arrived at Echo Street and immediately called the doctor. While he was upstairs with Hilda, their auntie and uncle told Jeanette and Connie that their father had suffered a huge heart attack while he was carrying out the pavement stock. The son of the Pakistani newsagent had called an ambulance and Tony had been taken to the East London Hospital, but he had not survived the journey.

By the end of the stiff little funeral ceremony Connie felt as if she were frozen. Her jaw and neck seemed to be made of some splintery material that was nothing to do with her own flesh and bone, and her eyes were dry as she watched the curtains briefly part and Tony's coffin slide out of sight.

Jeanette was crying. Silent tears ran down her pale cheeks and Hilda's arm protectively circled her shoulders, although it might equally have been that Hilda was using Jeanette to support herself.

After the cremation, and the inspection of the flowers laid out in the chilly wind with no grave to make sad sense of them, the mourners were invited back to Echo Street.

Mrs McBride and another neighbour from Barlaston

Road had made sandwiches and finger rolls and Uncle Geoff had unloaded two heavy, clinking cardboard cartons from the back of his Jaguar. The front room and the hallway and even the kitchen filled up with sombre people in dark clothes who quickly held out their tumblers to a shopkeeper from the Parade as he circulated on Geoff's instructions with a bottle of sherry in one hand and a bottle of whisky in the other.

Hilda sat in the front room, bright spots of colour showing high on her cheeks, and gravely accepted condolences. The cousins, Jackie and Elaine, were seventeen and fifteen. Jackie was already working as a hairdresser, and her fair hair was done to lie very smooth and flat over the top of her head and then to spring out around her ears in a flurry of sausage-shaped curls. Elaine would soon be leaving school to go to secretarial college, and like her sister she was accorded semi-adult status. The two girls sometimes called their parents by their first names. Geoff had given them a glass of sherry each without any questions asked, and somehow Jeanette had taken one too.

The level of talk rose perceptibly as an hour passed. Connie sat awkwardly on the piano stool, holding a glass of orange squash. The people who nudged up against her ruffled her hair, or patted her shoulders with hands that seemed to grow hotter and heavier.

'All right, my love?' someone asked her.

'Yes, thank you,' Connie mechanically replied.

After a time Connie noticed that Jeanette and the cousins were missing, and guessed that they had gone upstairs together.

The door to Jeanette's bedroom stood ajar. Jeanette was sitting on her green satin-covered eiderdown with

Elaine holding her hand. Jackie was standing in front of her, combing out her hair with long, gentle strokes. Fine silvery-blonde feathers floated upwards, following the teeth of the comb, and Jeanette's eyes were closed with the luxury of this tender grooming. Three sticky, empty glasses with nipped-in waists stood on the dressing table.

Connie edged into the room. The cousins glanced over their shoulders at her, then at each other. Nobody spoke.

'Do my hair as well?' Connie asked. Her voice sounded loud in her own ears. She hadn't spoken much in the last few days.

'Yours?' Jackie said. Connie's scalp immediately prickled, her dark hair seeming to spiral more tightly and thickly.

'Yes. Will you?'

Jackie sighed, glancing again at Elaine.

'I don't think I can do much with it.'

Suddenly, Connie was angry. From feeling shivery with cold a flash of heat ran through her, making her face burn.

'You know, you ought to be nice to me as well as Jeanette. My dad's dead, too.'

Elaine's face was flushed and her eyes looked strange. Her thumb massaged the back of Jeanette's hand, moving in slow circles.

'He wasn't your dad.'

Connie saw that Jeanette's eyes were open now. They were wide, and as blue as the sea.

'What do you mean?'

Jackie shook her head in warning and the comb dropped from her hand.

Elaine's flushed face turned darker, meaner.

'You're adopted, aren't you?'

Connie looked from one to the other.

She understood in that moment a mystery that had always been there, nagging like an invisible bruise under the eventless skin of her life, and she also knew with perfect certainty that it had been a mystery to her alone.

She bent her head and saw the pale brown of her wrists emerging from the knitted cuffs of her jersey. She felt the dusty twists of her hair, and the narrowness of her shoulders and hips, and then she looked with her dark eyes back at Jeanette, and Jackie and Elaine. They all had pale fine hair, like their mothers', and they had full breasts and hips and round blue eyes.

Jackie had drawn her lower lip between her teeth and Elaine looked hot and angry. Only Jeanette's expression was unchanged; she had heard none of those words of Elaine's that could never be withdrawn or unsaid, but she hadn't needed to. She looked like an angel in a painting.

Connie turned and left the room.

She went into her bedroom, closed the door behind her and sank to the floor with her back against the wall. She took up the position out of habit, because it was as far as she could get from the cupboard and whatever lurked within it.

There was a roaring in her ears, like surf in a storm.

SIX

They were both older, but Bill was the same. He was the same as he always was, no matter how many years intervened, and just as necessary to her.

He held his arms out.

'Thank you for coming, Con. I didn't know whether I should tell you. It's been worrying me for a long time.'

Connie lifted her head. He kissed her cheek, lightly and quickly, and then they studied each other's faces. He cupped a shoulder with each hand, then gently released her. She saw that Bill had grown thin. There were lines at the corners of his eyes and mouth, the same signs of age that marked her own, but the hollows in his cheeks were made deeper by the shadows of exhaustion. There was now much more grey than dark brown in his thick hair.

Connie said, 'It's much better that she told me herself. How is she?'

He shook his head. 'Physically? As brave and determined as you would imagine. But she's fighting a battle with herself as much as with the cancer. It's difficult for her to accept what's happening. If sheer willpower could change anything, she'd be healthier than you or me.'

'Where is she?'

'In the garden. She sits out there a lot of the time, communing with her plants. That seems to soothe her in a way not much else does. How are you, Connie? You look well.'

'I am. But for this.'

'Come and see her.'

Bill led the way through the house. Connie glimpsed a copper trough filled with pots of African violets and an expanse of polished parquet flooring divided into squares by the sun. It was very quiet.

'I'll leave you to talk to her,' Bill said.

The French windows stood open. Jeanette was sitting to one side of the big garden in the shade of a copper beech tree, her head nodding. There was a rug over her knees and a newspaper had slipped to the ground at her feet. Connie walked quickly over the grass, but it seemed to take a long time to cover the few yards to her side. Even in the sunshine it felt as if she was wading against a strong current. Their last parting had been hostile. Neither of them had envisaged a reconciliation.

As soon as Connie's shadow fell on the edge of the newspaper, Jeanette looked up.

– *Here you are.*

'Here I am.'

Automatically they used the private, pidgin version of sign language that had been their way of talking to each other ever since they were children. Nowadays Jeanette wore tiny hearing aids, but they were tiring to use because as well as individual voices they amplified all the ambient sounds into a confusing roar. She preferred to rely on lip-reading with everyone except Bill; she could distinguish what Bill said even without looking at him. They had been listening to and talking and interpreting each other for more than twenty-five years.

– *That was quick. All the way from Bali.*

Connie did her best to smile through her shock at her sister's appearance. The last time they met she had been

138

plump, pretty, and now she looked like a woman whose flesh had all dissolved and seeped away. Instead of fitting closely her skin clothed her bones in a wrinkled sack. Her blonde hair, once her shining glory, was a cap of colourless tufts that barely concealed her scalp.

'I came as soon as I got your email. Did I wake you?'
– *No.*

Connie made to kneel down on the grass beside her sister's chair, so that it would be easier for her to lip-read, but Jeanette stopped her.

– *Could you help me up?*

They hardly ever touched each other. But now Connie gently put her hands under Jeanette's arms and eased her to her feet. She felt as light as a child.

For a moment they stood uncertainly together, their cheeks not quite touching. Connie tightened her arms around her sister's shoulders. She wanted to find a way to reach beyond words, to leapfrog the impediment that wasn't lodged merely in Jeanette's deafness – that being only a kind of clumsy metaphor for a different and more enduring silence – and to hug her so tightly that nothing could come between them ever again.

'I'm glad to be here,' she began. She stroked her sister's thin hair, just once, very lightly.

We have to start somewhere, she thought.

– *I wanted to tell you the news myself. I didn't want you to hear from anyone else that I'm going to die. Not even Bill. But I didn't expect you to come straight away like this.*

'Did you *want* me to come?'

Jeanette suddenly smiled. Her teeth looked too big for her mouth, but the lines in her face eased and there was a light in her eyes.

– *Yes. You are the only one who remembers everything. That is odd, isn't it?*

'I know,' Connie said. 'I feel the same. All the way in on the train I was thinking about Echo Street. The day we moved in and we fought over the bedrooms. The garden shed and the piano. The nightmares I used to have.'

– *So much history.*

Connie nodded. She was turning a question over in her mind. Was it their entangled history that made them who they were, the two of them, or were those clashing identities rooted elsewhere, much further off?

'I'm so happy to see you,' she said, and it was the truth.

Jeanette's hand briefly masked her waxy face.

– *Looking like this?*

'Looking anyhow.'

– *Give me your arm. Let's walk.*

'Can you manage? Bill said he'd make us some coffee and bring it out here.'

Jeanette's eyes were also too big. Her gaze settled on Connie, then she looked away.

– *Coffee. Like sitting in some waiting room. Drinking coffee. Waiting for your name to be called.*

'Is that how it feels?'

– *Sometimes. Not always.*

They began to walk, a slow shuffle past the flower border. To Connie, used to the coarse brilliance of Balinese vegetation, the blooms looked ghostly pale with petals as fragile as damp tissue, the embodiment of restrained Englishness.

– *Look at my roses.*

'They're very beautiful.'

But Connie didn't want small talk starting to blur these first exchanges of their reunion. There was so much to say, right now, in case they should fall into the old evasions or even hostilities.

'I'd have come long before this, if you had told me that you were ill.'

– *Would you?*

Jeanette seemed to be examining the words for layers of meaning. Then she sighed, wearied by the effort.

– *I kept expecting to get better.*

Connie asked, 'Do you know for sure that you're not going to?'

– *It's in my spine.*

They took a slow step, then another, walking carefully in their new alignment.

If Jeanette had been healthy they would have maintained their distance. Now she was going to die, and the certainty was changing the attitudes of a lifetime.

Connie tried to calculate the combination of defiance and resignation that it must have taken for Jeanette to confess her condition.

Because Jeanette *would* regard it as a confession. For the whole of her life, it had been Jeanette's intention and her satisfaction to do as well as everyone else, and then a bit better than that. She had always wanted to be bigger than her deafness, and to make it incidental that she couldn't hear or speak like other people did.

In that, she had triumphantly succeeded.

So to succumb now to cancer might seem, in some guarded corner of Jeanette's determined being at least, to be a form of weakness. As would acknowledging it to her sister, with whom she shared everything – and nothing.

Her message to Connie had been a way of asking her to come soon, that was clear. What was it, exactly, that Jeanette wanted?

Connie caught herself. Wait. That wasn't the right way to pose the question.

What could Connie offer that might help her? All she had was a biting sense of how much had been missed, how much she had failed to do when she could have tried to make friends with her sister again, and how little time they had left to make amends.

'Are you in a lot of pain?'

How bald these questions are, she thought. What other way is there, to find out what I don't really want to hear in the way Jeanette wants me to hear it, which is from her, not from Bill?

– *The chemo was awful. I was sick all the time. There won't be any more of that, thank God. I have some good days, now.*

'Is today one?'

– *Yes. Today is one.*

Connie knew that was not just because she was in less pain.

Fifteen slow steps took them to the end of the flowerbed and the point where the lawn ran out into rough grass. Jeanette paused and shaded her eyes with her hand, and at first Connie thought the sun must be too bright for her. Then she saw that her shoulders were shaking. Jeanette was crying.

'Don't cry,' Connie begged.

She realised that she didn't know how to deal with this illness. She had never been ill herself, and had never looked after anyone who was suffering anything more serious than a dose of flu.

Quickly she corrected herself. 'I don't mean that. Cry all you want if that helps. What can I do? Tell me what to do.'

Jeanette sniffed and pressed the heels of her hands into her eyes.

– I don't want to die. You can't do anything about that.

The obverse of Jeanette's strength had always been anger. Connie could suddenly feel the dry heat of it coming off her thin skin, eating her up like a fever. Jeanette wasn't going to see another spring in her garden. She wasn't going to grow old with Bill at her side, or see her grandchildren, and she was raging at the loss.

– I am supposed to be brave. It's expected. People want to be able to say, 'She fought all the way. She was so brave.' But I'm not. I don't know how to be. I want to scream and yell. It's not fair that I'm dying. I don't mean just to me. To Bill and Noah as well.

Jeanette's hands chopped at the air, then her doubled fists knocked against her breastbone.

Connie stared miserably. 'That's what I always used to say, not you. That was my refrain, don't you remember? You never complained that life was unfair. You just lived it, made it do what you wanted.'

– But I can't now. I can't do this.

'Yes, you can. If anyone can deal with it, it's you. I'll help you.'

– Will you?

It was a fair question.

'If you'll let me,' Connie humbly said.

She caught hold of Jeanette's raised wrists and held them. For a moment it was as if they were having one of their old fistfights. Then Jeanette's eyes slid over Connie's shoulder towards the house. Connie let go of her.

– Thank you.

Connie didn't know whether her offer of help was accepted or dismissed.

A sudden smile glinted through Jeanette's tears. For an instant, with the flesh melted away from her jaw line and her eyes widening, she looked like a girl again. Without turning round Connie knew that Bill was coming.

– *Here he is.*

Jeanette's glance flicked back to Connie.

– *I love him. He loves me.*

She gave the signs an extra edge of precision, for clarity's sake.

Connie met her sister's gaze. She understood that one of the assurances Jeanette wanted from her was that she and Bill wouldn't share anything more than memories and kinship, now or ever.

She could give her that. In effect she had done it already, long ago. But even so, with the reminder of the bitterness that linked and divided them the day seemed to lose some of its warmth and softness.

'I know you love each other,' she answered steadily. 'There has never been any doubt about that.'

Connie held out her arm and Jeanette leaned on it again. They retraced their steps as Bill put down a tray loaded with cups and a coffee pot.

When they reached him he lowered Jeanette into her chair and tucked the rug over her knees, then folded the crumpled newspaper and laid it aside. He did everything deftly, clearly used to looking after her.

'Next week you'll be making the coffee for me,' he told her.

'If I have time,' she murmured. 'Busy, busy.'

Only Bill was trusted to distinguish her words without supporting signs.

Bill set up two more folding chairs in the shade of the copper beech tree, and they drew together in a triangle. If anyone had glanced over the hedge they would have looked like any family enjoying a summer's day in a garden flushed with lavender and roses.

The first time Connie met Bill was at Echo Street, in the early summer of 1978. She was fifteen.

'Stupid clothes,' Connie said, so that Jeanette could see her, but Jeanette was as good at ignoring what she chose not to pick up as she was at intercepting anything not intended for her. She went on ironing, meticulously smoothing the nose of the iron into the ruffles of her white shirt. Her hair was wound on big, bouncy rollers. In a moment she would brush it out and loose waves would effortlessly tumble round her face.

Hilda was cleaning. Her ally was a little battery-operated vacuum cleaner that sucked crumbs off the table and she switched it on now to drown out Connie's remarks.

Over the buzz of the cleaner Connie raised her voice to a shout.

'Who is it tonight? Four Eyes? Or Mr Physics Club?'

Connie despised all Jeanette's followers, as she despised almost everything except music and her tight coterie of like-minded friends. Jeanette whisked the finished shirt off the ironing board and held it up to admire her work. She slipped it on a hanger and took it upstairs with her, not even glancing in Connie's direction.

'Don't call Jeanette's boyfriends rude names,' Hilda warned. 'And don't leave all that rubbish piled on the table, you'll make this place look like a tip.'

Connie yawned.

'I said, don't leave all that rubbish there.'

'It's not rubbish. It's my homework. So who is he?'

Hilda began swabbing the corner of the table with a bunched-up cloth that smelled of bleach. Her red knuckles jabbed against Connie's wrist.

'He's a new one. You get a boyfriend yourself, you won't want us calling him names.'

Connie gave her a blank stare. *If only you knew.*

Connie was fifteen and she had been having sex with Davy Spencer for the last three months. She didn't really enjoy it; Davy pushed himself inside her, jiggled about for a few seconds and then came with a yell as triumphant as if he had just won a recording contract. But a lot of the girls in her year fancied him and he played the drums in the best band in their school – although that wasn't saying much. Sometimes, after he had finished, they cuddled up together and talked about the music they both liked and the places they would go once they left school. When they lay like that Connie felt close to him, although at other times she thought she hardly knew him. But when they were lying cosily in each other's arms, round at his place when his mum and dad were out, she could even convince herself that they were in love.

'What's his name, then?'

'Bill Bunting.'

Hilda was so proud of Jeanette's success and popularity, she couldn't keep any details to herself. She'd talk for hours to anyone who would listen about how boys wrote love letters to her and dropped them through the letterbox at Echo Street because Jeanette couldn't use the phone like other girls.

'My Jeanette, she was born stone deaf but she never

lets it stand in her way. She's a university student, you know.'

Connie gave a disbelieving laugh. 'What is he, some nursery-rhyme character?'

Jeanette came back. Her hair framed her glowing face and hid her hearing aids, her shirt ruffles were perfectly crisp and her tight jeans were tucked into soft suede boots. She trailed a waft of Charlie behind her, her favourite perfume. Connie slouched even lower in her chair. She was still in her school shirt and scratchy royal-blue synthetic-knit V-necked jumper.

'Here she is, Pete the Pirate.'

Hilda and Jeanette ignored her.

'Take him in the front room, when he gets here,' Hilda said.

– *It's okay, Mum. He's just an ordinary boy.*

The doorbell rang.

'He's here,' Hilda pointed. Jeanette performed a little pirouette of excitement before giving her hair a last shake and dancing to the door.

Connie deliberately stuck her nose in her English book. She heard his voice, and the busy silence of Jeanette's responses. She didn't look up even when they both came into the kitchen and Hilda was shaking hands and saying that she was pleased to meet him and he wasn't to mind the mess the place was in because when you were on your own with a family to look after you couldn't always have things looking the way you wanted, could you?

'No,' he said. His voice was distinctive: it sounded as though it had ripples in it. 'It must be difficult. But it looks fine.'

Then she knew that his eyes were on her.

Connie couldn't stop herself glancing up, even though she had meant to ignore all three of them.

She saw immediately that Bill Bunting was worthy of anyone's attention.

He had the sort of long hair that Connie liked, shaggy but not matted, and not self-consciously combed either. He was wearing jeans, old battered ones, and a not-too-ridiculous shirt. He had dark eyes and a clear sort of face, and one of those curly mouths that always look as if they are about to smile even when the owner is being serious. He was holding Jeanette's hand, without seeming to try to prove anything, but just as if he wanted to keep her close to him.

Connie swallowed.

'Hi, I'm Bill. You must be Connie,' he said.

What had Jeanette told him about her?

'I am Constance,' she replied stiffly. Her ears had turned red. She was conscious of the drips of something sticky and dark down the front of her jumper and her hair being a mess of dusty black spirals with plastic slides stuck in it, just like a kid.

He held his hand out. Hilda was asking him if he wanted a drink, a coffee maybe, or he could have a beer if he wanted one. Jeanette was leaning on him to indicate that they had to go.

In spite of herself, Connie shook his hand.

'What are you reading?' he asked. 'It must be really good.' He did smile now, his mouth curling.

'*Nineteen Eighty-Four*. It's my set book in English.'

'Yes. That's a good book.'

Connie would have liked to ask him why he enjoyed it, because she didn't particularly. It would have been interesting to talk to him, and a fully-fledged fantasy popped into her head in which she and Bill Bunting were sitting at an outdoor table in some exotic but unspecified place, drinking wine and discussing literature and music.

But in reality he was holding her sister's hand and telling Hilda that they couldn't stop, although he'd like to, because he was taking Jeanette for something to eat before they went to hear a new band at a place under a pub in Camden Town.

Jeanette was *deaf*. Why was he taking *her* to a gig?

Jeanette claimed that she didn't have to hear the music, she could feel the beat in her bones, which was the kind of pretentious thing she was always suggesting, but Connie knew that the evening would be wasted on her.

'Go on then, both of you,' Hilda said. 'Have a lovely time.'

Jeanette was almost bouncing with happiness, springing up and down in her little suede boots with the turnover tops. Connie thought that she was looking really pretty and sexy tonight, prettier and sexier than she had ever seen her look before.

'Bye, Constance,' Bill said. She knew that he was gently teasing her for having insisted on her full name, and she couldn't bear to be teased. It took enough concentration to keep the blocks of her life piled up in the right precarious order, without someone dodging in and out and threatening to topple them by laughing and making her feel ridiculous. Especially not this Bill Bunting.

Connie wouldn't look at him. She picked up her book again and stared at the grey paragraphs until he and Jeanette departed for their date. Hilda accompanied them to the front door, waved them off and then came back and picked up her cloth.

She resumed her rubbing and sighing.

Now that they were alone Connie was certain that Hilda wouldn't talk to her, the way Davy's mother and normal people talked, for example; she would just go on with the chores in a way that rejected any offer of help and never stopped implying that it was desperately needed. Hilda could make you feel superfluous and guilty all at the same time, even with her back turned. Being trapped in this house with Hilda and her martyred silences was what Connie disliked most, and it was happening more and more frequently these days as Jeanette's life blossomed. She still lived at home, but reading Biological Sciences at Queen Mary's College meant that she spent little time at Echo Street.

Connie sat and pretended to read for just long enough to make her motionless presence thoroughly irritating.

If Hilda suddenly boiled over and started shouting, at least that would be something happening. They would both have the release of an argument.

'What do you want for your tea?' Hilda asked at last, when there was no surface left in the kitchen that could conceivably benefit from further polishing, wiping, sweeping or disinfecting.

This evening, apparently, there wouldn't even be the equivocal satisfaction of a proper row.

Connie shrugged. 'Nothing.'

'You can't eat nothing.'

'Really? Can't I? What makes you think that?'

'I don't want any of your silly sarcasm, my girl.'

Connie gathered up her books and files.

'I might go out.'

'You've got the money for that, have you?'

In fact Connie did; she had a Saturday job in a record

150

shop up in Hackney although that was more for the chance to gloat over the new and second-hand vinyl than for the cash it brought in. She shrugged again and this goaded Hilda enough to make her demand, 'Why can't you be more like your sister?'

Connie let three seconds tick by, deliciously.

'You know why. You should have had another one just like her, if that was what you wanted.'

Hilda's face went tight and dark. Connie strolled out of the kitchen and it was only as she was going up the stairs that Hilda was able to call after her in a loud, harsh voice, 'You've got the devil in you, Connie Thorne. I don't know what you're doing in this house.'

Connie went into her bedroom and closed the door.

Anyway, she thought, I won't *be* in this house for much longer.

It took a very long time to grow up, but with every week and month that passed she knew with greater certainty that it would happen in the end. In a year, or not much more than a year, she would be able to leave school.

She was going to move out and leave Echo Street far behind her, and she was going to find her real mother and father. Once she had found them she could become the person she was born to be, instead of having to be Constance Thorne.

*   *   *

Connie wondered whether Jeanette remembered that evening. She knew Bill did, because they had once talked about it.

'You looked like an angry foal,' he laughed.

'A *foal*?'

'Yeah. With a sort of matted forelock hanging down over your nose and the whites of your eyes showing.'

'Oh, great. And I suppose thick knees and spindly legs, finished off with two pairs of unmanicured hooves.'

'I couldn't see your legs, you were sitting down.'

'I thought you were gorgeous.'

'I was pretty full of it in those days. I imagined that going out with someone who looked like Jeanette and who was deaf as well would make me look deeply cool and kind of committed and interesting.'

'Yes?'

Bill had laughed again. 'She outwitted me, though. Instead of being my accessory she made me hers.'

'You fell in love with her.'

Bill nodded.

Jeanette tasted two or three sips of her coffee then replaced her cup on the tray. The saucer rattled. Bill passed her a glass of water instead and she took a brown bottle of pills out of her cardigan pocket and swallowed two capsules, then gave the glass back to Bill. They did all this without a word or a glance, and Connie saw how practised they were at being just the two of them.

Jeanette leaned back in her chair.

– *What about you?* she asked.

Connie said, 'I've been at home, in Bali. Last week I was working on the music for a big commercial shoot.'

The bank clients and Rayner Ingram and Angela seemed already to have fallen into some distant other world. She was startled to think how recent the week's miniature dramas had really been, and how very little they mattered now that she was here.

When Jeanette was settled Bill sat down and crossed his legs. He was wearing deck shoes without socks, and Connie remembered that this was a sort of uniform for Englishmen at home on summer days. She was sufficiently unused to England to start noticing such things again.

'That sounds glamorous,' he said.

She laughed. 'It does, doesn't it? I had two groups of musicians to look after and I enjoyed that, and some of my neighbours were involved as well. It felt a bit strange, though, seeing London in Bali. I wasn't quite sure which environment was which. Life in the village isn't usually so busy.'

Jeanette followed all this. Conversations when each person took a turn didn't trouble her, only when everyone was speaking at once.

– *But you said at home. Is Bali your home?*

'Did I say that?'

– *Yes.*

Connie thought about it, and Bill looked at her over his coffee cup. 'I've been living there for a while now, so I suppose I do think of it as home.' This wasn't the time or the place to expand on anyone's definition of home.

– *What is it like?* Jeanette leaned forward.

Connie's face shone. 'Beautiful. Hot. Different. Exotic. And that doesn't do it justice.'

– *I would love to have seen it.*

'Would you?' Connie asked. Jeanette had never travelled much, preferring to take villa or hotel holidays with Bill and Noah in Italy or France. A flash of memory came back to her of Bill, in one of their snatched moments during the time long ago when everything hung in the balance between them, calling her his wild roaming girl because she was leaving him to go to Cambodia.

She'd go anywhere, in those days, anywhere in the world that was far enough to try to escape the problem that none of them could solve.

– *Wishful thinking now*, Jeanette indicated.

There was a small silence that was waiting for the comfort of words to be dropped into it. Bill rubbed the corner of his jaw with his thumb. A reddish patch in the skin showed that the gesture had become habitual.

Connie remembered that her camera was in her bag. She had dropped it in this morning before she left the apartment.

'I've got some pictures here,' she said.

– *Show me?*

Bill moved Jeanette's chair further into the shade so the sun didn't reflect on the camera's little screen, and found her glasses for her, and Connie leaned over her shoulder. Their arms briefly touched and Connie's warm skin looked darker next to Jeanette's hospital pallor.

'Press that button, the one with the arrow. There, that's the view from the veranda of my house.'

Jeanette studied the image. It was an early-morning shot. Mist clung to the lower slopes of the gorge and the row of palms that crowned the ridge looked as if they had been drawn in soft pencil against the silvery sky. Over Jeanette's bent head Connie pondered the contrast with the froth of roses clothing the back of this house, and the pots of agapanthus just breaking into flower on either side of the French windows.

The next picture was of a village festival. Men with drums and bamboo pipes, and laughing girls carrying towering piles of fruit and pyramids of flowers on their heads processed past a rank of snarling demons carved from tufa and winged dragons with jagged backs like dinosaurs. A line of scarlet and gold *penjor* flags flashed brilliance against the background mass of leaves.

Jeanette looked at that picture for a long time.

– *How beautiful.*

The next shot was of the pairs of exquisite Balinese schoolgirls dressed up for the bride commercial, and then there was one of Angela. Connie had caught her on the set with Ed and a couple of the other riggers. There were lights and cables everywhere, and darts of sunshine striking off the metal equipment boxes. Angela was standing upright among the chaos and giving her missionary-among-the-cannibals face straight into the camera lens.

'It looks like fun,' Bill said.

'Well, yes. It was really.'

The last picture was of the *gamelan* ensemble with their instruments, dressed and made-up for the shoot, with Ketut beaming in the centre.

'Who are these?'

Connie laughed. She was touched and pleased that Jeanette and Bill liked her photographs. 'That's my orchestra. But they'd soon tell you they're not mine. More like I'm their eccentric Englishwoman. They were on screen here for the commercial, playing a few bars of the music that I wrote for it, but usually it's me creeping along to play percussion with them and hoping not to make an idiot of myself. It's a big privilege; generally the *seka* – that's the village music club – is only open to men, but I suppose I don't count because I'm old and regarded as harmlessly mad. Ketut – that's him in the middle – is a very clever man, and a brilliant musician. He's a good friend. He only rates me because we were in his brother's café one afternoon and a local version of the old Boom commercial came on the telly over the bar. I told him I wrote the music and he was almost as impressed as if I'd said "A Hard Day's Night" was one of mine. Ketut's a very big Beatles fan.'

Jeanette was looking up at her, clearly trying to place Connie in a setting that was so remote from her English garden. Bill's expression was harder to read.

Connie shifted slightly.

'Actually my life's quieter than it looks from these. I sit and stare at the view quite a lot.'

Jeanette clicked back to the first of the pictures.

– *Do you? I think I would, too.*

There was a faint flush of colour over her cheekbones.

'It's a lovely place,' Connie agreed.

Bill hopped up and announced that he was going to go in and make some lunch, saying with a laugh he thought he was irritating Jeanette by always being under her feet.

Jeanette reached up and curled her fingers round his wrist.

– *You are not*, she told him. *Never.*

As Bill carried the tray back across the lawn to the house the two women settled themselves again.

'What's Noah doing?' Connie asked.

As when Bill had come out into the garden, Jeanette's face softened and brightened.

– *Noah's fine. He's a joy.*

She told Connie about Noah's job and his flat and the girlfriend he had just split up with because she had gone travelling, and added that Bill and she thought there might be some new love interest although they hadn't met her yet.

– *He's grown up now. That's one good thing.*

Connie remembered him as a teenager, protective of Jeanette, with a disconcerting physical resemblance to his father.

– *I hope it won't be too hard for him*, Jeanette added.

Her sister's tenderness for the boy moved Connie, and even without a child of her own she could imagine what anguish it must cause Jeanette to think of leaving him. But it also touched a place in Connie that she tried to keep covered up. Seeing a mother's love was like placing pressure on an unhealed wound, an old, deep injury that scabbed over and seemed on the point of disappearing, but which broke open when she least expected it and made her wince with the sharpness of the pain.

The sudden exposure of it made her push back her chair and drop to her knees.

She had to move to ease the hurt so she knelt down and gathered her sister into her arms, stroking her sparse hair and rocking her as if she were a baby. This time Jeanette didn't resist. Her head lay against Connie's shoulder in just the way Connie's used to do against Tony's when she was a little girl. This connection was made more precious by its fragility, its limited life, then as now.

Hot, uncalculated words broke out of Connie like fresh blood from beneath the broken scab.

'Jeanette. Jeanette, I'm so sorry. I'm sorry I haven't been here with you. So much in our childhood was wrong. It was nobody's fault, not even Hilda's. I ran away from home and from you. I was full of my own concerns, and I haven't been the sister you wanted or deserved.

'What I did with Bill was bad. But I didn't plan to fall

in love with my own sister's husband, you know. None of it was intended. Once you were married I should just have kept running, off over the horizon, before anything else happened. Bill was in the wrong too, but he's a good man. He loves you. He's not the first or the last husband to make a mistake and to regret it ever afterwards.

'I know you don't trust me, why should you? But I'm trying to say I'll do whatever I can now. If you let me. If you and Bill let me. If I knew Noah better, I'd promise you that he'll never need a woman's support while I'm here to give it.'

Over the years Connie had taught herself not to cry, but tears came now. They burned her eyes and the green garden blurred into splinters of silver.

She didn't even know how much of what she said was intelligible to Jeanette. Most probably it was nothing more than a vibration in the locked bones and channels of her bent head, but she held her and rocked her and slowly Jeanette lifted her arm. She put her hand on Connie's head and lightly stroked her hair, just once.

'It's not too late,' Connie said. 'It's not. It can't be.'

Jeanette made no response.

Silently they held on to each other.

Noah fell asleep with the lights and the television on, and the next thing he heard was a key in the lock. The front door of the flat opened and softly closed. He sat up and rubbed his face, then looked at his watch. It was ten past four in the morning.

'Hi, Roxana?' he called out.

The hall light clicked on and she appeared in the doorway. There were black marks like thumbprints where her thick eye make-up had smudged. She stood with her plastic handbag clutched across her chest, warily gazing at him. She looked dazed with exhaustion.

Noah stumbled to his feet. Roxana immediately took a step backwards.

He held his hands up. 'It's all right,' he mumbled. 'I just wanted to make sure you got back safely. It's very late.'

She shrugged. 'It is a club for men to enjoy themselves.'

Noah felt uncomfortable on behalf of his sex. 'Did you have a bad night?'

Roxana's mouth creased. Even when she looked plain, as she did now with her blotched make-up and late-night skin, her mouth made her beautiful.

'I earn money,' she said.

She burrowed her hand into the bag and brought out her wallet. 'If you like I can pay you some money for rent. Here.' She held out a note, but he wouldn't even look at it.

'Roxana, for God's sake, put your money away. Look, I don't know what's been happening to you and I don't know what you're afraid might happen next. But you're welcome to stay and I don't need any rent from you and I told you this morning, yesterday morning, whenever the fuck it was, you're safe here. I'm not going to touch you if that's what you're concerned about.'

She slid him a glance under her blackened eyelids. Noah thought, I shouldn't have promised that. Now I'm going to have to keep my word. With the flat of his hand he massaged the corner of his mouth towards his nose and sniffed hard.

'Would you like a cup of tea or something?'

Roxana raised her thin shoulders. 'I would like just to sleep,' she said.

'Go ahead.' He indicated the door of his bedroom.

She gave him an awkward nod. 'Good night. Thank you, Noah. You are a kind person.' She slid away and the door closed behind her.

She must have pulled off her clothes and dived immediately into sleep because he didn't hear any sounds of her moving about from then until he left for work.

Every evening of the following week Noah came home straight from work instead of going to the gym or stopping off at the pub, in the hope of overlapping with Roxana before she left for The Cosmos. If he was lucky he would find her still wandering between the bathroom and his bedroom with her hair wrapped in one of his towels, her muscled legs beaded with drops of water from the shower.

'Hi, Noah. Did you have a nice day? What work did you do?'

He took a beer out of the fridge or made himself a mug of tea, and while Roxana perched on the sofa to paint her toenails with deft strokes of silver glitter he told her about providing technical support to editors who could spend days honing a manuscript, somehow manage to lose all their work with a couple of keystrokes, and want him to recover it for them.

'It sounds highly responsible business. You have a good career.'

'Oh, I don't know that it's a career. I haven't made a policy decision on that yet. It's just a job.'

Roxana laughed. 'But you are lucky, aren't you?'

He was puzzled for a moment until he realised that it

would be a luxury, where Roxana came from, to be able to choose between a job or a career and to postpone one while indulging in the other.

When her hair and toenails were dry she would retreat into his bedroom and put on her street clothes.

'I have to go,' she would sigh. 'Mr Shane tells all the girls, even the Brazilian one that he likes, that if we are late we need not come back another time.'

'Don't you get a night off?'

Roxana teasingly smiled at him. 'Why do I need this? What will I do with a night off and not earning any money?'

'You could come out with me. You could tell me about Uzbekistan, talk about your life.'

'And why do you want to know about Uzbekistan, when you do not even know where it is?'

'I *do* know. You told me quite precisely.'

Their hour's overlap was already ending. Roxana took some small lacy items out of the tumble-dryer and placed them in a Tesco carrier-bag, together with an apple and a filled roll in a supermarket wrapper to eat during her break. He found it touching to think of her eating this humdrum meal in between dances, biting tidily into the doughy bread so as not to get blobs of mayonnaise on her chin or on her – whatever it was she wore, in order to take it off.

'What time do you think you will be back?' he asked, and then realised that he sounded like her husband. Or her brother.

She shrugged. 'When the club closes. I will see you tomorrow, Noah, when you come back from work.'

Noah's mobile rang and he dragged it out of his pocket. 'Yeah, hi mate. Ner, I didn't see it. Hang on a sec, will you?' Roxana was on her way out of the door. He gave her a wave and made an unthinking kiss in the air, as he would have done to Lauren. To his surprise Roxana laughed and copied the gesture and then she was gone.

'What's that, mate? I *am* listening. Who? Ner, it's a girl who's staying here while And's in Barcelona. No, I'm not. Nowhere near. I wish, in fact.'

He decided to wait for Saturday. On Saturday, he calculated, they should be able to spend the day together, and in the evening when Roxana went off to work he would go home again to see his parents.

On Saturday, Roxana didn't stir until two o'clock in the afternoon.

He made a pot of coffee, thinking the smell might tempt her, and when that one went cold he made a fresh one. At last he heard the small creaks of furniture and soft footsteps as she got up and padded round his bedroom. He didn't like the image of himself as an eavesdropper so he went to strip the covers off Andy's bed and made as much noise as he could putting the sheets in the washing machine. When he slammed the door and turned round she was standing in the kitchen. Her face was scrubbed and she looked younger, and miserable. Her greeny-blonde hair stood on end, like a child's.

'Hi. What's up?'

'Nothing.' She pressed the waxen wings of a carton of juice that he had left on the draining board and poured herself a glass. They stood in awkward silence as she drank it down and he knew that she wanted to be left alone. He supposed that he could go out for a while but then he thought, It's my flat. So he sat down at the kitchen table instead and busied himself with the *Guardian*.

Roxana went and took a shower and when she came back again she had on the pale jeans that she was wearing the first time he saw her and a grey T-shirt with the word *free* printed on the front. Her damp hair was combed flat.

'You slept for a long time,' he said.

'I like to sleep. It is easy. Easier than to be awake.'

'Is it? I suppose so. Listen, d'you want to come out for a walk? We could go down to the river and have a drink at a pub.'

Her first instinct was to refuse. Then she glanced at the slice of blue sky visible through the mansard window.

'All right.'

They walked down the road to the Broadway and crossed under the flyover. It was a bright, windy day with the leaves of the trees all tossed up to reveal their pale undersides. Roxana walked quickly, and he could see her brightening up with the fresh air and the sight of people busy with their Saturday afternoon pleasures. At Hammersmith Bridge they descended the steps to the riverside and headed west among the couples with buggies and the joggers and children on trikes.

Roxana turned to him and smiled. Her eyes were dancing.

'I like your Thames,' she said. He noted with a touch of regret that she pronounced it correctly now. 'I like all of London. In the daytime.'

Her English was improving and he wondered if he was only imagining that her heavy accent was fading slightly. Roxana was clever, there was no doubt.

'Only in the daytime?'

'Phhh. At night you see less of this . . .' she waved at the benign scene ' . . . and more of this.' She grabbed her own throat, lasciviously crossed her eyes and drooped her tongue from one corner of her mouth in such a comic evocation of sicko psycho drooling that Noah burst out laughing. Roxana laughed with him.

'Really?'

'Yes. Night bus, half the people. Believe me.'

'Harmless munters.'

'What is that?'

'This.' He grabbed his own throat and copied her face and Roxana gave a little scream and skipped out of his reach.

'What's it like where you come from?' he asked.

'I come from a very old city called Bokhara.'

'I've heard of it.'

'Very good. It has a small centre, the old city, where there are magnificent bazaars and *madrassahs*. You will have seen pictures, perhaps. And it has also a very big outside, very dusty, with railway lines and cement works and ugly blocks of apartments for the Soviet workers.'

'What part do you live in?'

'I live in London,' Roxana said coldly.

'Okay. Right. By the way, you know Andy, my flat-mate, is coming back from holiday this evening?'

'Yes. I remember this. I will have to move out. I will find a room, better than the last place. I was thinking this when I got up, and I was going to do it today, but now I am here walking with you.'

'Much better. It's fine, anyway. I'll be at my folks' tonight and I'll just leave a note for And, tell him who you are and not to leap up in the night assuming you're a burglar. After tonight I'll be on the sofa until you get sorted.'

She stopped walking and laid her hand on his arm.

'Thank you. I like staying with you, Noah. You have a good heart.'

They had walked a distance from the bridge and there were no people in the immediate vicinity. Roxana's face was close to his, close enough for him to be able to smell the scent of her skin and hair, and the promise of her mouth was suddenly too much for him. He came in closer and kissed her. He didn't intend anything heavy. It was supposed to be an appreciative sort of kiss, casually suggesting that there might be more to come if that happened to be acceptable.

Roxana's reaction was startling. She whipped away from him as if he had seriously assaulted her and her arms came protectively across her chest. She glared at him.

'Whoa. It's all right,' he murmured.

'It is not,' she snapped.

'Roxana, don't overreact. It was just a peck.'

'Perhaps you believe that because I am just a lap dancer, I am for anyone? Perhaps now you will offer me some money? Or perhaps you think you let me stay in your flat and I am free?'

He gazed at her in dismay. 'I don't think any of those things. I think you're pretty, and I like you. I've got no reason to believe you dislike me, in fact you just told me I've got a good heart. We've known each other a couple of weeks, I gave you a very quick kiss. It's what men and women do. At least, they do in London.'

That touched a chord, as he had known it would. Roxana hoisted her shoulders towards her ears and with a long breath let them fall again.

'I see.'

'Here. Let's sit down for a bit.' There was a pub with wooden trestle tables and benches set out parallel to the river. They sat down facing each other at one end of a table, both of them reminded of their first encounter further downriver, with the robot man and the borrowed bicycle.

'I am thinking you are the same,' Roxana muttered.

'The same as what?'

Her fingers drew a circle in the air.

'My stepfather. My teacher. Dylan at my other house. Mr Shane at my work.'

Noah was aware that there was a big tangle here that he and Roxana might have to unravel together if they were to go any further. He picked at the nearest thread.

'Mr Shane?'

'He is the man who owns The Cosmos. He likes one of the Brazilian girls, Natalie she calls herself. But last night he came when I was in my break and tried to make some games with me.'

'What did you do?'

Roxana laughed. 'I know how to handle this by now, don't you think? I am pleasant and I make him feel that he is big, but no, he doesn't get me. Perhaps I can't say no for ever, though. The worst is that Natalie is now my enemy. Soon I will find that I am given less good times to dance, and maybe some of my belongings will disappear while I am on stage.'

'Roxy, you have to leave that place. You're bright and lovely. You could get a completely safe, normal job. Even if it was in a bar, or as a waitress, for the time being.'

Roxana laughed again. She had the gift of good spirits. 'Not for this.' She rubbed her thumb against her bunched fingers.

'Money isn't everything,' he told her pompously.

'Maybe not for you, Mr Noah Bunting. But I need to make a good life here in England. I work, I save, and some day I will be somebody. I always keep this in mind, you know.'

They looked at each other, smiling but also weighing one another up.

'Shall we have a drink?' Noah asked after a moment. 'This time, I'll buy one for you. What would you like to have?'

'All right, thanks. Just a half, then.'

He watched her, walking head up with her dancer's poise through the knot of people at the doorway of the pub. A minute later she came out again, frowning.

'You didn't tell me a half of what drink?'

'Beer, Roxana. A half of best is what you ask for.'

She came back with two halves in straight glasses, carrying the drinks as if they were molten gold.

'Cheers,' she said, and took a long swallow. She wiped her mouth with the back of her hand. 'Is that what you say?'

'Yes, it is. Very good. Cheers, Roxana.'

They clinked their glasses.

SEVEN

Andy came back from Barcelona, leaving a lava trail of damp and pungent clothing between his room and the washing machine. He was very large and suntanned.

'Uh, hi,' he said, when Roxana emerged from Noah's room early on Sunday afternoon.

'Yes, hi,' she said quietly. They exchanged some pleasantries but it was impossible not to feel like an intruder while this young man was scratching himself and frying sausages in his own kitchen. Roxana packed her work clothes into a carrier-bag and went out into the bright afternoon. She turned in the opposite direction from the way she and Noah had gone yesterday, and found herself thinking it would be nice if he was with her now. She remembered how amused he had been at the pub, when she hadn't known what drink he wanted a half of, but he had been laughing about it, not at her. Noah was very kind.

There was a McDonald's in the main street, with a lot of empty cartons outside blown into the gutter and against the gritty walls. She went inside and bought a burger and a waxed cylinder of cola and sat in the window to eat her meal. The seat was uncomfortable because it was sloping, and a girl in a nylon uniform was wetly mopping the tiles close to Roxana's feet. She was troubled by the thought that in Uzbekistan a visit to

McDonald's had been a rare treat, whereas in London it seemed a less satisfying experience. She was realising that to become an English girl might just mean exchanging one set of things that you wanted for a different set.

'Excuse me,' the girl with the mop said to Roxana, and Roxana answered her in Russian.

The girl shrugged wearily. 'Polish,' she muttered, and went on mopping.

Roxana ate slowly but the meal only took fifteen minutes to consume, which left her with three hours to fill before she need even think about taking the tube to The Cosmos. She went out into the sunny, cheerfully dirty street again and saw an open shop with a lot of pictures of apartments in the window. On impulse she went inside and was waved to a seat across a desk from an Asian boy wearing a smart tie and a very clean, large-sized shirt. She told him that she was looking for a place to live.

Yes, near here.

It would be good to be close to Noah. It was dawning on her that Noah might after all just want to talk and laugh and have fun at first, the way people did in some of the movies she had seen. Maybe the way he had kissed her meant that it was just a kiss and not a prelude to something worse. What had he said?

In London, it's what men and women do.

Roxana's experience in Uzbekistan was entirely different, and she would not think about that just now. Even in London, with Dylan and Kemal and Mr Shane, and the men at the club, it had been much the same as back there. But, just conceivably, Noah might be like none of these men and more like a guy in a film.

She felt full of a sudden longing for a new world

that for the first time since she had left Bokhara seemed three-dimensional, and close enough to grasp.

'One bedroom please,' Roxana heard herself grandly saying. She hadn't been able to specify what her price range was because she had no idea, none whatsoever, how much it would cost to rent a flat that was like Noah's, and also close to Noah.

The Asian boy stabbed at his computer keyboard.

'Here you go. Brook Green, yeah?'

He turned the screen to face her. Roxana saw photographs of a gleaming steel kitchen and a bed with layers of covers and pillows.

'How much?'

'Four nine five. Might take a near offer.'

'Pounds?'

'This is London, innit?'

'Pounds, is that, a month?'

Roxana saw a flash of contempt. In a much less polite voice he said, 'A week. Two months in advance, plus one month deposit. Minimum one year, six-month break clause.'

She did the mental arithmetic, then hardened her voice.

'I want something cheaper.'

'Not a lot round here. If you're looking at a small studio, maybe.'

'I see.'

Half out of his chair, he was looking at his watch.

'We close at four, Sundays.'

Roxana stammered, 'Where do people live who are not rich?'

He hesitated, then took pity. 'Rent a room in a shared flat, innit? Look online, or in the free sheets.'

Roxana stood up, hoisted her carrier-bag, squared her shoulders.

'Thank you.'

She walked quickly away from the place so that he wouldn't be able to watch her through the big windows, then slowed her pace to an aimless meander.

A bus came towards her, trundling over the McDonald's litter that blew into the road. A small file of people stepped forwards as the doors swished open, and Roxana joined the line. She made her way up to the top deck and found a seat next to the window, near the front. She had no idea where the bus was heading, but she had time and nothing else to do. She rested her temple against the glass and stared out as they began to sway and rock through London. The traffic was lighter than usual because it was a Sunday, and the bus seemed to move quite fast. She could see over a hoarding into a parking lot chequered with cars, and over the hooped roof of a big supermarket, and into a little park with tennis courts behind wire lattices and boys playing football with clothes for goalposts, just like the boys did in the evenings in Bokhara.

Now they were passing red-coloured apartment blocks with heavy white facings round the windows, and she could see over net half-curtains or between grey loops of torn material into crowded rooms with the tiny busy screens of televisions and lines of washing and a bed all stirred up after a long night.

To her surprise, Roxana didn't feel as lonely looking at all this as she had done when she first came to London. She was curious, even affectionate, as if she had suddenly slipped from the outside into familiarity.

The bus turned a corner and the scenery changed.

Here there were trees, big ones, taller than the bus, all together in a leafy clump like a slice of forest, but set around with high white houses. The houses had steps up to grand doors, and little lacy iron balconies, and window boxes planted with green and silver leaves. Parked all round the squares were BMW and Mercedes cars. Roxana had never seen this part of London before and she stared out on it as hungrily as if she were going to eat it.

Then everything changed again and they were passing the plate-glass windows of glittering shops. Here elongated mannequins stood in hips-forward poses, and there little velvet recesses contained a spot-lit blaze of jewels. All the abstract wealth and beauty and grandeur that she had dreamed of in London seemed scooped together and made real in one place, with majestic trees and glimpses of polished houses giving way to the rows of prosperous, shining commercial facades.

It wasn't even a matter of wanting in much the same way but on a different scale, as she had suspected earlier in McDonald's. Roxana was suddenly quite certain that whatever had happened in the past, whatever was written in her passport or bred in her bones, whatever history or heritage might otherwise suggest, here in these wide streets was where she belonged. The Cosmos, Mr Shane, a room for herself, her illegal status, what to do next, all of these were just details and she would find a way to deal with them.

She was at home. Just to know it was almost as good as possessing it, she thought.

She smiled as she looked out at the gilded day. London was a wonderful place, so wonderful that she would have liked to share the discovery with someone who would understand how far she had already travelled. Most of all, she wished that person could be Niki, even though he would disapprove of all these material goods.

Niki. Roxana's smile faded. It was still hard to come to terms with a world that didn't have her brother in it.

There was always Yakov. She owed him a letter because he had helped her to get here. She thought of him in his curtained room, always reading, with the books piled up to the ceiling and stacked in pyramids on the floor. Yakov had been her mother's friend, though. He was well-disposed to Roxana, even though she sometimes had to move out of range of his plump hands, but it wouldn't be like telling someone of her own age.

Then she thought of Fatima, her old friend from school, who she had last seen when they were both briefly studying in Tashkent. She had an email address, Roxana knew that; Fatima was very proud of her business skills these days.

Maybe, Roxana thought, she would find an internet café and send her a message.

It was 4 a.m. when she returned to the flat in Hammersmith. She tiptoed in without turning on a light and almost immediately collided with the sofa end. Noah was wrapped in a blanket, his large bare feet sticking up over the low arm, and he was gently snoring with his broad, good-humoured face creased up against a cushion. Roxana went into his bedroom and climbed into the now familiar bed.

The next afternoon she left the flat early, before either Noah or Andy were home from work. She had bought a copy of the newspaper and circled some rooms to let that she reckoned she could afford. Until she had found a place, she thought, it might actually be possible to live at Noah's without him or Andy ever having to bump into her. Except for Noah on the sofa, it was a good arrangement. She decided to tell Noah that it would be better if *she* took the sofa.

On Tuesday, she discovered the Best Little Internet Café on the Planet. It was in a side street, a very dingy street that was full of bagged refuse from fast-food restaurants. The pavement outside was slippery with grease and the air was rank with the breath of kitchen ventilators. But still, the café itself looked inviting. The funny name was printed above the window, in square red letters. Inside at the front there was a handful of small wooden tables, with mismatched chairs and old-fashioned glass salt and pepper sets. At the back, on a slightly raised section of the floor, she caught a glimpse of a row of terminals. Some young men who looked like Asian students were perched in front of them.

Roxana went inside and ordered a Greek coffee, as the menu described it. The café proprietors were Greeks, obviously. One of the Asian boys got up from his terminal, tapped the others on the back, and paid some money to the owner.

'See you,' the man called after him.

Roxana asked if she could use the terminal that was now free.

'Sure,' the owner answered. 'Half an hour, or one hour?'

She sat down in the still-warm seat. There was a lam-inated card with printed instructions taped to the table-top. Roxana read it carefully.

Fumbling with the English keyboard, she chose an

Uzbek-language portal offering news and cultural commentary. Obligingly it came straight up, headed by a tourist-brochure picture of four sky-blue tiled majolica domes surmounting four brick minarets. It was the Chor Minor, gatehouse to a ruined *madrassah*, one of the most famous of the many famous buildings in Roxana's home town of Bokhara.

Roxana blinked at the domes, and at the sky behind them that was even more brightly and intensely blue with the heavy pulse of heat within it. The view was very familiar, but she needed to feel her distance from the alleys and concrete blocks and the hot white light of Bokhara. Outside the café, taxis reassuringly rumbled in the city street.

There was a boy leaning back in the next seat and covertly eyeing her.

'Excuse me?' Roxana said to him, quickly closing the window. 'How do you send email from here?'

That night at The Cosmos was the worst yet. None of the men had wanted a dance from her, however hard she worked at making eye contact from the pole. There had been a sour, uneasy atmosphere in the club and Mr Shane had been vicious to all the girls, even Natalie.

Roxana was about to get her period, so her face looked pale and spotty and her stomach was distended. She felt ugly and bone weary and contemptuous of the men who lined the bar at the back of the club, staring at her as she went through her routine as if she were meat in a market. If she couldn't make them do what she wanted, she felt naked instead of clothed in self-confidence.

As soon as she closed the front door of the flat with the softest possible click, she knew that Noah was awake. She moved as silently as she could, to the bathroom and from there into the bedroom. When she lay down in the darkness, she saw a stripe of light under the door. She suddenly wanted very much to see Noah and talk to him.

She sat up abruptly, swung her legs out of bed, adjusting the vest and shorts that she wore to sleep in.

Noah was in the kitchen, two hands wrapped round a mug. His hair stood up at the back of his head and he was yawning and blinking. He took a gulp from the mug, looking at Roxana over the rim.

'I knew you were awake,' she said.

He nodded. 'You should get to bed, though. You look really tired.'

They looked at each other under the twinkling, over-bright kitchen lights.

'Do you want some tea?' he asked. They were speaking very quietly, not wanting to risk disturbing Andy.

'Tea? Okay, why not?'

He juggled with a teabag and a mug and the kettle, then handed the mug across to her. They sat down at the kitchen table.

'How are you?' she asked. 'I have missed speaking to you.'

'I come home at the usual time, hoping to see you, but you're never here.'

Roxana pushed out her lower lip and he studied the faint indentations in the fullness where her teeth had rested.

'I don't want to be in the way, for you and Andy.'

She drank some of her tea, put the mug down and spread her hands flat on the table. Noah matched the gesture and without speaking or looking directly at each other they slid their hands closer until the tips of their middle fingers were just touching. After a moment of this most tenuous connection Noah ventured to raise his hands to cover hers. When he glanced at her face he saw that she was blushing, and the contrast between what she did and what she was like touched him deeply.

Behind her the fridge shuddered and the motor began its low hum. Roxana stirred herself and withdrew her hands from beneath his.

'It is very late.'

'When can we see each other?' he asked.

'We are seeing each other now.'

'You know what I mean.'

She said abruptly, 'Yes. Of course I know.'

'And so?' He might as well be persistent, he thought. You could only get so far with tact and circumspection.

Roxana appeared to consider. 'I would like to be friends.'

For Roxana this was an offer of far greater value than mere sex, because sex was handed over in a transaction or taken in violence. For Noah, it was a brush-off. They misunderstood each other.

He sighed, and then smiled.

'Okay. So we will. And now I think it will be best if I take myself off to the sofa.'

They both stood up, bumped into each other as they tried to place their mugs in the sink, stepped quickly back again, turned awkwardly aside. Roxana saw him resignedly ease himself down on the sofa, bend his long legs to fit the shorter space and pull the cover up to his chin. She clicked the light off at the wall and retreated into the bedroom.

She lay down too, but sleep was a long way off. All

she could think of was Noah's face, crumpled against the cushions, and the way the tip of his finger had nudged against hers. She was lying in his bed, safe under his roof, with the New Zealand boys who played rugby lined up downstairs like a row of innocent, beefy bodyguards. In spite of her uncertainty, in the darkness she laughed. Then she kicked off the bedclothes and marched back to the door. She switched the light on again and Noah sat up, blinking at her.

'Come in?' she asked.

He hesitated, but it was an invitation that he was physically incapable of refusing.

Still, he went slowly, knowing that she was offering herself because she felt indebted to him, because he had manoeuvred her into an awkward position. Roxana lay down on her side, her knees drawn up and her hand curled out towards him.

The edge of the mattress gave under his weight. He lay down with his body as far away from hers as possible, then he gently took her hand. She sighed and clasped his in return. Noah looked up and saw that there was grey light creeping round the edges of the skylight blind.

'Close your eyes,' he murmured, stroking the back of her hand with his thumb. 'Everything is all right.'

To his surprise, he fell almost immediately into a deep sleep.

When he woke, the first thing he saw was Roxana's shoulder and the rounded swell of her upper arm. He lay without moving, listening to the sound of her breathing. He heard the water running as Andy took a shower, then a series of bumps and a brief snatch of music before the radio was turned down. The smell of burned toast made Roxana stir. She rolled onto her back and in the pale light he saw her eyes open.

She turned her head towards him, her face still filmed with sleep.

'Hello?' he said.

'Hello Noah.' Her mouth curved in a smile and they lay looking into the worlds within each other's eyes. Slowly, Noah shifted himself towards her. She didn't move back or try to push him away. Her smile broadened slightly, and then his lips touched hers.

There were some more thumps, and finally the door slammed as Andy departed for work.

'What time is it?' Roxana murmured when the kiss ended. Noah's fingertips gently traced her jaw line, then ran down to the warm notch at the base of her smooth throat.

'No idea. Half eight?'

'You have to go to work.'

'I think . . . I think I might pull a sickie.'

Roxana's eyes were dancing.

'What is that?'

'A sickie is when you don't go to work for a whole day. You stay in bed, like this. Doing this . . .' His fingers trailed downwards, found a small round breast.

'I see,' she sighed. Her spine arched, like a stroked cat.

'Come here.'

She didn't move. But she was still smiling. 'Why don't *you* come *here*?'

He slid across the remaining inch or so of sheet and suddenly connected with the whole silky length of her body. Her arms snaked round him and held him tight.

'Now I have you.'

'So you do,' he agreed. He took her hand, and guided it.

Andy came in at about seven o'clock.

Roxana had left for The Cosmos and it was eight hours before Noah could even hope to see and touch her again. He'd wanted to take her to work, and to stay there to watch over her, but she had absolutely forbidden him to do anything of the kind. She had plastered her two hands over his mouth as a gag.

'No. No. Do you understand me?'

He broke away and rolled on top of her. 'Not really. You have this very, very strange accent.'

'Listen to me. Dancing is just dancing. It doesn't mean anything.'

He kissed the inside of one wrist. 'I know. Just come back soon, right?'

She had gone, and now he was sitting watching the *Channel 4 News*.

'All right, mate?' Andy said. He let his bag flop off his shoulder.

'Yeah, thanks, not bad at all.'

'How was your day?'

'I didn't go in.'

Andy reached into the fridge and took out a beer. He popped the ring and expertly captured the rising froth beneath his upper lip. He took a long, eager swallow.

'Ah. That's better. So, are you shagging her yet, then?'

Noah raised his eyebrows. He didn't even need to glance about him to see their shared quarters in full detail. There were magazines and last weekend's colour supplements on the floor and sofa, interleaved with takeaway flyers. Clothing belonging to both of them hung on the backs of chairs and there was a jumble of trainers in the niche to the left of the front door. It wasn't squalid, but it wasn't orderly either. They both understood the unwritten rules of sharing, one of which was that they should conduct most of their sex lives elsewhere. More recently, in Noah's case, it had happened at Lauren's neat flat. When he had removed her teddy bear from its place of honour on the pillow.

When Noah didn't answer, Andy grinned. 'I'll take that as a yes.'

'Take it as whatever you want.'

'Uh-huh.' Andy drank some more beer, settled himself into his usual chair and paid a minute's attention to Jon Snow.

'So,' he began again. 'Does it look serious?'

'Too soon to tell,' Noah conceded. Remembering the details of the day made him almost lose the studied cool he and Andy maintained around each other. He allowed himself a smile, though. 'Maybe.'

'Look, mate. Whatever. It's just that . . .' Andy waved his hand to indicate the limitations of their space.

'I know,' Noah interrupted. 'It's only till the weekend. She hasn't a clue about the Western world, let alone London. I'll help her find a room, and then she'll be sorted.'

Andy nodded and returned his attention to the television. 'Sweet, mate.' He found the remote down the side of his chair and began to click through the channels. 'Isn't the athletics on now?'

'No idea,' Noah sighed.

Bill fanned the coals until they glowed, and then stood back to watch the scarlet fade to ash-grey. It was a warm Sunday in July, and therefore, in theory, the perfect opportunity for a family barbecue.

In many ways his marriage to Jeanette had been a

conventional one. He had built up a business, a City PR firm that had remained small but was now well-regarded and quite successful, while Jeanette had run their home. Once Noah was old enough for school, with Bill's encouragement Jeanette had built on her undergraduate science degree by taking a postgraduate diploma in plant taxonomy. She had discovered a passion for botany and plant classification. For years she had worked at a botanical garden, with a small team of long-standing colleagues who specialised in plant diversity and conservation techniques. It was stimulating work in an environment where her deafness was not a serious impediment, but it had also left her with enough time to be a regular wife and mother.

Lately, though, Bill had had to take over responsibilities around the house. He thought his cooking was improving, and Jeanette insisted that it was, but still a barbecue had seemed the best option for today. Bill had always done the barbecuing.

Noah was coming to lunch, and he had asked if he could bring his new girl. He wanted Jeanette to meet her. *Both* of them to meet her, he had corrected himself, without managing to withdraw the implication that Jeanette didn't have much time to take the measure of new girlfriends.

Connie was coming too.

Jeanette had asked for this, and Connie had accepted the invitation.

It was going to be a family party. Bill could count the precedents for this on the fingers of two hands.

Jeanette was sitting in her usual place in the shade of the tree. She was wearing a straw hat, her head bent to deepen the shade over her face, intent on shelling peas into a colander. Bill straightened up to look at her.

It was simple, he thought. After twenty-five years loyalty and affection and habit took the place of love. Or perhaps at some point in their history, love had become these things. Whichever way it was, when he remembered that next summer she would not be here in her garden, he found himself in tears. He often cried these days. The tears came without warning, like a child's or an old man's. Then, just as suddenly, the grip of sorrow released him again.

Whereas where Connie was concerned, nothing was simple.

All their long history had been constructed out of negatives: out of guilt and then denial, pain, then more guilt and absence, and long silence.

And yet still, with the knowledge that soon he would see her, even with his dying wife quietly shelling peas a few feet away from him, Bill was fired up with anticipation as fierce as a boy's.

The coals in the barbecue pan were breaking into surreptitious flames. From his array of barbecuing equipment, mostly past birthday offerings from Noah, he selected a metal spray canister and spritzed the flames into submission. When he looked up again Connie was walking across the grass. She was wearing jeans, flip-flops, a basket slung over her shoulder.

'There was no answer to the bell so I came round the side,' she called.

He met her halfway, grasped her by the wrists and kissed her cheek. She was warm, flushed with the sun, and her hair was damp at the nape of her neck.

'Glad you're here,' he said.

Jeanette sat up. Connie turned so she could read her lips.

'How are you? How's the week been?'

– *Good. Quite good today*, Jeanette answered. – *How about you?*

Connie knelt beside the chair and Jeanette leaned forwards, pushing back the brim of her hat so their cheeks touched. From her basket Connie produced a row of little gifts: a magazine with an article on plant names, a jar of manuka honey, a ridged wooden cylinder that you were supposed to roll beneath your feet to massage away tension.

Bill watched as they passed the various items back and forth between them. There was no physical resemblance, of course, but their gestures mirrored each other. At a glance you might assume that they were siblings, and then wonder why you had jumped to that conclusion.

'Let me get you a drink, Con. Glass of wine?'

'Please.'

– *Me too*, Jeanette indicated.

'Coming up.' Bill carried the colander full of shelled peas into the house, tipped them into a pan, took a bottle of white wine out of the fridge. When he went out into the garden again he saw that Connie was sitting on the grass beside Jeanette. They were not quite looking at each other and a pool of silence spilled between them, but even so, for the first time that he could ever remember, it was Bill who felt like the outsider.

He poured wine into three glasses. Jeanette lifted her head and smiled at him; as Connie reached upwards she angled her legs and her ankles showed under the turned-up bottoms of her jeans. All three raised their glasses in a wordless toast. There were wood pigeons throatily cooing in the tall trees.

Noah and a girl emerged round the side of the house, the same way that Connie had come.

'Hi, here we are. Mum, Dad, this is Roxana.'

Roxana was wearing a denim jacket over a short full skirt made of some sort of sweatshirt material that revealed an almost unfeasible length of leg; it wasn't a reticent outfit, but her expression contradicted her appearance. She looked taken aback by the size of the house and the expanse of the garden.

She shook Jeanette's and then Bill's hand very quickly and stepped back beside Noah.

Noah turned to his aunt. This was not the time to let the faintest wrinkle of uncertainty crease the smooth surface of goodwill. Noah gave her a generous hug and Connie embraced her nephew warmly in return.

'Hello Auntie Con,' Noah said. 'How've you been?'

'Noah. It's so good to see you,' she smiled. He had filled out and lost the accusatory glare of adolescence, and the resemblance to his father had deepened.

He introduced Roxana. Roxana's hand was cool. She gave Connie a quick glance under mascara-heavy lashes.

'You are Noah's aunt, he told me.'

Connie was thinking how striking she was.

'Yes. Jeanette and I are sisters.' It sounded simple enough.

Jeanette stood up. She was the shortest of the group anyway, and so reduced now as to seem hardly bigger than a child, but she commanded attention. She took Roxana firmly by the arm.

'I like your garden very much,' Roxana told her politely, then glanced to Noah for confirmation that she was doing the right thing.

'Mum can follow everything,' Noah told her. 'You'll be surprised. It's difficult for her when everyone speaks all at once, but otherwise it's no problem. And she can talk. You'll get the hang of it. It's stopping her that's the problem, half the time.'

He grinned and Jeanette shook her head at him. She held on to Roxana's arm and pointed towards the length of the garden. With a sweep of a hand she encompassed her flowerbeds.

– *Come with us*, she beckoned Connie. Connie took her other side and they began a tour of the borders.

Bill and Noah watched them.

'It's okay that Connie's here, then?' Noah said in a low voice.

'Yes. Your mum wants to see her. I'm glad of that.'

'It still feels a bit weird to me.'

Bill put on an apron with *Natural Born Griller* printed on the front, another of Noah's offerings.

'Cool pinny, Dad. Suits you.'

'Yes. Thank you. Everything about dying is weird, isn't it?'

'Yeah. How are you with it?'

'Death?' Bill used a pair of tongs to lift chicken portions out of a marinade, and laid the meat on the barbecue. Dripping juices caused the red coals to sizzle and spit. 'I'm finding the inevitability, the non-negotiability, quite hard to accept. Just at the moment. I'll probably get my mind round it.'

'I know what you mean. I keep on thinking, look, this isn't right. Surely we could do this, or that, and she'll get better. Even though we know she won't. I was asking more about Connie being here, though.'

'I see. Well. Jeanette and Connie predate you, you know. They predate me as well. It's right that they should come back together now, in spite of all the problems in their history. It's important. It's all that matters, in fact.

I'm full of admiration for your mother, for having the will to make it happen. And I admire Connie too.'

Noah put an arm round his father's shoulders. 'You're such a good, good person, Dad, you know?'

Bill laughed briefly. 'You didn't always think that.'

'You know what kids are like.'

'Righteous.'

'A total pain. But I'm a grown man now, I'm not insisting on black or white. I can acknowledge grey. You know, Dad, I love you.'

'Yes,' Bill said, as composedly as he could. He turned a chicken portion, revealing a browned underside frilled with burned edges. 'I love you too.'

They could say these things to each other now, whereas once it would have seemed impossible. Bill told himself that here was something to hold on to, at the very least. He slung the tongs over the rail at the side of the barbecue burner and wiped his palms over the *Griller* slogan. He nodded his head towards the three women, who were just reaching the end of the garden.

'She looks like an interesting girl.'

Noah beamed. 'Roxana is an *amazing* girl,' he said. 'I have never met anyone like her.'

'That's good to hear. I'm very pleased. I'm looking forward to getting to know her. Now, how are we doing with this food? Noah, will you go in the house for me and put the potatoes on? Just the spuds, not the peas yet, otherwise the peas'll be . . .'

'. . . Yeah, Dad, right. I'm not a total loser in the kitchen, as it happens.'

'Just do it.'

'Christ,' Noah sighed.

Roxana gazed at the tall blue spires and the low misty-blue mounds and the clumps of grey velvet leaves. She had never been in a garden like this. She had no idea what the flowers were called, she had never even seen most of them. Noah's mother and aunt were making a kind of duet out of telling her about them. They seemed to talk fluently, with only one of them speaking.

'Those are delphiniums. Those, I don't know – Jeanette? Oh yes, it's nepeta.'

Jeanette made a low sound and Connie added, 'Catmint, yes.'

'These, um, roses, what a nice colour. I have never seen one like this. What kind are they?'

At least she knew roses. Roxana was trying hard. Her jaw muscles strained with politeness, and all the time Noah's mother was looking at her with inquisitive eyes.

The two women conferred. Noah's aunt was quite tall, and interesting to look at. Her plain white shirt with rolled-up sleeves set off her beautiful skin and she was wearing a very thin gold bracelet around her right wrist. Roxana thought she looked very *chic*, so much so that she made Roxana want to tug at the hem of her own skirt and straighten out the creases in her jacket. It was difficult to make the same sort of appraisal of Noah's mother, and Roxana knew that that was because she was very ill. Her face had an ageless look to it, so that she might have been sixteen or sixty, with too-big eyes and faded hair as thin and tufty as a young child's. She and Noah must once have looked quite alike, with similar mouths and cheekbones, but now Noah was more like his father. They had the same fair, faintly reddish tinge to their skin and the same amused quietness in their manner that still expected to be heard.

'It's called Buff Beauty,' Connie said.

Jeanette released their arms and leaned into the flowerbed. She broke off one of the blooms and put it into Roxana's hands. The outer petals were pale cream, the colour of elegant, expensive paper, but in the tight centre they were apricot gold. Noah's mother's scrutiny made her feel exposed, and she felt uncertain with these two women and their family party and this big house with about fifteen windows blinking at them, and the scented depths of their flower garden.

Whenever Roxana had thought or dreamed of England, it was London in her mind's eye. She had never even considered that there would be places like this, set behind hedges and buried in trees. There were houses quite close at hand because she had seen them as she passed by with Noah, but from here she could see nothing but the birds. Only a week ago she had felt her place in the rich city streets, and now she was where Noah belonged and she was out of her depth all over again. It was quite likely, she thought, that she would never be able to fathom what Englishness meant. It would keep evading her, and then where would she be?

'It's nice,' she said flatly, turning the rose in her fingers.

Connie took it from her and twisted the stem in the buttonhole of Roxana's denim jacket.

'There. That looks good,' she smiled and lightly touched her shoulder.

Jeanette nodded her approval. They began to walk again, slowly. Leaves brushed against Roxana's ankles, releasing aromatic scents.

At the far end of the garden, partly screened by tall bushes and backed by trees, they came to a little green-painted structure with a low door and a pitched roof.

Both of the women stopped walking.

Connie said, 'Do you know what I remember?'

Jeanette made a little roof shape by placing her fingers together and then moved her bunched fingertips to her lips and on upwards in an extravagant arc. She was laughing. Connie was laughing too.

'Yes, yes.'

They had forgotten Roxana. There was a ladder leaning against the trunk of one of the trees. Connie ran forwards and seized it, propped it against the side of the hut and clambered up. She balanced in a duck-walk, arms outstretched. She perched unsteadily, feet on either side of the roof ridge, struck a pose and then began singing. In a high, loud voice. About a prince, and when he would come to carry her away.

Roxana gaped, thinking that the two of them had perhaps been drinking. She peered back towards the house and saw Noah carrying plates out to the round wooden table, and his father shaking out the folds of a big umbrella.

Jeanette was leaning back against the trunk of a tree, laughing so much that she seemed hardly able to stand, so much that Roxana wondered if she ought to try to help her. But Connie slithered down the roof and vaulted back down to the grass. She ran to Jeanette and the two of them fell into each other's arms. The noise Jeanette made was loud, a hoo-hoo sound against Connie's lighter, normal laughter. Then there was a point when they both took a breath and looked into each other's faces.

They weren't laughing any more.

Connie touched her sister's cheek, and then Jeanette's head slowly came forwards until it rested against her shoulder. They stood there, swaying a little, arms round each other.

Roxana walked a few steps onwards, not wanting to intrude on this, and stared over at Noah. He was wiping cutlery and laying it on the checked cloth that had been spread over the table. He looked up and saw her watching him, gave her a wave and then blew a kiss.

After a minute or two the women rejoined her.

Connie said, 'We were just remembering when we were little. We used to have a shed at home, quite like that one. I used to . . . sing.' They were both shaking with laughter again, and Roxana wondered if they were perhaps not drunk but a little bit crazy.

With an effort, Jeanette composed herself. She put her hands together and inclined her head, making such an eloquent apology that Roxana was disarmed. She fell into step when Jeanette indicated that they were to traverse the opposite side of the garden.

This was the shadier half, and here there were big dark leaves splashed with silver, and wiry stems that held up bronze leaves shaped like hearts. Noah's mother made some more of her quick gestures and his aunt translated them into words.

'What do you think of England?'

'I like it very much,' Roxana answered, choosing the obvious response. She added carefully, 'And Noah has been kind. Now I am looking for a flat to share. There is a room in, what is it, North Ealing? Noah says he will come with me to look at it. London is a big city, and it's very expensive, but I have a job. Perhaps Noah will have told you what work I do?'

Both women casually nodded, careful not to place too much emphasis on knowing about it.

'Are you going to stay in London? Don't you miss home?'

'Not so much. Uzbekistan is a poor country. People work hard, there is some discontent, little freedom to speak. We don't have too much of anything, except cotton fields and policemen.'

Jeanette smiled, but Noah was right, his mother didn't miss anything. She signed again, and Connie spoke for her. 'Noah told us about your brother. I'm sorry.'

'Thank you,' Roxana said.

She did not want to think about Niki now, although the memories of the Friday Massacre, the images of the main square in Andijan under a rain-heavy sky and the armoured trucks full of men with guns were seldom far from her mind. She added, because it seemed that she ought to say something more, 'Niki was a good boy. A Muslim boy, and he believed in certain things. Me, however, I am not so good.'

To underline her point she did a couple of little dance steps and the folds of her short skirt swung around her thighs. 'And now I am here in England,' she finished.

– *That's good*, Jeanette indicated.

Noah's family were kind, like him, Roxana decided.

Noah's mother wanted to find out about his girl-friend. That was all right, Roxana thought philosophically. Any boy's mother would want to know things about her, she had arrived from nowhere, that was natural. She wished she had a family of her own exactly like this one. But at least she was here, included in the lunch party, just as if she were an English girl. Suddenly she smiled, basking all over again in the white light of freedom and opportunity.

Connie saw the smile. She was thinking, This girl is quite formidable.

Jeanette pointed. Bill was waving the barbecue tongs, beckoning them.

'Lunch,' Connie said.

They all sat down under the shade of the big parasol. Jeanette supervised the seating. She put Roxana opposite her where she could see her face more clearly, and there followed an interval of drink-pouring and complicated passing of various dishes of food. Roxana watched covertly to see what Noah did and then copied him. He glanced across and winked at her.

When they all had some of everything, Bill filled Jeanette's glass with wine and Jeanette raised it in Roxana's direction.

'Cheers,' the other three all said.

Roxana put her hand over her heart. '*Za vashe zdorovye.*'

Jeanette ate hardly anything, but she sipped some of her wine and she followed the conversation. The others seemed to orbit around her, and whenever she broke in with her signing or the occasional unformed, liquid syllables that they seemed to understand perfectly well, they all stopped to listen. For all her physical fragility, her strength was evident.

'How's the music biz, Auntie Con?' Noah asked after a while. 'Connie writes music for films and commercials, Roxana. Very big-time.'

Roxana liked Noah's mother and father, but it was Connie who increasingly drew her attention. She seemed different from the others, and not just in her appearance. Roxana was very interested to hear what she did.

'Really? What is the work like?'

Connie raised her hands now, laughing and twisting back her dark hair. 'It's a circus. Always has been. I was at the EMMAs in the week. That's the Electronic Music Marketing Awards,' she said for Roxana's benefit. 'The ad industry is one of the best there is for awarding itself awards.'

'Were you nominated for something?' Noah asked.

'No. I'm *way* out of touch. I went with a friend of mine.'

Connie had been Angela's guest.

'Please come,' Angela had begged her. 'The cat-food commercial's up for best use of classical-style music in a thirty-second TV spot. The client's a total nightmare, but you needn't have anything to do with him. You know everyone, anyway.'

So Connie had taken her place at Angela's company's table for twelve clients and agency people.

To her surprise, she found herself sitting next to Malcolm Avery of GreenLeaf Music.

Her first job, when she had turned sixteen and could at last leave school, had been at GreenLeaf.

Full of determination to make her escape from Echo Street by finding work in the music business, she had taken a bus and then the tube up to Soho one Saturday morning and walked into all the recording studios. The studio manager, Brian Luck, admitted that they needed a teenager to do odd jobs. They wanted a boy, really, but Connie insisted that she could make better tea and what's more she could start at once. She added that they might as well give her the job right now, because she was going to sit there in the studio until they did.

When the job was hers, she bought a copy of the *Evening Standard* and went through the accommodation ads until she found a room she reckoned she could just about afford. She went home that first night to Echo Street, but it was the last time she ever slept in the house.

Once she was at GreenLeaf, she learned how to make herself useful and then indispensable. She gradually made friends among the loose tide of drummers and singers and keyboard artists who spent their days swirling around the studios and sitting in at recording sessions for whoever needed them. She did her share of playing and singing too, and in time a way of life established itself. It was an existence that centred on drinking heavily in Soho pubs, and rolling spliffs in stuffy rooms at the back of clubs, and from there watching quite a few of the people she knew descending into abysses of their own creation.

Connie didn't fear the abyss for herself. She was learning that she was her own safety net, and probably always would be, and therefore it was important to keep the structure in good repair.

Constance Thorne acquired a reputation for being good for a laugh but quite straight, and therefore reliable in an emergency. Everyone at GreenLeaf was busy and she began to get odds and ends of commissioned work that led to writing jingles for commercials. Connie was too used to being poor, and the effect of having some money once in a while seemed to shoot straight into her veins like her own version of a fix. She worked feverishly, jazzed up by the earning potential, and soon she had a useful little showreel of her work.

She lived like this for four years, sharing a dingy flat in Perivale and keeping irregular hours, not seeing the sun often enough and always juggling with work and money. She had plenty of friends and few intimates. The digital age was arriving, and the old studios were slowly going out of style. Jingle writers could come up with a tune on the way to a meeting with agency or television people, then call up and order a drummer, a flute-player and a violinist, record the separate tracks and mix them, sample some more, and the job would be done. Unusually for a woman, Connie watched and learned how to use the new equipment. She worked on a retainer for GreenLeaf during the day, then freelanced in the evenings, using the company's studios for her own work.

Then one of the founding partners of GreenLeaf, the amiable but lazy Malcolm Avery, ran a deadline too close. The brief was to write a jingle for the launch of a new chocolate bar called Boom Bar.

Malcolm slumped in his studio chair at six o'clock in the evening, his headphones hanging around his neck like a noose and dark circles under his eyes.

'I've got nothing here for the agency and I'm scheduled to meet them at ten tomorrow,' he groaned.

Connie had a date, for once with a man who wasn't a penniless drummer or trombonist. He was an agency account man, and he had even promised to buy her a meal rather than expecting her to stand alternate rounds in the pub.

'I'll have a go,' she said to Malcolm.

'Yeah, go on then. I'm going home. We'll play them whatever we've got tomorrow morning, and promise them the earth in a couple of days' time. See you, Con.'

Connie called to put off her date. The man didn't sound pleased.

When GreenLeaf Studios went quiet for the evening, Connie sat down at the eight-track EMU 2 with a jug of coffee and the brief for the Boom Bar jingle. She worked all night, and in the morning the tune was there.

At eight o'clock, with traffic building up in the street below and the lift beginning to hum in the old building, she picked out the tune on the keyboard one more time. *Boom boom baboom ba ba . . .*

She went out to get coffee and a danish, finished this breakfast at her desk in the corner by the stairs, and waited for Malcolm to come in.

When he arrived she played the jingle to him. His face flashed with cunning and then went flat.

'Well, yeah. Not genius, but not bad. I'll chuck it in with the others, mix 'em up, see what the agency thinks. Give me the tape.'

Connie was red-eyed and wired from her sleepless night. Her hand shot out and caught Malcolm by the wrist.

'No. I'm coming to the meeting. I'll play the tape, and I'll make sure everyone knows whose work it is.'

Malcolm laughed. 'Whose brief is it, whose studio is this, who do you work for?'

Somehow, Connie found it within herself to shrug and turn away with the tape in her pocket.

'Suit yourself. I did it in my own time, so it's mine. Go and present whatever you've got.'

She could almost hear Malcolm Avery making calculations. It was an important commission, for a big agency, for a major product launch.

'Oh, what the fuck,' he sighed. 'Come with me if you feel so strongly about it.'

The agency team and the clients all went mad for Connie's tune.

For the first time in her life Connie found that she was able to call the shots. She agreed to split the commission fee with GreenLeaf, and gleefully put a cheque for a thousand pounds in her bank. But she made sure when she signed the contract that royalties would come to her alone.

Almost at once, the Boom tune became a huge hit.

By the time she was twenty-three Connie was living in her own large flat in Belsize Park, with a room in it converted to a studio. In time she formed her own company and employed a manager to run the business side, and to go to meetings and take the music briefs from advertising-agency creative departments or television producers, while she concentrated on writing the music. She could spend days at a time shut away in the soundproof studio, working less with live musicians and more and more via the spiralling trajectories of new technology.

She never wrote another Boom song, although the title stubbornly clung to her, but she was a good composer. Her work won some awards, her showreel gathered depth and range. After the first flood of royalties, her income was steady rather than spectacular, but she had come a long, long way from Echo Street.

Eight years later, when numbers of her friends were marrying and having babies, Connie was certain that neither option was open to her because she was deeply, unwillingly in love with the man who was already married to her sister.

Then one day she went along to the recording of the orchestral music she had written for a television serialisation of *Dombey and Son*. The orchestra was under the baton of Sébastian Bourret.

They edged together, over the space of a year.

Connie liked being with Seb because he was actually as rootless as she felt. Seb was Australian by birth, half Belgian and half South African by parentage. Home for him was wherever he was rehearsing the current ensemble, and Connie fitted well into that structure. She was as happy as he was to move on from Geneva to Philadelphia to Tokyo. The topic of marriage or the possibility of children was never seriously discussed, though, and that was as much Connie's choice as Seb's. She couldn't envisage having children by anyone except the man she still loved.

Then came Sung Mae Lin. Connie didn't want to go back to Australia, and when she thought of London the streets were crowded with shadows. The Balinese village house with the veranda and the view stopped being a staging post and became her home.

Time had not treated Malcolm Avery kindly. He was three stone heavier and his cheeks were mottled dark mulberry red.

'Christ. It's Boom Girl, isn't it?'

'Hello Malcolm.'

'Don't see you around much these days. Are you still working? Wait a minute, you married Simon Rattle, didn't you?'

Connie said, 'I was with Sébastian Bourret for a few years. We never married, though. I live in Bali these days.'

'Bloody good idea. Better than sodding London.'

Malcolm refilled his own glass with the not-bad California merlot and sloshed the remaining inch or two from the bottle into Connie's.

There was a big silver-plated wine cooler in the centre of the table, filled with ice and bottles. Across the top of it Connie caught Angela's eye and they smiled at each other. It was going to be a long evening.

Once the dinner had been cleared away, the moderately well-known comedian and the blonde television presenter who were jointly compering the event took the podium. There was a lengthy session of jokes and banter.

'Bloody get on with it,' Malcolm said, not quietly. He was an award nominee, having devised the music for the cat-food commercial. He poured three inches of brandy into a balloon glass as the presentation of awards finally began. Nineteen minutes later Cosmo Reiss of Gordon Glennie Music lifted the award for the best use of classical style in a thirty-second television commercial over his head as if it were the World Cup.

Malcolm shouted, 'Bollocks, mate.' The cat-food client looked furious and Angela covered her eyes with one hand.

After the awards had all been presented the table-hopping part of the evening began. Among the well-dressed executives the composers looked like skinny angular children at a party for plump old relatives. Connie excused herself and went to the cloakroom. Angela came in a minute later and tossed her Lulu Guinness bag down beside the basin. They peered into their reflections in the mirror as Angela applied red lipstick.

'Bad luck about the award,' Connie commiserated.

Angela raised one eyebrow. 'Worse luck for Malcolm. He needs it. But next year, darling, it'll be yours for your Bali bank music. Trust me.'

'I do, I do,' Connie smiled. 'Ange? How are things with . . . ?' Women were coming in and out behind them so she didn't say Rayner Ingram's name out loud.

'All right. Well. You know. Quite difficult, actually.'

Angela looked unhappy, but determined to conceal it.

Connie couldn't think of anything she could say that might improve matters. She murmured something anodyne, and they went back out into the party together.

At the end of the evening Connie returned to their table. Waiters had carried away all the debris except for the wine cooler, which now contained only a couple of detached wine labels and a scum of melting ice. A couple of agency account men were attempting to haul Malcolm Avery to his feet.

Malcolm rather thought he would like one more drink, and resisted their efforts to hustle him. He gripped the table edge and rotated his head as if he were blind in one eye. Then he stood up, hauling on the cloth for support. The cooler slid towards him.

'Check this,' he suddenly roared. He moved fast, considering how drunk he was. He grabbed the wine cooler by its two little handles and tipped the contents over his head. Waves of icy water gushed over his shoulders and poured down his clothes. He gasped and shook himself like a walrus emerging from the sea. Constance gasped too, because quite a lot of the water had splashed over her.

'There you are. Sober as a judge now. Sober as Constance,' Malcolm shouted. He took off his shoes and tried to empty water out of them.

Connie told this story, complete with mime.

Jeanette and Bill and Noah all laughed, and after a second Roxana joined in too. She watched Connie admiringly as she pretended to wring water out of her hair, then glanced quickly round the table. This family laughed a lot, eagerly seizing every opportunity.

Bill sat back in his chair, grinning broadly.

'What did you do?'

'I personally saw him into a taxi and gave the driver forty quid to take him to West Hampstead.'

'Bravo, Auntie Con,' Noah applauded.

Connie didn't tell them what one of the account men had murmured to her.

'Poor sod, his wife's just left him.'

Roxana said, 'I thought it was only in Uzbekistan, like this.' She tipped her left fist towards her mouth, thumb and little finger raised.

'Ah, no. I am afraid you will encounter mass drunkenness in the UK. Even here in Surrey,' Noah said gravely, as he poured more wine for everyone. They all laughed again.

Bill had made a summer pudding. They all admired the crimson, slightly sunken dome before he stuck a spoon into it and rivers of juice escaped. Noah and Roxana ate most of it between them, then they cleared the table and went into the house together, claiming that they were going to do the washing-up.

Jeanette immediately raised her eyebrows at Bill and Connie.

Bill pretended to consider. 'I like her . . . skirt.'

Jeanette pointed at him and sliced her finger across her throat. She turned to Connie.

'She's impressive,' Connie said.

– *She liked you*, Jeanette indicated.

They faced each other, and the faintest shadow of ancient rivalry seemed to dim the afternoon sun.

Connie leaned forward and touched her sister's hand. 'I expect she just wants to get into advertising.'

Jeanette met her eye, and then smiled.

– *She'd be mad, from the sound of it. Plant taxonomy would be far better.*

There was relief in their laughter. Connie wondered, Might it have been as simple as that all along, to defuse the hostility? Why do you have to *die* for us to find out?

Noah and Roxana did most of the washing-up. Then they wandered through the house and Noah led her into his old bedroom. Roxana rested her elbows in the deep window embrasure and peered down into the garden. Jeanette and Connie were lying on a rug in the shade of the big tree, seemingly asleep. Bill sat in a deckchair beside them, reading a newspaper.

'Your mother and your auntie are not very like each other.'

Noah leaned behind her and kissed the back of her neck.

'They're not but they are, if you see what I mean. They're not real sisters, Auntie Connie was adopted. I haven't seen her for years. Not since my grandmother's funeral, come to think of it. Mum and Auntie Connie really didn't get on.'

'Why is that?' Roxana asked. Noah was thoughtfully sliding his hand over her hip.

'Well. My dad and Connie. They had a sort of relationship, long ago. An affair, I think you'd call it that. Yeah. I was only a kid and I didn't know much, but my mum was wild. She's always loved my dad extravagantly. My dad went very quiet and dignified about it, even though you could tell he was massively confused and in pain. He hated hurting my mother, he's always protected her by encouraging her. That's partly why she's been a successful scientist, he saw his job as enabling her, not further disabling. Connie was the loser in the end. She just sort of evaporated. Went to live abroad, and we never saw her. Dad kind of made a point of being exemplary after that, making up for it all. I mean, I don't think it was a penance because I know he loves Mum. There are different kinds of love, that's stating the obvious. But once the blood-letting was over there was a silence around it all. Taboo subject, you know, don't mention. Elephant in the corner. And then it's too late to mention anyway, because it's got hidden behind the rest of the furniture. It takes the prospect of someone dying to get anyone to expose the old carcass again.'

He looked over Roxana's shoulder at the tranquil scene in the garden. Then he buried his face in the nape of her neck.

'English middle-class silence. Profound deafness has got nothing on the silence of comfortable family dysfunction.'

Roxana was quietly working out where an elephant fitted into this plush house, and why its presence seemed to matter so much.

Noah added hotly, his lips against her skin, 'I want my family, the family I *will* have, to talk to each other all the time. No silences.'

Roxana tilted her head and wriggled round to face him.

'Of course. You can have the family you want. You can make it that way.'

He gazed at her. Her belief was so strong, and yet she was the one who was a stranger to this house and alone in England. She didn't seem particularly shocked about his father and Connie, although his father's betrayal and his mother's distress was the single biggest trauma Noah had had to deal with in his life, up until the present one.

Roxana had lost her mother and father and her only brother and left her whole world behind. He didn't know what she had suffered at the hands of her stepfather after her mother died, although he could guess.

He held her face between his hands and smoothed her broad Asian cheekbones with his thumbs. Compared with Lauren and her predecessors, who had had to deal at the very worst with an overbearing mother, or a father who ran off with his secretary, Roxana's experience was unfathomable.

'I love you,' he blurted out.

Roxana laughed. 'Is that the truth, or are you saying what men say?' Her mouth was the loveliest shape he had ever seen.

'It's the truth,' Noah said humbly. 'Do you love me?'

She turned serious. 'Yes. Maybe. That is a difficult question. I want to give a proper answer.'

'Then let's leave it at yes, for the time being,' Noah advised. 'Here. Lie on my bed for a minute with me. See, up there, the cracks in the ceiling look like a map. When I was a kid I made up a whole imaginary country to go with it. I called it Outlandia.'

Connie opened her eyes. The leaves overhead created an abstract pattern shot through with darts of light. The remains of sleep, the scent of grass and the sun-warmed wool rug made a complex net of memory that held her captive. With an effort of will she turned her head and saw Jeanette asleep on her back a foot away. Her mouth was slightly open and a tiny snore repeatedly caught in the back of her throat, and this was part of Connie's memory too.

Bill's shadow fell over her.

He was holding out a mug of tea to her. She pushed herself to a sitting position and took it from him.

A picnic. That was it. The day and the place and the time swam out of her subconscious and delivered themselves to her, complete. Connie shook herself.

'How long have I been asleep?'

'Maybe an hour.'

'I'm sorry.'

'Why? You looked very comfortable, both of you.'

'Where are Noah and Roxana?'

Bill rubbed with his thumb at the raw patch near his mouth. 'Upstairs. No, here they are.'

They spilled out of the door leading to the kitchen. They were scuffling, trying to trip one another and grabbing at each other's arms for support.

'They're very young,' Bill said quietly.

Jeanette stirred. She coughed and sighed, and he went to her and helped her to sit up.

'That was a good nap,' he said, holding her against him, and she nodded, still dazed with sleep.

Noah and Roxana chased across the grass and came to a panting standstill in front of them. Roxana tugged at the hem of her skirt again and composed her face, and Connie involuntarily smiled. This girl was endearing, as well as formidable.

'Dad? Mum? We might have to head back quite soon. I'm going to take Rox to North Ealing to look at the room.'

Connie sat more upright. There were midges coming out as the sun sank, and she had to put her mug aside to slap at her exposed ankles. An idea had taken shape.

'Roxana? This might not suit you, but I've got a spare room. It's a big flat, and I'm not there all that often. You'd be welcome to stay. It's not all that far from where you work.'

Roxana's self-possession finally deserted her. She looked from Noah to his parents, then back at Connie. Jeanette was fully awake now, following the conversation intently.

'With you? In your place?' Roxana stammered. Her face flushed with surprising colour.

'Yes. It might not be what you want at all, but until you get your bearings and decide what you really need?'

'Connie?' Bill murmured.

Roxana nodded very quickly. 'Thank you. Yes, please. If you think it would not be a trouble. Thank you.'

Connie wondered, too late, if Jeanette might interpret the offer as an attempt to infiltrate Jeanette's family, and Jeanette did seem to struggle with herself before she responded. But then she nodded.

– *That's kind of you, Connie. What a good idea.*

Directly to Roxana, Connie added, 'Maybe you and Noah could come back via my place this evening. You could take a look at the room.' She felt suddenly absurdly pleased with the thought of company, of Roxana's company, in her bare white apartment.

'Noah, can we do this?' asked Roxana.

In his easy-going way, Noah said, 'Yeah. Sure we can. Thanks, Auntie Con.'

EIGHT

June 1979

They drove out of London on a Sunday morning, the four of them in Bill's old car, Hilda taking the place of honour in the front passenger seat and Jeanette and Connie corralled in the back. Jeanette kept angling her left hand towards the light in order to admire the sparkle of her diamond engagement ring. Connie turned away from this spectacle and pressed her forehead to the window glass as the suburbs finally gave way to countryside. She was a few days short of her sixteenth birthday.

The picnic had been Hilda's idea.

'We should have a family day out together. Jeanette, what do you say? To welcome Bill to this family? Tony and I – that's Jeanette's dad, Bill, of course – we had a picnic to celebrate *our* engagement. We went in Geoff's car. He was doing nicely for himself even in those days, you know. There was Sadie and Geoff and Tony and me, and we drove all the way up to Constable country. That's on the river Stour, in Suffolk.'

'I expect Bill knows where Constable country is,' Connie interrupted.

Hilda ignored her. Bill's interested expression didn't change but Connie caught a glimmer of – what? Complicity? – behind his eyes. She stored up that one look as if they had shared an hour's private conversation.

'My Tony's family originally came from up in Suffolk, Bill. Farm workers, they were, generations of them. It was his father who moved down to Essex, to work for a butcher. My family were quite different, proper East Enders, bombed out in the war. My granddad worked on the docks.'

Connie listened even though she had heard all this before from Tony, many times, and Hilda's retelling made her miss him. She was interested in the old stories, though, because *everyone* had their stories. Somewhere, in a place that she hadn't yet discovered, her own story was waiting for her. Maybe her real mother was waiting, too. Some day she would find out exactly what painful circumstance had forced this unknown woman to give her up, and then she would be able to dress herself in her own history.

She thought often about this process, imagining it as if the details of her bloodline were glamorous garments that she could pull on, transforming herself like Cinderella from Connie Thorne into . . . well, not a princess, that was just a kid's idea, one she used to play with once she had worked out what her cousin Elaine's words on the day of Tony's funeral really meant. She had long ago discarded that babyish fantasy. Today she was thinking that perhaps her mother was an opera singer. Or maybe she was French, something like Edith Piaf, or possibly Simone de Beauvoir.

She would find out.

In the meantime, she pushed her hands into her pockets and sat expressionlessly as Hilda chattered on to Bill.

'It was a perfect day, I remember. Warm; sunny. Sadie and I made a lovely picnic. Cold chicken, and that was when it was a real luxury, not like these days. Meat rationing only ended in 1954, you know, and this was just a year later. We lay on the riverbank and it was as beautiful as any picture.'

'It sounds it,' Bill said.

'We stopped at a country pub on the way home. We sat out in the garden, in the twilight, drinking cider. There were bats flying between the trees and Sadie got quite hysterical, moaning that one of them was going to get tangled in her hair. Tony and Geoff laughed at her, the mean things. I'll always remember that day. He was a wonderful man, my Tony.'

– *Yes, Mum, he was*, Jeanette gently agreed.

'I'm sorry I never met him,' Bill said.

Connie was pondering the fact that once people were dead, you didn't speak ill of them. It was as though they turned into a different person, just through having died. While he was still alive Hilda had always been going on at Tony. She would go on until he couldn't put up with it any longer, and then there would be an argument. Usually it was about money, and how Sadie and Geoff lived in a detached house with a front garden and garage parking for two cars, or else it was about Jeanette and how the Joseph Barnes School for the Deaf wasn't giving her the right opportunities, not with her abilities, until Tony gave in and agreed to the expensive private speech-therapy lessons.

And the lessons had made a big difference.

'She's doing well, our Jeanette,' Tony had conceded. 'You were quite right, love, to send her for extra help. I'm sorry, I should have seen it for myself.'

Tony never believed in letting the sun set on an argument, whereas that was one of Hilda's specialities. Hilda could bear a grudge as though she had invented the process.

After Tony died, though, their marriage could only be viewed as perfect, its shining face never having been rippled by discord. Tony was a hero. Hilda would not hear a murmur to the contrary. Connie knew that this tribute, too late, ought to have pleased her, but instead the distortion made her feel angry.

Money was short. The piano lessons that Connie loved so much had to stop, but Hilda managed to go on paying for the speech therapy. She couldn't afford to keep the shop going once the creditors were paid off. They would have had to put a manager in and there wasn't enough turnover for a man's wage as well as an income for the family. Corner hardware shops couldn't compete with the DIY stores that were opening up along the North Circular. The shop was sold as a going concern, quickly and not very well.

Hilda took a part-time job in a school, preparing and serving dinners, and Jeanette became her lieutenant in the house. She did more of the cooking and cleaning, and delegated a proportion of the rest to mutinous Connie.

Uncle Geoff helped out financially. He never missed an opportunity to remind them, in a low, almost prayerful voice, of how generous he was being. Hilda was usually thin-lipped and long-suffering, sometimes seeming actually to vibrate with the effort of bearing all her burdens. Occasionally her veneer of control shattered into fits of hysterical weeping. Jeanette would fill a hot-water bottle and give her headache tablets. When an attack became more serious than Jeanette thought she could deal with, she would indicate to Connie that it was time to call in Auntie Sadie. Connie would telephone, Uncle Geoff would drive Auntie Sadie over in his red Triumph Stag, and Auntie Sadie would sit with Hilda in her bedroom until the weeping subsided. Eventually Hilda would emerge, white in the face and swollen-eyed, and make no reference to the outburst.

Their mutual difficulties might have brought Jeanette and Connie closer, forging a bond in adversity. But what happened in fact was that Jeanette's increased confidence, and the responsibilities that she was shouldering, lifted her forward onto a different plane. She simply stepped ahead of Connie. From being Connie's near-equal and constant adversary it seemed that in a matter of weeks she became an adult, moving beyond childish fistfights, out of Connie's realm altogether. From a chaotic sea of grief, the messy aftermath of Tony's business affairs and Hilda's shaky control of herself and their lives in Echo Street, the deaf and nearly speechless daughter sailed like a swan.

It was Connie who didn't deal well with her loss.

After Hilda had given her a brief and featureless account of her adoption – *We didn't know who your mother was. We adopted you through a council home in North London. It was done properly, formally, through a court order. We wanted Jeanette to have a little sister* – this new, immense piece of information wasn't manipulated at all. It was just left there, knocking up against all the other new truths; that Tony was dead and the shop was bankrupt and Hilda, who had once seemed made of iron, was threatening to dissolve.

Tony had been Connie's champion and now he was gone. She would have liked to run away from home, and dreamed of doing it, but she didn't have enough life or daring in her. Instead she took refuge in her music. She played the piano as much as she could and she listened almost obsessively to pop on the radio. She made up her own charts, and squirrelled away tunes and trends. She loved Roxy Music and hated Abba. Connie knew that she was waiting for her life to start.

Hilda had forgotten the whereabouts of the first picnic spot.

Bill obligingly turned the car off the main road and they followed country lanes through villages on the Suffolk border until it became clear that they were pursuing a dream rather than a memory. The objective became to find any secluded place that offered a riverbank, shady trees, an unspoiled view, and no cows because Hilda was afraid of them. The discussion was happy and animated at first, but quite soon became impatient.

Bill made the decision for them. He swung the car into a field-gate opening and turned off the ignition with a decisive click.

'This will be a good place,' he announced firmly.

Beyond the gate there was a rough field, with no livestock visible, and a line of trees indicating the course of the river.

'Are you sure?' Hilda demurred.

Jeanette swung out of her seat and opened up the boot. She began lifting out baskets and a rug and the insulated picnic box that had been bought for the occasion. Connie saw her framed in the rear window, and was struck again by how happy Jeanette was. The word that came into Connie's head was *joy*. Joy shone out of her sister's face like a searchlight. Bill got out and went round to join her. He quickly kissed the back of her neck and then they began passing camping chairs to each other, laughing and enjoying the job.

Connie unfolded herself. Her limbs were stiff, she had hardly moved all through the journey. She stood beside the open car door, yawning and rubbing her upper arms.

'Here, Con,' Bill said. He passed her a heavy basket and she took it from him, and she bowed her head submissively as he draped the rug around her shoulders. 'Can you manage that?'

'Yeah. Course.'

They marched in a line down the edge of the rough field, skirting patches of nettles. The river lay at the bottom of a small incline. There were a few trees, mostly stunted alders, but the view was of a field of young corn opposite and a copse on the higher ground beyond. There was a small crescent of dirt at the near margin of the river, deeply pocked with dried-out animal prints, but the grass at either side looked quite inviting, although it was thistly. Jeanette was beaming her approval.

'Are you sure there are no cows in this field?' Hilda wondered, peering back up the rise.

Bill and Jeanette were already trampling down the thistles. Bill kicked aside a dried cowpat and took the rug from Connie's shoulders. He spread it on the grass and set up four low chairs with seats and backs made from faded green canvas.

'If any cows come, Hilda, I'll defend you,' he laughed. Jeanette unwound the ties of her espadrilles and balanced over the hoof-marks in dried mud to the water. She paddled in, found a couple of stones and weighted the six-pack of beer that she had brought for Bill. But the current was deceptively strong and as soon as she turned away the pack toppled and was dragged downstream. She waved her arms and plunged after it, and Bill vaulted in off the bank shouting 'Catastrophe!' He rescued the beer and Jeanette, and brought them both back to dry land. Jeanette happily squeezed river water out of the hem of her floppy skirt.

Bill rummaged in the bag that he had brought with him and produced a bottle of white wine.

'Hilda, this is for you,' he said.

Hilda flushed with pleasure and told him that he really shouldn't have.

The picnic was a success, only slightly marred by the large orange flies that hummed from the cowpats to the Tupperware. Bill and Jeanette waved them away as they talked about the future, touching on Jeanette's plans to find a job as a laboratory assistant, her imminent exam results, Bill's job that he had now been doing for a year, a possible date for the wedding. Bill and Jeanette had agreed that they should wait for at least a year, maybe two, until they had saved some money. Bill asked Connie what she was going to do next year at school, as if he expected that she would have plans and intentions like everyone else. She couldn't think of what to say, as the idea of another year at school seemed real only in its utter implausibility.

'I dunno,' she shrugged, and hitched her black sleeves over her knuckles. Connie had made no concession in her clothes to the occasion or the weather, and was layered in shapeless dark garments as usual. Next to Jeanette in her floaty skirt and white pin-tucked top she felt hot and grubby, and the wrong shape.

'With all your opportunities, I'd have thought you'd be full of ideas, Connie,' Hilda reprimanded her.

Jeanette smoothed back a ripple of blonde hair, momentarily exposing the heavy hearing aid she wore. She was so comfortable with Bill now that she didn't try to conceal it from him.

– Mum, she's all right. Don't go on at her.

It was Jeanette's defence of her that was almost the hardest to bear. Connie frowned hard and chewed her lip.

When the food had all been eaten and the bottle of white wine was empty, Jeanette lay on the rug with her arms outstretched. Hilda sat in her canvas chair and looked through *Woman's Own*. Bill and Connie carried the plates and cutlery down to the water to rinse them before packing them away. Connie passed each piece to Bill and he swilled it clean, then handed it back. They worked comfortably together, and with the cool water swirling round her ankles Connie felt better. She caught his eye, and grinned at him.

'There,' Bill said as the last plate was done. He looked into her eyes. 'You okay?' he asked, and she was sure that he was concerned for her.

'Yes,' Connie said.

Hilda was reading, and after two glasses of wine Jeanette had drifted off to sleep. Bill wandered away down the bank of the river. Connie would have liked to go with him, but she was too shy to follow. Instead she lay on the rug beside Jeanette, taking care to leave as much space as she could between them.

In the afternoon's humid silence she fell asleep too.

When she woke up, disorientated and with her temples throbbing with heat and wine, she turned her head and saw Jeanette asleep a foot away. Her sister's mouth hung open and a tiny snore clicked in the back of her throat. Bill was sitting in the nearest chair, and it was as if he had been watching over both of them.

Not long afterwards a few heavy drops of rain fell.

Jeanette yawned, stretched, and sat up. A smile lit her face as soon as she saw Bill.

'It's going to pour down,' Hilda said. The light was purplish, as sore as a bruise, and there was not a breath of air. They packed up the remains of the picnic, folded the chairs, and trudged back along the field edge to the gate and the car.

They drove back towards London, but the thunderstorm never managed to break. After forty minutes Hilda leaned towards Bill and murmured something.

'Sure, of course we can,' he said at once. 'I'll look for somewhere.'

A mile or so further on he stopped just past another field gate, waited for a car to pass, then reversed into the gateway. There was a high hawthorn hedge separating the field from the road.

'Will this do?' Bill asked. 'Behind the hedge?'

Hilda peered out. 'I should think so. Won't be long.'

Jeanette went with her. The next thing Connie registered was Hilda's alarmed voice calling out that she couldn't go here, there were cows in the field.

A car was approaching, travelling fast. Connie saw a second blurred image, swinging across the path of the oncoming car. There was a long, jarring screech of brakes and an explosion of metal, a deafening *whump* that discharged itself in breaking glass and Connie's scream. The blurred thing had been a motorbike and rider, and now it split into two parts and she saw the bike skidding sideways in one direction and the dark shape of the rider bumping and rolling down the crown of the road. The noise seemed to last for a long time, and then it stopped abruptly, apart from tinkling glass and the creak of buckled metal. The car was in the ditch, rear-end up. The motorbike lay on its side, handlebars askew like broken limbs, one wheel still revolving. The rider was a motionless hump.

Jeanette and Hilda ran out of the field.

Bill was already out of the car, and Jeanette followed him into the road.

Hilda began moaning, 'Oh God.'

Connie knew that she must do something, but every fibre in her body told her not to move, not to go and see what lay there in the road. Jeanette had already dropped to her knees beside the prone biker.

From the crashed car Bill shouted, 'Connie, run to those houses and call an ambulance.'

In the distance, back down the road with the broken white line seeming to point straight to it, was the brick and flint end-wall of a cottage. Connie started running, over broken glass and the black skid marks and then along the verge. Her footsteps pounded in her ears and gravel crunched under her feet.

She reached a pair of cottages and an old man came to the door.

'An accident? What kind of accident?' He had a pendulous lower lip, and a huge stomach with shirt buttons straining across it.

Connie gabbled out the account again and pointed back down the road.

'Telephone?' the old man repeated after her, as if she was using a foreign language. She made him understand at last.

After he had called the ambulance the old man struggled to get his arms into the sleeves of a stained fawn-coloured jacket. Connie noticed the incongruity of a pink rosebud secured through a buttonhole in the lapel.

He followed her back up the road.

Jeanette was sitting with the biker's helmeted head in her lap. The black sheen of the helmet was scraped and dented. Her head was bent and blonde hair waved around her cheeks. Her lips moved as she seemed to talk to the injured man.

There was a second man sitting at the roadside, propped up against a tree trunk. There was blood down one side of his shockingly white face.

Bill walked across the road with the picnic rug in his arms. He went round to the passenger side of the crashed car, shook out the rug and covered up the person who was still sitting in the passenger seat. Connie began moving towards him but Bill held up his hand.

'Don't come over here,' he said quietly. Then he pointed to Hilda, indicating that Connie should go to her instead. Hilda was leaning against the bonnet of Bill's car, the heel of one hand pressed into her mouth.

'The ambulance is coming,' Connie heard herself say. Two more cars had arrived. People began to pass across Connie's line of vision, but all she could really see was Jeanette in the broken glass and tyre marks, cradling the injured biker. She couldn't see much of the biker's face, just enough to note that his skin was a terrible grey colour. His eyes seemed to be open and he looked straight up into Jeanette's face. She was smiling and silently talking, words of encouragement and reassurance that only the two of them could understand.

Hilda was shivering and weeping.

'Mum, why don't you sit in the car?'

A police or ambulance siren sounded in the distance.

The old man from the cottage mopped his face with a red handkerchief.

Five minutes later the emergency services were doing their work. Bill and Jeanette watched the ambulance crew tending to the biker. Bill's hand rested on her shoulder, but her attention was still entirely fixed on the injured man. His eyes closed as they all bent over him.

The police wanted to take their names and addresses, and brief witness statements. Jeanette would not be distracted until the biker had been put on a stretcher and lifted into the ambulance.

Connie gave a brief account of what she had seen. The biker had fatally turned in front of the oncoming car.

'Are you certain of that?' a policeman asked.

She nodded her head. She had been certain, but now the images were melting behind the biker's grey face, Jeanette's bowed head, the rosebud in the old man's buttonhole. She was trying not to see a knot of uniforms over by the crashed car, lifting out the passenger's body still blanketed in tartan, laying it at the roadside. The driver was trying to walk, but his legs would not carry him. The ambulance men supported him on either side.

A policeman tried to speak to Jeanette. She shook her head and Bill said tersely, 'She's deaf.'

'I see, sir.'

It seemed that they were at the roadside for a long time, but at last the police indicated that they could go. The front of Jeanette's white pin-tucked top was covered in blood. A policeman beckoned them out of the field entry, pointing to the line they were to take so as not to drive over any evidence.

Bill drove with exaggerated care. Raindrops starred the windscreen. Within seconds, rain was sheeting down. The windscreen wipers whined, struggling with torrents of water. Words similarly began to flood out of Hilda as if a tap had been turned on.

'I've never seen anything like that, not as bad as that,' she kept repeating. 'Not even in the Blitz. It was so sudden, one minute just the birds singing and then *bang*.'

Jeanette couldn't have known what she was saying, but she leaned forward and stroked her mother's neck and shoulder. Bill didn't take his eyes off the road. Hilda's hands shook.

'I've never seen anything like it. Just like that, it happened so fast. I couldn't believe my own eyes.'

The torrential rain slowed the traffic and it took a long time to get back to Echo Street.

They trudged into the house, carrying the bags and chairs. Jeanette stood in the kitchen, seeming to notice her bloodstained clothes for the first time. She stared down at her blouse.

– *I need to change.*

'Come upstairs, love. You should have a hot bath,' Hilda insisted. Now that they were back in the house she was regaining her equilibrium.

When Hilda and Jeanette had both gone Bill carried out the folding chairs and put them away in the shed in the garden. Connie wondered what she could do, and then remembered that at times like this people made tea. She filled the kettle and clicked the switch, and while she was waiting for it to boil she tipped some of the picnic litter into the kitchen bin. Bill came back, shaking off the rain.

He said, 'Tea, that's a good idea', so warmly that she felt useful. Carefully she poured a cup and passed it to him.

He drank some and looked at her. 'You look very pale.'

Images of the accident flickered in her head.

'I've never seen anyone dead before.'

'Neither have I,' he told her.

'Was the . . . was the bike man going to die as well?'

'I don't know.'

'Jeanette comforted him.'

'Yes, she did. She was amazing.'

Connie hunched her shoulders. Everything to do with the day was raw, bulging and swollen, and she felt as if the slightest pressure would puncture a membrane and out would come spilling all kinds of things that she feared and tried to keep hidden because they were bad and secret and known only to her. Her jealousy of Jeanette was only one of them.

'Connie . . . ?' Bill murmured. Then he put down his tea and gathered her in his arms. He pulled her closer until her cheek and the corner of her mouth creased up against the collar of his shirt, which was warm and slightly damp and smelled of him. He combed his fingers through her hair and rocked her against him, settling her head in the crook of his shoulder. He rubbed her shoulders and her back.

'You're shocked. I'm not surprised. Listen. Terrible things happen, Connie. They happen every day, and there's no reason, and all you can do is try to help out and then be grateful that it wasn't you or anyone you love in that car or riding the motorbike. You have to just go on doing what you do, and try to do it as well as you can, and be happy doing it. That's all life is.'

To her surprise, Connie's body was loosening and relaxing.

She whispered, 'Yes. I know.'

Her shoulders dropped as she felt her weight supported

in Bill's arms. They stood locked together, gently swaying. Then a different feeling spread through her, like a tide of warm honey, thick and slow. Connie had long ago left innocence behind, but none of the boys she had known, dirty-minded and fumbling and of a different species as they were, had ever made her feel like this.

She wanted nothing more than to turn her mouth to discover Bill's bare neck beneath the shirt collar. Then she wanted to lick her sister's fiancé's skin, and measure out her hips and the length of her legs against his. Somewhere close at hand, tantalisingly close, mysterious and yet obvious, there was a connection that would answer all the questions that teemed around her.

For a second, a brief interval of delight as brilliant as a flash of lightning, she was certain that Bill felt the same and wanted exactly what she did.

She felt rather than heard him draw in a breath, and they seemed poised on the edge of a great space through which they might fall or fly.

Then he abruptly withdrew. He patted her hair with the flat of his hand as if he were her uncle, and at the same time pecked her on the cheek.

He was suddenly so awkward, so unlike himself, that she knew he was trying to disguise feelings that were not avuncular at all. She was bewildered, and it was bewilderment that made her suddenly want to scowl and even punch him with her knuckles, as if she were nine years old again.

She stared at him with reddened cheeks.

'Drink your tea,' Bill said gently, moving away from her and leaning back against the pock-marked old kitchen cupboard. 'Put some sugar in it. Sugar's good for shock.'

Connie turned her back on him and began unpacking the picnic dishes that were smudgy with river water. There was a frond of weed trapped between the tines of a fork. Her racing heart slowed, and she began to breathe again.

A little later Jeanette came downstairs. She was pink and shining from her bath, and her dressing gown didn't quite cover her breasts. Her damp hair was pinned up on the top of her head, but tendrils escaped to frame her face. Hilda came too, having changed her clothes and dabbed some make-up on her face. They all sat down round the kitchen table and began to talk about the accident. Hilda reached across for Connie's hand and squeezed it.

'Don't be too upset, love, will you?'

Jeanette smiled at Connie too.

– *You were good. You ran for help. They came quite quickly, didn't they?*

'It seemed a long time to me,' Bill said.

He and Jeanette kept glancing at each other, and even though they were talking about death, about how one person was dead and another might die, they couldn't help covertly smiling. All of them knew how capable Bill and Jeanette had both shown themselves to be in the emergency. They were justified in feeling proud of themselves and even excited. Connie was thinking that she and Hilda had appeared in quite a different light.

It was almost as if *she* were Hilda's real daughter and not just the adopted one, which was another disorientating thought.

Dry-mouthed, Connie looked down at her plate.

Out of the corner of her eye she could see Jeanette's left hand with the diamond ring lightly resting on Bill's thigh. She knew with sudden and absolute certainty that she could not go on living at Echo Street. If she stayed here she would have to watch Bill and Jeanette touching and smiling and kissing each other. She wanted Bill to do those things to her. And Bill was her sister's fiancé.

I have to get out of this place. Just as soon as I can.

Suddenly she stood up.

'Do you feel sick, Connie? You've gone white.'

'I'm okay. I'm going upstairs.'

She closed her door and sat down on the bed. She tried to empty her head of sudden death at the roadside. She thought about Bill instead, guiltily and hungrily.

The following Saturday, the day after Jeanette learned that she had gained a 2:1 in Biological Sciences, Connie turned sixteen. The planned family celebration was dinner with Uncle Geoff, Auntie Sadie, Elaine and Jackie in an Italian restaurant, the invariable festivity for each of their birthdays. Connie got up early, before either Hilda or Jeanette, and left a note on the kitchen table saying that she was going up to the West End to do some shopping and would be back in good time. By ten o'clock she was in Soho.

She had no idea, back then, what a fluke it was to find the manager of GreenLeaf Studios in his chaotic office cubicle at any time on a Saturday. That her appearance at his door should coincide with his tired acknowledgement that they could do with a kid to help out, somebody who wouldn't mind a bit of hard work and didn't have too many ideas above his station, seemed no more than an average stroke of good luck. It was only when she was established in the business that she understood the scale of improbability. Once she had her foot inside his office, though, she had been determined not to give in.

'I can do the job. Just let me try, and I'll show you,' Connie begged. Something had happened within Connie since witnessing the accident. She defined it approximately to herself as *What have you got to lose?* You could choose to be polite, you might feel that it wasn't right to stand in a man's office and insist, refusing to budge until you got what you wanted, but that would achieve nothing and nobody really cared about you being a nice, considerate person, did they?

Bill found out that the motorcyclist had died in the ambulance on the way to hospital.

Jeanette turned away in tears when he told them, but Connie just gazed back at him thinking that it could happen to her tomorrow, to him, to Jeanette, to anyone at all. The way it had happened to Tony. You might as well live the way you wanted while you were here and while you could. She was tired of waiting, and now there was the other reason as well. Sometimes, when she looked at Bill she found that he had been looking at her first. They would both turn away, sharply, and Connie felt her face burning.

'Shall I start now? Look, I could make you some coffee and then I could clean up a bit,' she persisted. The GreenLeaf Studios were a mess. There were dirty cups and full ashtrays and collapsed heaps of tapes, the waste bins overflowed and the kitchen cubicle smelled of sour milk.

'We've got cleaners,' Brian Luck said.

'They're not very good, are they?' Connie rejoined.

Brian laughed. 'Go on, then. See those tapes? Check the label, or put them in the player there, find out what's on 'em, work out a filing system. Can you do that?'

'Yes.'

She worked all day. At lunchtime, Brian went out for a sandwich and brought one back for her. While she ate it they talked about music. He knew a lot, but he also listened quite kindly to what she had to say about writing songs and singing with the band at school.

By six o'clock, when Brian said he was locking up, Connie had catalogued the tapes and made space on shelves to store them.

'I'll come in on Monday morning, shall I?'

Brian said he would have to consult his partners.

'I'll come anyway. They can't decide without taking a look at me, can they?'

There were still three weeks to go before the school year ended. But Connie already knew that she wouldn't be going back.

She was late getting home to Echo Street. Uncle Geoff's new car was already parked outside when she jogged breathlessly up to the house. Geoff and Sadie were sitting with Hilda in the front room, Elaine had gone with Jeanette and Bill to the pub for half an hour while they all waited for Connie to reappear. Jackie wasn't coming; she had been married for two years but whenever the name of her husband had been mentioned recently she sighed and looked up at the ceiling. Tonight it seemed that there was some kind of crisis. Sadie and Hilda had been discussing the situation in low voices while Geoff watched football on television.

Hilda jumped up. 'Connie! Where have you been all day? You've worried us half to death. Your auntie and uncle have been here since seven o'clock.'

'Sorry. I told you, I went up west. There wasn't a bus for ages.'

Sadie was wearing tight cream trousers and a low-cut top. She checked her lipstick in her compact mirror then arched an eyebrow at Connie over the disc of gilt.

'Happy birthday, love. Where's your shopping? What did you buy?'

'Thanks, Auntie Sadie. I didn't really see anything I liked. Shall I just quickly run up and change, Mum?'

'All right,' Hilda sighed.

When Connie came down again, Jeanette and Bill and Elaine were filing in through the front door. Blushing, Connie submitted to birthday wishes and kisses from everyone except Bill. Bill didn't kiss her, he just gave her his curly-mouthed smile.

When they were all crammed into the front room Uncle Geoff made a show of telling everyone to hush. Then from a carrier-bag he produced a package.

'Now, young lady, this is from your Auntie Sadie and your cousins and me. Many happy returns.'

Connie took the package, shook it and listened to it. She knew that Bill was watching her. Hilda sat on the edge of an armchair, smoothing the folds of her skirt over her knees. Jeanette and Elaine leaned against the closed piano keyboard, looking alike except that Elaine was the 'before' version and Jeanette the 'after', in some advert for a miracle beauty product perhaps.

'What is it?' Connie murmured.

'That's for you to find out,' Uncle Geoff smiled.

She undid the wrappings, and discovered a Sony Walkman.

Uncle Geoff's presents to the Thornes were always generous to the point of being slightly embarrassing, because they highlighted the difference between what the two families could afford. Personal cassette players had only just come on to the market and Connie was amazed to receive one.

She went to Geoff and hugged him. 'Thank you, Uncle Geoff.'

He put his arm round her waist and kept it there. 'Sixteen, eh? Big day. It doesn't seem a minute since you brought in this little scrap of a black-haired thing to show us all, Hilda, does it?'

There was a pause in which everyone seemed to be waiting for someone else to mention adoption, and at the same time willing them not to. Connie moved hastily to Sadie and hugged her too.

'We're all family, aren't we?' Sadie said, as if this point needed clearing up.

Geoff began showing Connie how the Walkman worked (although she knew already what every function was) and telling her that she must handle it carefully.

Bill said, 'I've got a present for you, too.'

He handed over two small rectangular packages and Connie opened them to find the new Police and Ian Dury albums in cassette form. This gift of music seemed to speak to her so personally that she couldn't quite look at him in case she gave herself away. From beneath the veil of her hair she murmured, 'How did you know about the Walkman?'

'I heard,' he said drily. This meant he had thought about her birthday, talked about it, and then gone to a record shop and made a choice just for her. He did it out of affection, nothing more, but she felt riven with love for him and with dismay at the impossibility of her situation.

It's all right, she reassured herself. You're going to move out. You won't *be* here any longer.

'Thanks a lot,' she muttered.

To her relief Hilda and Sadie were getting ready to leave for the restaurant. Elaine went with Bill and Jeanette in Bill's car, and Connie with Hilda in Uncle Geoff's. His latest car was a silver-grey Jaguar that he parked right outside the window of La Osteria Antica, where he could keep an eye on it.

'It's this young lady's sixteenth birthday today,' Geoff announced to the maître d'. The man seized Connie's hand and kissed it, murmuring *bella, bella signora*. By accident, Connie caught Bill's eye. His mouth curled extravagantly and she knew that he was on the point of bursting into laughter. It would be so easy to laugh with Bill, she thought; there were so many ridiculous things. It would be as easy to laugh as to be serious.

Once they were seated round the centre table and had ordered their various tagliatelles and saltimboccas, Uncle Geoff and the others wanted to hear all about the accident. Hilda covered her eyes with one hand and shuddered, so Bill gravely told the story again, with signed interventions from Jeanette. Next there was Jeanette's degree to discuss. She was the first person in the family to graduate from university.

'This is a double celebration,' Uncle Geoff said. 'We should drink to two fine young women.'

These days Jeanette easily outshone her cousin, who worked in a bank. Elaine compressed her lips slightly but she drank the toast with everyone else. Uncle Geoff didn't look for interventions from his wife and daughters.

He was in his stride now. 'So, Connie. You'll be following in your sister's footsteps, I expect. Which A levels are you going to choose?'

Connie gazed at the red tablecloth and a slice of tiled

floor. She was overtaken by an irresistible impulse not to be patronised by Uncle Geoff, not to do what was routinely expected of her, and most of all not to place herself next to Jeanette in Bill's eyes.

'I've got a job,' she said quietly.

'Holiday job? Very good. It's important to get some practice in the real world. It's a harsh climate out there. Nobody knows that better than I do.' Uncle Geoff was chewing and pointing at her with his fork.

Connie raised her voice. 'It's a real job. In the music business. I'm not going back to school next year.'

Six faces stared at her.

Hilda said sharply, 'Don't talk rubbish. You're staying at school. While you're under my roof, you . . .'

'I start work on Monday morning. I'm leaving home.'

Hilda laid down her knife. Elaine smiled.

She hadn't planned this, not in any way, but Connie's head swam with sudden elation. The Osteria Antica was lit up with the insanely flickering glow of burning bridges. If she didn't get a job at GreenLeaf Music, if Brian Luck and his colleagues decided they didn't want her, she would find a different place to work. She saw that the door of Echo Street was opening and all she had to do was walk – run – out of it.

The waiting was finally over.

'What do you mean, leaving home? How do you think you'll cope on your own, my girl?'

She had no idea, but already she was improvising temporary solutions. Ideas cascaded through her head. Her one-time boyfriend Davy's parents had just gone away on holiday to Spain for two weeks, so she could almost certainly sleep round there for a few nights. She had a little money saved from her Saturday job, so she'd get a room somewhere. She had never experienced such a moment of euphoria. She was sharply aware of Bill, across the table, and it was only later that she wondered if she had correctly read admiration in his eyes. Jeanette turned her head between them and the bell of hair swung round her jaw.

Uncle Geoff's eyes bulged. 'Don't you think, young lady, that after all she has done for you in sixteen years, from the moment she took you in, you owe your mother a debt of gratitude?'

The clamour in the restaurant seemed to die away.

'I will find a way to repay my debts,' Connie said.

Then she stood up and weaved between trolleys and waiters to the cloakroom.

When she came out of the cubicle, breathing more calmly and with the elation already draining away like water into sand, leaving her feeling cold and shaken, she found Jeanette standing by the basins.

– *Did you mean all that?* Jeanette asked.

There was a smell of liquid soap and air freshener, and an echo of dripping taps.

'Yes.'

Their reflections glanced back out of the peach-tinted mirror. Connie caught a glimpse of how different they looked, angel and demon.

– *Why do you really want to leave home?*

She could hardly tell her sister what had actually precipitated the decision.

'It's time. I want to find out who I really am.'

Jeanette raised an eyebrow.

'Well, I don't know, do I?'

– *No*, Jeanette agreed. She turned to wash her hands, carefully soaping around her diamond ring. Connie

232

stared at her bent back, wanting to fight her as much as she had done when she was six, and at the same time thinking that love and hate were so close as to be nearly the same thing. Like sisters.

Jeanette stood upright again and shook water from her hands.

– *You've spoiled your own birthday.*

'Yes,' Connie agreed. There was something definitively Thorne family about the disintegration of the evening. They tottered against the clanking roller-towel holder as laughter swept over them.

'Have I got to go back in there?' Connie murmured, when she could speak once more.

– *Definitely.*

'I'll go if you come.'

They went. At the table Hilda was smoking one of Sadie's cigarettes, looking as tragic as if she was bereaved all over again. Geoff was telling Bill that when he was his age, he already owned his own business and didn't owe a penny to a soul.

Hilda always maintained afterwards that Connie left home just like that, walked out on them on the day she was sixteen and never came back.

It was true that she left Echo Street quietly the following morning, with a rucksack containing her clothes and Uncle Geoff's Walkman, and went to stay at Davy's house. The job at GreenLeaf Music paid twenty-eight pounds a week, and she managed to live on that when she moved to her room in Perivale. The only times she ever went back to Echo Street were for Sunday lunches. A square meal was welcome, for one thing.

Three weeks after the birthday evening, she and Hilda

and Bill went to Jeanette's graduation ceremony. The hall was packed with hundreds of parents. Before Jeanette's turn a blind boy, led by his guide dog, crossed the platform to shake the hand of the Vice-Chancellor and collect his degree. The dutiful, bored applause from the audience rose into a wave of cheering and foot-stamping in acknowledgement of his achievement.

When Jeanette came up in her dusty black academic gown and rabbit-fur hood, she looked the same as all the other young women in her group. There was no extra volume of clapping as she took her scroll and descended the steps from the stage to take her seat again.

Afterwards they emerged into the July sunshine. Hilda had brought her camera and she made them all pose in every possible permutation with Jeanette, who smiled serenely from beneath the tilted edge of her mortarboard. It was one of those family-album, framed-photograph days. Connie knew that these pictures would always be with them, capturing a momentary theorem of family life that reality constantly disproved.

'If only Tony could see you today,' Hilda sighed.

Connie protested, 'Nobody knew you were deaf. You should have had all the extra clapping and cheering, like that blind guy did.'

Jeanette took off the mortarboard and slipped the gown down her shoulders.

– *Better for no one to know. That makes it more of an achievement. Anyway, I wouldn't have heard them, would I?*

'You did well,' Connie said simply.

Jeanette suddenly laughed with pride.

– *I did, didn't I?*

Hilda needed to change the film in the camera and Bill

showed her how to do it. Jeanette took Connie's arm and steered her to one side.

– *Are you coming back home?*

Connie shook her head.

'No. I can't.'

The way she was living now was far harder than she had imagined it would be, and she was lonely, but she was not going back to Echo Street.

– *Can't?*

'Won't, then.'

– *Mum misses you.*

'Does she?' Connie could not quite believe the transparency of this. It went with the family theorem, sunny for a day, for the camera's benefit.

– *And I'm not going to be there. Not for ever.*

Jeanette and Bill were going camping in France. They were talking about moving in together, once Jeanette had started work.

Connie looked back over her shoulder, at Bill with the body of the camera open in his hands, at Hilda in her summer dress, both of them dappled with sunlight. She felt the pull in too many directions, responsibility quartered with desire, selfishness shot through with an unwieldy sympathy. The only way to extricate herself seemed to be to move out of this magnetic field altogether.

She found the self-interest to say what she really meant.

'I want to live on my own.'

Jeanette studied her. Don't judge me, Connie thought hotly. I'm doing this for you as well as me.

The ground between them was too complicated, too obscured, for her to map it out. It always had been.

Hilda called out, 'Bill's done it. I want one more picture. Jeanette, come here.'

She took a picture of the two of them, Jeanette standing in the circle of Bill's arms, sun on their heads, both of them looking into the long lens of the future.

This was the image that Connie took away with her.

NINE

Until she saw his parents' house and its garden full of flowers, Roxana thought that Noah's flat in Hammersmith was the most comfortable place in the world. Now Connie unlocked the door to her apartment on the top floor of a tall, anonymously modern building – not so very far, Roxana worked out, from the bad house where she had stayed with Dylan.

'Come in,' Connie said.

Noah and Roxana shuffled in behind her.

Their first impression was of a space that opened straight out into the sky, a smoky summer's-evening London sky now fading from amethyst into horizontal bars of grey and rose-pink cloud over tower-blocks and trees and the spires of city churches. The wall facing the door was an almost complete run of plate glass.

Noah looked about him. The family rift meant that he had never been here before.

'Nice place, Auntie Con,' he murmured.

Worrying a little that she might be leaving dirty foot-prints, Roxana walked over to the huge window and looked out. To her right was the strange bulging tower that Noah referred to as the Gherkin, the domes of St Paul's Cathedral bathed bronze by the floodlighting, and the arrow shape of a descending plane given definition by its winking lights. In the distance to her left was another group of towers, seeming to float in the purple twilight. Below her spread layers of rooftops bisected by orange-lit streets, the crowns of big trees – the jumble of London that she was beginning to know, smelling at ground level of dirt and fast food, clogged with traffic, and crackling with the jolts of human static electricity discharged through sudden snarling altercations – and yet which, from up in this eagle's nest, looked serenely beautiful.

The room itself was almost empty. There were no ornaments, hardly any furniture. A pair of sofas faced each other across a low table. A lamp hung on a swan's neck of arched metal. In the distance, in the dimness, Roxana could see a countertop that looked as if it was made from some kind of stone, the glinting metal curve of a tap, some glass shelves.

This emptiness struck her as immensely restful, as well as opulent.

At home in Bokhara the ordinary places to live, her stepfather's apartment among them, were in cheap Soviet-built blocks made of stained and crumbling concrete where the walls excluded no sound louder than a whisper and where the decoration consisted of pungent oilcloth table coverings, gaudy Chinese rugs, tin trays, and bulbous glass vases in shades of orange and purple bathed by the flickering light of the television screen. In the old city, down alleyways behind wooden doors, the old houses were kept dark against the heat, lined with ornamental plaster-work and painted into every cluttered crevice with brilliant patterns and colours. All of it was bright, in a monotonous desert landscape, but it was not restful.

To Roxana this pale apartment of Connie's went with

the glimpse of London that she had caught from the top deck of the bus. This huge city was a mass of contradictions, and of systems of possession and exclusion that she couldn't fathom, but her hunger to be a part of it was steadily increasing. Noah's family very obviously had their established place, which made her want even more to be accepted and included by them.

From the little she knew of Noah's auntie's history, and seeing her apartment, she reckoned that Connie had launched herself onto this glittering, wide London river with notable success. She herself did not have the advantage of being a genuine English girl, but Roxana would find her own way.

She breathed deeply, pushed her hands into the pockets of her denim jacket with the paper-coloured rose wilting in the buttonhole, rocked upwards on the balls of her feet and lengthened all the muscles of her back and her bare, dancer's legs.

She became aware that Noah and Connie were both looking at her. She quickly lowered her weight back onto her heels, extricated her hands and let them hang at her sides.

'I'll show you the spare room,' Connie said, clicking on the swan-shaped lamp and creating a pool of pale gold light.

Roxana followed her down a high, pale, empty corridor and they came to a flat door in the bare wall. Connie pushed it open.

The room was unfurnished except for a small double bed framed by built-in cupboards and the air smelled unused, faintly stuffy. The window came higher up the wall, giving a slice of a different view. Connie nudged open an inner door and this time Roxana saw a small bathroom lined with some light-coloured stone. Glass and polished mirrors showed her reflection and Connie's retreating into infinity, but otherwise it was completely bare. She frowned.

'Where are your . . . things?' she began, imagining that Connie's talcum powders and face creams must be hidden away somewhere.

'This would be yours. My bedroom's at the other end of the flat, and so is my bathroom. The room's almost self-contained, so I thought it might be good for you.'

Awed, Roxana understood that this amazing apartment must have *two* bathrooms.

She remembered briefly the alcove screened with a plastic curtain where she had washed when she was growing up, soaping her developing breasts and afterwards pulling on her clothes as quickly as she could, not always in time, before Leonid came and caught her. At Dylan's house the bathroom was a reeking cave that she had avoided as far as possible, and even at Noah's the basin was speckled with shaved bristles and the towels tended to accumulate in damp drifts against the bath's side. Here, Roxana allowed herself to imagine that she might have hours to soak and dream, safely alone, with all these mirrors gently fogged with steam. There would certainly be hot water here, endless hot water, she was sure of that.

'It's very nice,' she whispered.

Noah hovered in the doorway. He didn't look as pleased as Roxana expected. They filed back the way they had come.

'What do you think?' Connie asked. She moved into the distance, began opening concealed cupboards to reveal treasures of stacked white china, shining glassware, rows of bottles and jars.

Roxana's excitement was draining away. Even Noah seemed smaller, somehow scruffier in this setting.

How could she possibly, even momentarily, have expected to be able to live here?

'I don't think,' she sighed. Connie's head turned, her fingers pinching the edge of a cupboard door. Their eyes met. 'You see, I don't think I will have money, *enough* money for rent.' She remembered the Asian boy with the big shirt and the rental prices he had reeled off.

Connie resumed her search in the cupboard.

'I don't really need rent. Not right now, anyway. If you wanted, you could just stay here while you're getting used to London. Until you're ready to decide exactly where you'd like to be.' She spoke tentatively, almost as if Roxana were the one offering to do her the favour. Roxana glanced at Noah, lifted her shoulders interrogatively while Connie's back was turned. Noah shrugged with a touch of sulkiness, miming *Why not?*

'You are very kind,' Roxana began.

Connie turned back to face them again. 'I'd be glad of some company now and again,' she smiled, as if all this was unremarkable to her. Perhaps it was, Roxana reflected. 'What do you think?'

Roxana smiled back. 'So I would like to. Thank you.'

Noah said he could drive her over with her suitcase, if she wanted, but not before the next weekend because their work hours didn't allow any time off in common.

'I think for Andy, maybe it will be better if I come by myself before that. I don't need to bring everything.'

Noah frowned again. Connie went away and came back with a pair of keys on a metal ring. These she dropped casually into Roxana's pocket, adding, 'We're fixed, then. Come when you're ready. What about a drink now, to celebrate? Or would you like something to eat? I'm just having a look to see what there is.'

The kitchen area somehow didn't have the appearance of being much used.

Noah said quickly, 'Thanks, Auntie Con, but we'll be on our way. Work in the morning and all that.' He kissed his aunt lightly on the cheek. 'It's been really good to see you again. And thank you for coming to see Mum. It'll make a difference to her.'

'I'm here. I want to be.'

Connie and Roxana said a quick goodbye, hardly looking at each other. They were already flatmates; it was almost as if they were conspirators, Noah thought. He was silent in the car as he and Roxana headed west.

They were on the elevated section of the route through London when Roxana asked him, 'Are you angry with something, Noah?'

'No. Why?'

'Maybe it was rude, saying we would not like to stay to have something to drink and eat?'

'That's your culture. Not necessarily ours. You're going to be living there, anyway. You'll have plenty of time with Connie.' Noah had seen Roxana's hypnotised expression as she followed Connie round her apartment, and his normal equanimity was shadowed with jealousy. He didn't want to have to share Roxana with anyone, let alone his aunt. There was too much history here, peering over their shoulders.

He sighed. 'Sorry. I'm sounding a bit pissed off, aren't I? I'm really glad you've got somewhere decent to stay, you deserve it, and I know you can't go on staying with me and Andy. It's just that for years Auntie Con hasn't been popular in my family and I'm getting my head round thinking differently about her. And I'm also wondering when you and I are ever going to see each other. I mean, you work every night.'

Roxana's hand slid across the handbrake and rounded itself on his thigh. Her little finger stroked a tiny circle, making him shift on his haunches and wish that they could get home a bit faster.

'I am here now,' she reminded him.

'Mm. So you are. Rox, do you have to work *every* night?'

She turned her face to him. Streetlights and oncoming cars swept light across it and he glimpsed her set expression.

'Yes. I need money. I need it to make myself into somebody,' she said.

He couldn't disagree with her absolute determination. It seemed familiar to him, surprisingly and closely connected to his own being even though he judged himself as slightly lazy, and he loved her for it.

'But you are already somebody.'

Roxana didn't answer.

Andy was already at home, occupying his usual end of the sofa, with the television turned up loud. There was an empty pizza box at his feet.

'Hey, you guys. Had a good day?' Remembering Jeanette he added quickly, 'How's your mum, mate?'

'She's about the same, thanks. She was pretty cheerful today, her sister was there. Actually, Roxana's got a room over at her place. We've just been there to take a look at it.'

'A room at your mum's?'

'No. My Auntie Con's.'

'It is beautiful,' Roxana put in.

'Ah. Oh. Well, cool. That's really great.' His gaze slid back to the television. Noah put his hands on Roxana's hips and steered her briskly across to his bedroom. Once they were inside with the door closed he hooked his knee behind hers and tipped her expertly onto the bed, as he had been wanting to do ever since they had left his parents' house. They rolled together, giggling and wrestling until Noah found a way to pin her down and kiss her. He caught the hem of her tiny skirt and edged it higher.

'God, you're beautiful.'

'And you, Mr Noah Bunting, are a very kind man.'

'Right. Is *kind* as far as it goes?'

She pretended to think. 'You are, um, pushing for a compliment, I think?'

'*Fishing*. It's fishing for compliments. Quite an old-fashioned expression. Your English isn't perfect yet, my Uzbek girl. Although it's pretty damn good, come to mention it. You never told me how you learned.'

'I had a teacher called Yakov. He knows a lot of languages. And I worked hard at it.' He waited for her to expand, but she did not.

In the end he said, 'Yes, I bet you did. I love you, Rox.'

Her expression lightened, and they were connected again. She touched her mouth to his. 'Good. I am pleased to hear.'

She never said *I love you* back to him. But there was time, Noah thought. She would in the end.

It was a few days before Roxana stopped feeling like an intruder at Limbeck House, which was the name of the building crowned by Connie's apartment. She half-expected, as she tapped the security code into the panel at the street door and then rode up in the hushed lift, that some security official would seize her by the shoulder and march her outside again.

But, gradually, she became accustomed to the place. She hung up her few clothes in the cupboard, and stuck her beach postcard right next to the side of the bed. She liked to see the picture when she opened her eyes, although it no longer represented her only idea of Paradise. Where she now found herself came quite close to that.

By the time Roxana got up Connie had usually gone out, and when she came back from The Cosmos her flatmate was always asleep. Roxana didn't mind at all being alone in the apartment. She unfurled, slowly, like a new leaf.

At first she stayed in her room, watching the clouds and the planes passing her window. She took long, hot baths and stared at herself in the misted mirrors, not quite recognising the scrubbed, leisurely person who looked back at her.

Then she acquainted herself with the other rooms. The daylight in the big living area changed with the hour, and according to the weather. One afternoon there was a storm, and she watched the rain sweeping towards her like fine scratches over the city towers.

She looked in the cupboards in the kitchen and in the huge fridge. There wasn't much food, and anyway she didn't think she should help herself to what there was. She left the flat in the middle of the day and went back to the Best Little Internet Café. The owner greeted her warmly, and served her a plate of souvlaki and salad. The fatty meat and chopped salad and the flat bread served with them reminded her of the food at home in Bokhara.

After she had eaten, she checked the email account that the Asian student boy had helped her to set up. There was the latest email from Fatima, responding to Roxana's news that she now had an English boyfriend as well as a job.

Fatima said she was glad that Roxana was having such a good time. *You struck lucky, all right!*

Fatima was working in the travel industry in Tashkent, mostly with the Turkish *biznez* men who came to invest in the new post-Soviet developments. It was okay, she wrote. *You know.*

Roxana rattled off a euphoric description of her new home. When they were little girls, she and Fatima had played with pebbles and pieces of stick in the shade of crumbling walls. It gave Roxana great satisfaction to think what different circumstances they found them-selves in now.

The café owner called a friendly goodbye to her as she left, and that made her happy too. She was a regular cus-tomer, recognised and valued.

She called in at the grocer's store on the corner of the street and bought milk, tomatoes, bread and cheese to take home to Limbeck House. She put the food in the fridge, seeing how lost it looked in the cavernous interi-or, and wondered what Connie liked to eat and whether she should cook something for her. She didn't, in the end, but that was because she didn't really know how to cook anything that would be good enough.

In the early evenings she went out to The Cosmos, and after the cool neutral air of Limbeck House it was like breathing in a toxic compound of smoke, sweat, alcohol and men's lust. But she was rested now, feeling almost dizzy with the lifting of anxiety, and she was able to work much better. More punters wanted private dances and they paid more money for them, perhaps because her smile was convincing. She earned good money and she didn't even have to worry about keeping the thickening wad of notes safe. It lay in an envelope, on a shelf within one of the cupboards in her sanctuary.

She came home at three thirty in the morning, her clothes and hair stinking of The Cosmos, and found a note from Connie on the kitchen counter.

I helped myself to milk and bread, etc. Hope you don't mind. C.

It was beautiful that Connie should be so polite when this place and everything in it was hers.

The solitary hours of the next day flowed past. Roxana ventured beyond the living area to Connie's end of the flat. She peered into the room where Connie spent most of her time when she was at home. From the doorway, she saw a bank of unfamiliar machinery with dozens of sliding keys, a musical keyboard, computer screens. A pair of headphones was hooked over the back of a swivel chair. There was a separate desk covered with papers, a big diary and a telephone. The inside of the room felt flat, dead of vibration, as if it had been soundproofed. Roxana silently retreated.

The only other door led to Connie's bedroom.

It was tidy. The white bedcover was smooth and flat and there were no scattered clothes. Roxana knew that this was an intrusion but she couldn't help herself. She tiptoed across to take a look into the bathroom. There were tiers of white towels, glass shelves with neat rows of cosmetics, a faint drift of Connie's spicy perfume.

Roxana glided across and opened the nearest cupboard door. Inside, Connie's clothes were ranged on hangers, like so many ghosts of her. Roxana rippled the tips of her fingers over the fabrics. Suddenly she stepped closer, lifted the sleeve of a dress made of some diaphanous greeny-grey stuff, and buried her face in the fabric as if she could breathe in the essence of the other woman. As if she could make herself into Connie. The perfume was much stronger here.

Nothing happened. She was still a taller, thinner, younger woman, whom none of these clothes would fit.

Embarrassed by herself, even though there was no one to see her, she dropped the sleeve and closed the cupboard door, turned quickly and retreated to her own room. The silence in the flat seemed to roar in her ears. Soon it would be time to go out to The Cosmos again to dance for men.

Connie saw her manager and discussed the current state of the music business, had two lunches in Soho with two producers she had worked with in the past, and called in to see Angela at her production company. They watched the first edits of the bank commercials, and Angela said how pleased she was with them. Connie thought her music was good enough, but no better than that. Ketut and the other musicians looked wonderful for the brief second that the camera lingered on them. She gazed intently at the little wedding temple, the clearing in the jungle greenery and the tropical beach, and the sight of them brought back the thick, humid warmth of Bali. She particularly missed her veranda and the rolling green wave.

She was also quite aware that wherever she happened to be, it was becoming increasingly unlikely that she would ever feel perfectly at home.

Angela raised one eyebrow. 'What's funny?'

'Not much. Are you doing anything this evening? Shall we go and see an early film?'

Angela's face clouded. 'I'd like to, I really would. The thing is, though, Rayner said he might be able to slip away for an hour before he has to be home. We haven't seen each other for a week. We've got a couple of work things to discuss,' she added, lifting her chin.

'We'll do the cinema another evening,' Connie reassured her.

Bill mentioned to Connie that Jeanette would like to see her. So she drove down to Surrey one morning, against the flow of traffic, arriving well after Bill had left for work. Apart from Jeanette's cleaner, who hoovered in the distant reaches of the house and laid a tray for coffee, they were on their own.

It would probably be the longest time they had been alone in each other's company, Connie reckoned, since she left Echo Street.

The weather had turned. It was cooler, and there were sharp bursts of rain. Jeanette sat in the room that opened onto the garden, small in her large armchair. She had her mobile that she could use to text for help if it was needed, a small tray with a glass of water and several vials of pills, her book and the newspapers and a radio arranged on the low table next to the arm of her chair. In the afternoons a nurse came in for an hour, and twice a week a beautician visited to wash and set her hair.

– *I am well set up, you see*, Jeanette said.

Connie sat down.

'Do you want to talk?' she asked.

They exchanged a glance of mutual amusement.

– *Yes*.

At once, Connie's tongue felt thick and awkward. Jeanette gazed out into the garden.

Connie began almost at random.

'I was remembering the picnic. The day we saw that terrible accident. You and Bill, I remember you especially, were so capable. You were brave, and you knew exactly what to do. You sat in the road and held the biker in your arms. You were talking to him, all the time we waited for the ambulance to come. I was just afraid of what I might see.'

– *You were only a girl*.

Connie protested. 'I wasn't. I was grown up, or I thought I was. I don't think I felt any different in those days from the way I do today, I've just seen and lived through more things since.'

Jeanette nodded.

– *Why were you thinking about that day?*

'The picnic was to celebrate you and Bill getting engaged.'

– *Of course*.

Jeanette calmly reached out for her coffee cup, took a sip, replaced it on its saucer and adjusted the teaspoon that lay next to it.

– *We could talk about the old days*.

When she raised her hands her loose sleeves dropped back, exposing her wrists and forearms. A bracelet hung around her right wrist as if it encircled bare bone. Connie felt the dislocation between ordinary life, the present desire for harmony by not causing pain from old injuries, and the steady approach of death.

Their relationship was changing. It wasn't too late. Connie's throat tightened.

– There are times that only you and I remember now. Only the two us, in all the world.

So Jeanette was thinking back to long ago, before Bill. This was safer ground.

'I know. I've been conscious of that too. Remember how Tony used to tell us stories? He didn't make them up, he always said he didn't have the right sort of brain for inventing anything. But he was really good at painting a word picture. I used to think I could actually see the old Parade the way it was in the Thirties, just from the way he described it. That little supermarket, Gem Stores, used to be a butcher's shop with sawdust on the floor, and beef carcasses hanging on hooks. The sawdust would be darkened with spots of blood, directly underneath where the animal's head had been cut off. Where the café used to be, remember, he said there was a dairy. The milkman delivered to the houses with a horse and cart. What was the horse's name?'

A smile lit Jeanette's face. She didn't hesitate.

– Nerys.

Connie was amazed. 'Nerys. You're quite right.'

This was comfortable, and comforting, for both of them.

Connie pressed on. 'Remember the trains, at Echo Street? I could hear them rumbling through the cutting, when I was waiting to go to sleep and when I woke up in the morning.'

The tip of Jeanette's fingers touched the rim of her ear then her hand stretched out. The fingertips fluttered, describing the faintest vibration, and the diamond in her engagement ring briefly caught the light.

– I could feel them.

The same experience, Connie thought. Differently perceived.

Talk, she exhorted herself. Before it's too late. Talk about anything, while it's still possible. You've got the words and Jeanette hasn't.

'Remember those Sunday lunches, at Auntie Sadie and Uncle Geoff's?'

They both laughed. There was no need for either of them to say any more.

There had been the queasy car journey up to the better part of Loughton, to Geoff and Sadie's house. '*Detached*,' Sadie pointed out. Hilda was tense with anxiety and Tony would drum his fingers on the wheel as they waited at traffic lights, whistling through his teeth in an attempt to appear relaxed. When they reached their destination Jackie and Elaine would scoop Jeanette up and take her off to one of their bedrooms to listen to a record or admire a new pair of shoes. Connie would be left mutely scowling and eavesdropping on the adults' talk.

'Roast beef. Three different veg, in serving dishes,' she said anyway.

– Orangeade. Blue glasses.

'Sherry beforehand for Mum and Sadie, beer for the men.'

Sadie and Geoff had divorced after Sadie found out that Geoff was having an affair with his receptionist at the garage.

'How are Elaine and Jackie?'

– The same. Jackie's oldest is almost a barrister now.

'Really?'

Connie was thinking that families were more alike than

they were different. Children grew up. Grandchildren were born and then became lawyers or IT consultants. The unknown woman who had borne her most probably had grandchildren, a row of them. She'd have framed photographs, similar to the ones of Noah at various ages dotted round this room. Connie hoped that she did, anyway. She wondered if, when the woman looked at her photographs, she imagined another child's face among them.

Suddenly she asked, 'What was it like for you, before I came?'

Jeanette signed quickly, laughing.

– *Heaven.*

'*Was* it?'

She shook her head.

– *Mum said I'd have a little sister called Constance. Then you were there. In a cot. Black hair, red face.*

Jeanette screwed up her eyes, opened her mouth and balled her fists in a swift impression of a howling newborn.

– *I wanted you to disappear. But you stayed and stayed.*

'That must have been annoying. No wonder older siblings get jealous.'

There were threads of rain stitched across the glass. Connie could just hear the sounds of Jeanette's cleaner working in the kitchen. Alarm and claustrophobia made her think of the fresh air outside, away from the faint smell of illness and the pressure of recollection, but she sat still. It was extraordinary, but Jeanette and she had never discussed their childhood like this.

'Can I ask you something? Before Elaine told me, did you understand about adoption?'

– Yes.

'What did you think?'

– I was angry.

'Angry?' Connie wondered, but she suddenly understood something. They were racing ahead, skipping pages of history, just as they skipped words and whole sentences when they communicated in their speech shorthand.

Jeanette lifted her head and looked Connie full in the face.

– They didn't want another like me. So they picked you.

In her adolescent cruelty, Connie had taunted Hilda with this. Yet it had never occurred to her that Jeanette might have believed exactly the same thing.

Connie could see and smell the old house. Steep stairs, aerosol polish, gloss paint, the sagging fence at the end of the garden weighted with ivy, the low pitch of the shed and its curled tar-paper roof.

Within those neat, cramped rooms Hilda had constructed a brittle edifice around Jeanette, trying by ambition for her daughter to compensate for heredity.

She had drilled into Jeanette the absolute necessity to succeed in spite of being deaf, and – amazingly, brilliantly – Jeanette had met her expectations. She had gone to university, an unheard-of achievement in those days for a child from a deaf school.

While she did so, Connie had fulfilled her equal and opposite role of being unlike Jeanette in every way. And faithful, loyal Tony had done everything that his wife asked of him – except to stay alive.

Thinking of these things was like holding together pieces of a broken china dish. The shape was re-created, but the function was gone.

Connie said awkwardly, 'You couldn't have known they didn't want another you. You were only five.'

– *Not then. But soon.*

'How?'

Jeanette gestured, a small sweep of her hand that nevertheless took in herself, Connie, and the distance between them. Connie knew that the information had come from Jackie and Elaine, the drip-feed of family secrets, exchanged behind closed bedroom doors.

– *We were different,* was all Jeanette would concede.

'We were alike in some things. I was angry as well.'

– *I know that. You were terrible. What were you so cross about?*

'About not being you, of course.'

Jeanette stared, and then she started laughing. She laughed so much that she had to wipe the tears from her eyes.

– *I see. Yes. That's funny.*

Connie nodded. 'It is. I don't think I ever saw anyone's point of view but my own.' She added, 'Poor Hilda.'

– *Mum would have been touched to hear you say that.*

'Would she?'

– *She was afraid of you.*

'Afraid?'

– *You were the unknown. And then you were gone, and then a huge success.*

Connie was going to protest that she had arrived as a baby, two months old and helpless, and in any case Hilda hadn't been forced to take her in. But she understood that they were talking about Hilda, and from that particular standpoint her own concerns were incidental.

Jeanette's head fell back against the chair cushions. Talking and laughing had tired her. Connie realised how weak she was becoming.

'Are you all right?'

– Yes.

The door opened and the large shape of the cleaner appeared.

'Mrs Bunting, love, I'm off now. Your lunch is all ready,' she shouted. 'Mr B., he said make sure you eat something. There's a nice piece of quiche, some tomato salad. You've got your sister here, she'll see you're looked after.'

'I will,' Connie promised.

The woman beamed at them and withdrew.

Connie helped Jeanette to her feet.

– She shouts, doesn't she?

'She certainly does.'

They went into the kitchen. Food was set out and the table was laid. Once they were eating, Connie said, 'Old Mrs McBride, in Barlaston Road.'

– Yes?

She pointed with her fork for emphasis. 'You told me that she was a witch. I was terrified. Most of my early life was badly affected by extreme fear of our downstairs neighbour.'

Jeanette's eyes were round and as innocent as dawn. She chewed and swallowed.

– Broomstick. Every full moon. Without fail, I promise you.

Connie left her when the nurse arrived. Jeanette asked Connie if she would come back again the next day.

When she reached home Roxana had already gone

out, but Connie guessed that she had only just missed her. The flat retained the warmth of another presence, nothing more than a breath in the air and a faint indentation in a cushion, but it was enough to make the place feel inhabited. Connie liked the idea of her being there.

Roxana had taken to leaving food in the fridge, and yesterday there had been a punnet of strawberries placed on a saucer in the centre of the polished counter, with a note saying *For you*. Today in the same place was a small marguerite bush in a brown plastic pot. A piece of kitchen paper had been folded into a square and placed underneath, so as not to leave a mark on the counter. Connie went in search of a better pot for the plant, humming as she looked through the cupboards.

Later she sat down and tried to listen to music, but she kept getting up and walking to the window to look down at the roofs and the streets spread below. A young couple who lived at the top of a terraced house in the middle of the nearest street were lighting a barbecue on their roof terrace. Connie stood and watched them fussing with food and plates while the blue smoke curled up behind them. Suddenly she turned and went down the corridor to Roxana's door. She felt guilty about prying, but she told herself that she was just checking to see that she had everything she needed.

The bed was made, and there was a Russian–English dictionary and an English language course-book lying on the bedcover. In the bathroom, a roll-on deodorant, a lip-salve and a tube of toothpaste shared a glass shelf.

As in the main part of the flat, Roxana's presence made an impression, but only a faint one.

Connie inched open the wardrobe door and saw a brown envelope, two pairs of neatly folded jeans, some tops dangling from wire hangers. On the wardrobe floor were two pairs of shoes, one flat and one high-heeled, both with worn-down heels and creased toes.

She noticed a postcard stuck to the side of the cupboard next to the bed, and leaned forward to study it. It was a picture of a beach, turquoise water and a rim of white sand, with a fringe of palm trees. Straightening up again, Connie thought how brave the girl was to live in a strange place with so little, so precariously, and with almost nothing to conjure up other places and other times except a picture postcard.

Connie herself did not like to feel insecure, not physically or financially or emotionally. She had, she supposed, devoted a lot of energy to work that shielded her in the first two cases and to retreating from the demands of the third.

She went back and turned off the music. She rolled back the section of wall that hid the television screen, and sat down to watch that instead.

– *Would you mind driving me there?* Jeanette asked.

'Of course not. Shall we go now?'

Jeanette had been applying lipstick, holding up a compact mirror towards the light. She rolled her lips to smudge the colour, then ran her fingers through the blunt spikes of her hair. The make-up looked too bright against her skin.

– *Yes*.

Jeanette had said that she wanted to call in at work, to collect some papers and other belongings. They drove the short distance and Connie parked the car next to a red-brick building set in the middle of a botanical garden. The arms of willow trees trailed in the water of a small lake.

Connie followed Jeanette through a set of double doors and up in a lift, then along a green-painted corridor. Jeanette's office was a big room lined with desks and big chests of drawers made of dark wood. A handful of people had been working in silence, but they all looked up as Jeanette came in. A woman at the nearest desk was bending over a bound catalogue of drawings, then studying a section of a plant through magnifying lenses attached over her spectacles. She took off this apparatus and leapt from her seat.

'Here she is, back to cause more trouble,' she shouted.

The other taxonomists, quiet-looking people, pushed back their chairs and called greetings. They smiled warmly, and they didn't stare too hard at Jeanette. The first woman patted her on the arm and told her she was amazing, she was, and she was looking great. Jeanette introduced Connie, and Connie exchanged small talk with the first woman and the man at the desk next to hers. The strip lights overhead hummed faintly, and a younger woman in a skirt that might have been woven from hemp slid open a drawer near Connie's knee and took out a specimen sheet layered between sheets of protective paper. She peeled back the paper to reveal the tiny components of a plant, fixed and labelled in minute brown handwriting. The room was stuffy and smelled of dust.

Jeanette sat down at her desk. The others hovered, and then turned uncertainly back to their work. She indicated to Connie that she would need a few minutes, and that there was a coffee room on the ground floor if she wanted somewhere else to wait. Obediently Connie descended in the lift again, and sat looking out at the miniature flanks of a rockery while she drank a cup of coffee from a vending machine. A gardener in green work clothes was stooping among the tiny alpines, picking twigs and debris from the cushions of leaves.

When she had finished her coffee Connie wandered back upstairs again. Jeanette nodded and began to gather up her papers. She put a book and a sheaf of notes into her briefcase, and rearranged more papers in neatly labelled folders. Her colleagues got up once more from their work and Connie watched as they said goodbye to her. They all agreed jovially that they would see her soon, but she wasn't to rush back, not until she was good and ready.

'When you do get back we'll go out and have that dinner, all of us. A proper night out,' the woman with the magnifying lenses cried as Jeanette passed between them.

But nobody looked her straight in the eye.

It was as if her sister was already a ghost, Connie thought.

In the car on the way home, as they queued up at a roundabout, Jeanette patted her briefcase.

– *The Early Spider Orchid. Rare in Britain. I have been following a conservation project. The results are here.*

'That's interesting,' Connie said.

– *I want to go back to work. In a week or so. Part time.*

'Good. If you think you can, that is.'

They had only been home for a few minutes when Bill's car turned into the drive. Connie was making tea, opening and closing cupboard doors as she searched for cups, and Jeanette was reading the papers she had brought with her. Her head lifted at once, even though she couldn't have heard the crunch of car tyres on gravel. Before his key turned in the lock she was touching her hair.

He came into the kitchen and Jeanette went straight to him. He folded her in his arms and rested his cheek on the top of her head.

'Hello, Jan. What sort of a day have you had?'

Connie spooned tea into the warmed pot. She was conscious in this kitchen of weighted years of joint domestic life, drawer handles worn to the touch, a tea towel brought back from a trip to Dublin, pot basil on a sunny windowsill showing bare stalks where leaves had been picked off. The steps from the oven to the fridge, the view of trees and sky from the window over the sink, these would be as familiar to Bill and Jeanette as their own bodies. As each other's bodies.

She loved them both.

The lid of the teapot clattered as she awkwardly dropped it into place.

After a moment she was able to turn and look at Bill. He looked formal, in a business suit with his tie loosened at the neck.

'Con,' he said quietly.

She smiled. 'I saw where Jeanette works.'

'The plant kingdom,' he nodded. He unwound his arms from Jeanette's shoulders.

– *Tea in here?* Jeanette wondered.

'I should get home,' Connie said.

– *Stay for dinner.*

'Yes, do,' Bill added.

'Just tea. A quick cup.'

The next morning, Connie knew as soon as she opened her eyes that she wasn't alone in the flat. There wasn't a sound, but she could feel the comforting emanations of another person. She put on her dressing gown and shuffled into the main room. Roxana was standing by the window looking out, but she spun round as soon as Connie appeared.

'Hi. You're up early,' Connie said.

'I did not sleep so well.'

'Would you like some coffee?'

'Yes, please.'

'How was your week?'

'Fine. I have made altogether four hundred and seventy pounds.'

'I think that's pretty good,' Connie laughed.

She opened a new vacuum pack of espresso coffee. Roxana came and stood by her elbow, watching closely as Connie pressed the ground coffee into the little holder and locked it into place. When she gave her the cup, Roxana took it and sat next to her on a high stool at the counter.

'Thank you for the plant.' Connie stroked the feathery leaves with the tips of her fingers. 'And the strawberries.'

Roxana flushed. 'I am glad you like them.'

Connie splashed some milk into the strong coffee and Roxana did the same.

'What are you doing today?' Connie asked.

'I am going to meet Noah. He says we will see an art gallery.'

'Very Saturday metropolitan.'

'Yes. Then I must go to The Cosmos Club, of course. Noah is saying that he will be coming to watch me dance. He makes the threat, at least.'

'You don't want him to?'

Roxana jumped off her stool. Using the countertop as a pivot she gathered her face into a sultry pout, turned

262

away from Connie while still holding her gaze, and mimed the slow removal of her top. She cast the imaginary garment away from her then rotated to face forwards with her hands coyly folded across her chest. She flung her head back and circled her tongue over her lips, sighing with apparent desire.

Connie coughed with laughter and a drop of coffee ran down her chin. Roxana snapped upright again.

'You see? This is ridiculous, but I have to do it. I don't want Noah to think that I am ridiculous.'

'I don't think he would, actually.'

Roxana raised an eyebrow. 'Or, what might be worse, I would see him there with all the other men who come, with their money rolled up in their pockets and sit like *this* for their private dances.' Now she sat on the stool with her legs splayed, hands in pockets and head cocked, more than filling an imaginary space. 'And I'd think that he was the ridiculous one, for being the same as the rest. You see, when you go to work you can be one person. And then at home again you can be completely another. I think it is better that way.'

'Yes, that's quite true,' Connie agreed.

They had finished their coffee and there was a clink as they both replaced their cups.

Roxana was suddenly beaming. 'Yesterday I did some shopping. The first clothing I have bought since I was in Tashkent, with my friend Fatima. Except for stupid things, for working, I mean. I'd like to show you. Shall I bring it?'

'I'll come,' Connie said. She followed Roxana along to her bedroom. There was a Topshop bag on the floor beside the wardrobe. Roxana reached in and brought out a short blue canvas jacket with oversized buttons. It was very like one that Connie owned. Roxana slipped it on, instinctively tweaking the cuffs and collar into a flattering shape. It suited her.

'Do you think this is nice?'

'I do.'

Carefully Roxana took it off again, smoothing the seams. She took a hanger out of the cupboard. The brown envelope still lay on the shelf. She sighed.

'It cost thirty-five pounds. Is this too much money?'

'No, Roxana, I don't think it's too much. And if it was, so what? It's the money you earned from lap dancing, which must be extremely hard work. I can't imagine doing it, not even if I had a body like yours. You can spend it exactly how you like. Although better if not on cocaine, perhaps.'

Roxana made a disgusted sound. 'Some of the girls, Natalie and others, they do this. Myself, I think it is the most stupid pastime in the entire world.' She picked up the envelope and opened it to show Connie a wad of notes.

'After I had bought the jacket, I thought that before shopping I should really give you money for rent.'

'Thank you. But I said you didn't have to. If you're here for a while, we can talk about you making a contribution towards the electricity bill, something like that.'

Roxana reflected on this. Whichever way she considered it, however pessimistically, it did not sound as though Connie was telling her to go.

'I think you should put that money in the bank, though.'

'I don't have a bank.'

Connie considered. Roxana was almost certainly in the country illegally; she had no resources except her dancing and no one to stand up for her except Noah and Connie herself. However tough she might appear to be, she was vulnerable too. All Connie's instincts were to help her as much as she could.

'I can help you with that, if you like.'

Roxana looked pleased.

Connie's eyes fell on the beach postcard again. 'Where's that? Did you go there on a holiday?'

'A holiday? No. This place is my fantasy. My paradise. Whenever I was in a very ugly situation, before I left Uzbekistan or when I was here in London before I met Noah, I would stare very hard at this picture. I would tell myself, somewhere in this world that place exists. There is the heat of the sun and the cool water and lapping of waves. You are not here, you are there. Or', Roxana shrugged as if to brush off the memories like a cobweb from her shoulder, 'some day, you will be. The truth is that I have never seen the sea.'

'Never?'

'How would I have? Uzbekistan is a country that has no coast. Not even the countries that border it have any coastline.'

'I didn't know that,' Connie said, embarrassed by geographical ignorance. 'Would you like to see the sea? I'm not saying the beaches in England are anything like that one, but we have plenty of coast. Or no, wait a minute, you'd rather go with Noah, wouldn't you? I'm sure he'd like you to see it with him.'

They looked at each other.

'I would like to go with you,' Roxana said.

'Then we'll do it.'

TEN

October 1980

Hilda wanted a big wedding for Jeanette – *a proper wedding*, was the way she described it.

Jeanette gave the impression that she was going to perform like a feature out of *Brides* magazine, wearing an ivory slub-satin dress and carrying a bouquet of stephanotis and white freesias, just in order to please her mother, with the implication that if left to themselves she and Bill would really have been just as happy to slip off to the registry office in their ordinary clothes and be back at work the same afternoon. But Connie suspected that even though Jeanette was now a lab technician who would frugally walk almost three miles to work in order to put the tube fare into the savings fund she and Bill were building up towards the deposit on a flat, she was actually almost as in love with the full bridal notion as Hilda was.

Connie steered clear of most of the early discussions about arrangements.

She knew that Jeanette and Bill had settled on a date, and that a church and a location for the reception had also been chosen. Beyond that she partly chose to be vague because she didn't want to think too much about Bill being her sister's husband anywhere in the near future, and partly it was inevitable anyway because she worked at GreenLeaf Music from the moment the studios opened in the morning until the last person left at night, and then either went out or groped her way home to Perivale to sleep before starting over again. Her only real contact with Hilda and Jeanette was during Sunday lunches at Echo Street, and on some of these occasions Connie was concentrating too hard on staying awake or on facing down her hangover from Saturday night to take in much of what was being said.

She was taken aback, therefore, to realise that over one lunch the bridesmaid's dress was being discussed with the understanding that she would be the one who was wearing it.

'Apricot's a nice warm colour, yes. But with Connie's complexion, maybe there's too much orange in it? What about a lovely pale blue?'

Connie chewed and swallowed a mouthful of Hilda's granite-coloured roast lamb, and then put down her knife and fork. Bill was sitting directly opposite her at the kitchen table with which Hilda had recently replaced the old one that came with them from Barlaston Road. He flicked a glance at her, then ducked his head again. But not before Connie had seen the curl of his smile.

'I don't know anything about being a bridesmaid. Jeanette? What's this? I don't want to be a bridesmaid. Thank you, and all that.'

Patiently, Jeanette fluffed the blonde wings of her new shorter hairstyle over her ears, in case her hearing aids were protruding.

– *Why not?*

'I just don't. Get Jackie or Elaine.'

Hilda clicked her tongue. 'Jackie's due six weeks after the wedding, she can't possibly do it. And Elaine, what will people think if she's Jeanette's bridesmaid and you aren't?'

'They'll probably think how pretty Elaine is, and how lovely she looks in pale-blue satin. I'm just not doing it, all right? Anyway, wouldn't it have been a nice idea maybe to *ask* me?'

Bill watched her. He wasn't smiling now.

'I've tried to talk to you about plans, I don't know how many times, Connie. Haven't we, Jeanette? You're never, ever at that flat of yours, wherever it is. And even when someone else answers the phone they sound half-witted.'

That wasn't surprising, Connie thought, given what went on. And it was true that she was rarely there. She was making unpredictable new friends, and it was fun to go out after work to drink with them in a noisy throng at the French pub or to fuel up with moussaka at Jimmyz.

'And I can't ring you at that place you work.'

'No, please don't. I'm not allowed to have personal calls.'

Connie felt fierce about GreenLeaf Music. After more than a year she was still only a glorified cleaner and messenger but she was learning, every day, and she was making herself useful. She was superstitiously afraid that if she relaxed her attention even for a moment, she would miss the one crucial detail that would enable her to impress Brian Luck or Malcolm Avery or one of the others.

'Well, then. You see what I mean.'

Hilda was going to pursue the subject to the point of combustion, but Jeanette held up her hand.

– *We'll talk about it.*

These days, Jeanette was very calm and practical.

After the apple pie and ice cream, Connie went out into the garden. She kicked damp leaves off the path and walked the short distance to the shed. A train rattled through the cutting and as another handful of yellow leaves drifted towards the earth she became aware that Bill had followed her outside. He took out a pack of cigarettes and lit one, then stood on the path and looked at the cobwebs spun between the dead twigs of border plants.

'Can I have one of those?'

He offered her the pack without comment, and struck a match for her. Connie inhaled and watched him through a slice of her hair.

'What will *you* have to wear for this wedding?'

'Lounge suit. Flower of some sort in buttonhole arrangement. Sheepish smile.'

'Why?'

'Why? Because I love Jeanette. Because if that's all it takes for us to get married, it's nothing. Even if I have to wear a Tarzan suit I'll do it.'

Shit, shit, Connie thought. I didn't want to hear that. The pain it caused her was like a meat skewer stabbing between her ribs straight into the thick muscle of her heart. She had to breathe in hard to stop herself actually wincing.

She managed to say, 'I suppose you think that if I love Jeanette too, I should dress up in whatever she wants me to wear on her wedding day and be happy for her?'

Bill hesitated. 'I think you should do what you decide is right, Connie.'

They were standing quite close together. There seemed to Connie to be a light directly behind Bill that gave him a bright outline and trapped tiny rainbow filaments in the nap of his clothing. She could see the fine hairs on his wrists and a pulse in his throat just above the line of his collar.

She wanted to confide in him about how she didn't love Jeanette, not the way you were supposed to do when you were sisters, because sometimes she hated her and the rest of the time she felt mostly indifferent. She didn't think he would even be that surprised. Bill had always given her the impression that he noticed and understood what went on at Echo Street. But the very idea of mentioning love, and Jeanette and herself, and including Bill in the equation, was much too dangerous.

She said with her teeth clamped together, 'I'll do what's right, then. I'll be a bridesmaid if I have to.' But I'll be doing it for you, she silently added. Just for you.

To her dismay, and choked delight, Bill put one arm around her and drew her close as she had seen him do with Jeanette.

'Good,' he said into her ear.

Connie shivered. She pulled away from him, hard, and threw the glowing end of her cigarette into the next garden. Bill watched its trajectory.

'You should have put that out. You could start a fire.'

'It's soaking *wet* everywhere.'

'But the man next door might just have left a crate of firelighters on his lawn.'

'Yeah,' Connie said. They both started laughing.

Before she left Echo Street that afternoon she told Jeanette and Hilda that she'd do it.

'Well, now you're talking sense, thank goodness. Why would any girl not want to be her sister's bridesmaid?' Hilda wondered.

Jeanette squeezed her arm with unusual warmth.

– I'm glad. Thank you.

'All right. Just promise me that it won't involve powder blue or baby pink.'

A busy period followed. GreenLeaf were commissioned to compose and record the music for the television serialisation of a Le Carré novel, and Malcolm Avery's solution required a choir of twenty gospel singers that Connie had to book and then look after for two days. Next she found herself flying to Switzerland at two hours' notice, to dress up as a Bavarian milkmaid and sing on camera for a chocolate ad. This was the first time she had been abroad. On the plane home one of the other musicians, drunk on duty-free whisky, told her that he loved her. It was fun. Connie was having a good time.

From a swatch of fabrics posted to her by Jeanette she chose a pale gold not-too-shiny satin. She examined the rough sketch that accompanied the material. The dress looked as if it would at least be quite plain, close-fitting, nothing too extreme.

The next thing she heard, she was summoned to a measuring and preliminary fitting. Jeanette's dress and her own were being made by the sister-in-law of old Mrs Polanski, Connie's one-time piano teacher. The dressmaker lived somewhere not very accessible, in Bow, and Hilda told Connie that to save time Bill would give her a lift from work. He was going to be in the West End that afternoon, and he could drive her out to Mrs Tesznar's.

Connie walked down the gritty stairs. There was a session in progress, and a clash of cymbals and then a ponderous drum roll made the walls vibrate. She saw Bill from above, sitting on the battered sofa with musicians dashing past him and a slice of busy street visible through the open door. He was chatting to Sonia who worked on the reception and switchboard.

'Hi,' Connie said. He stood up at once.

'Hi. Are you ready to leave?'

'Yes, let's go before anyone finds something else for me to do.'

'Bye, Bill,' Sonia called. She gave Connie a wink.

Outside it was smoky and damp, the lights were coming on and it was easy to remember that in only a couple of weeks' time it would be winter-dark at five o'clock.

'That's an interesting place to work,' Bill remarked. 'Are you happy there?'

Connie skipped a couple of steps and he grinned down at her.

'Yes. It's really pretty cool, sometimes. Elvis Costello came in the other day with a keyboard player who was doing some work. He sat in reception in exactly the same place as you. Where's your car?'

'On a meter in Wardour Street. Actually, there's been a change of plan. Hilda rang, with a message from Jeanette. There's some drama with her dress, the woman's cut it too big and there's more complicated work to do. I'm not certain, but I think that's the gist. Anyway, apparently they're going to concentrate on that this evening and start on yours next week. So you and I are surplus to requirements tonight.'

Connie stopped walking and Bill bumped into her. They apologised simultaneously and Connie hesitated.

'Does that mean you've got to go?'

'Not really. I thought we might have a drink,' Bill said. 'You'll pass for eighteen,' he added.

Connie skipped again, full of excitement at the legitimate prospect of having Bill all to herself.

'It's only a few *months* off. I'm in pubs all the time.'

'Are you really? Come on, then. There's a place off Regent Street that's quite respectable.'

'What? What do you mean? I don't need *respectable*.'

'Maybe not. But I do.'

They went to a wine bar, densely furnished with twining plants in wicker baskets. Connie found herself sitting opposite Bill in a ferny alcove scented with damp earth, drinking wine and talking, talking as if a cork had been drawn out of her as well as from the bottle. She told him about Switzerland and the flat in Perivale and some of the friends she had made since leaving Echo Street.

'You're very independent, Con.'

'I am, aren't I?'

She gulped some more of her wine, feeling that what she was saying was interesting, and that Bill was very easy to talk to. People in work suits passed their alcove, carrying drinks. The volume of noise was rising.

'Anyway, who else can you depend on but yourself?'

'Family?' he answered. 'Friends?'

Bill talked a lot, too. She found out things about him that she had never known before. He had elderly parents and he had grown up as an only child in a suburb in the Midlands. His mother had suffered for years from agoraphobia, and rarely left the house.

Connie's eyes widened. With her increasing freedom, she was just discovering the thrill of travel.

'That's tragic,' she breathed. 'Doesn't she go *anywhere*?'

Bill grinned at her dismay. 'No. And that means my dad doesn't either. But they're not unhappy, Con. There are many worse situations.'

He told her about the PR business he was setting up with two partners.

'You can really make a difference. For instance, we're doing some work for a charity that raises money to buy special wheelchairs made in Germany, for badly disabled children. We've just had a promise from the sports minister that he'll look into putting some government backing into a nationwide series of wheelchair athletics, and we managed *that* because one of my partners is related in some way to Mrs T and got himself invited to a reception at Number Ten.' He was leaning forward in his seat, full of enthusiasm. 'It's about connections, but not using those connections in a crass way. Of course, we have to take on some less – um – *radiant* accounts to underwrite that sort of work. But I love it, you know. You place a little piece in a newspaper for your client, and it's worth thousands in direct advertising.'

Connie was dazzled. She could feel a hot wire running beneath her cheekbones. They had almost finished the wine, although Bill had drunk more than half.

'It's not that I'm fixated on making money,' he said earnestly. 'But I want to be able to take care of Jeanette, and our children if we have them. That's not very modern-sounding, but it's the truth. I know Jeanette could look after herself, of course she can, she's the most determined and capable person I've ever met, but I want to make it so that she doesn't *have* to. I do feel an extra responsibility because she's deaf. Not that we've ever talked about it. She wouldn't want to admit that her deafness makes any difference and I suppose I've joined her in a kind of conspiracy that it doesn't matter, doesn't really even exist. I've never spoken about this to anyone. Do you mind, Connie?'

'No.'

Yes. But she didn't want him to stop confiding in her.

'It's so good to talk to you. I can tell you that before I asked Jeanette to marry me, I thought very hard. But the deafness and her determination are so much part of the person she is, I can't untangle them. I can't say to myself I love this part of her and if she wasn't that it would be easier for me. She's a whole person and that's the person I'm going to marry, and once I'd worked that out, it was simple. I knew what I had to do. I won't let her down, you know. You can rely on that. I do love her very much.'

Bill drank the last inch of his wine. When he put his glass down his hands rested on the tabletop and it seemed the most natural thing in the world to Connie to reach out her own to cover them.

'I know,' she said. Although she did wonder, *So why do you need to say it*?

She stared very hard at some drops of wine that had spilled on the varnished wood.

He squeezed her hands and then released them.

'Well. Time. I've got my car, too. I shouldn't drive before having something to eat.' He hesitated. 'I wonder – shall we go somewhere and have dinner? I know you've got to get home. But at least it's not all the way from Bow.'

'Yes, let's do that,' Connie said hastily.

They went to a place a few doors further down the street. There were red tablecloths and oversized pepper grinders, and they ordered food without Connie paying an instant's attention to what it was going to be. They were both reminded of La Osteria Antica and Uncle Geoff, and Bill did such note-perfect imitations of Uncle Geoff and the waiter's Italian that Connie coughed into her third glass of wine and Bill had to thump her on the back until she caught her breath. She mopped her eyes with her napkin.

'You're not about to choke to death, are you?' he asked.

She nodded, and laughed some more.

As they ate they went on talking. There seemed to be a lot to say, and there were none of the awkward pauses or sudden speaking over each other or moments of incredulity at what the other person was saying that Connie was used to with other men. It was like a dream to be facing Bill across the red tablecloth, sharing an order of fried potatoes, and at the same time it felt as natural and easy as it had in the wine bar.

This was an evening when nothing could go wrong, whatever she said or did. She was slightly drunk, but it was happiness and not wine that made her feel giddy.

Was this what being a couple was like?

She wondered if Jeanette felt like this every day. Probably she did.

She was telling Bill about finding out that she was adopted.

'What did you feel?' he asked.

She thought hard, because she wanted to give him a true answer.

'It was the day of my dad's funeral. That was why Elaine and Jackie were there. It was very bad, because it seemed to cut me off more from him. As if I didn't quite have the same right as Jeanette and Mum to be sad, to miss him so badly, because I wasn't his and he wasn't really mine. I felt as if I'd been cut out of another picture, a completely different one, and I couldn't blend back into the Echo Street family photograph any longer. It made me realise I probably never had done. In a way, after a while, that was a relief because it explained a lot of things that had bothered me and I'd never understood. Then I started wondering who I really was – Hilda didn't tell me very much – and I made up for the loss of Constance Thorne *and* my dad by making up all kinds of fantasies for myself. Pretty childish ones. You know. Princesses and great tragedies and stupid stuff like that.'

She took a big swallow of wine. Bill was watching her face, and the sympathetic way he bent towards her made it suddenly seem vital that he shouldn't feel any sorrier for her.

She added brightly, 'I don't do that any more. I'm fine about it. It's probably quite an ordinary story.'

She almost said that the rest of the episode was the strange part. That she was taken into Echo Street, where Jeanette's deafness at the centre of the house sent ripples of silence spreading outwards. Like one absence balancing another, nothing that mattered in the Thorne family was ever openly spoken about, not anger or death or disability or the vast mystery of her adoption. Outbursts of any kind were forbidden. Furniture was dusted, exams were passed, and funerals and weddings were done properly. Hilda saw to that, and Connie recognised with a flash of adult understanding that she maintained her rigid ways because she was afraid of the mess of exposure. The only time she had almost collapsed was when Tony died, and with Jeanette's help she had fought her way back from that.

It was fear that made Hilda afraid. A sudden faint sympathy for her mother buckled and creaked under the skin of Connie's antipathy.

Connie had opened her mouth to talk about Jeanette

and her deafness, and the effect that it had had on both their childhoods. But she closed it again, like a fish. It was the one subject she found she couldn't talk about to Bill, because, because . . . *I do love her very much.*

Another silence. Ironic, that's what it was.

Connie wanted to laugh again but she suppressed the urge because she could already hear the crazy note it might contain. She was definitely drunk now. The room was blurred at the edges and her head felt as if it might float off her shoulders. Luckily she had had quite a lot of practice lately at dealing with these symptoms. She sat up straighter in her chair, took several deep breaths, and pinched the flesh of her thighs under the tablecloth to the point at which the pain became too much to bear.

Bill said, 'Have you ever thought about finding your natural mother? It might be easier to know the story than to speculate about it. I think I read somewhere that adopted children can trace their original families now.'

'I could. Maybe I will.'

He touched her wrist. 'If you don't want to do it on your own, and you might not want to involve Hilda or Jeanette, I'll help you.'

She took these words inside her, wrapping them up with the knowledge that she could come back to them whenever she needed to.

'Thanks,' she said. 'I mean, thank you. I'd like to. It's just, I haven't decided anything yet. I'm at GreenLeaf and I go to the pub or a gig afterwards and then I get home and go to sleep and then it's another day. I'm quite busy.' A bubble of laughter did escape her now, like a breath of relief. Bill laughed too.

'I see. I know. That's good, isn't it?'

'Yes,' she agreed.

She wasn't waiting, she realised. *Now* was what counted, a perfectly crystalline moment, in this restaurant with Bill.

Her glass was empty, and so was her plate. Time had telescoped and the dinner was paid for and they were standing up with the table wobbling between them. They walked outside into the fine rain and hesitated, pulling up their coat collars under the shelter of the restaurant awning. Droplets glimmered on the scallops of canvas. Connie knew from past experience that fresh air was likely to affect her in one of two ways. Luckily, tonight her head cleared.

'I'll walk you to the tube,' Bill murmured. They fell into step and without thinking about it Connie slipped her hand into his. Their fingers interlaced. She felt as if she had grown a million new nerve endings. Heat ran up her arm and radiated through her body. They were moving as if they were one person. She could feel his breathing in her chest, his words in her head before he uttered them.

'Connie . . .'

They stopped walking. The small side street was deserted. Raindrops slanted into the puddles, splintering the reflected lights. She turned her face up to his and they kissed. The electric shock of it passed through them both and Connie heard his sharp intake of breath. They pressed their bodies closer, fitting shoulder and hip together, arms winding as they kissed more deeply.

'*Connie.*'

With the greatest difficulty Bill stepped back and broke the circuit. He lifted his hands to cup her face, and Connie remembered the contrast between cold rain on her skin and the warmth in his fingers.

'Don't,' he whispered. 'We can't do this.'

She crowded herself against him imploringly, but all he did was drop his hands to her shoulders and gently hold her at arm's length.

'This is not what you want,' he insisted.

'It is. It *is*.'

It was what he wanted too, she knew that whatever he might say to try to convince them both otherwise, and out here in the rain in the street emptied by the downpour – in this deserted world in which they seemed to be the only two living things – nothing and no one else mattered.

'No. With somebody, yes. But not me. You're seventeen, Con. Everything has still got to happen to you. And it will, I know that.' He tried to inject conviction into the words.

Enough has happened already, Connie thought sadly. There were raindrops on her eyelids and lashes. She blinked quickly, and his face blurred. Bill's thumbs smoothed the corners of her mouth and when he came into focus once more he was smiling down at her. Somehow he had made sure of himself again. He was Jeanette's fiancé.

'Come on, or we'll get soaked. Let's go for the tube,' he said. He kissed her forehead, then took her arm and linked it beneath his, drawing her after him. From somewhere beyond herself Connie could see what they looked like. Like a Victorian brother and sister walking to church.

She was cold, and then hot, and then angry. She tramped through the puddles, careless of the icy water filling her shoes.

They turned a corner and a crowded bus churned past them. At the end of the street was the mouth of Oxford Circus tube station. When they reached it the fuggy, familiar smell rose up the steps and they were caught up in the crowd of people hurrying for shelter.

The lights in the ticket hall were very bright. Connie winced and ducked her head, not wanting Bill to see the confusion of her anger, nor that she was close to tears.

'Have you got a ticket?' he was asking.

'I'm not *twelve*.'

'I know that, Con. I really do.'

She took a breath and lifted her head. 'I'm going home now. Thanks for dinner.'

Their eyes met then, and reflected shock and uncertainty and a glimmer of pure madness. Bill blinked.

'What happened back there was my fault,' he muttered. 'I'm sorry.'

Connie marshalled herself. 'It was just a *kiss*,' she said precisely. 'Nothing to worry about.' Then she flicked him a smile. 'See you,' she said, and turned to the ticket barrier.

She was in love with Bill Bunting.

She had no option but to be nonchalant now. She would have to be nonchalant and sisterly around him for the rest of eternity; her pride depended on it. As she descended into the depths she searched inside herself for the vestiges of anger. Anger was good; better than despair. Anger was cauterising.

Bill stood and watched her go. Her dark head and thin, square shoulders floated down the Central Line escalator and sank out of his sight. It was as if a part of himself had just been torn away.

He wanted to call her back. He wanted to leap over the barrier and chase after her, but he denied the impulse.

Where could it lead, but into pain?

The wedding was predictable, or slightly worse than Connie might have predicted. Her dress was too tight, and the gold satin turned out to be much shinier than it had appeared in the sample. Jeanette was ravishing – happiness transformed her china prettiness into serious beauty. Uncle Geoff walked her up the aisle, and at the altar she turned to Bill and her smile lit up the church. Bill looked proud and pleased. In his speech at the reception he praised Jeanette's lovely bridesmaid and thanked Hilda for her generosity in the same sentence.

After the reception, exactly on schedule, Jeanette changed into her jade-green going-away coat and came out on Bill's arm. The wedding car was waiting for them; some of the technicians from Jeanette's lab had scrawled lipstick messages over the windows and Bill's friends had tied the usual assortment of junk to the rear bumper.

The door of the car was held open for her. With Bill's arm circling her shoulders Jeanette searched the crowd of guests for Connie. Catching sight of her, she held up her bouquet and threw it.

Connie's arms stayed stuck at her sides. To catch her sister's bouquet was her last obligation of the day but she couldn't make herself dive for the tumble of petals that would promise her a husband, not Bill. Instead there was a pecking of high heels on the gravel and Elaine's hand shot out. She swung the bouquet upwards, then pressed her flushed face into the flowers.

A laughing Jeanette blew a kiss to Connie, who returned a small wave. She saw Bill as a dark shape but she would not let herself look directly at him. She gazed at the car instead and kept her smile fixed in a final blizzard of confetti as the newlyweds stepped into the back. She smiled all the time, as the doors slammed and people shouted and the car trailed its cargo of tin cans over the gravel and away.

There was a party to go to almost every night of the week – the music business took Christmas seriously – but for the first time Connie felt seriously out of key with her new world. The Soho streets seemed full of laughing, drunken people and the pubs overflowed, but however much she drank and danced Connie couldn't capture the Christmas spirit. From being pleased with her independence she found herself longing to be loved: a proper, intimate love, not the kind that seemed to be all that was on offer for her, involving a lot of drink or dope and a sexual encounter under a pile of coats at a party.

Everyone else in the world seemed to have a lover, a family, a child.

The window of Liberty's that fronted onto Regent Street featured a nativity scene. Mary and the infant Jesus were surrounded by life-sized sheep and a patient donkey.

Connie wondered where her real mother was this Christmas, and whether she ever thought about her baby.

One Saturday morning Connie went out to the local library. She looked up Adoption Services and wrote down the information she found there.

During her lunch hour on the following Monday she walked through the crowds of Christmas shoppers and found her way to the General Records Office at St Catherine's House. It was a big building with a municipal feel to the interior. Hurrying feet clicked over the stone floors, names and numbers were called out to waiting lines of people. A Christmas tree decorated with blobs of cotton wool and bulbous lanterns blinked in a corner. It was strange to be standing in a queue of coughing people in overcoats, waiting to find out the name of the woman who had given birth to her. Connie wondered if there would be an address. Maybe even a telephone number. How did you begin such a conversation?

When her turn came, she found herself across a wooden counter from a clerk with a red birthmark spreading across her neck. Almost relieved to have a different point to focus on, Connie concentrated on not staring at the mark while she explained what she wanted. The woman sneezed and whipped a tissue from a box at her elbow. She blew her nose and Connie waited until she was ready to speak. She was imagining a ledger, somewhere close at hand. A finger running down the columns of names and stopping at her own, written under another name.

Your mother is . . .

My natural mother, she practised.

The clerk said, 'I am afraid we cannot give you access to your file.'

'Why is that?'

'Adopted people born prior to 1975 may only access their records through an intermediary, a counsellor nominated by the Registrar General.'

Connie frowned, trying to make sense of this. The clerk said that she could make an appointment to talk to the approved social worker, if she wished, but there was a waiting list. In the meantime she could apply to receive a copy of her birth certificate but it would only be a shortened version, revealing no details of her original parentage.

'I see,' Connie said. There were several people waiting

in the queue behind her. 'I . . . thank you. I'll think about it.' She turned away from the counter, and fled.

Although it was only two o'clock, the light was already fading. Connie trudged back to the studio.

In June, she turned eighteen. By the end of the year, Connie was learning the new musical digital technology as rapidly as GreenLeaf took it up. She began mixing and sampling tracks, working up her own compositions after-hours on the eight-track in the studio.

Jeanette announced that she was pregnant.

Connie had hardly seen her sister and brother-in-law since their return from honeymoon. They had bought a flat in Stoke Newington and were busy renovating it, and Hilda tended to go over there on Sundays. Jeanette underwent a series of tests, and when the results came back they indicated that the baby was a boy and was highly unlikely to have inherited his mother's deafness. Once this news was confirmed Jeanette sailed through her pregnancy. Bill sawed skirting boards, sanded floors and put up shelves. Hilda made curtains and covers and knitted piles of blue baby clothes.

Connie worked harder. She claimed to have too little time to go to Stoke Newington or Echo Street, and this was true. But it was also much easier not to have to see Bill in his decorating clothes, unshaven and happy, with splodges of pale-blue paint in his hair. She also had a boyfriend now, a thin boy called Sam from Newcastle, who was a student at the Royal College of Music.

'Can't you ever bring your boy home to meet us?' Hilda asked, on one of the rare Sundays when Connie did see the three of them together. Bill and Jeanette were nestling on their Habitat sofa, and they seemed responsible and dauntingly mature compared with the anarchic Sam and the rest of the post-punks and drummers and students she spent her time with.

'Yeah, one of these days,' Connie said, knowing that she would not. She liked Sam and he suited her and she was doing everything she could to convince herself that he was what she wanted. And all the time, compared with Bill he was utterly insubstantial.

Bill didn't say anything, and he didn't even look at her. He rubbed one corner of his jaw with his thumb.

Noah was born. Connie went to see him and Jeanette as soon as they came home from the hospital. She had never had much to do with babies and his helplessness and the crimson miniature limbs with their fine down of hair made her cry so suddenly and unexpectedly that she couldn't hide it from Bill and Jeanette.

Jeanette misunderstood.

– *He's fine. We both are. Do you want to hold him?*

'No. I've got to go soon.'

Bill followed her out of the room.

'Seeing him made you think of you, didn't it? When you were that small?'

'Yes. But so what?'

He sighed. 'Connie, you don't have to try to be so hard-boiled all the time. Look, can't I help?'

'Maybe. Not right now,' she said abruptly. It was too difficult to be this close to him and she wished she hadn't come.

She went back to St Catherine's House, and this time she saw a different clerk. She told the woman yes, she did understand that the only way to proceed was by agreeing to talk to a specialist social worker. She made the appointment, and waited for the date to come round.

It was spring again, but the interview room only had a small high window in a gloss-painted wall and no sunlight reached into it. Connie sat and waited while the counsellor fetched her file. She studied the backs of her hands and the shape of her fingers, wondering if they resembled her mother's.

'Here we are,' the woman said. She had introduced herself as Mrs Palmer. Connie stared at the thin buff-coloured folder that Mrs Palmer laid on the desk in front of her and then shielded with her hand. It was odd to think that such an anonymous-looking piece of officialdom contained her personal history.

'I understand,' Connie nodded at the end of a lengthy explanation of rights and procedures that she hadn't listened to. She went to take the folder as Mrs Palmer lifted her hand, but the woman held it away from her.

'I am afraid I'm not allowed to give you direct access to the contents of the file. I can read out the documents to you.'

Connie felt a pulse hammering in her head but she forced herself to be calm.

'All right.'

Mrs Palmer put on her spectacles, fumbling for what seemed like five minutes. She took out one slip of paper, then adjusted her glasses again.

'You were found on the night of 17 June 1963.'

There was a silence. From an anteroom Connie heard the metallic scrape of a filing-cabinet drawer.

'You were taken to the Royal London Hospital, where you were described as being between one and two days old.'

'Found? What does *found* mean?'

'I'm sorry. There's not much information here. Do you know what a foundling is, Constance?'

The word had a Victorian, melodramatic ring to it that was out of place in this utilitarian setting. But she did know what it meant. Somewhere out of sight the cabinet drawer was slammed shut again. Stiffly she nodded her head.

Mrs Palmer extracted another flimsy sheet of paper. 'At the Royal London, the medical staff reported that you were healthy on arrival but hungry and dehydrated. You remained at the hospital for two weeks, and were then transferred to St Margaret's Children's Home. From there an adoption order was made, let's see, two months later. Mr and Mrs Anthony Thorne. The Order states that you were a foundling.'

Connie had imagined a variety of histories for herself, but this one had never occurred to her.

'Found,' she repeated. 'Is that all?'

She could see that there was nothing more in the file.

'That's usually all there is, in these circumstances.'

'Where was I found?'

Mrs Palmer consulted the first sheet of paper.

'In the garden of number fourteen, Constance Crescent, London E8. At the hospital you were given the name Constance. That's quite usual. The hospital staff choose what seems appropriate.'

The name of a *street*.

'There must be some more. What do I do next? How can I find out more information?'

Mrs Palmer looked back at her. Connie could see sympathy in her eyes but she didn't want that. She kept her gaze level.

'I'm afraid I don't know. It's difficult, with cases like this. You have to understand that it is a criminal offence to abandon a baby. So the woman, whoever she is, might have to face charges. Very rarely do they come forward.'

Connie looked away. What circumstances could have driven a woman to make such a decision? An image of tiny Noah Bunting came to her.

'Constance? Are you all right?'

'Yes, thank you. It's a surprise.'

Mrs Palmer gathered the fragments of Connie's history and slid them back into their buff folder. She folded her arms protectively across it.

'If there's anything else I can do?'

Connie felt for the seat of her chair, gripped it and stood up. She held on to the back of it for a second until she was sure that her legs would hold her. Then she said goodbye to Mrs Palmer, turned and walked back down the corridor, into the open area with the clerks at their counters, and finally out into the thin April sunshine. Everything looked precisely the same as it had done an hour ago.

She was supposed to go back to GreenLeaf, but she began walking in the opposite direction. She crossed the Strand and continued southwards over Waterloo Bridge. The river water was flowing fast, and debris swirled against the wooden piles and rusty ironwork lining the Embankment.

Constance Crescent.

The image of herself, a day old, kept separating and then fusing again with that of Noah Bunting, and her mother was a slip of a figure on the margin of her imagination, refusing to come forward even though Connie stopped on the very centre of the bridge and closed her eyes, trying to bring her into focus. She longed to reach out to that woman and hold her, and be held in return, but her hand opened and closed again on nothing.

She walked on, a long way, into unfamiliar South London streets. When she was too tired to walk any further she sat down on a bench and then she cried.

Holding the A–Z open on her lap, Connie told Bill to take the next left turn.

'Then it's the third on the right,' she said.

They were in an area of medium-sized semi-detached villas and smaller terraced houses, no different from many others in London. There were trees in the streets, now coming into full leaf, and front gardens either clogged with wet old furniture or gentrified with clipped hedges screening polished windows. Bill followed Connie's directions in silence, and then they both craned forwards to read the name plate at the street corner.

Constance Crescent was a quiet curving street set back from the busier road. All the houses here looked well-tended. There were window boxes on some of the lower sills, brass door-knockers and letterboxes, and several of the white-painted door surrounds had French-blue enamel number plates. Number 14 was one of them.

Bill stopped the car. A woman came out of the front door of number 12 and bumped a baby's buggy over the front step and down the path to her gate. She pushed the buggy past the car, glancing at them as she passed.

Connie got out, and her jerky movements caused her to bang her elbow against the car door. Tingling pain shot up her arm and she rubbed her funnybone as she stood and looked around her. There was a privet hedge, recently clipped, separating the garden from the street. A path tiled in red and black diamonds and triangles led to the dark-blue front door, a pair of black dustbins on the house-side of the hedge had 14 painted in tidy white numerals on the lids. The wrought-metal gate stood open.

Bill had got out of the car too and she was conscious of him standing just behind her.

'It's just a street,' she said.

He didn't ask her what else she had been expecting, although she knew it would have been a fair question. There was nothing here in this patch of urban garden, spruced up with evergreen shrubs, to give her a scrap of information about herself or who had left her here. It had been, she now understood, absurd to believe that it might.

Almost nineteen years ago her mother had walked along this quiet street, carrying a baby in her arms. Then she had walked away again without her. The thread of this connection was too fragile to take any strain, Connie thought. As soon as she tried to pull on it for more infor-mation, or to reel in some comfort, it silently broke away and the end was left floating in an infinity of space.

'Let's go,' she muttered.

Bill put his hand out, didn't quite touch her arm. To both of them, the inch of space between his fingertips and her wrist was charged with unnatural significance. 'Wait. We should talk to whoever lives here.'

He walked up to the blue front door and pressed the bell. Connie listened to the drone of traffic and a police siren in the distance. No one came to the door.

'They must be out at work. We can come back one evening,' he told her. 'They may have been living here when you were found, or at least they may know a neighbour who was. Somewhere there is going to be somebody who knows what happened, and all we have to do is ask questions until we find them.'

Connie nodded, without much expectation. She looked again at the path, the dustbins, the rim of grey earth beneath the hedge. Then she retraced her steps down the path and back to Bill's car. She felt stiff and rather cold.

'Let's go and get a coffee,' Bill said. He drove along the curve of the street and Connie watched the houses slide by.

An ordinary street, in an ordinary corner of East London. It didn't provide much of an identity to cling to, she reflected, when she had been hoping to find a solution for herself that didn't depend on Hilda and Jeanette, or particularly on Bill.

It was just dawning on her that she was not going to find her mother.

There was a coffee shop on the corner, empty in the dead time between the end of the lunch hour and the beginning of children coming home from school. Connie sat looking through the window while Bill fetched two coffees from the counter. She stirred sugar crystals into hers and then watched brown liquid drip from her spoon.

'Thanks for coming with me. I don't think I'd have done even this on my own. But now I know my place of origin, don't I?'

'Does it help to have seen Constance Crescent?'

'Not really.'

'Con, don't you think perhaps you should talk to Hilda? She may be able to give you a lead.'

Connie considered this from all angles.

'I don't think I can. She'd be offended, wouldn't she?

292

She'd interpret my wanting to trace my real mother as a criticism of her as an adopted one. Hilda does that, you know. She edits what isn't about her until it is. I can't imagine how our talk would go on beyond that, either. It's not really our family thing, is it? Warm and affirming heart-to-hearts, opening up to each other?'

Bill said nothing.

'Well, *is* it?'

'You're angry, Con.'

'I am not,' she snapped. 'I just want to know who I am.'

His eyes held hers then. 'Don't you already know that? Truly? I think *I* know who you are. You're what you've made yourself, and will make. Regardless of what or who you were born as.'

She wanted to hurl herself against him, crying, *I don't know. Tell me, help me.*

Bill's hands lifted, ready to take hers, but then he withdrew them and sheltered them beneath the table, out of danger. They never touched each other, not since the night they had kissed in the rain.

'Does Jeanette know that you've come here with me today?'

She saw his eyes flicker.

'No.'

It was only a lie by omission, of course. Jeanette didn't ask him what he did every lunchtime.

Connie thought she might feel a small satisfaction that they had a secret between the two of them, but instead there was a hopeless weight bearing down on her, bending her neck and compressing her spine and making it difficult for her to expand her lungs. Her decision to trace her mother was private to her, and Bill would respect that, even – maybe especially – where Jeanette was concerned. Months ago he had offered to help her, and he was doing no more than keeping his promise.

'Well. Thank you again,' she murmured.

Bill shifted sideways on his plastic seat and looked out of the café window. A crack ran diagonally from the bottom corner and it had been sealed with brown parcel-tape.

'We'll come back and talk to the people in the house. That's the next thing to do.'

'Perhaps.' With the weight pressing down on her, Connie had lost her enthusiasm for detective work. She changed her tone and asked brightly, 'How's Noah?'

Bill smiled. 'He's great. He's sitting up. His favourite game is banging saucepans with a wooden spoon. And how is Sam?'

'Sam is fine, thank you.'

'Good,' Bill said. He began rubbing the skin at the corner of his jaw with the side of his thumb. Connie knew by now that he only did this when he felt unhappy. She was sorry for him, and she was sorry for herself too because he was so near to her and familiar and necessary, and also absolutely desirable and equally forbidden. Love and what she hoped was contrary determination made her sit up and reach for her bag.

'Come on,' she said gently. 'I've got to get back to work. They'll be wondering where I've got to.'

ELEVEN

'The weather forecast's not that great,' Connie said. She put her foot down and overtook a horsebox with wisps of straw rustically blowing out of the tailgate. 'I was hoping it would be sunny.'

Roxana laughed delightedly. She laced her arms beneath her long thighs and hugged herself.

'I am not worried about sunny,' she said. 'Today I am going to see the sea.'

In Uzbekistan the sun blazed relentlessly out of an invariable, dust-whitened sky, or else it was harsh winter. But the weather in England was for ever changing from sun to rain and back again, with an endless sequence of halfway states in between those two. Sometimes there was even rain and sun at the same time, and the wind could chase away heavy grey clouds and leave a sparkling sky in the space of a single hour.

'We'll be there quite soon,' Connie told her. They were driving towards the east coast, for the first part of the way following the same route that she had taken with Hilda and Jeanette and Bill on the day of the long-ago engagement picnic.

Connie made the simple plan and Roxana told Mr Shane that she would not be working for one night. He frowned and said that he preferred to employ dancers who wanted to dance, not take half the week off.

'Just this once,' she coaxed. 'A friend of mine has invited me to make a trip to the sea. This will be my first time.'

At last, grudgingly, he agreed that she could go.

Connie caught some of Roxana's excitement. They accelerated out of London as if they were heading for somewhere much more exotic than the Suffolk coast.

'What did Noah say about this outing, by the way?' Connie asked.

Noah hadn't been very pleased.

'What is it with you about Auntie Con, Roxy? If you're actually going to take time off work wouldn't you rather come for a lovely weekend at the seaside with me?'

He coiled his arm round her waist and tried to pull her closer to him, but Roxana held herself just a little apart. Noah could sometimes be more affectionate than she really wanted him to be. Occasionally she could feel her resistance to his demands breaking out all over her skin in tiny tremors of impatience. Of course, she told him, she would have liked to go to visit the beach with him. But Connie had invited her, and it was very kind of her, and so they were going.

'Is it still so far?' Roxana asked now, peering through the windscreen as if she could make the waves materialise out of the fields ahead. 'I thought England was only a small country, but it seems very big.'

Now it was Connie's turn to laugh. It was like having a child in the car on Christmas Eve.

They turned eastwards, off the main road, and drove across a flat landscape hummocked with gorse. As they approached the coast the sky hollowed out and the light turned hazy.

Connie had given some thought to where would be the best place for them to make the first sighting. She knew this part of the coast because Sébastian had conducted a series of concerts at the Aldeburgh music festival a few miles away. While he was rehearsing she had driven for hours, exploring the salty inland creeks and the shingle spits that poked out into the changeable sea. She had taken long, solitary beach walks and sheltered with her book in hollows in the sand dunes. Thinking back to this time, as she headed down narrowing roads, it occurred to her that she had been lonely. She was glad of Roxana's company now. Her anticipation of reaching the sea suddenly sharpened to match her passenger's.

At last the lane swung into a sharp bend and petered out. There was a cluster of wood and tar huts around a patch of broken tarmac dusted with sand, and beyond them an undulating line of dunes.

'Is this it?' Roxana asked.

Connie opened the car door. A gust of salty air swept in.

'Yes. Can't you smell it?'

Roxana sprang out. The beach café was closed and theirs was the only car in sight. Seagulls shifted on the ridge of the nearest hut, a rusted tin ice-cream sign swung and creaked in a rising wind and the undertone was the constant dull murmur of breaking waves. Connie pointed to a rough path through the marram grass, up the slope of the dune. Roxana's eyes were wide with expectation now.

They started out at a walk but Roxana's pace quickened as the path led upwards and for the last few feet they were sprinting, sinking into the loose sand with the grass and sea thistle clawing at their ankles. Neck and neck, panting, they reached the crest of the dune.

The fierce onshore wind snatched their breath away. Roxana would have exclaimed, but all that came out of her lungs was a gasp.

A curve of coastline expanded like a scribble of silver wire, from a low headland to the north away southwards to the dull glimmer of a tiny, toy-sized town etched against the sky and water in the far distance. The two extremities were joined by the broken combs of surf, rolling out of the mass of sea and pounding on the vast sweep of shingle. Towards the still horizon, patches of water shone an unearthly pale gold where sun broke through the towering clouds. Seagulls looped and screamed over the waves.

Roxana galloped down the steep face of the dune, straight to the gentler slope of shingle beach. She staggered as the surface changed, managed to right herself, and ran the few steps onwards to the sea. The tide was at its highest point and the waves smashed in front of her at hip height. A yard from the water she spun round and waved her arms to Connie in a wide, exuberant arc. Her mouth was a slash of glee. She kicked off her clumpy sandals and even as Connie was racing towards her, the wind snatching her shouted warning and hurling it away, Roxana dashed straight into the surf.

For an instant she was a flat shape, a cartoon of limbs cut out against a lacework of receding water. Then with the sea sucking at her calves she stumbled on the lip of a shelf, where the beach dropped invisibly away. The next wave smashed against her and knocked her off her feet, her laughter turning into a shriek of alarm. As Connie reached the waves, Roxana was thrown forwards in a tumble of surf and then dragged away in the undertow.

Connie gasped with the shock of the cold water as a

wave slapped her thighs. For two seconds that stretched into an age she lost sight of Roxana under the surf. Then she spotted her, arms and legs flailing.

She had never seen the sea.

Of course she couldn't swim.

Roxana went under again.

Connie threw herself into the waves and kicked off to the point where she had seen her disappear. The water was icy and the beach shelved very steeply. Another wave caught her and she paddled hard to crest it, then glimpsed Roxana in the next trough. She swam as fast as she could towards her and as the undertow caught her they were thrown together. Roxana flung her arms around her neck, yelling words Connie couldn't understand as she was dragged down. With a massive effort Connie broke free from Roxana's grasp and caught her under the arms. Another wave smashed over their heads.

There was a swirl of green water and then darkness as they tumbled over. Connie had no air in her lungs. She clenched her teeth, willing herself to hold on against the bursting pain in her chest and the urge to breathe.

Then the water rolled backwards again and somehow she was the right way up and still holding on to Roxana. Their heads broke the surface. Connie gulped in a lungful of air and kicked towards the pewter gleam of the shingle. Roxana churned in the water beside her, heavy as a barrel, but Connie's efforts and the next wave together flung them over the lip of the shelf and their arms and legs and cheeks were suddenly scraping the sharp pebbles. Connie clawed herself to her knees and hoisted Roxana beside her. Struggling before the next wave hit them she staggered to her feet and dragged her burden into the lacy curl of foam and detritus at the high-water mark. She tottered another couple of steps, grasping both Roxana's wrists, and then they collapsed beyond the reach of the sea.

Roxana lay in a heap on the shingle. She coughed and opened her eyes. Her eyelashes were glued into spikes with salt and mucus and her face was a mask of superficial scratches and grey-black dribbles of ruined mascara.

Connie knelt beside her.

'You're all right,' she kept repeating. 'It's all right. You weren't going to drown.'

Roxana began to shiver. Within seconds her teeth were chattering.

Connie made her sit up.

'In a minute,' she said with her mouth close to the girl's ear, 'we're going to stand up and walk slowly back to the car. Then when we're out of this wind we can get dry and warm again.'

The thunder of the waves was getting louder, and the wind was rising. Connie helped Roxana to her feet. Slowly, holding on to each other and coughing to clear the salt from their lungs, they plodded like wounded creatures to the slope of the dune and began the ascent. Connie was shivering too.

At the summit, Roxana shook herself like a dog. Drops of water spun out of her hair and her clothes. She looked backwards at the pounding waves.

'My God,' she gasped.

As soon as they descended it was quieter, and almost warm. They trudged through the sand and Connie had a moment of panic before she discovered that the car keys were still wedged in her sodden back pocket.

'It's all over now,' she told Roxana.

It was less than ten minutes since they had left the car park.

It was only when they had stripped off the outer layers of wet clothes and were in the warmth of the car that Roxana spoke. She sat in the passenger seat, staring towards the dunes as if what lay beyond might still reach out for her. Her lips were blue.

She started to gabble. 'I am so sorry, Connie, to be stupid and make you jump into the sea for me. Don't be angry with me.'

'I didn't expect you to run straight in, or I'd have warned you, but of course I'm not angry. You're safe, that's all that matters. Are you warmer now?'

'You saved my life.'

Connie said, 'No. No, nothing nearly as heroic as that. They were big waves and the sea took you by surprise, that's all.'

'You saved my life,' Roxana kept repeating.

Connie started up the car and drove to the nearest village. There was nowhere to buy dry clothes and Roxana looked in urgent need of a hot drink.

'Let's go in here,' Connie said. There was a teashop open in the main street. She gave Roxana an old jumper she unearthed from the car's boot, and wrapped herself toga-style in a picnic rug. The teenaged waitress stared at their costumes and at the fresh grazes on Roxana's face, but fortunately they were the only customers.

Connie put a cup of hot tea into Roxana's hands.

'We weren't going to drown, you know. It was just the shock and cold, and losing your balance. You'd never seen the sea before, you didn't know what to expect,' she comforted her.

'But I think in England many, many people must die by drowning.'

'Some do,' she conceded. 'But not us.'

Roxana put down her teacup. She stared at Connie. 'I

didn't want to die. When I was under the water and it was filling my mouth and eyes, I was thinking no, no, it's not time for me, I am in England now and I have met Connie, and Noah, and soon all the dreams I had in Uzbekistan will come true, and now I'm going to die and everything is wasted.'

Connie said gently, 'That's a good response, isn't it? To know that life is precious and you can't bear to lose it?'

Finally Roxana nodded. 'I am still alive. I will try harder to be who I want.' Her gaze was fixed on Connie's face as if she could draw the essence out of her.

Connie was thinking that when the time came, she didn't want to die without knowing what she wanted to live for. A sense of isolation descended on her. What was she doing, sitting here with Roxana, in a place she was familiar with only because of Seb's absence?

Suddenly she longed for Bill. She wanted to hear his voice, to close her eyes and touch her forehead to his, submerging herself in the comfort of him.

No. No, you can't wish for that. Not now, not ever.

To Connie's dismay, Roxana's eyes had flooded with tears. The girl bent her head to hide it, but it was too late.

The waitress, idling beside her display of scones, was pretending not to eavesdrop.

'What's wrong, Roxana? What is it?' Connie implored.

But Roxana would not be drawn. She screwed up the paper napkin that had been placed underneath her mug and scrubbed at her face with it, then winced as she rediscovered the grazes.

'If you've finished your tea, let's go,' Connie said quietly. 'We won't find anywhere to buy clothes this late in the afternoon. I think we should stay up here tonight. You can have a hot bath, and we'll dry out our things and go home in the morning.'

They drove along the coast towards the town that had been visible in the far distance. The weather was deteriorating and the sea was an angry expanse of white horses.

Connie called ahead and booked two rooms in a pub she had once been to with Seb, across the road from the sea front. She saw Roxana into her room and told her to take a hot bath, then went to her own and tried to read until it was time for dinner. The print kept dancing in front of her eyes.

When she descended again she found Roxana waiting for her in the bar with an unopened bottle of wine and two glasses on a tray. Apart from the scratches on her face she looked her normal self again. She leapt up as soon as she saw Connie, her mouth wide in a smile.

'I want to say thank you for saving my life.'

The barman opened the wine for them and Connie raised her glass to Roxana.

'I hauled you out of the water, no more than that. But here's to life. Here's to us.' *Whoever we both are . . .*

'To life and us,' Roxana echoed in triumph. She was exuberant with relief and pleasure in being alive, and her elation rubbed off on Connie. The wine quickly disappeared, and Connie ordered a second bottle.

They ate dinner in the restaurant off the bar, which was decorated with nets and fishing floats.

Roxana kept shaking her head in wonderment. 'That sea, my God. It was *not* blue and smooth as glass, and there was *no* white sand like there is in my picture. I could not see one single palm tree, only grey stones. And such cold. Like Siberia, I should think. I thought my breath would never come again.'

'Your picture's of Thailand. The sea can sometimes be blue in England in September – but not all that often, come to think of it. There are no palm trees here. Well, maybe there are in Bournemouth or Torquay, I'm not sure. I should have told you more beforehand, and most of all I should have warned you that the North Sea wasn't going to look anything, nothing *at all*, like Koh Samui. I was so concerned with not spoiling the impact that I didn't think hard enough. I'm sorry you were disappointed.'

Roxana's eyes opened wider.

'Disappointed? I was not, not one bit. That sea, it was like a wild monster. It was alive, roaring, coming to swallow us up. I have never seen a sight like the waves coming, and to be caught by it like that, snatched up in its jaws and shaken, I could not ever have imagined such a thing. I have lived only in Uzbekistan, you know. The desert is a different animal. It lies coiled up like a snake, heavy, and only a very few times does it move. It is dangerous always, but not like your sea. I will never forget today, if I live for ever.'

'No,' Connie smiled. 'I don't think you will forget.'

It was only the very young and determined, she was thinking, who could conceive of living for ever.

Jeanette had been intending to return to work at the centre for taxonomic studies today. Connie found herself wondering how she had managed it.

'You are the heroine,' Roxana insisted.

'No. Really. I've swum off this coast before, that's all.'

'To me, you are.'

'You'd better not tell Noah I led you into trouble.'

Roxana nodded. 'If you think that is best, I will not say a word to him.'

'I didn't mean you had to keep it a secret,' Connie laughed.

The second bottle was empty and they had finished their dinner. They could hear the *whump* of waves driving against the sea wall. Spray hit the windows with a rattle like thrown gravel. In the bar the barman was polishing glasses, talking to a fisherman about the storm at sea.

'Rough night,' said the fisherman.

'Good night, ladies,' the barman called.

Connie went to bed and slept for three or four hours, then woke up again. For a few minutes she lay listening to the wind and the pounding waves. She waited to see if she was going to fall asleep again, but the roar of the surf swelled until it pressed inside the bones of her skull. She sat up, switched on the light and got out of bed. When she pulled aside the curtains, the streetlights on the sea front seemed to flicker through the streaming rain and spray. As she pressed her forehead against the chilly glass she heard the floorboards creak in the next room. The storm had woken Roxana, too.

She returned to bed and picked up her book. She heard a soft knocking. Roxana was standing out in the corridor, wearing her jacket with big buttons over a long T-shirt.

She said in a small voice, 'I am afraid that the waves will knock this house down.'

'No. It's quite safe. Come in here.'

Roxana followed her in. The room was small, and the only place to sit apart from on the double bed was the stool in front of the old-fashioned dressing table. They caught each other's eyes and started laughing.

Roxana raised her shoulders to her ears. 'I don't understand this sea of yours,' she repeated.

'I know. But this pub has probably been standing here for three hundred years, and the storm will have blown itself out by the morning.'

Connie opened the minibar and took out a couple of minia-tures. 'Let's see. Whisky? Or brandy?'

'Either one.'

'Sit on the bed. Might as well be comfortable if we're going to have a small-hours drinks party.'

They stretched out, side by side, and Roxana let her head fall back against the pillows. Companionably, they lay and listened to the sea.

'Such waves. It is like . . . nothing I know, that's the truth. I am trying to imagine. Maybe, let me think, this little room is like a ship. Maybe we are in a wreck. We have to cling on for our lives.' She gripped the edge of the mattress as if she was about to be tossed into the depths. 'I am lucky, and so are you, Connie. We are alive on our ship, and we are not going to drown. Not today. Maybe never.'

Roxana reached for her glass and drank. The rim clinked against her teeth.

'I wish my brother was on our ship with us.'

'Yes.'

'But Niki is not lucky. Not at all. He did not travel to England, and he has not been into the sea, like me.'

'Were you thinking about him, this afternoon in the café?'

Roxana didn't answer. Her chin was tipped forwards and she was staring at the tumbler balanced on her diaphragm.

'You could talk about him, if you wanted,' Connie gently prompted.

The glass clinked again as Roxana drank.

'I cried more for myself, if you want to know the truth,' she said abruptly. 'There is no point in tears for him, because he is dead. He did not have much life, and now it is over. Me, I am still here without him.'

'Go on.'

'Go on to what?'

'Well. Let's see. What happened to your brother? And to you? Why are you here, in this ship? And where are you sailing to?'

'That is many questions, Connie.'

'You don't have to answer. You can tell me to shut up, if you like. Or you could take them one at a time.'

There was a silence.

'I will be needing more whisky, to talk so much.'

'That can be arranged.'

Connie slid off the bed and opened the minibar again.

'My brother Niki, I told you about him, that time in the garden at Noah's house. He was two years older than me. Even when times were very bad, he was funny, and brave, and always company. Then, because my friend Yakov helped me, I was able to go to Tashkent, away from our stepfather and from our home in Bokhara, to study the dance. Niki, when he grew older, became more serious. He went to the *madrassah* with his friends, he read the Koran and went to the mosque. But he was not angry; Niki was never an extreme person. He believed only in each person's right to follow their beliefs, without threat from the government. But that is not easy to do, in our country.

'When I was away Niki went with his friends to stay in Andijan, which is in the far east of Uzbekistan, in the Fergana Valley. This is a very poor place, very traditional. There was an uprising there, a protest because some men were arrested for religious crimes. I am not sure if this was right or wrong, but the protest grew in Andijan until thousands of people were gathered in the square before the government houses. Then soldiers came and sealed off the square, and they started shooting.

'Many hundreds of men and women were killed. This was exactly one year and four months ago.'

Connie waited.

'I didn't hear from my brother, not a word. I feared for two months, then I went by bus to Fergana and in Andijan at last I found one of his friends who was not in prison or already dead. This boy told me that he had seen Niki that day. It was raining, the stones of the square were shining with water. Then the tanks and soldiers came, and the bullets. People were running and screaming and falling down, and then the stones shone with blood. He said to me that when he saw Niki he was lying on the ground and people were tripping over him and he didn't move. He was dead, this friend told me. I hope he did not suffer much.'

'Roxana, I'm so sorry. Was there any compensation, or a trial, or an official inquiry?'

She waved her hand. 'This uprising was said to be a crime of extremist people who were unlawfully trying to create a state for Islam in Fergana. That is the way it is, in my country. It is sad, and life there is hard for many of us. But there are also beautiful places and good people, I have not forgotten that.

'Without Niki, there was no reason left for me to stay. My stepfather Leonid is a bad man. But Yakov, who was my mother's good friend, and who has some care for me too . . . he helped me to get a passport, and a visa from the British embassy to come to England for a tourist visit. So here I am, and now I will be a new Roxana. Since I have luckily not drowned in the sea, after all.'

'Was it Yakov who helped you with the dance studies and taught you to speak English so well?'

'Yes.'

'He must be a good man. Is he still in Uzbekistan?'

'In Bokhara. He is like men are, you know. Some good parts, some bad. I have not always done the best things in my life, Connie, but I have done what it seemed needful to do. And I am glad that you think my English is good. I try hard.'

'Your English is excellent. You know – if I can do anything to help you, I will.'

'You have let me stay in your home, that's quite enough. I am saving all my money and soon I'll have an apartment of my own.'

'Soon you will be ruling the world,' Connie murmured, only half-joking. She was wondering what Noah's long-term chances were with this girl of his.

'I hope so. So that's my life,' Roxana smiled. 'Not much like yours. Your life is *beautiful*.'

Connie considered. In most of the ways she could bring to mind, compared with what Roxana had actually described and the likely history behind that, it was true. Her life was enviable.

'Yes,' she agreed. 'In some ways. Although like most people's lives, probably, it feels different inside from the way it looks.'

'Tell me one thing. Why do you not have a husband?'

Connie took a mouthful of her drink. 'Never met the right man,' she said lightly.

Roxana gave her a hard look. 'How can that be right? You are pretty and you are rich, and you are a

309

good person. If I was a man I would ask you to marry me right now.'

'Thank you. But if you were a man, I would also have to want to marry you. It takes two to make that decision, doesn't it?'

'Yes, you are right.' There was a pause. 'Noah told me, you and his mother are not real sisters.'

'Oh yes, we're sisters. Not by blood, but we're sisters just the same. I am only just realising it, but our childhood together made us that. There are times in my life that only Jeanette remembers, and times in hers that only I do.'

Connie was surprised by the speed and ease with which she made this admission, but there was no doubt in her mind that it was the truth. Even though she and Jeanette had never shared even a single hour of drink and talk like this one.

'Me and Niki, too. When you lose that person, and your memories, it is like a death of part of you.'

I should be with Jeanette right now, Connie thought. That's where I belong.

'Noah said to me that it is difficult in your family, for years you did not see him and Mr and Mrs Bunting.'

'Did he say that? And did he tell you why?'

'In about one word only.'

'That was a bit indiscreet of him.'

'Maybe. But,' she puffed out a breath, 'I'm a stranger. What do I matter?'

'It all happened a long time ago,' Connie mused. And it might just as well have been yesterday, she thought.

She closed her eyes and let her mind wander. She was drowsy, and the din of the wind and waves had become soothing.

'Shall we try to sleep for a bit?' she murmured. When she turned her head on the pillow, she saw that Roxana had already drifted off.

It was daylight when she woke again. Roxana was still asleep, lying on her side with the bunched pillow creasing her cheek. She looked very young. Connie slid out from under the bedclothes, taking care not to disturb her. With an awkward, motherly gesture she pulled the covers up over the girl's shoulders.

When she came out of the bathroom, showered and dressed, Roxana was up and gazing out of the window.

'Look,' she said. Huge, glassy waves were driving against the sea wall and occasionally breaking over into the road. A delivery van crawled past, sending up grey plumes of seawater. It had stopped raining, and there were streaks of brightness showing in the fleecy sky. 'Let's go out.'

'You want to risk it again?'

'Of course I want to, before we have to go back to London.'

The pub's breakfast room was heavy with the smell of frying. Connie thought that when Roxana had seen enough of the sea they might try to find a coffee place. They went out into the salt air and ran along the road beside the sea wall, listening for the warning thump of the biggest waves and then dodging the spray that came over the wall. Roxana was radiant with exhilaration.

Ahead of them stood the lifeboat station. There was a knot of cars beside it, men in orange oilskins and a scramble of other people. Connie pointed and shouted.

'I think they might be going to launch the lifeboat.'

'What is this?'

In the shelter of a sea-front kiosk they stood to watch. There was a whine of power winches and the high prow of the boat emerged from the station and rocked above the short slipway. It dipped forwards, gathered momentum and crashed into the sea, sending up a double arc of water almost as high as the mast. It wallowed dangerously and then as the propellers bit the water it corkscrewed forwards. The orange blobs of the crewmen swarmed on the heaving deck.

Roxana's eyes were completely round.

A man in chest-waders passed by. Connie asked him what was happening.

'Trawler with engine trouble. They're going to take the crew off.'

'What?' Roxana repeated. Connie told her what the lifeboat did and she shook her head in amazement.

'I think these brave men must be paid a lot of money.' The boat was breasting the huge waves, heading straight out to sea.

'No, it's voluntary. They do it for nothing.'

'My God,' Roxana breathed. 'My God.'

They watched it go.

'I think I'm ready for a cup of coffee,' Connie said firmly, once it was out at sea. She steered Roxana into the town. Shaking the drops of spray off their hair, they opened the door of a new coffee shop.

There were only two other customers, sitting knee to knee at a corner table away from the big windows that overlooked the street. Connie glanced at them, and then stopped in her tracks.

It was Angela with Rayner Ingram.

There was no way that either pair could pretend not to notice the other, although Angela and Rayner would clearly have preferred it.

'Ange, hello,' Connie called, trying to inject sympathy and apology into her smile. Angela looked as if she might have been crying. It was clear that they had been arguing.

'*Connie?* I mean, what are the chances of this happening? Rayner and I are . . . up here scouting locations for a shoot.'

'Why don't you join us?' Rayner drawled. He hooked a chair forwards.

Connie said, because there was no alternative, 'Well, for a quick coffee. We've just been watching the lifeboat go out. This is Roxana, she's my nephew's girlfriend and she's staying with me at the flat while she's working in London.'

'Hi,' Roxana said. Rayner looked at her as she folded herself into a chair.

They ordered breakfast. Angela put on a pair of glasses with tinted lenses and with her little finger surreptitiously smeared some coloured gloss on her lips. Chiming in together, Connie and Angela told Roxana about the Bali shoot. Adopting her enforced-contact-with-a-highly-contagious-disease face, Angela said she had been doing some more work with Tara. Rayner curled his arm over to reach the back of his head and raked his hair with his fingers.

'You did well out there, working with that bunch,' he told Angela, and her tense expression softened at the compliment. He added to Connie, 'The commercials turned out a treat, considering the problems we had. The bank loved them. Blinding music, by the way. Awards material, no question.'

'Thank you, Rayner.'

Roxana watched and listened. Connie could feel the force-field of her concentration on these new people.

'What are you doing in London?' Angela asked in her friendly way.

Quickly Roxana answered, 'I am going to study, English and business. I have some part-time work, not very interesting, and Connie is very kind to let me stay with her for now. I am from Uzbekistan.'

'I thought you might be Russian,' Rayner put in. He stirred his coffee and raised one eyebrow as he drank.

'My father was from Novosibirsk, my mother from Bokhara, where I was born. I speak Russian, of course.'

'We're just setting up some work in St Petersburg. It's not the easiest location to shoot in,' Rayner sighed.

'You have to know the people,' Roxana smiled. 'I do not mean the people individually, of course, but I think no one from the West knows how a Russian thinks. The only person who does is another Russian.'

Connie waited, wondering if Roxana was now going to ask for a job, and if so how she would go about it. But all she did was bite into a triangle of toast and smile again. 'It is more interesting to be in England. Yesterday, for example, was the first time in my life I saw the sea. And I almost drowned. Connie saved me.'

Rayner's eyebrow flicked again. Angela wanted to hear what had happened so Connie told them, relating it as a comedy rather than a drama. Roxana kept chipping in with contradictions, making it sound as though Connie had hauled her from the jaws of death. Angela laughed. She was enjoying herself enough to remove the shield of her glasses.

'Is this actually the same day you're both talking about?'

'Oh, yes. I was there,' Roxana insisted.

Rayner turned his chair a little aside to take a call on

314

his BlackBerry, then began checking his messages. Breakfast was clearly over.

'We're heading back to London today,' Connie said.

'But I would like to know first that the lifeship has not sunk.'

Angela corrected Roxana, 'It's lifeboat. That's the first slip I've heard you make, though. Is your Russian as good as your English?'

'Much better. Russian and Uzbek, these are my own languages.'

Angela nodded thoughtfully. Rayner put away his mobile and looked at his watch.

'We're going to have to make a move. We've got a couple more locations to check out,' Angela said at once. She gathered up the papers and notes she had piled on the table. Connie wished she didn't always jump with such alacrity to do what Rayner wanted. 'Amazing to bump into you like this. I'll call you, Con. We'll have that movie night together.'

Rayner was ready to leave. He raised one hand in an all-purpose salute and settled his sunglasses on his nose. Angela was looking through her wallet. She found a card and handed it to Roxana.

'All set, Angie?' Rayner asked, as if she was keeping him waiting.

'Bye,' Angela said to both of them.

After they had gone, Roxana tucked the card away in her plastic zipper purse. 'Your film people are very interesting, I think.'

Back on the sea front beside the lifeboat station, they learned from the onlookers that the trawlermen had all been taken off. Connie said she didn't think they had time to stay to watch the boat come in again.

'I know,' Roxana sighed. 'We have work. Always the same story.'

But as they drove up the small hill that led out of the town, she begged Connie to stop for a moment. She scrambled out of the car and stood looking at the sea. In the distance the lifeboat could just be seen, pitching through the waves on the way back to the shore. Roxana stared at it, and sucked in a great gulp of the salt air, as if she were trying to fill her eyes and lungs and carry the coast away with her.

Once they were finally out of sight and sound of it, and the nacreous light was fading into flat grey over the fields, she shook her head and gave a deep sigh.

'Amazing. Totally amazing,' she sighed. 'Thank you for showing it to me.'

Connie noticed that she gave the pronouncement exactly the same upwards inflection as Angela would have done.

'I enjoyed myself more than I've done for ages,' Connie said with a smile, and it was the truth.

'How is Jeanette tonight?' Connie asked Bill on the phone that evening, once Roxana had gone off to work.

'Not very good,' he told her. 'She was practically transparent with exhaustion when I got her home. She went straight up to bed. I couldn't persuade her even to try to eat something. I don't see how she can go back tomorrow, although she insists that she will.'

'She wanted so much to prove she was still strong enough to do some work, didn't she?'

'Not to me, or Noah, or you.'

'To herself,' Connie said, stating the obvious. 'I'll be there tomorrow,' she promised.

'Have you been away?' Bill asked.

'Just one night, in Suffolk. I took Noah's Roxana, she wanted to see the sea and we ended up staying over. I'll tell you about it.'

'I'd like to hear.'

His voice in her ear was as warm as ever, and as familiar, but there was also a note of imprecision in it.

Everything else, all their history together, the joy and the long denial, now seemed compacted and whittled down to this single, brittle point of caring between them for Jeanette.

'Tomorrow,' Connie repeated softly.

* * *

Jeanette was sitting in her chair with a shawl round her shoulders. She was looking out into the garden, a green and buff expanse of fading leaves and grass now, with the evening sunlight slanting on spiders' webs. It was a moment before she sensed that Connie was there, but then she turned her head. Her eyes burned in their deep sockets.

– *I had to come home today after just two hours.*

'That must have been tough.'

– *I opened my files. I sat there. My head was useless. Everyone looked at me, then pretended not to. Full of sympathy. Embarrassed, as well. Other people's weakness is embarrassing, isn't it? I felt as if I was already dead.*

'No,' Connie tried to soothe her. 'You've just gone back there too early after the operation. Rest for another week or two, then see how you feel.'

Jeanette lifted her hand again. Connie was almost surprised that the light didn't shine through it.

– Too early. Too late. They overlap, don't they?

There was a new, mordant edge to her anger at what was overtaking her.

'Jeanette, try to be a bit patient. You're too harsh on yourself.'

Jeanette regarded her. Then she jerked her head.

– I will have to do something else. I can't just sit here. Waiting.

Bill brought in a bottle of wine and some glasses. From the slope of his shoulders Connie could see his despair.

'It's not waiting, Jan. It's being with us.'

There was a pause.

– Yes. Of course it is. You're right. I'm sorry.

Connie stared into the garden, not wanting to risk seeing the look that passed between the two of them. She felt her own spike of anger at the finality ahead.

'Here.'

Bill put a drink into her hand. Jeanette took hers, the finger of wine heavily diluted with water, and sipped at it. Her lipstick left a pink print on the rim of the glass, and Connie remembered the night before last with Roxana in the storm, when talking to another woman had seemed so easy.

It still wasn't easy to talk to Jeanette: their legacy still affected them.

Change that. It's not too late, Connie told herself.

'I think we should have a holiday, instead of worrying about plant taxonomy,' Bill said.

A glorious idea delivered itself to Connie.

'Why don't you both come out and stay with me in Bali?' As soon as the thought came to her she was longing to take Jeanette straight there, to the green wave. 'It's

318

beautiful, and it's always warm. My house is comfortable enough. There's a view from the veranda you could look at for ever.'

– *For ever?*

She met her sister's gaze.

She guessed Jeanette would be wondering about moving from her own safe realm into Connie's unknown one, and whether it would be risky to allow her sister and her husband to spend so much time together.

Then, just as clearly, Connie saw her dismiss the questions. They didn't matter any longer. Jeanette's face changed completely, flowering into a beam of excitement. She held out her hand towards Connie, and they matched their palms together. Affection seemed to flow like a current between them.

– *I'd like that so much.*

Then she remembered how weak she had become and turned to Bill.

– *Can I? Can we? Those pictures Connie showed us, remember? They were wonderful.*

Bill said, 'Of course we can. We'll go as soon as you want.'

It took a week to finalise the arrangements. Connie was to fly out first, to make the house ready, and Jeanette and Bill would follow her two days later.

The night before she left London, she spoke to Angela.

'Sounds a good idea, Connie. Bali will do your sister good.'

'I hope so. I think it will.'

'Email me, let me know how she is, and how you are.

By the way – did you know that your friend Roxana came into the office to see me?'

'No, I didn't know that.' They had hardly seen each other in the past week. Connie had been working, but she'd had the impression that Roxana was tactfully absent so as not to intrude on her.

'She turned up in reception and very politely but very insistently announced that she would wait there until I was free to see her.'

'Yes?'

'I had her into my office and she sat down and told me exactly how she wanted to help me with setting up this shoot in Russia. I made the point that we work with the Russian Film Institute, and that I deal with difficult foreign locations every day. But she insisted that she could make herself useful in reading between the lines. With the Russians, you have to appreciate the nuance, she said. *Nuance* was the word she actually used. I was fairly impressed, I can tell you.'

'That sounds like Roxana. So what's the deal?'

'I had to give in. I'm going to employ her informally for a few hours a week, on the phones, looking at the contracts, finding suppliers out there, that sort of thing. Twenty quid an hour, cash in hand.'

'Informally or otherwise, that's her entry into the film business. You know she'll probably be running the show within a couple of months?'

'Very likely,' Angela agreed. 'Who am I to stand in the way of ambition? Anyway, Rayner liked the look of her. There's one other thing, Con . . .'

'What's that?'

'When she came in she was wearing your Chloé suede jacket, or an identical version of it.'

'I expect it looked better on her than on me?'

'Oh, I wouldn't say that.'

They both laughed. 'Thanks, Ange.'

Connie was almost ready to leave for the airport when she heard Roxana moving about in her room. She opened her door as soon as Connie knocked, and beamed at her.

'Are you all prepared to go?'

'Yes, just about. I talked to Angela last night; I hear she's offered you a part-time job.'

'That's right. I am very lucky.' Roxana's face glowed. She looked very young and beautiful, Connie thought. 'And I owe thanks to you, Connie, yet another time.'

'I'm glad about the work. That's good news. But Angela also told me that when you went in to see her, you were wearing what looked like one of my jackets.'

Roxana stared, and then drew her lower lip between her teeth. Colour flooded into her face.

'I . . . I wanted very much not to – not to appear like a girl from Uzbekistan. I wanted to seem like a London girl.'

'I understand that. But you went into my room, and looked through my cupboards?'

And I did the same thing myself, Connie remembered. *The only real difference was that there was nothing among her few possessions to appeal to me.* She felt her own colour rising.

Roxana nodded unhappily. 'I wanted to be like you,' she whispered.

Like me? And who is that?

'You are yourself. Why do you want to be someone

else? To be Constance, or anyone? Why not be proud of being Roxana?'

Roxana still stared, with a light kindling in her eyes that seemed to indicate that she had never properly explored this question. She had just made the assumption. She shrugged, unwillingly.

'I have not always done good things.'

'Maybe you haven't always had the chance. You've had a hard life, up until now, haven't you?'

Roxana shrugged again.

Connie said quickly, 'You're going to stay here in my flat, while I'm in Bali with Noah's parents.'

'Please, if I can. Perhaps now you don't want . . .'

'I don't want to turn you out. I've got two homes, you have nowhere to live. But can I trust you, if you live here without me, to look after my home and respect my belongings?'

Roxana put out her hand, then drew it back again. 'Yes, yes, I promise.'

There was a moment when Connie stepped forward and Roxana began to duck away, almost as if she expected to be struck. Instead Connie put her arms round the girl. As she hugged her she felt the wary set of her shoulders, the taut line of her neck.

'All right,' she murmured. 'It's all right.'

Roxana's shoulders loosened. They held on to each other for another moment.

'How old were you when your mother died?' Connie asked.

'Nine. Niki was eleven. We stayed with Leonid, my stepfather. This was not what we chose, you know, but we had no other place where we could go.'

'Can you remember your mother?'

'Not so well. A little.'

Connie could guess, just from the touch of her, that Roxana hadn't known much mothering.

'I don't know who my real mother was.'

'No,' Roxana acknowledged.

The simplicity of her agreement reminded Connie: there it is. That's the truth. Now and always will be.

She dropped her arms. 'Oh, Lord. Look at the time. I've got to go or I'll miss the flight.'

Roxana stood back at once.

'Have a safe journey,' she said. 'I am sure it is very nice in Bali.'

'There are beaches. White sand and palm trees, even.'

'That will be good for Mrs Bunting. Myself, I prefer Suffolk.'

TWELVE

A tiny basket made from plaited coconut leaf and containing a few grains of red and white rice, a sliver of lime and a betel leaf lay on the veranda step. The thin white trail of smoke from a burning incense stick drifted in the still air.

Wayan Tupereme prayed for a moment after he had placed the offering. He waved his hand three times, to send the essence of the offering towards God, and then padded quietly down the path to his own house. The Englishwoman was back, and now she had guests staying with her. Putu, the taxi driver who had brought them up from Denpasar, was a relative of his wife's and she had heard from Putu's wife that the lady who had arrived was very sick.

Wayan was certain that a stay in his village would help to balance her again.

Connie had moved into the smaller bedroom in her house, to give Jeanette and Bill more space. When she woke up she had to open her eyes before she was able to work out where she was, and then the rooster in the nearest yard started crowing.

She got out of bed and wrapped herself in a sarong. The heat of the coming day was gathered in the corners of the room, waiting to reach out and envelop her. She padded across the bare floorboards to fold back the window shutters and immediately the early sun gilded the bare walls.

At first glance the veranda looked deserted. But then a tiny movement caught her eye. Jeanette was sitting in the rocking chair watching a cat-sized yellow-green lizard that was splayed on a corner of the decking, half-hidden by a fan of pleated leaves.

Connie slid open the screen door and stepped outside. The lizard blinked once, then flowed over the edge of the deck and vanished. Jeanette turned her head. When she saw Connie she pointed to where it had been a second earlier, chopping a bookends gesture with her two hands to indicate its size.

'I know. He's a big one. He lives under the boards. If I feel like some company, I feed him. He particularly likes ham, and cocktail olives.'

Jeanette smiled.

'How do you feel? Did you sleep?'

Connie was thinking that she looked a bit better than she had done yesterday, although that wasn't saying very much. When she had met them at the airport, Bill was pushing Jeanette in an airline wheelchair. Her face looked the colour and texture of tissue paper and she had seemed to lack the strength even to lift up her head.

'Bad journey,' Bill murmured.

'It's not far now,' Connie rallied them.

She was shocked. Jeanette looked so weak and defeated, she was afraid that she was going to die there in the midst of the airport's callous scramble of taxis and tour buses. She ordered their frightened driver to get them home, back to the village, as quickly and smoothly as he could.

And now, less than twenty hours later, Jeanette was

325

up, her hair was combed, and she had dressed in a shirt with kindly folds that hid her sharp bones.

– *Better. Thank you*, she answered. – *I was very tired*.

Connie could only admire the depth of her sister's resolve. However much pain she was in, however exhausted, if she wanted to get up she would somehow do it. She pulled a stool across and sat down next to her. They gazed out at the view.

Veils of mist were drawn upwards from the bends of the river. Diaphanous layers silvered the opposite wall of greenery and where the sun touched them droplets of moisture trapped in the fingers of the leaves twinkled with tiny points of light, as if the branches were hung with jewels. The palms on the farthest ridge were pale grey feathers.

Without taking her eyes off the line of sunlight as it slid down the side of the gorge, Jeanette let her head fall back against the cushions. Her arms dangled over the sides of the chair as if her hands were heavy weights. Her bare feet were planted flat, toes turned out.

Connie could hear the warring dogs and the buzz of traffic, splashing water from the spring and the screeches and chuckings of the various birds, but all Jeanette had was the vast green intricacy of the view, and the gentle pressure of heat and humidity.

– *Look at it*, she said. – *It's perfect. And it's so hot.*

Connie was solicitous at once. 'A breeze gets up later. Come inside for now. It's cooler. There's air-con, I'll turn it up.'

Jeanette shook her head. Her face and throat were lightly sheened with sweat.

– *I like it. I'm usually cold.*

'If you're sure.'

Connie thought that she must be all right. Jeanette's body looked heavy, as if her sore bones were softening.

A long moment passed, comfortably silent.

– *So many trees. I don't know half of them.*

'Neither do I. We'll get a book.'

– *Good idea.*

Another moment passed.

– *Connie?*

'Yes.'

– *I'm so happy we came.*

'I thought the journey was too much for you. I was angry with myself for having suggested you should come out here in the first place.'

Jeanette rolled her head and sighed.

– *I threw up all the way. The shame. I hate Bill to see me like that.*

Bill had told Connie that the motion of flight had disagreed with Jeanette almost from the moment of take-off. She hadn't been able to keep down even sips of water. He had wanted to stop the journey at Singapore, but Jeanette had insisted on making the connecting flight. – *I want to see Bali,* she'd said, and kept saying it.

– *But I'm all right now I'm here. In this place. It's more beautiful than I imagined.*

'I'm glad you're here,' Connie said.

Jeanette shot her a sudden glance.

– *It's a long way from Echo Street.*

The exotic walls of the gorge and the solid sunshine emphasised the physical distance, but Connie shook her head. 'Only in miles. Sitting here with you, I feel as if we could be back there.'

The steep stairs rising from the narrow hallway, the residue of damp left by Hilda's mopping, the piano and the line of photographs – Jeanette with Connie propped on her knee, Jeanette in her graduation gown – shapes, smells, ghosts. The architecture of these memories felt as real between them as the deck beneath their feet.

There was another glance.

– *Bad or not bad?*

Connie said, 'Neither. Or both. It's what connects us. Echo Street.'

The last time they had been there together, four years ago now, the rooms were being emptied. Two sweating men hoisted the piano onto a wheeled trolley and rolled it away. Dusty rectangles showed on the bare walls, and the living-room carpet was dimpled with brown-rimmed hollows where the same furniture had stood in the same places for more than thirty years.

That was the day they discovered the old cardboard box, the one with *Fray Bentos* printed on the sides in rubbed blue lettering and sealed with packing tape that had turned brittle with age.

That was the day when they had their last, seemingly irrevocable quarrel.

The last time they communicated with each other, until Jeanette emailed to tell her sister that she was dying.

Connie bowed her head. The arches of her sister's feet were netted with blue veins and the five tendons fanned out like sash cords. The toes were absolutely white, bloodless, the nails as chalky as if they belonged already to a dead woman. She pulled her stool closer and lifted the feet into her lap. She began to massage them, running her thumbs over the ridges and feeling them slide away from the pressure, cupping the heels and squeezing the tired ligaments, as if she could rub the life back just by the force of her will and the warmth of her own flesh.

After a moment Jeanette sighed, and her eyes closed.

That was how Bill found them, Jeanette fallen into a doze with her mouth slightly open and Connie with her head down, stroking her feet.

* * *

– *What do you do here?* Jeanette asked later. – *Every day?*

Connie had brought out a bowl of salad and a dish of mango and guava and they ate the simple meal at the table drawn into the deepest shade at the back of the veranda, from where the afternoon sun striking two yards away was as powerful as a blow.

Bill sat in the rattan chair next to Jeanette's rocker, checking her from time to time with a glance, but otherwise he was almost silent. Connie had read from the lines in his face precisely how exhausted with nursing and perpetual anxiety he was. To be so close to him, to know his whereabouts and what he was doing every hour, made her skin feel slightly raw. Even in the heat, goose bumps prickled on her arms.

She answered brightly, 'What do I do with my time? You wouldn't believe how busy it can be here. And that's when I'm not working. When I've got a commission I have to lock myself away or it would never get done. There's my orchestra, for instance. That's Tuesdays, for rehearsal. Sometimes we put on a performance. There are other *gamelan* concerts, and shadow plays and temple festivals to go to. On a normal day if I just call in to the market in the village, it can take half a morning by the time I've greeted everyone I know and asked after the children and grandchildren. I visit my neighbours, the Balinese ones, and they visit me, on a strict turn-by-turn basis.

That's not to mention the Europeans, their drinks parties and swimming-pool barbecues and gallery openings . . .'

Bill said, 'That's busy.'

Connie thought, Yes. I am busy, because I need to be. It's the life I've made for myself.

She smiled at him. She wanted him to know she had her place in the village. She was not an object for concern, and she was certainly not to be pitied.

'Take today. There's an invitation to go to my neighbour's house, just over here.' She pointed to the thick palm hedge that separated her garden from Wayan Tupereme's house compound. 'Wayan and his family have a big celebration coming soon, and today's party is in preparation for that. All his relatives, the women especially, are coming to the house to help to prepare offerings for the ceremony. The men will be starting to build a roof to provide shade on the day itself. There's a lot of work to be done, but it's a social event too.'

Connie wondered if now was the right time to explain that the big event that was being so elaborately prepared for was the cremation of Wayan's father. The old man had died more than a year ago and was buried in the village cemetery. The most auspicious day had been fixed on months ago, giving the best possible circumstances for the dead man's *atman*, his immortal soul, to continue on its journey to heaven.

She added quickly, 'You're both invited too, of course, as my family. Wayan made a special call, to insist on that. But you are tired . . .'

Jeanette sat up.

– *I would like to go to the party. Very much.*

Her eagerness had a feverish glitter. Bill leaned forward to touch her arm, but she waved off the restraint.

– *Why not? We are here. If you will take us, Connie?*

Connie nodded. 'Of course. And they will all want to meet you. They are very curious, always, about new people.'

Jeanette touched her fingers to her mouth in a question, and Connie wondered how she should answer it.

She picked an orchid flower from the vase on the table and placed it in a triangle with her water glass and a spoon. This was a difficult concept to sign, but she would do the best she could.

'In Bali, everything is a matter of balance. Each living or inanimate thing is part of an ordered universe, each stands in relation to every other. This is called *dharma*, and our personal actions or *karma* must harmonise with our duty to *dharma*. To do this, Balinese Hindus try always to look at the world with regard for others, not themselves. To be old here is a matter for reverence. A new baby is pure and treated almost as a god. For a person to be deaf, or lame, or a stranger, this is also part of the balance of the universe. If a Balinese does not accept these differences, and acknowledge the grace in them, he causes disorder. Or *adharma*.'

Jeanette reached forward to stroke the flexed and velvety spotted petals of the orchid.

Slowly she mouthed the words.

– Dharma. *Balance.*

Bill sat with his hand shading his eyes.

– *What time?* Jeanette asked.

'We should be there at about five o'clock. Once the day starts to cool down, but before it gets dark,' Connie told her.

Jeanette took the orchid and tucked it behind her ear. It lent her a look of reckless gaiety.

– I will lie down for an hour.

Bill edged back his chair. 'I'll come with you,' he said at once.

Jeanette shook her head.

– Stay here with Connie.

Connie followed her into the bedroom. The shutters were closed and the ceiling fan stirred a draught of cool air.

'Is there anything you need?' she asked, as Jeanette lay down in the dimness. The flower glimmered against her temple.

Jeanette smiled.

– Dharma, she repeated.

Connie left her to sleep.

Bill had carried the plates and glasses into the kitchen. He was opening cupboard doors to find the right place to put things away, and keeping his face averted. Without needing to see, Connie knew the depth of pain in his eyes.

'Those go in there,' she pointed.

'Thanks. And these?'

'In the drawer.'

She was thinking about the kitchen in the Buntings' house in Surrey and the way that the familiarity of their domestic routine, of their marriage itself, was printed all through it. Here in her own kitchen it would be difficult, after he had gone home again. She would look at this handle, that cup, and remember how he had touched them. He had been here, moving around in her small and self-contained universe, and from now on she would be obliged always to see the shape of him printed in the old rattan chair, and to direct herself away from the image of his long body curved into the yield of her mattress.

It was only a matter of weeks since the invasion of the film team, and it was strange now to remember how apprehensive she had been about this disturbance to her ordered life. In the end Angela and Rayner and the others had come and gone, bringing London to the village and then bearing it away again, and had left barely a trace of themselves except that the villagers still talked about the visit of the movie people.

It would not happen like that with Jeanette and Bill. Their impact on the village would be negligible, but for her everything would be changed.

Connie blinked. When she opened her eyes he was still there.

Bill collected up the salad trimmings and rinsed the sink, in the practised way that showed how he had learned to be cook and cleaner in the past few months.

The light surrounding them seemed to have turned very pale and crystalline.

She would remember exactly how he scraped the chopping board clean and rinsed it, and the way he had to stoop a little to do these tasks because the counter was too low for him.

What would Bill do when Jeanette was gone?

It seemed impertinent, almost, to speculate about his grief.

What will *I* do? Connie wondered. A stab of pure pain made her gasp.

Bill folded a cloth. His movements were very slow, indicating that he was experiencing some difficulty that she could only guess at. She resisted the impulse to touch him for comfort's sake.

It dawned on her that she had barely thought about *afterwards*. All her concentration had been on the progress of the disease, on Jeanette, and on the business of dying and death. Afterwards remained a vacuum.

The only certainty was that it would not hold out any prospect for herself and Bill. That was implicit in *before*.

'Thank you. That's all done,' she smiled.

'It didn't take long,' he said, reflecting her own neutrality back at her.

Connie went into her room. There was still an hour or so before it would be time to go to Wayan's house.

'I should explain,' Connie said, 'before we go.'

Bill and Jeanette were ready. Jeanette had made up her face. They looked expectantly at Connie.

'This evening marks the beginning of the send-off for my neighbour Wayan's father. The cremation itself is next week, on the most auspicious day.'

Bill's thumb moved to the corner of his mouth.

'We're going to a funeral? A sort of *wake*?'

'Yes. And no, in fact. Of course it is a funeral and it's a sad occasion because the family and friends are saying a final goodbye, but the old man died quite a long time ago.'

Jeanette was following the explanation carefully.

– *How long ago?*

There was no point in being evasive. The arrangements were according to Balinese custom, and Bill and Jeanette might as well hear about it now.

'A little more than a year. A big, grand cremation costs a lot of money for the family, and they have to save up for it as well as wait for the auspicious date in the calendar. So the body is temporarily buried, and then when everything is ready they dig it up again in order to cremate it and set the spirit free. It tends to be a wild party.'

Jeanette started to laugh. The surprising sound of it bubbled out of her throat.

– *I have to see this, don't I?*

Outside Wayan's house, scooters and parked cars lined the narrow lane, and dozens of pairs of sandals and shoes were lined up at the step. The *bale*, the house pavilion, was overflowing with people. The bamboo pillars that supported the palm-leaf roof were decorated with strips of coloured cloth and the roof itself was swathed in more folds of colour. Most of the men wore white or crimson head-cloths and bright sarongs. The women's long skirts were intricate *ikat* fabrics and frangipani and hibiscus blossoms were plaited in their hair. Children in their best clothes chased and played between the adults' legs. The effect was of a brilliant moving sea of patterns and faces and smiles.

As the visitors passed through the outer gate into the open compound, Wayan and his wife came forward to greet them. Connie made the introductions, formally, in polite Balinese. Dayu, Wayan's diminutive wife, placed her hands together and bowed to each of them in turn.

'You are welcome,' she said in English. 'Please come to join us.'

The guests were crowding towards the family temple, placed in the most sacred corner of the compound and separated from it by a gate. Connie bowed her head to the nearest people she recognised in the throng.

A priest in white robes was preparing to make the offerings.

Chairs were ranged in a loose row for those who needed them, and without drawing attention to it Wayan made sure that Jeanette found her way to one. The priest lifted a small bronze bell and rang it. At once the talk and laughter died away.

A small group of *gamelan* musicians were gathered with their instruments in the inner enclosure. One of them struck a long, shivering gong note. It resonated in the warm, damp air. The daylight was fading, and the guttural boom of the first frogs could be heard against the brittle rasp of crickets and trills from birds hidden in the foliage. Thick wafts of incense rose through the leaves and coloured cloth hangings and twisted into the smoky evening sky.

The musicians began to play. It was sombre temple music, the metallophones with their bamboo resonators laying down a skeletal rhythm that was filled in with the drums and gong-chimes. Connie listened with close attention.

The priest was chanting. He lifted and placed the offerings in turn, silver plates of rice cakes garlanded with flowers and bark-frilled bamboo skewers of fruit. The guests mumbled or chanted their prayers, holding a blossom between their fingers and pressing folded thumbs to their foreheads. The priest's attendant came through the crowd with a clay jug of *tirta*, the holy water. Bill was somewhere behind Connie in the crowd, but she watched Jeanette observing and copying her neighbours. When Jeanette's turn came she held out her cupped palm for the water as the others did, sipped three times at it, then dripped the remainder over her hair. She took a pinch of sticky rice too, and following the grandmother beside her she pressed a few grains to her forehead and temples.

The tempo of the music changed. It rippled now, faster, like running water with a silvery thread in it.

The prayers were over and people were turning away,

laughing and gossiping again. Connie was struck, as she always was, by the seamless way that spiritual and secular life were woven together in the rituals of the village.

A small group of women had been in one of the enclosed rooms during the prayers. Now they came out, carrying huge bowls of rice and baskets of coconut leaves. The working part of the evening was about to begin. In the centre of a knot of young girls, Connie spotted Dewi. Her baby son was wrapped in a sky-blue shawl and tied against her, his smooth brown head just visible.

'Dewi,' Connie smiled and waved.

The girl flashed a smile in return and ducked through the crowd towards her. Jeanette reached Connie's side at the same time. The grains of rice were still glued to her tissue-thin skin.

'This is my friend, Dewi. She is Wayan and Dayu's daughter. And this is their grandson,' Connie told her. The unfamiliar Balinese names took time to sign and Dewi waited, her bright eyes on Jeanette.

'My sister,' Connie completed the introduction. Dewi was too polite to show her surprise at the difference in their looks. She made her graceful bow, and Jeanette's fingers fluttered close to the baby's head.

Beautiful, her gesture said, and Dewi smiled proudly. She gestured in return, *Would you like to hold him?*

Jeanette opened her arms. One hand cupped the baby's head, the other supported his tiny weight against her breast. She breathed in the scent of him and touched her lips to his gleaming cheek.

'He's a strong boy,' Connie said to Dewi.

'Oh, yes. Like his father,' the girl beamed.

There were more people to greet. Wayan's cousin Kadek from the village store came to touch her hand.

'Good evening, *Ibu* Connie.'

Kadek was a relatively wealthy man. He and his brothers and all the other cousins would be helping to pay for the cremation. Connie had heard that three other families would also be sending off their relatives during the same ceremony. It was not unusual for people to club together to meet the heavy costs.

The women were settling at tables with the bowls of rice and coconut leaves spread between them. Connie talked to Dayu, and when Jeanette finally parted with the warm bundle of baby she joined them. Her face was faintly coloured under her make-up. She rocked her empty arms.

– *That baby. The scent they have. The hollow at the back of his neck. I wish Noah had a son.*

'Maybe he and Roxana will.'

– *Not in my time.*

Jeanette's face was smooth. Connie could see no bitterness or anger in it now.

'He will some day,' Connie murmured.

– *I wish he could see this, too. The colours. The people. He would love this place.*

Bill and Jeanette and Connie herself had all suggested to Noah that he should come out to Bali with them. But Noah had replied that he was busy at work and with Roxana, and that in any case his parents should take the opportunity to enjoy some uninterrupted time with Connie. Bill had confided to Connie that he hadn't had the heart to push the suggestion any harder. He didn't think Noah had acknowledged to himself how little time there was left.

Jeanette leaned closer.

– *Will you do something for me?*

'Of course,' Connie said.

– *If. When. Will you be a grandmother in my place?*

Connie took a breath. 'Yes. I promise. Whatever Noah wants.'

Composedly, Jeanette nodded her head.

– *Good. Thank you.*

All round them, women were working. Some of them were scooping up handfuls of rice, coloured bright pink or yellow or pistachio green, and dextrously moulding them into animal shapes. These would be left to dry, and then incorporated into the high tiers of offerings on cremation day. Others were weaving strips of tough palm leaf into baskets. Their fingers flashed, folding and turning and skewering with sharp slivers of bamboo. They talked while they worked, hardly even glancing downwards as the intricate baskets took shape. The musicians played sweet, liquid music over the frog chorus.

Connie had been to one class, aimed at Westerners living in the village, on how to fold the simple triangular baskets used for daily offerings.

'Shall we have a go?' she said now. 'Rice pigs or palm baskets?'

Dayu beamed her encouragement and gave them both a fistful of leaves. The women moved up on the benches, patting a free space among them. Connie and Jeanette took their places and spread out the leaves between them.

'Hold like this. In and out.' Immediately Connie's leaf split, while Jeanette's splayed into its fibrous components and all the women broke into peals of laughter.

Connie laughed too. 'Wait. You fold, I'll stick the skewer in.'

She and Jeanette began to work, clumsily, in tandem.

It was almost dark now, and the lights in the compound had come on. Some of the men were carrying in bales of leaves that would provide temporary thatch for the open compound. Others were putting up bamboo poles to support the new roof or carry long strings of lights. Connie saw Bill in the middle of one group. He stood head and shoulders taller than the other men, and they were using him as a prop to hold up a pole with one hand and run up a length of cable with the other. There was the usual village cacophony of waving and shouting and running about as the work progressed, with Wayan and Kadek directing the business. Bill pointed and gestured at another loop of cable, indicating where it should be fixed. He was good at fitting in. It was just one of the reasons why Connie loved him.

Between them, she and Jeanette managed one misshapen, ragged basket with a stray corner of palm leaf sticking out like the ear of a lame dog. Dewi held it up and the women giggled behind their hands, the flowers nodding in their hair. Dayu had left the tables to oversee another cohort of women in the kitchen, preparing food for the workers, and now they began to emerge with bowls heaped with hot food. It was important for the prestige of the dead man that everything should be of the best quality, and laid on in abundance. The musicians abandoned their instruments and the men put down their tools and cables. The women served them with big, steaming platefuls. The noise of talk and laughter grew louder. Children squirmed away from the attention of the adults, and some of them took up the musicians' mallets and began picking tunes from the percussion instruments. A tiny, plump child was patting out a rhythm on one of the drums.

Someone tapped Connie on the shoulder. She turned round to see Ketut.

'Connie, will you play? I think we should not let the people eat without music to help their digestion.'

She beamed at him. 'Ketut, I didn't see you in this crowd. You're asking me to play one of my drum pieces? I think that baby's doing better than I could.'

'You have not been practising. We have missed you. You have been in London, I think?'

'Yes, I have. Jeanette, this is Ketut, my friend and music teacher. Ketut, my sister.'

He bowed. 'You have heard Connie play Balinese music?'

'Jeanette is deaf, Ketut.'

Ketut bowed again in calm acknowledgement.

– *I would like to see you play*, Jeanette indicated. Connie passed this on to Ketut, who lifted his hand.

'This shall happen. Connie, we have enough friends here to make some music while this ensemble is enjoying the food. Wait one moment, please.'

'What have you done?' she sighed to Jeanette.

Ketut darted off through the crowd. He whispered to several people and persuasively patted their arms. A minute later Connie was propelled to the corner where the instruments were set up. An impromptu, giggling group of musicians closed round her. She was relieved to see that she knew most of them from her regular ensemble. Ketut marshalled them into position.

'Connie, you will play . . .'

'Please, Ketut, not the *kempli*.'

The horizontal gong was the metronome of the group, providing the even beats that underpinned the texture of the music and incorporated the constant changes of tempo.

'Perhaps not this evening. Maybe tonight you will take the *wadon*.'

Connie recoiled. This was even harder. The female drum was usually the leader of the ensemble, playing learned patterns that linked to the gong structures but which also had to be built up with considerable personal improvisation.

The other musicians were taking up their mallets and Ketut positioned himself in front of his regular instrument, the large gong. A couple of shy young women with frangipani blossoms in their hair took the paired cymbals. The crowd was still eating and chatting, but they were also waiting to see how the new performers would measure up.

It was too late to back out. Connie swallowed hard.

Ketut bent solemnly in front of his big gong. He took a pinch of rice and laid it on the floor beside the gong stand. The stand was carved in the shape of a giant tortoise, on which according to Balinese mythology the entire world rests. An offering to the spirit of the gong would ensure a harmonious performance.

A second of quiet gathered, broken only by the scrape of frogs and crickets.

Then Ketut struck a single note. The powerful reverberation sailed out over the walls of the compound and slowly faded away into the darkness. He gave Connie the conductor's bow of introduction; she obediently settled the drum on its brocaded cushion on her lap and lifted her head.

You play with your head high and your heart open, Ketut always told her.

Jeanette was sitting in the chair from which she had watched the prayers. Connie didn't try to look deeper into the crowd for a glimpse of Bill.

She struck the drum head with the flat of her left hand, and then another beat with the thumb of her right. She had begun with the certainty that she would forget the pattern of this sequence but now, miraculously, the first notes came back to her. Facing her was Bagus, a thin, bespectacled schoolteacher, who had taken the *lanang*, the male drum. His beats interlocked with hers and the metallophones and the gongs and cymbals fell into place, each pair of instruments tuned slightly apart so that the music breathed in and out, shimmering like rain caught in sunlight. The musicians' dark heads dipped and their bodies swayed as the pulsing rhythms swelled and diminished.

Some little girls edged forwards and began to dance, tugging their mothers with them. The women extended their arms, the hands flexed and the fingers eloquently raised. The bright threads in their clothes shone as they circled their hips and the children wove between them. A flutter of laughter and appreciation ran through the crowd.

Connie let herself float away into the music. The pattern of drum beats, *kap pek kap pek kum pung kum pung*, that had started as a rigid imperative suddenly loosened its hold and turned into a platform from which her own pattern launched itself, gathered momentum and soared away. Bagus's drumming was a sinuous thread, confidently rising and knitting with hers, seeming to know where she was heading before she led him there. Like the best of lovers, Connie would have thought, if she had not been too caught up in the music itself. The bronze and bamboo instruments elaborated the melody, all the time like waves breaking over the sonorous rock of the great gong. As the splash of the cymbals rose to her lead she knew for sure, here and now, what belonging meant.

The music reached a crescendo with a blare of bronze, and then the sequence unravelled again, simplifying itself down to the last drum beats, *kap pek kum pung de tut kum pung*.

The dancers let their arms fall to their sides. Laughing with exhilaration and the pure pleasure of being part of the music, Connie looked up at last. She saw Bill at the back of the crowd, his eyes fixed on her.

Ketut struck the last thrilling gong note.

The piece had been a short and simple one, but Wayan and Dayu's guests and even the regular musicians were appreciative. Ketut's ensemble all smiled at each other, and Connie formally shook hands with Bagus. Her hair was glued to her forehead and her shirt was damp against her back.

'It was fairly good. You were a little stiff,' Ketut said judiciously. 'You should try to be more fluid in the arms, perhaps.'

'I will try,' Connie promised.

Jeanette was clapping her hands, and her eyes shone.

– *How beautiful and graceful. I wish I could have heard it, but I felt the rhythm in here.* She tapped her chest with the flat of her hand.

Bill appeared beside them. Connie pushed her damp hair back from her forehead and grinned at him.

'That', he said simply, 'was the best music I've ever heard.'

'Oh, come on.'

'It was,' he insisted.

Jeanette nodded in agreement and as she sat between them Connie felt a wave of pride and happiness. Dayu brought a carved wooden dish of fruit and laid it in front of them. The proper *gamelan* players were taking their seats again.

It was late when the three of them made their way back to Connie's house.

Bill opened the window onto the veranda and the night's noises flooded into the room on warm, scented, moist air.

'Do those frogs ever pipe down?' he groaned.

Connie shook her head.

Jeanette spread her hands in a gesture of satisfaction, and all three of them laughed.

It was raining.

Fat raindrops slapped on the broad leaves, trickled from the fronds of the roof and drummed on bamboo pipes. The rush of water in stone drainage channels drowned out all the other island noises. For four days it had been thundery, and in the late afternoons swollen masses of cloud had sailed over the gorge and the rice paddies and blotted out the pale-blue cone of Mount Agung. Now the rain had finally come.

Jeanette spent most of the days reclining in the rocker. She studied the book of trees that Connie had brought back from the European bookshop in the village. Connie usually sat with her, while Bill sometimes went out with Wayan and his brothers and cousins to work on the building of the *wadah*. This was a bamboo cremation tower, with the tortoise and two dragon-snakes at the bottom, representing the universe. Successive tiers rose to a height of thirty feet, to a little pagoda that stood for heaven. It was a big construction job. Bill's practical contribution was welcomed.

When it was ready the huge structure, with a symbol of the old man's body in the *bale* within it, would be carried by his male descendants through the village to the cremation ground.

The hammering and sawing had been audible all day but the rain stopped the work. Connie and Jeanette sat and looked out through a curtain of falling water. The gorge swam with mist, and a miasma of damp rose between the planks beneath their feet.

– *Is it often like this?*

'It rains sometimes, yes.'

Jeanette rocked gently.

– *It takes a long time. Getting ready for the cremation.*

'Months.'

– *I like that. The proper rituals. Everyone doing their part.*

'It's seen as part of a natural cycle. Grief and the work going on. The body is only a container. The better the ceremony, the more likely that the spirit eventually becomes one of the deified ancestors.'

Jeanette's head fell back. Connie was used to the way she would suddenly fall asleep, and then wake up and continue talking as if no interval had passed. But instead of drifting into a doze she said,

– *I didn't know it took so long just to die.*

'Does it seem so long?' Connie kept looking at her sister's hands.

– *Yes. I thought death came quick in the Thorne family.*

'It seemed that way,' Connie agreed.

She had been away with Seb.

Sébastian Bourret with the Sydney Symphony had been a big event in Hobart, Tasmania. After the series of concerts they had gone up for a few days' holiday in Cradle Mountain Park. It was cold, but fine clear weather. Seb had been irritable after the rehearsals and performances, and had wanted to get as far away from the music world as he could. On the spur of the moment they rented a motorhome intended for backpackers, and drove out into the park wilderness. For five days Seb fished in the lakes while Connie read, and in the evenings she grilled the fish he caught over an open fire. They went for walks and spoke to no one, and it had been an unusual interlude in their lives. Connie thought that they were happy, so far away from memories and the pull of desire.

On their way back through Hobart, Seb picked up a message that was waiting for him.

He studied it for a moment, then turned to Connie.

'It's for you,' he said quietly. 'I'm afraid it's bad news.'

Bill and Jeanette had failed to reach her in London or in Sydney, and as a last resort had tried Seb's management company.

Connie learned that her adopted mother had died one night, alone at Echo Street, of a cerebral haemorrhage. The funeral was taking place more or less as she stood trying to take in the news on the opposite side of the world.

'Hilda is dead,' Connie repeated, disbelieving.

Seb took Connie in his arms to comfort her. 'I'm so sorry,' he said.

Connie didn't cry, but her eyes burned and she felt that there was a tourniquet around her throat, coming close to strangling her. In a voice quite unlike her own she whispered, 'I never felt that she was my mother, even when I didn't know that she wasn't. I don't think she ever convinced herself that I could be her daughter. It makes it harder to believe that she's gone, because now it's too late.'

'Does her death make you think of your natural mother?'

'Yes,' Connie said.

The funeral was over; there was no reason to hurry home to London.

When she did get back, Jeanette was already clearing out the house in Echo Street before selling it.

Jeanette opened the door to her. The smell of the old house flooded into Connie's face. The past was like a vapour, spiralling into the chambers of her head. Behind Jeanette the stairs that had once seemed to rear like a cliff-face now just looked awkwardly narrow and steep. A fragment of the old red-curdled lino was revealed again where the more recent carpet had been taken up. They stood and looked at each other.

– *You're here.*

'I would have come before now, Jeanette. You know I would. Given the chance.'

– *I couldn't postpone the funeral until you turned up.*

'That was your decision to make, of course.'

Two overalled men edged out of the kitchen doorway, hauling Hilda's old refrigerator between them. In the confined hallway Connie and Jeanette had to flatten themselves against the wall. Connie remembered the day in 1969 when they moved into the house, when Tony and another set of removals men had carried in their belongings from the old flat and the new rooms had seemed big enough to echo with emptiness. The memories nudged against her, years packed on years, jostling for her attention. She could hear piano music. *Für Elise*, picked out by small fingers.

To get out of the way of the removers she angled past Jeanette and climbed the stairs.

Her old bedroom was already empty. Noah slept there when he stayed with his grandmother, and a couple of crumpled pages from a boys' comic lay on the floor. The corner cupboard stood open. Connie rested her fingers on the old-fashioned latch that was swollen with a teardrop of gloss paint, trying to recall exactly why the musty enclosed space had frightened her so badly.

Jeanette had followed her. Now she stood framed in the doorway, her plump body held as taut as a wire. Connie turned.

– *Bill's not here*, she indicated, as if Connie might have come up the stairs in search of him.

You are so bloody difficult, Connie thought. *Why can't you let it go, just for today?*

Anger inflated like a balloon inside her. It swelled under her ribs and within her head, compressing the memories into shadows that had no depth, only darkness.

She said coldly, 'Hilda has just died. Can't we be civil to each other?'

Jeanette seemed to rear up.

– *Civil? Was what you did civil?*

'No. It was wrong. We know that. But it's over. It was over years and years ago.'

That's all true, Connie thought. *But I think of Bill every day. Does that make me guilty, still?*

The balloon of anger collapsed again. The sound of heavy furniture being shifted came up the stairs.

She began again. 'Today is not about what happened between Bill and me. It's about Hilda, and you and me, the two of us, and what's left in this house. If you can't see that, shall we try to do what we've come here for? Then I'll go.'

Jeanette lifted her chin.

– *You think you can run away. You always did.*

'*Jeanette*. For Christ's sake. Shut up. Shut the fuck up, and *stop it*. Stop *attacking*. I'm not your enemy, I never was.'

– *You are shouting.*

It was true, she was. Connie rubbed her face with her hands.

It became very important to make Jeanette understand what she was trying to say. She took two steps across the room and caught hold of her.

'I didn't think Mum would just go and die like this. It's a shock. I still thought there would be plenty of time for the three of us to work out the . . . the resentments. They were always there, weren't they, long, long before Bill? In this house. At Barlaston Road, even. Isn't that right? That must be what you feel too?'

Jeanette's flesh was solid under her hands. She was angry too, Connie could feel the heat of it.

– *Resentment?*

'Yes. Couldn't we talk about it?'

– *Talk changes nothing.*

Jeanette made a twist, away from Connie, then beckoned. Connie followed her into Hilda's bedroom.

The place where the divan base had rested was outlined in grey furry dust. The dressing table with the triple mirror was gone, and the bedside tables. In the bay window, the curtains with the garland pattern sagged in loops from their tracks. Connie looked at what had once been familiar, and wondered how a person's absence could be so tangible.

A pyramid of cardboard boxes stood in the middle of the floor. Some of Hilda's clothes had been packed into them. Connie recognised a checked tweed coat.

– *Do you want any of this?*

Connie looked again at the boxes of clothes.

'No. But thank you.'

Hilda hadn't owned much jewellery, and rarely wore any apart from her wedding ring. On a plain cushion cover on the floor, a few costume brooches and a couple of necklaces were laid out. Connie reached down to touch the tweed coat, and then the small heap of faded glitter.

It was cold, and she had the sudden sensation of great distances and a wind blowing across them.

There was nothing, nothing at all to keep her in this house. It was as if she had never belonged or even lived here.

She reached down and picked up a brooch more or less at random. It was a ring of polished stones in a vaguely art nouveau setting.

'May I take this?'

Jeanette nodded.

– *And there is something else. It's yours*, she added.

She pointed out to the landing, where the square trap giving access into the roof space stood open. There had never been anything much up there, apart from a broken stepladder, some paint kettles with cracked residue in the bottom, a pair of deckchairs with the canvas frayed beyond use, and ancient cobwebs thick with soot.

– It was up there.

A smaller cardboard box stood a little apart from the others. It had once contained tins of corned beef. Connie stooped down. She pulled aside the tape that had been used to seal it, grown brittle with age, and opened the flaps. A puff of dust rose. Inside the box, under some folded paper, she found an old brown leatherette shopping bag. It had looped handles, and the plastic material was torn around the rivets to reveal the yellowed padding beneath.

'What's this?' she asked, although she already knew. Her heart was banging like a drum.

– You had better look.

Inside the bag, folded up together, lay a knitted baby's blanket and a tiny yellow cardigan. As Connie unfolded the cardigan an ordinary cheap brown envelope fell out. Her hands were shaking as she opened the envelope's flap. Into her uncertain hand an earring fell.

It was a little pendant of marcasites with a rod and a screw fastening for a pierced ear. She gazed at it, her mind racing. This, surely, had been her mother's earring. The pair to it, she must have kept for herself.

Breathless, Connie closed her fist on it. It was more precious than the biggest diamond in the world.

'These things are mine. They belong to *me*.' She stared into Jeanette's eyes. 'Why didn't Hilda give them to me?'

Jeanette shrugged.

– I suppose because you didn't need them. Mum gave you a home, a new family. Why would you want those things?

'Why? *Why?* Because these are mine. *This* is my identity.'

Angrily Connie shook the blanket at her.

Jeanette looked incredulous.

– An identity from someone who put you in a bag and left you under a hedge? You were lucky that Mum and Dad took you in. Even though you were what you were.

Connie kept her fist tightly closed. 'What I was?' she asked, dangerously.

– Not one of us.

Not creamy-skinned, plump, blonde, like Hilda and Sadie and their three pretty daughters. Different. Unidentified. Unidentifiable.

The divide had always been there.

At Barlaston Road, where old Mrs McBride brewed up her prejudice like a witch with a cauldron.

Inside the pin-neat rooms at Echo Street.

Not spoken of, never, of course not. But scrawny little Constance Thorne had always been different, with her loud voice and her singing, her tight hair and her skin a shade darker than anyone else's in the street or the school. Not different by very much, but just enough for her to have to stand up to the schoolyard bullies and the casual taunts of girls like Jackie and Elaine.

Connie had learned to accept that she would never know her birth mother and father, or where they had come from or what their stories were.

There were tests, of course, modern ones, that would indicate exactly what mixture of blood ran in her veins. But no test, however elaborate, would tell her who she really was.

She folded the blanket, awkwardly because her hand was still closed on the earring. She tucked it and the cardigan away inside the bag.

'"Lucky",' she said aloud.

Jeanette stepped close, putting her face up against Connie's.

– *Yes. Lucky.*

'Why did Hilda *want* to adopt a foundling?'

Jeanette's face suddenly blazed with fury. She grabbed Connie by the shoulders and shook her. The loose words tumbled out and spit flecked Connie's face.

– *Why? Why do you think? Because of me. Deaf. Deaf. Deaf. They didn't want another like me, did they? And with one deaf-and-dumb kid in the family, they weren't going to get given a nice new pink baby. They were only going to get one like you.*

Connie breathed in sharply. It was like being children again, fighting and scratching, trying to damage each other by any means.

'You are a bitch, Jeanette.'

Jeanette ignored her. She was caught up in her own resentment.

– *And what did you do in return? Tried to take my husband.*

'I didn't try to take Bill from you. I made the mistake of loving him. I regret what I did.'

– *If I am a bitch you are a liar.*

Connie pulled away from her. She had to get away, out of the room before one of them hit out. She snatched up the bag, made sure of its contents, and ran down the steep stairs past the gaping removals men.

She heard Jeanette's bellow.

– *'Running away.'*

The front door stood open. She ran out and slammed it behind her.

Leaving Echo Street for the last time.

She held the marcasite earring so tightly that the metal post dug deep into her palm.

It was still raining. The waterspouts gurgled with the rush of water and the palm leaves dripped a few inches from where they sat.

She glanced across at Jeanette.

'Are you asleep?' she whispered.

Jeanette opened her eyes and licked her dry lips.

– *No.*

'Would you like some juice? A cup of tea?'

– *No. My back aches.*

It was an hour before she could take more of her drugs.

'Shall I massage your feet again?'

– *Would you?*

Connie shifted her place, gently lifted her sister's feet.

– *What's the time?*

She told her and Jeanette smiled.

– *Bill will be back in a minute.*

THIRTEEN

Noah stood aside in the kitchen to call Roxana on her new mobile. Andy went on unloading shopping from supermarket bags and flinging open the doors to cupboards.

'Forgot the bloody bog roll,' he shouted.

Noah stuck a finger in his free ear. 'Rox? Can you hear me? Where are you?'

Roxana had just left the offices of Angela's production company. She was out in the street, dodging the home-going crowds on her way to the bus stop. She rocked on the edge of the kerb, her bag hitched over her shoulder and her phone clamped to her ear, then dived confidently through the stream of buses and taxis.

'What is that? I am in the street, Noah. I am going to work, I can't be late.'

She had done three hours on the telephone in Angela's office, talking in Russian to unimportant officials in the Russian Film Institute who would eventually open the doors to conversations with the more senior officials who had the power to grant the production company the permits they needed to film in St Petersburg. Angela seemed pleased with her. Now she had to get to The Cosmos before Mr Shane noticed that she was late.

'When can I see you?' Noah asked.

'I am not sure. On Saturday?'

'That's four days' time.'

'I know that. What can I do?'

Roxana could see her bus, stalled in the traffic a hundred yards down the road. She attached herself to the crowd of people waiting at the stop, then began the process of slipping between them to bring herself closer to the point where she calculated the jaws of the bus would open up.

Noah frowned. He admired Roxana's capacity for work, but her availability as a girlfriend was severely limited by it.

'You can let me pick you up from the club tonight.'

'No.'

'Why not?'

'I don't want you to see me in that place. You don't understand why, but I don't want it.'

'I do understand. Sort of,' Noah sighed. 'But . . .'

'Noah, here is my bus. I will call you tomorrow.' She chirped a kiss to him. She was at the front of the crowd now, and as the doors opened she skipped inside and inserted herself into a just-vacated seat.

Roxana couldn't help smiling. She kept counting them up, as if the wonders of her life might otherwise be snatched away. She had two jobs, one of them in the *film business*. She had an English boyfriend who called her more often than she needed to hear from him, a savings account, a mobile phone, an Oyster card, and a place to live that made her feel as if she was in a movie. She was a London girl.

The bus lurched and a man fell against her. He took longer than necessary to get up again.

'Sorry, love.'

Roxana straightened her skirt over her thighs. 'No

worries,' she said, as the production-company receptionist did about a hundred times a day.

Noah helped Andy to put away the rest of the shopping. He balled up the empty bags and threw them into
the cupboard where they kept the ironing board.

'You okay, mate? Is everything all right with you
two?' Andy asked him.

'Yeah. Sure. Well, in a way. Roxana seems full-on, but
at the same time you know that she's keeping quite a lot
back. She's protective of herself. I suppose that's the way
you have to be, where she comes from, and after what
she's been through. But I wish I could convince her she
doesn't have to be like that with me.'

Andy eyed him. 'You're serious about her.'

'It takes two to make a relationship serious, I find.'

'Yeah. It does. I thought when you first brought her
back here that she might turn out to be just a gold-dig-
ger. But she's not like that. What are you going to do?'

'I'm going to see her tonight, for a start. I'll pick her
up and take her home from that pole-dancing club.'

'Right. Need any help with that? You know, I could
come with you, take a look round, see if any of her
friends need to work on their self-revelation issues?'

'Yes. No thanks, mate. I'll manage.'

'Sure?'

'Certain.'

It was a quiet night at The Cosmos, which was always
harder than when it was busy. When there weren't
enough customers to fill the bar and the tables, even the
low lighting couldn't quite conceal the tatty fittings and
grimy carpets. Roxana worked the pole as enthusiasti-
cally as she could, exaggerating every undulation of her

body. She locked eyes with each of the men in turn but she couldn't make a single one of them pay for a private dance. Towards the end of the interminable evening, Mr Shane sent for Roxana to come to his office. Scarlet, the girl who delivered the message, wiggled her hips and smirked.

'Fuck off,' Roxana hissed at her.

Mr Shane took his cigar out of his mouth and exhaled a swirl of dirty blue smoke.

'Shut the door. Come here.'

Roxana took one small step forwards.

'Here,' he indicated with the butt of the cigar. 'That's better. Well, now. Hmm.'

His manicured hands twitched her lace top away. He put the cigar back in his mouth, reached up and with a deft, insolent movement unhooked her bra.

Roxana looked straight over his bald head. She wouldn't give him the satisfaction of reacting.

Casually he fondled her. 'You were late tonight, weren't you? But you're quite good, the punters like you. Do you enjoy your job here?'

'It is a job.'

'Like to keep it, would you?'

Now his hands slid over her breasts and insinuatingly over her hips. There was no doubt what Mr Shane had in mind. The same thing as Leonid. Always the same. Hatred stabbed through her.

'Yes.'

'Take that thing off,' he ordered. His legs splayed on either side of her. His lower lip was wet, glinting in the light.

Roxana smiled down at him now. She reached behind her, undoing her miniskirt with deliberately slow movements as Mr Shane waited. The smoke from his cigar drifted into her face. She slid the skirt down over her hips, further down to her knees. Then she raised her leg, as if she was about to step out of the little garment. The man's eyes travelled down the length of her thigh and calf, down to the stiletto heel of her shoe.

Roxana let her skirt drop. She jack-knifed her knee to her chest, then used the momentum to stamp her foot hard into his crotch.

There was a liquid gasp, like a bubble of air escaping from a blocked drain. As Mr Shane doubled up into his own lap, Roxana grabbed her skirt and ran for the door. Scarlet and one of the other girls were smoking in the corridor and they gaped at her as she pushed by. In the cubby-hole that the dancers used as a dressing room she collected up her belongings and stuffed them into her bag. She put on her outdoor coat and hurried up the customers' stairs to the ground floor. A large group of flush-faced drunken men mobbed the entrance, trying to get into the club past the Maltese doorman who was barring the way and insisting that they must pay for membership first.

Roxana knew that this was her last-ever moment inside The Cosmos Club.

She felt no regrets.

She elbowed her way out through the crowd before Mr Shane could send anyone to catch her and repay her for stamping on him.

'Some guy was in here asking for you,' the doorman shouted after her.

Roxana ignored him. She let the heavy door swing shut. The night air tasted cool and fresh.

Noah had been waiting only a few minutes. He saw

her erupt from the club, the light briefly catching her blonde crop. He also saw that she was laughing. Roxana slowed her pace and strolled away down the street, her stilettos click-clicking and her bag swinging from her shoulder. He jumped out of the car and ran to catch up with her.

Roxana heard the hurrying footsteps, and then an arm caught hers. She wheeled round, two hands grasping her bag with the intention of using it to batter her attacker rather than to secure it.

'Hey. Hey, Roxana, it's me.'

'Noah, what are you doing here?'

'Picking you up from work.'

'I said not to.'

'Not inside the club. Nothing wrong with waiting outside, is there?'

'No, I suppose. Anyway, there is no argument. I won't be going back there again. I don't have a job any more.'

'Why's that?'

'I kicked my boss in the testicles.'

'What for?'

'Roxana shrugged. 'The usual reason.'

Noah shouted, 'What? What did he do to you? I'm going to go in there and do worse than just kick him in the balls, I'll tear them off and stuff them down his *throat*.'

Roxana let herself briefly imagine what would happen if Noah tried to do anything of the kind, and what he would look like after Maltese Mike and Mr Shane's driver had finished with him.

'Thank you for the idea, but you don't need to. I have looked after myself already.'

Noah wound his arms round her and kissed her. She

was tough, but she was vulnerable too and the combination seemed to him almost unbearably lovely.

'That was why you were laughing, when you came out of there?'

She kissed him back. 'If you knew Mr Shane, you would be laughing too.'

'Would that be before or after I ripped his balls off? Come on, let's go. I'm taking you back to Auntie Con's place.'

With their arms round each other and Roxana's head tipped on Noah's shoulder, they retraced their steps to the car. A few late-night pedestrians passed by, and Roxana remembered the night when she was leaving The Cosmos and had seen a boy and girl together, just like she and Noah were now, and how lonely she had felt because all the world seemed to be made of couples hurrying home to bed together. To anyone looking at her it would seem that she had joined the lucky people, and yet now she was here she knew the world was still a precarious place where you could lose your job in a flash of anger.

Even so, she was glad she had kicked Mr Shane where it really hurt.

Roxana noticed that the man was there again, waiting in reception with his laptop case.

He sat with one leg crossed over the other, the shiny toe of his loafer gently tapping the air. Once he turned back the immaculate blue cuff of his shirt with his little finger and glanced at his thin gold watch. He caught Roxana's eye again through the glass door of the office where she was working, raised one eyebrow by a millimetre, and flashed a smile back at her. This was his second visit to Oyster Films, and Roxana had been aware of him right from the start because he kept looking at her. He would smile and not seem at all embarrassed to be caught staring.

He was very good-looking. He looked rich, too. She wondered who he was.

'Mr Antonelli?'

The unfriendly girl who was the boss's PA had come downstairs. The man got up and followed her out of Roxana's sight.

Roxana went back to work. Angela had asked her to obtain the details of several Russian companies who might supply catering on location in St Petersburg, and to compare their quotes. In the back of her mind, as she tallied the boring figures, was worry about money and finding a new job. Working a few hours a week for Oyster Films was fine, better even than fine, but it paid next to nothing. Money was what counted, in the end.

Roxana did everything that Angela might possibly want, but at half past six there was nothing left to deal with. Noah was playing football tonight for his office team, and the prospect of an empty evening ahead of her was unfamiliar and slightly unwelcome. She put on her jacket with the buttons and went out into reception. Zoe had already chirped *no worries* for the last time that day, switched the phones to the night answering service and gone home. Then the lift doors slid open and Mr Antonelli emerged.

'Hello,' he smiled. 'Finished for today?'

He held open the street door, and when she began walking he fell into step beside her.

'How long have you been working at the company?' he asked in a companionable way, as if they already knew and liked each other.

'Not so long. But it is a good job, I like it very much.'
She wasn't going to let on quite how menial or how temporary her role was.

He gave her a glance. 'Are you a producer?'

'No, in fact. I am, er, a translator.'

He looked impressed. 'Is that so? What languages?'

'I am working in Russian. I am from Uzbekistan, but now I live in London.'

'Of course.' Mr Antonelli nodded, as if something had fallen into place. They reached the end of the street and he glanced at his thin gold watch again. 'I have an hour before my next appointment. Would you like maybe to have a drink?'

Roxana considered. Mr Antonelli was obviously important. Maybe he could be a useful person to know.

'Thank you,' she said. 'That would be very nice.'

He seemed to know his way around. He briskly steered her towards a place she had often passed but never thought of going into. Even this early in the evening, a big man wearing a black suit and a headset was guarding the doorway.

'Good evening, sir; good evening, madam,' he said, as they swept past.

The bar was flooded with soft golden light. The low furniture was all made of brown leather, wall mirrors reflected the backs of the women's smooth blonde heads and the shoulders of men in City suits. There were waitresses in black uniforms, and low music playing. Mr Antonelli steered them to a table in a little alcove. Roxana blinked as a glass of champagne materialised in front of her. When she went out with Noah it was to pubs, or to indie music gigs in underground venues in Camden Town.

'I am Cesare Antonelli.' He took a card from his wallet and slid it across to her. Underneath his name it said *Film Director*, with an address in Rome. Roxana sat up. This was exactly the sort of person she needed to meet.

'My name is Roxana.'

'How do you do?' Cesare Antonelli clinked his glass to hers. He leaned back against the leather seating.

'So, Roxana. Do you do some acting, or modelling perhaps, as well as translating? You look as though you might.'

Her attention sharpened even further. This could be an opportunity much bigger than making phone calls to Russian caterers.

'Not at the moment,' she smiled. Her fingers moved on the cool stem of her champagne flute. 'But I am interested, of course.'

'And you are a good dancer, that is always useful.'

She stared at him. A flush rose from her throat to her cheeks and Cesare lightly gestured. 'I was at The Cosmos Club with some Japanese business associates, after a long evening, you know what it can be like, and I saw you dance. You were really very good.'

Roxana was embarrassed. She had been thinking that Mr Cesare Antonelli recognised her talent, but it was only that he had seen her pole dancing. She was fairly sure she hadn't done a private dance for him, at least, although she had become quite good by the end at blocking out the men's faces, even at blocking out the fact that they were people at all.

Now she would have to make little of The Cosmos and at the same time convince Mr Antonelli that she could easily do whatever acting or modelling work he had in mind.

She lifted one shoulder. 'I don't work at that place any longer,' she said coolly. Which was turning out to be a blessing. 'I am concentrating on Oyster Films and my work across the board in the movie and advertising business. Are you going to direct a picture for them, perhaps?'

He said that he was setting up an Anglo-Italian co-production deal for a big feature film, which he would be producing and directing, and he had been visiting Oyster Films to see if they might be a suitable partner for the enterprise.

'But they are not really in the big league, you know. They are mostly commercials and small stuff. Nice people, but I don't think I am going to be able to make it work with them, very unfortunately.'

In answer to his questions she told him about Noah and, without quite mentioning Connie, about living in her beautiful apartment, making it all sound as though she had lived in London for a long time. She liked talking to Cesare. He was never short of something to say, and yet he paid her the compliment of listening to her.

Cesare kept looking at his watch. When they had finished the bottle of champagne he said that he was afraid he would have to go and meet an associate to discuss some business over dinner. He hesitated, then added that if Roxana didn't think that would be too boring, she could perhaps join them? His colleague might be a useful contact for her.

Roxana was thinking the same thing.

They took a taxi to a restaurant, another place with rich golden lighting. Some of the women at the tables glanced at her as she passed. Cesare's associate was waiting at a table for two, but it was quickly re-laid for three.

The man was called Philip. He was younger than Cesare and his clothes were scruffier. He had a tiny patch of hair sculpted under his lower lip.

Roxana waited until the introductions had been made, then she excused herself and went to the cloak-room.

The lighting was quite dim, but she came up close to the mirror and studied her reflection. The women in the restaurant looked smart, but then they were mostly quite old. She rubbed some more foundation on her face, thickened her mascara and finally stroked her eyebrows into place with a licked fingertip.

Critically, Roxana met her own gaze.

Noah constantly told her she was beautiful. She wasn't sure quite how much she would be telling him about this evening; that would depend on whether it led to a job. But the thought of him made her face soften into a sudden smile. Now, she thought, she looked all right.

Over dinner she learned that Philip was a photographer. Fashion, glamour, he said airily. He looked round the room as he talked, clicking his lighter to the cigarette he held in the corner of his mouth and inhaling with one eye half-closed against the smoke. An understanding had arisen that Roxana would be doing some as-yet-unspecified work in the area of business that he and Cesare dealt in. Before anything could go ahead, though, she would need to get some shots in her book. He thought he could help her with that. Cesare listened to all this, but without much enthusiasm.

They encouraged Roxana to order food from the big, tasselled menu.

When it came it was delicious, the most elaborate food she had ever tasted, with layers of little crispy pancakes and soft, glistening meat and small puddles of unctuous sauces. She ate everything and tried hard not to look too greedy. Cesare and Philip had similar dishes but they only took a few mouthfuls. They smoked and talked, and drank wine followed by whisky with a lot of ice in short, chunky glasses. Roxana drank quite a lot too. She sank into a honeyed daze of optimism.

Of course she could be an actress, or a model.

After a while, the food and the drinks and the series of espressos that followed were all finished. They were out in the twinkly night, and Cesare hailed a taxi. Both men insisted that they couldn't let her go home unescorted. Roxana confidently gave the driver the address of Limbeck House. When they reached her building, to her faint dismay they got out and Cesare paid the fare and the cab drove off. They were talking about coming up with her for a final nightcap.

Roxana hesitated. They had bought her dinner, and she was going to be working with them. She had talked – yes, too much – about her beautiful apartment. They took the lift to the top floor.

Once they were in the big white room the two men strolled to the window and gazed out at the city.

'Nice place,' Cesare said.

'Live here on your own, do you?' Philip wanted to know.

'I . . . have a flatmate. She is away tonight.' As soon as she said it, she cursed her stupidity. She should have said she would be back any minute now.

Philip wanted whisky. Cesare examined the music stacked on the top of Connie's grand piano.

'Are you a musician, too?' he smiled.

'No.' Roxana searched through the cupboards. She

knew that Connie kept drink somewhere, but she couldn't remember where she had seen it. Cesare took pity on her and said that he would like a cup of tea. She filled the kettle and while she was waiting for it to boil she drank a glass of cold water. The room settled into clearer focus, and she realised she very much didn't like the way Philip was wandering about picking up Connie's possessions and putting them down again. Cesare was all right, but she didn't care for this Philip. He saw her watching him and grinned at her. Very casually, he produced a little camera from the pocket of his jacket.

'Now we're here, shall we take a few pictures? Just some nice informal shots?'

'Perhaps it is too late for that,' she said.

'It's early. Isn't it, Cesare?'

Roxana closed the door of the last cupboard with a snap. 'I am sorry that I don't have whisky.'

Philip studied her through half-closed eyes. 'What have you got?'

A shiver of apprehension passed through her, followed by a dull sense of familiarity, disappointment and absolute recognition.

Model, indeed. Actress, ha ha.

She could forgive herself the first mistake of the evening, which was assuming Cesare might be useful to her, instead of the other way round. But now she found herself in the middle of a much bigger mistake.

'Nothing. It's time for you both to go.'

Philip came at her. 'Come on, darling. A nice picture or two. On that lovely sofa, eh?'

'No. If you don't leave I will have to call for the police.'

Her hand stretched out to the telephone on the counter. Philip caught her wrist and Roxana squirmed in his grasp, trying to bring her knee into his groin.

Is this all that is ever going to happen to me? she wondered.

The answer came at once. Noah had never given her cause to kick him in the balls.

If only he was here now.

Cesare dashed forwards. He looked genuinely distressed. 'Now, now. Don't spoil a beautiful evening. Stop that, Philip. If the lady doesn't want you to take her picture, you can't force her.'

Philip let go, reluctantly. He slicked back his hair with two hands and adjusted his expression.

'There we are. All friends again,' Cesare smiled. 'And Roxana is quite right. It's late, and past everyone's bedtime.'

She breathed again. 'Thank you,' she said.

'I'll just use the bathroom before you throw us out,' Philip muttered. Roxana silently pointed along the corridor.

While he was out of the room Cesare apologised for him. He hoped very much that Roxana hadn't been upset.

'I am all right. Thank you,' she said stiffly.

There was no more talk of opportunities in the film business.

When Philip reappeared his coat was done up and he stood by the front door without coming back into the main room.

Cesare kissed her on the cheek. 'Goodbye, Roxana,' he said.

Roxana locked the door after them, and slid the chain

into place. She let her head fall against the heavy door, her shoulders sagging in relief. Then she walked down the corridor, past the cloakroom door and glanced into Connie's bedroom. In the shaft of light falling from behind her, the room seemed undisturbed.

In the morning, even though the girl was so unfriendly, Roxana casually asked the boss's PA about Mr Cesare Antonelli.

'Him? Oh, turns out he's just a bullshitter. Max checked him out, then told me not to set up another meeting. Why?'

Roxana only shrugged. 'I wondered.'

'You get all sorts,' the PA said, as if Roxana might not have noticed this fact.

Jeanette slept better than she had done for months. She explained to Bill and Connie that the heat was soporific. It drew some of the pain out of her.

The pace of the village matched her invalid rhythms. Dewi would come to call, and sit drinking tea for an hour at a time with her baby shawled against her chest while Jeanette rocked in her chair. Sometimes Jeanette would make a slow walk to the market with Connie, and sit on a stallholder's plastic stool while Connie tested the mangoes for ripeness.

'*Selamat pagi*,' Kadek and the other shopkeepers greeted them both.

Jeanette went with Dayu once or twice to the village temple with an offering, and came back with the symbolic grains of rice pressed to her temples. She said that for almost the first time since she had fallen ill, she didn't feel that the whole world was racing ahead and leaving her like a piece of broken machinery at the side of the road.

Bill and Connie dovetailed their days around her. When she was awake and wanted to talk or just to look out at the view they sat beside her, and when she was asleep they stepped quietly through the house and spoke to each other in low voices.

The wet weather persisted. One afternoon Connie looked into the bedroom while Jeanette was taking a rest. Rain rustled in the palm thatch and dripped from the water spouts outside the shutters, until the whole house seemed enveloped in a thick cocoon of damp that furred all the cushions in the house with a silvery nap and tried to embroider their leather shoes with mossy green patches. Jeanette was fast asleep, lying on her back with her mouth slightly open and her hands, palm up, defencelessly uncurled. Connie thought she could see daylight between her ring finger and the wedding band.

Bill had come from the opposite direction with the same intention. He stood close behind Connie, looking over her shoulder as if they were a mother and father checking on a sleeping child. It was as if with the progression of the disease they had become Jeanette's parents, Connie thought. They fed her, and encouraged her with affectionate words, and watched over her. Only they weren't proudly watching her grow up. They were bringing her towards death.

She turned abruptly, almost colliding with Bill. As always, her skin felt minutely sensitive to his nearness. They were only six inches apart.

Gently, he cupped her face in his hands. He kissed her forehead and then involuntarily they folded together, listening to one another's breathing and the steady drumming of the rain.

Connie wondered how it was that you could love one person so much, for so many years, and yet have so few shared memories. So little to sustain you, and no hope left at the end. Except for those few months when neither of them had been able to stop themselves, everything between them – chains of days, months and years – had been made up of absence.

Bill traced the line of her cheekbones. The palms of his hands were very warm. She thought how much she wanted to kiss him. She wanted it so badly that she felt dizzy, and now she asked herself how desire could sprout so nakedly and unashamedly out of the desert of Jeanette's illness.

Tears gathered and ran out of the corners of her eyes. Bill trapped them with his thumbs and then touched his mouth to her wet skin.

'Don't cry,' he said. 'I can't bear it if you cry.'

Connie made a sound in her throat that wasn't a word or – not quite – a murmur of pure pain. She turned her head to escape his scrutiny, then pulled herself out of his arms.

'I'm going out,' she managed to say. 'I'm going for a walk.'

She pulled on a nylon jacket and ran into the rain. Outside Wayan's house was a row of scooters and bicycles belonging to the relatives who had come for the last flurry of preparations. Tomorrow was the day of the cremation.

Connie began walking. The raindrops landing on her face and lips felt warmer than blood temperature. The dirt road was reduced to a muddy ribbon threading through khaki puddles. Ahead of her a young woman hitched up her skirt and ran with her black umbrella bobbing over her head. Under all the awnings and shelters families were gathered, white-robed grandmothers and men in sweat-ringed T-shirts, mothers and impassive toddlers, sitting and staring out at the downpour. Even the dogs had crawled away to find cover.

She walked a circle round the outskirts of the village and came to the entrance to the monkey forest. The peanut vendors had withdrawn under the canopy of leaves, and only a small handful of tourists shrouded in plastic rain capes hesitated and discussed whether to abandon their itinerary for the nearest cappuccino bar.

Under the trees inside the forest enclosure, though, only occasional drips fell from the interlaced leaves to spatter the grey dust with percussive insistence. The macaques were drawn up in size order on the temple walls, tails dangling like inverted question marks. Connie squeezed some of the water out of her hair and strolled down the nearest path. The light was greenish, subaqueous.

Her intention had been to shut out all the thoughts of Bill, hurrying away from him yet again and closing up her mind as if she were preparing the defences against a tidal wave. But the wave smashed through the barriers and swept her away.

She was submerged in memories.

Bill and Connie saw each other at Christmases and birthdays, marking the milestones of the years. Without ever speaking of it, they had tacitly agreed never to hug each other like a brother- and sister-in-law, because they knew such an embrace would never be fraternal. They never even allowed their hands to touch.

Then came Noah's tenth birthday. There was a football party, with Bill acting as referee for twenty boys who ran up and down the Surrey garden.

In the kitchen, Connie ('I've only dropped in for an hour, just to bring Noah his present, I've got to go back to London for a screening tonight') helped Hilda to lay out plates of sausages and bowls of crisps.

At the end of the game the pack of boys chased into the house. These days Jeanette didn't enjoy parties or crowds, and she was white in the face with the strain of communicating with children who didn't understand her signs and who tried not to giggle at her blurted words. Her jaw and back were rigid with determination to make her boy's party a success. Noah was flushed and boisterous and he pushed past his mother to get to the table. In doing so, he knocked a big bowl of sliced fruit off the counter and onto the tiled floor. Chunks of pineapple and chips of broken china flew up into the air. Jeanette swung round in mute, boiling anger. Up to her ankles in fruit and unable or unwilling to strike out at Noah, she raised her hand at Bill as if to hit him.

A flash of loathing passed between them.

Connie saw it. A terrible, wild excitement shot through her.

Bill caught his wife by the wrist and gently steered her away from the mess. Hilda dashed forwards with a cloth and a bucket and the boys cheered and began like a multi-headed monster to stuff food into its many mouths. A minute later Bill was telling knock-knock jokes and Jeanette was triumphantly bearing the birthday cake to Noah at the head of the table.

Connie waited just long enough to sing 'Happy Birthday' and then hurried away.

All marriages go through dark patches, she told herself.

Jeanette was by then studying plant taxonomy in the spare hours that were not devoted to Noah. She was a committed mother. Everything that was done for and by Noah Bunting had to be the best.

Perhaps Jeanette the perfectionist, Jeanette who loved her husband so much, who had never thought or dreamed of any man but Bill, had not left quite enough room in her arrangements for the awkward reality of Bill himself, the man and not the ideal.

Connie told herself that in any case whatever was happening between the two of them did not, *must not*, mean anything to her.

Then, a month later, she went to the party given by the agency in Docklands.

Bill was there and she walked towards him, knowing that she should turn and run, because if she didn't it would be too late.

But that night, the will and the determination to keep on running finally deserted her.

Bill was waiting. He knew as surely as Connie did that they had reached the point of no return. He had been drinking, but he was clear in his mind. His marriage was a shaky edifice and the woman who came towards him was solid reality. She was light and warmth and food and water to him. To hold her at arm's length tonight would have been to ask his heart to stop beating.

They left the party. As soon as they had taken a single step out of the room, there was no going back. Every evasive action that they had both taken over the years now seemed to have been leading directly to this moment.

Instead of extricating herself and sending him home to Jeanette, Connie took Bill home with her.

All Bill's careful structures of duty and responsibility were burning down, and he let them blaze and then collapse into ashes.

They stumbled into the refuge of her flat, and the heat of passion melted and fused them.

He said, 'I want you. I can't sleepwalk through one more day.'

She tightened her arms round him and he kissed her as if he were a starving man.

'I have been so lonely without you,' she whispered.

'I've been like a machine. But without you, everything's starting to break down and run out of power.'

He undressed her, there in the hallway. She pulled off his clothes, just as greedy as he was. Reckless, laughing, they scattered a trail of discarded shoes and shirts behind them.

Bill was familiar to her, the shape and even the scent of him, but he was also brand-new. She had never seen this insistence in him.

'Connie, Connie,' he whispered. He marched her backwards, step by step, until they fell onto her bed.

There were no miracles, but Bill's presence in her bed, in her body, closed a circle. Connie felt for a brief few moments that she wasn't searching the landscape for signposts or trying to decipher a mysterious language. For the first time in her life she was at home, where she belonged, in a place that wasn't defined by time or history.

Afterwards she held him against her.

His breathing slowed and steadied.

'Why tonight?' Connie whispered.

'Because I can't go on persuading myself that what's true is not. And you?'

'Truth and reality aren't necessarily compatible, are they? The truth, if I'm going to admit it, is that I fell in love with you the minute you walked into Echo Street on your first date with Jeanette. Before I even saw you. As soon as I heard your voice.'

'Look. You're blushing,' he smiled. His finger touched her cheek.

'We're talking about truth, remember? It's often embarrassing. Reality is that you are Jeanette's husband. But tonight the truth is that I still love you and you are here with me. I don't know about tomorrow. I don't even care.'

He held her closer.

'Remember the day of the picnic? The motorbike accident?'

'Of course I do.'

'You were such a contrast to Jeanette. Jeanette was sunny. You were so dark and intense, coiled up in the back of my car.'

His mouth moved over her face. 'And do you remember the wet night just before the wedding, when we kissed on the way to the tube station?'

'Oh, yes.'

'That was a shock. You were supposed to be just a kid.'

'I was seventeen.'

'And then I took you out to find Constance Crescent, that empty street that didn't tell your story, and afterwards I couldn't stop thinking about you. You wanted so much to find where you came from, and I wanted to tell you that it mattered much less than where you were going. I don't know if it was then that I realised it, or if it came to me more gradually, but I was beginning to suspect that I might be marrying the wrong sister. I told myself that it was absurd, plain wrong, imagination, a trick of the light, a vertigo sufferer's compulsion to haul himself to the edge and pitch himself over the precipice . . . all kinds of explanations. Justifications. But I couldn't escape the conviction. It was there.

'It wasn't that I didn't love Jeanette, because I did. I do still. And Noah. I have to tell you that now, Con. But how many variations of love are there? I kept seeing you and wanting to know you more; it wasn't desire precisely – even though it was that too. Sometimes I could hardly be in the same room with you, I had to go outside and walk up and down until the urge subsided and it was safe for me to venture back again. It was more a certainty – I'm putting this very badly, and it isn't as if I haven't thought about it constantly – that if I could get close enough to you, if you would allow me to, if I could suspend all the other realities, then I would find – I don't know – *yes, I do* – the love of my life. I'm making this sound so narcissistic, I'm sorry. All I can do is try to tell you the truth. The truth as it seems to me, in my heart. I know that your truth is likely to be different. Jeanette's will be totally other, God knows.'

Connie tried to interrupt, to tell him that she knew what he was trying to say and that it was the same for her, but he gently put his fingers to her mouth.

She understood how much he needed to talk.

'You seemed opaque. But inside here, Connie,' he touched his fist to her forehead, 'I knew you were as clear as spring water. Does that sound fanciful?'

'No. Although I don't think I'm either clear or opaque. Just a mixture, like everyone.'

'It's a matter of contrasts. You see, Jeanette is the opposite of you. Is this presumptuous of me, telling you what your own sister is and is not?'

'No.'

'On the outside, Jeanette is translucent. Her pale skin. That smile. But I made the classic bloke's mistake of confusing looks with character. Jeanette's inside is your outside. It's dark. Of course she's angry, that's understood. You would be, I would be, if either of us had to contend with what she does.

'I know it's her anger that gives her the will to shape her life the way she wants it. That's all right, it's admirable. It's just the silence, Con. It's the *silence* I can't bear. Not the deafness. In a way that's only external. I mean the real silence.'

He tightened his arms, as if she might try to escape from him. His face was hidden in her hair but she could hear the grief in his voice.

'I know,' Connie said.

Echo Street had bred that deeper silence. It was rooted in the cultivation of appearances, the fear of exposure, the pin-neat, net-curtained, buttoned-lip and averted-glance rebuttal of the unwieldy and passionate world, as invented by Hilda and upheld by Jeanette.

After Tony died, those standards had gone so much against the grain for Connie that she had run away as soon as she was old enough to be alone.

'At Noah's birthday party. You saw what happened when he smashed the bowl.'

'Yes.'

'You or I would have yelled at him. Or just yelled. But that's not what Jeanette does. Her only outlet is me.

Everything is channelled through me. I am her lightning conductor.'

'It looked for a second as though you hated each other.'

'We do, sometimes. I don't want to be a lifeline, Connie. All I can be is a man.'

There was a break in his voice that she had never heard before. She couldn't see Bill's face, but she was sure that he was close to tears.

In all the time she had known him, she had never before felt that he needed her or that she could help him, instead of the other way round. The wash of tenderness that came with the recognition was as powerful as desire. She hadn't guessed that it was possible to love someone so much.

She rocked him gently in her arms. She talked in a low voice, words that were hardly connected, telling him that everything would be all right.

She couldn't see how, but maybe they would find a way.

After a while he collected himself.

'I have to go soon,' he whispered.

'Please don't go yet.'

'Con, what are we going to do? This is all we'll ever say to each other.'

'I know.'

'Just a few more minutes.'

He made love to her again, roughly this time.

'I want to go on holding you for ever,' Bill said.

'I want you to.'

She stretched herself beneath him.

She was discovering that it was possible to be wildly, exotically happy, even when you were in despair.

Connie walked back through the village, calculating that Jeanette would be awake by now. People had emerged from beneath their awnings and were hurrying to the market, and the street was noisy with the buzz of scooters. The puddles gaped like lunar craters. She jumped aside to avoid a tiara of spray as a scooter shot through the nearest one.

She found Bill and Jeanette sitting in their accustomed places on the veranda. The low sun had emerged into a broad band of pistachio-green sky, and the margins of the banana palm leaves were glinting gold. Steam gently rose where the sun struck the thick-knit vegetation and the frogs were clearing their throats for a long night.

Jeanette pointed, beyond the greenery, over towards Wayan's house.

The upper storeys of the thirty-foot-high cremation tower constructed over the past weeks that had been shuddered and tipped sideways. Jeanette's hands flew to her mouth as the whole edifice lurched and threatened to topple over. There was an echo of shouting and laughter before it righted itself again.

'Don't worry,' Connie said. 'Now they are decorating the *wadah*, ready for tomorrow.'

As the dusk gathered, Wayan emerged from his house compound. Two bamboo poles, one tall and one short, were planted beside the entrance. From the shorter one hung a bird woven from bamboo and decorated with coloured feathers, and from the taller a coconut-oil lamp covered with a white cloth. Wayan used another pole to unhook and lower the lamp. He cleaned the wick and filled the oil reservoir, then made sure that the flame was bright before he raised the lamp into its place once more.

It made a pale glow in the fading light.

The bird was the watchman and the lamp was kept alight to guide his father's soul back to its home. It would burn until the cremation was over.

FOURTEEN

At midday Wayan unhooked the coconut-oil lamp from the pole at his gate. The lane was so packed with people he could hardly turn.

'Everyone from the *banjar* is here,' Connie said. 'The whole neighbourhood.'

The latest arrivals noisily greeted her as they passed her house. Kim and Neil the property developers waved from the other side of the lane and Werner the sculptor accompanied by his latest boyfriend positioned themselves in the best place for taking pictures. Drums and gongs were pulsing from inside Wayan's compound. Some of the young girls began dancing.

'It's like a huge party,' Bill said.

'That's just what it is. A send-off for the spirit.'

A big group of laughing young men pushed by. They wore long tunics with bright yellow sashes, and headcloths knotted round their foreheads.

Jeanette's eyes glittered as she watched. She was holding Dewi's baby in her arms. Dewi was wearing her best clothes, a brocade skirt with her upper body tightly bound in pale gold cloth. Her head was crowned with flowers and the baby reached out his fat hands and tried to pick off the petals. Jeanette stopped him by whirling him away and burying her face in his brown neck. He turned his attention to her hair and she let him tug at it with his fists.

In the middle of the lane towered the *wadah*. It was

decorated now to the tip of the highest tier with a mass of coloured streamers, tinsel and branches and garlands of flowers, and on the back of it a grotesque painted mask bared its fangs over the heads of the crowd. The monster had huge paper wings on bamboo frames that flapped and creaked.

'Look,' Bill pointed. Out of the house compound came a group of relatives, carrying an object wrapped in white cloth. Two dozen pairs of hands grabbed it and hoisted it onto a shelf within the level of the tower that represented the world of men. He muttered, 'That's not the body?'

'An effigy. The real body's been buried in the ground all these months, so it's impure and can't be brought to the house. They'll have dug it up and it'll be waiting in the cemetery.'

'I see.'

The tower shook as two boys scrambled up it. They wedged themselves among the decorations and waved to the cheering crowd. There was a fresh burst of shouting and laughing and further down the lane the throng parted. A pair of horns was all that was visible at first, but then a larger-than-life carving of a black bull appeared, standing tall on four splayed legs and borne on a platform of bamboo poles by yet more of the dead man's family and neighbours.

The carving of the bull was realistic, down to the last detail. One of the men obligingly demonstrated that its large penis was moveable. The streamers and strips of cloth with which it was decorated fluttered and everyone laughed and cheered.

A loose procession began to form. Kadek waved his plump arms to marshal the crowd. At the head of the line, a young cousin lifted the coconut-oil lamp to guide the spirit to its destination. The bull came lurching and capering to the front and another boy jumped up onto its back. The sweating men carrying the platform tilted and swung it to try and throw him off but he clung on like a rodeo rider. The rows of women in their gold and best brocades came next, balancing silver dishes heaped with rice cakes and fruit and with flowers on their heads. Dayu and her sisters were carrying bamboo poles speared with carved pineapples and papayas. Dewi held out her arms for her baby before taking her place, and Jeanette reluctantly handed him over. He surveyed the scene with mild interest.

A long white cloth was unfurled over everyone's heads. A mass of people rushed underneath it, reaching up to grab a handful of the cloth. Connie explained to Bill and Jeanette that the cloth was for everyone who couldn't carry the tower itself to share in bearing the dead man's remains to cremation. At the tail-end of the procession the strongest men were straining to lift the poles supporting the tower onto their shoulders.

The bull sarcophagus, the pyramids of multicoloured offerings, the cloth, the tower and the hubbub of supporters began the journey through the village. The procession moved slowly enough for Jeanette to keep pace without difficulty because the bull kept wheeling away from the route and making feints into the crowd. The bearers capered and spun in circles to confuse the spirit, so it would never be able to find its way back to the house and haunt the family.

Jeanette clapped.

– *So remember, twice round the roundabout on the way to the cemetery for me*, she ordered Bill.

He caught her hand and kissed the knuckles.

Under its own momentum now, the procession roared through the market, past the clicking cameras of packs of tourists. The boys in the tower pelted the crowd with handfuls of rice and the crowd threw flowers. The bull danced under rows of coloured *penjor* flags, and a man with a forked pole hoisted low-slung power lines along the route so the *wadah* could pass beneath. Young men in the procession chucked water at each other and soaked the onlookers, and the fighting spread until dozens of hooting people were scooping handfuls out of the puddles and splashing it over everyone within reach. The insistent rhythm of drums and metal gongs grew louder and the men carrying the tower sweated and staggered beneath the weight.

As they came to the cemetery, they could see three more towers bobbing over the low roofs of the houses. Wayan's family procession merged with the other three funerals and hundreds of people surged towards the cremation ground.

Connie gasped as a scattered handful of rice stung her cheek. She took Jeanette's hands and they guided her away from the mob.

– *What happens now?*

Connie pointed.

In a quiet corner under the shade of a huge tree, the robed priests were waiting in a circle of musicians and dancers. The bull and the *wadah* were manoeuvred into place.

The musicians began to play. As the chains of notes swelled against an expectant hush, the people pressed round a pavilion hung with plain white draperies. The bull was carried into its shelter and set down, with a collective groan of relief from the bearers. At the side, on a low platform, a bundle wrapped in white cloths lay waiting.

The music grew louder and the whole crowd surged three times round the pavilion. Wooden cages were opened and chickens flapped and squawked to freedom, with dozens of pairs of hands waving them off in the auspicious direction.

There was a roar from the crowd. The hinged back was torn off the bull as the body was snatched up from its resting place. As it was manhandled to the sarcophagus, the cloths fell back to reveal a little heap of bones and hair and leather skin.

Bill put his arm out to shield Jeanette but she shook her head. She was watching intently.

The family piled the remains into the belly of the bull. More people tore the shrouded effigy from the shelf within the tower and crammed it in alongside the real bones. A jingling skeleton of human form made from pierced coins was thrown in on top. The priest poured holy water from an earthenware jar, then smashed the jar to fragments.

Now Wayan and Kadek and the other men packed kindling and logs into the space that was left. Brushwood was piled between the bull's legs and the two boys reluctantly jumped from their perch in the *wadah*.

The stench of kerosene was momentarily overpowering.

Wayan stepped forward with a blazing torch. Flame leapt in a sheet and tore a long *aaaaah* from the throats of the crowd. They stumbled backwards as heat singed their faces. The *wadah* was torched in the same way, causing the monster's paper and bamboo wings to arch and swoop just once as the heat rose, as if the creature would take flight from the fire. Flames licked from the snakes and serpents twining at the base and up towards the pagoda roofs of heaven.

Black smoke swirled through the crowds, and the brass music rose as the funeral dancers chopped and sliced with their swords, defending the spirit from evil as it made its way upwards.

Connie and Bill and Jeanette sank down, huddled together against the trunk of a tree, mesmerised by the blaze and showers of sparks that shot over the treetops. The other pyres were blazing too and the cremation ground became a nether world of drifting smoke, gyrating dancers and milling soot-blackened faces split into white smiles of elation.

The priest leapt onto a platform in the midst of the crowd. Over the crackle of the fires and the patterns of drums and gongs he shouted mantras at the sky. Processions of women laid their offerings in the flames as the bull and the tower and the bones were gradually consumed.

It took a long time for everything to be burned.

The musicians mopped the running sweat from their faces. The wood and metal patterns slowly unwound and separated into falling notes.

The priest's arms fell stiffly to his sides and the dancers slowed to a shuffle, their heads drooping.

A stillness spread through the cemetery, and flakes of soot drifted through the leaves and settled like black snow.

Jeanette's eyes followed the smoke up into the sky. The sun would soon be setting.

– *Just bones*, she said. – *Dry bones on the blaze and the spirit set free. I like that.*

'So do I,' Bill murmured.

Connie's throat and lips were burning.

She took a bottle of water out of her bag. Jeanette and Bill gulped thirstily, and Connie finished what was left. Water trickled down her chin and when she wiped it with the back of her hand she saw a slimy trail of soot. Jeanette's face was similarly smirched, but it was smoother than it had been for weeks. Her head rested against the rough bark of the tree and the soot flakes spiralled past her.

Bill rested too. When she stole a glance at him, Connie caught another brief glimpse of the young man of thirty years ago.

The smouldering ashes were finally doused with jars of water, and children raked through them with sticks to collect the coins. The families had been kneeling on the grass to pray, but now they brought urns and scooped up the ashes. Carrying the filled urns between them they began to leave in slow groups, walking through the twilight. Bill and Connie and Jeanette followed them, out of the cemetery and back towards the village. After the tumult of the day, people were quietly gathering in their house compounds to eat and talk. Lights shone across the village street and long shadows flickered whenever someone crossed in front of the lamps. Bats had come out as they always did with the darkness, and now they swooped in complicated skeins between the power lines and the overhanging trees.

Back in the lane, Wayan's immediate family climbed into a line of waiting cars.

– *Where are they going?* Jeanette asked, as they stood aside respectfully to let them pass.

Connie said, 'They are taking the ashes down to the

sea. They'll wade with them into the water, and then the tide will carry them away. The body has been reduced to its five elements, earth, water, fire, air and space, and the spirit has started on its journey. That's all there is. It's over.'

The three of them stood still, watching the red tail-lights of the vehicles until they turned out of sight.

'Wayan and Dayu will be pleased. It was a good cremation.'

Jeanette surprised them with her smile.

– It was. The sea, you said? I'd like to go and see the sea, before we leave.

'I know a place,' Connie answered. 'We can go there. It's on the way to the airport.'

In two days' time, Bill and Jeanette would be flying back to London.

* * *

Connie made a picnic, and the airport taxi driver took them down a winding road that turned away from the high-rise hotels and cheap shopping malls that blighted most of the coastal strip.

The beach was a thumbnail curve of silver-grey sand overhung by coconut palms, and the midday sea was a sheet of sapphire scalloped with foam where the tiny waves tipped over into the sand. It was Roxana's picture postcard, almost to a detail.

Connie smiled as she thought of her insistence, 'But I prefer Suffolk.'

They paddled along the water's edge. Bill carried Jeanette's flip-flops for her. Connie picked up bleached shells with salt crystals in their ribbing and Jeanette held out her hand for them, cupping her palm and smelling the ocean trapped in the whorls. But after only a hundred yards she was tired.

Bill spread out a blanket in the shade of the nearest clump of trees and Jeanette lay down, propping her head on one hand. A jet crossed in front of them, on a direct line to the airport.

– *Will we really be in England tomorrow? I don't want to leave this place.*

Bill and Connie glanced at each other. They were expert collaborators now in giving Jeanette whatever she wanted.

'You don't have to. You could stay here with me,' Connie said at once.

Jeanette shook her head.

– *It's time to go home. I miss Noah.*

She stretched out her arms and sifted warm sand through her fingers. She had given up pretending to eat, but Connie and Bill peeled fruit and drank white wine out of the cool box.

– *Remember that day?* Jeanette asked. Sand spilled out of her fists and she dug her hands more deeply.

'The picnic,' Bill said.

We are too wound up in our damned memories, Connie thought. Jeanette had been brave and capable when the accident happened, and Bill was loving and good, and I was afraid and angry. But that's not all each of us was, or is. It's only what we remember. Is it our memories that make us what we are?

She wished it were possible to step out of the past, and the deep parallel grooves the three of them had worn, separately and in their pairs.

Connie and Jeanette, Bill and Jeanette, Bill and Connie.

Within her sister's changed face she could see again the girl she had once been, just as at the cremation ground she had glimpsed the young man in Bill.

If we were young again, she thought. If we could do everything again, and differently, with more words and less bitterness, what would we say and do today, now we are nearing the end?

Sadness gripped her. They were sitting on the sand together just a few hours before Bill and Jeanette had to get on a plane. Jeanette was going to die before many more weeks passed, and here she was still thinking *if* and *if*.

Connie said, 'It isn't *then* that's important, is it? We can make *now* matter, this minute, instead of Echo Street and whether it was harder for you to be born deaf or for me to be a foundling.' Without glancing at Bill she went on, 'We could forget what Bill and I did. Or we could acknowledge it and say *that was a mistake*, and not let it matter any more. Could we do that?'

She knelt down in the sand, stretched out and took her sister in her arms.

Jeanette's eyes widened.

'I love you,' Connie said.

She had to strain to catch the blurred syllables of the answer.

– *'Do you? I haven't always been lovable.'*

'I love you now. And I always will.'

– *'I love you too.'* The words almost inaudible now, from Jeanette who usually spoke much too loudly. Her breath was warm on Connie's cheek.

Bill lay down on the other side of Jeanette. He folded himself against her spine, knees pressed into the crook of her knees. As they would have lain for a lifetime of nights, Connie thought, in their marital bed. They cradled

Jeanette between them. Connie felt the ancient scabs of jealousy as if they were peeling off her skin and drifting like the flakes of soot.

'I'm sorry,' she breathed.

Jeanette studied her. Connie could see the mesh of wrinkles that netted the loose skin beneath her sister's eyes, and the beads of sweat caught in the fine hair above her top lip. Light filtered by the palm leaves patterned her skin, and beyond her shoulder it caught the thatch of grey in Bill's hair. It seemed that each of them was holding their breath, in case a clumsy word or movement from anyone might divide them again.

– I am sorry, too. But we are here now. I am so happy that the three of us are here.

Bill looked up into the clear sky. It was harder to speak than he could have imagined, and he was the one who had long ago railed to Connie about the damage of silence. The two women seemed to slide together, Connie's warm brown skin enveloping his wife's brittle bones, Jeanette's vowels filling Connie's throat.

He wanted to tell Jeanette that he loved her, and honoured her, but there would be enough time and privacy for that. He wished he could have told Connie out loud that he held her in his heart, then and now and always, but he believed she knew it without his bathetic words.

'Connie is right,' he said. He could just see the pulse beating beneath his wife's ear. 'What matters is now.'

Through the band of colourless, shimmering air between blue sky and sea, another plane roared towards Denpasar. The airport was waiting, already full of people, each of whom was shuttling around the globe like a restless atom, charged with their own concerns, winging towards families or taking flight from them, children and patriarchs, brothers and sisters and parents, healthy and sick, weighted with schedules, laptops, souvenirs, notes for meetings, all the travellers with their guilt and good intentions, each with their dreams and memories.

Jeanette watched the diminishing arrow of the plane.

– *I want to go home to Noah, but it's hard to leave Bali. I'm not ready to die. But I'm ready to consider the prospect.*

Bill reached for Connie's hand, found it, and drew it across Jeanette's shoulder. They held her more tightly between them and Jeanette smiled at the sky.

– *I smashed a table, you know*, she said.

'How did you do that?' Connie asked.

– *Didn't Bill tell you?*

'No.'

– *After I came home from the hospital. After the operation when they couldn't do what they planned. I saw the glass coffee table we used to have. Smooth and whole. And I couldn't see why a table should be like that, and not me. I smashed it to pieces. Pounded it with a paperweight.*

'I never liked that table,' Bill said.

– *You were shocked.*

'Yes, that's true. It was so unlike you.'

– *Dying was unlike me.*

Not *is*, Connie noted. She was finding it very hard to keep back her tears.

'Did smashing it make you feel better?' she asked.

– *No. Not at all. I was shocked at myself. But you know what? Bali has helped me. Your green wave, that was beautiful. The smell in the village of earth, pig-shit, rain, incense. The bodies burning, the party. It was apt. Just life and death. It made me think of Mum and Dad. Us three. Even*

Noah, some day. Only bones. And then the spirit set free. Maybe. You never know.

Her face split suddenly into a pumpkin-lantern smile.

– *You could say, Bali has helped me see the bigger picture.*

It was so like Jeanette not to try to speak of spiritual enlightenment or any kind of epiphany. The bigger picture was as big a metaphor as she was likely to use.

'That's the best recommendation for the island I've ever heard,' Connie replied.

They lay back with their heads in the sand. A line of giant ants ran from a coconut shell into the coarse grass at the back of the beach, and another plane roared and dipped out of the sky.

Jeanette yawned.

– *Have I got long enough for a nap?* she asked.

Connie looked at her watch. 'Maybe half an hour?'

They released her and she curled up on her side, sighing with satisfaction as she pillowed her cheek on her folded hands.

In the wake of the plane the air seemed to expand, the rustle of the waves and the palm leaves exerting an unwelcome pressure in Connie's ears. Bill shook himself and sat up.

'I'm going to have a swim,' he said.

Jeanette seemed already to be dozing.

'I'll come with you,' Connie said.

She was thinking of the unoccupied rattan chair on her veranda, of returning to her own bed and trying to sleep, and the knobs and handles in her kitchen where his fingers had rested.

They walked down to the water's edge and waded in. Bill stared out to sea.

Abruptly he said, 'Has Jeanette ever talked to you about afterwards? About what is supposed to happen when she's gone?'

A breath of wind dragged puckers across the surface of the water.

'Only at the beginning, that first day when I came down to Surrey. She told me then that she loves you and that you love her, and I agreed that there has never been any doubt of that.'

'Did you?'

'It's true, isn't it?' Connie heard herself say. 'And I've been able to share the weeks since then with the two of you. I've been included in her dying, even though the three of us made it impossible to share life. And I am grateful for it,' she truthfully concluded.

Like Bill, she kept her eyes fixed on the horizon.

'Yes,' Bill agreed. 'I understand.'

He stripped off his shirt and threw it onto the sand, then dived under the skin of the water. Connie stood and watched him swimming powerfully out to sea as if he would go on and on, over the various bars of paler and deeper blue to the glittering line of the horizon, and never turn back again.

The telephone used to ring in the flat in Belsize Park and she would hear Bill's low voice.

'I could see you for an hour, this evening.'

And without a thought even taking shape in her head she would answer 'Yes', blinded by a flash of delight at the prospect of a single hour. That was how it was.

From their first evening together after the Docklands party, they both knew that there was no hope of a happy ending. It was even true that to be stalked by the twin threats of imminent discovery and impending pain gave an extra edge to their temporary ecstasy, defining it with the same sharp glitter as the rim of frost on a dead leaf.

Connie told herself that it was enough – more than enough – to revel in the time that Bill could spare away from Jeanette and Noah.

From being an independent woman with money and freedom she willingly became the embodiment of a cliché, the lover of a married man, who sat waiting for him to telephone and who counted the hours until their next snatched meeting.

'Why?' Bill asked her.

They were lying in each other's arms and she pressed her face to his so that their mouths touched.

'Let me think.' She played for time, trying to come up with an answer that wouldn't sound needy or grandiose, when she needed him so much and loved him with an intensity that – in anyone else – she would have called dangerous. Or insane.

Then she laughed, giving up the struggle. 'Because it's what I want.'

'Hm,' he said. 'Don't you think it's extraordinary, magical, that it's so exactly what I want too? How often does it happen that two people stumble on a passion like ours?'

'Rarely. Eloise and Abelard? Maybe Antony and Cleopatra?'

'Ha. Don't cheapen us with pale comparisons, Connie Thorne.'

'Sorry. Never before, then. Not in the history of the universe.'

He cupped her face in his hands, holding it away from his so he could search her eyes.

'That is how I feel,' he said.

Bill could switch from playful to serious in half a sentence, and she knew he did it with her just because he could. She tried never to compare herself with Jeanette where Bill was concerned – but Jeanette couldn't hear the alteration in his voice from lazy to imperative, or the dip from elation into melancholy, and Connie hugged that advantage to herself with guilty greed. To Bill, the shorthand intimacy of some of their exchanges was as much of a luxury as their long, rambling conversations about music or Italy or food.

Most of the time they spent together, in the fourteen months before the end came, was snatched in brief hours after work when Bill could plausibly have been with clients. They retreated to Connie's apartment and set about constructing a miniature universe together.

'I know this isn't real,' she said once, sadly. 'We long for each other so much, and every meeting is like drinking champagne on Concorde. We never see each other on irritable weekday mornings, or when one of us has flu, or when we've been spending so much time together that there isn't anything particular left to say.'

'It's real to me. The benchmark of reality isn't necessarily sharing the breakfast cornflakes.'

'What would it be like, if we were married?'

As soon as she asked, she wished she had resisted the temptation. But Bill didn't hesitate.

'It would be wonderful. I imagine it all the time. To be together like this every day, to see you in the instant before I fall asleep and as soon as I open my eyes. And don't you think I ask myself every day, how has this happened? How is it that I am married to the wrong sister?'

There was a bitter edge in his voice that was quite unlike him.

'Bill, I shouldn't have asked.'

'Why not? I don't want there to be even one forbidden topic between you and me.'

Maybe not, Connie thought, but there will be. Not now, but once the inevitable happens.

'But I can't leave Jeanette and Noah, you know. I won't ever do that.'

'Have I ever asked you to? Even hinted at it?'

'No, you haven't,' he said humbly. 'What we have now isn't enough for either of us, but it's all there can be. Will you forgive me?'

'No. Because there's nothing to forgive. We made this choice together. And it's good.' Her voice cracked.

'It's not good. It's all wrong, but I love you so, so much.'

A handful of times, when Bill was legitimately away on business, they managed to spend a night together. Connie would travel separately to a hotel in Manchester or York or some other place she had never been to before in her life, check into a hotel, and wait for him to join her. The anonymity of hotel bedrooms, the signs to dangle on doorknobs and the miniature packaging of toiletries and minibar drinks became almost unbearably erotic. The few hours that followed contained the essence of happiness.

And while her affair with Bill continued, for the first time in her life Connie stopped probing at the riddle of her identity. She defined herself simply as a woman in love and all her being was concentrated in the present. It was possible, she discovered, to live almost from one breath to the next.

Just once, they spent three days in Rome.

Bill crammed three days of meetings with an Italian client into a single day. For the rest of the time they walked the streets, drank coffee in tiny bars, and sat in the shadows of baroque churches. They went to *Il*

Trovatore, and came back hand in hand to the home they had made out of a hotel suite.

Then, very suddenly, the end came.

Connie and Bill had flown back from Rome, and they were standing at the carousel at Heathrow waiting for their bags. Two whole days and nights with Bill had lulled Connie into a wifely rhythm. She linked her arm through his as streams of luggage circulated on the belt, then stretched up to kiss the corner of his mouth.

An instant afterwards they turned their heads, sensing that they were being watched.

The moment froze into horror for ever afterwards.

Cousin Elaine – who was returning with her best friend from a fortnight in Tenerife – was staring at them across the revolving suitcases.

It was immediately clear to all three of them that a bomb had silently exploded in baggage reclaim and that the fallout was going to affect every corner of their lives.

Within twenty-four hours Elaine had told Jeanette exactly what she had seen.

('Well. Not to tell would have implicated me in the affair, wouldn't it? You couldn't expect me to enter into that sort of conspiracy with Bill and *her* against my own cousin. No right-thinking person would do such a thing. No, I did what was right and proper and I'm not ashamed of it.')

Jeanette made an unprecedented journey to Belsize Park.

She marched into the flat with her coat pulled round her body as if to let it fly loose might expose her to lethal contamination. She refused even to sit down. Instead she stood in Connie's kitchen, her eyes burning and the muscles in her throat working as she fought for the words.

She told her adopted sister that she was a despicable adulterer, ungrateful, a liar and a cheat, and not worthy of having been taken out of council care and welcomed into the Thorne family.

– *That's what we did, and this is your response.*

Connie stood and silently took it all. In the grip of hurt and fury Jeanette looked like an avenging angel in a Renaissance painting. With a kind of bleak detachment, Connie had to admire her magnificent passion. Back came the memories of clawing and scratching at each other as children. Those battles seemed almost affectionate compared with this one-sided fight.

– *You are not my sister. You never were*, Jeanette said.

Connie didn't point out that the biological bare fact was hardly news to her. And if Jeanette now chose to sever the remaining connection, with all its patina of Echo Street and the crannies and knobs of resentment that had accumulated over all their years – then Connie couldn't really blame her.

– *You will not see my husband again.*

Connie couldn't disagree with that either. She said that she was very sorry, and ashamed. She could have tried to add that Jeanette loving Bill so much herself might at least have lent her some sort of understanding of why Connie should love him too, but her fingers felt too cold and heavy to sign one more syllable and her face was stiff with misery.

– *I don't want to see you ever again.*

Connie tipped her head in silent acknowledgement. Jeanette wrapped her coat even more tightly around her and swept out of the flat.

After she had gone, Connie stood behind her front door and listened to the silence. She had never felt as lonely as she did then.

'How bad was it?' Bill asked in a low voice.

Connie pressed the receiver to her ear as if that would bring him physically closer.

'It was bad. What about you?'

'The same.'

'Where are you?'

'I'm at the office. I want to see you.'

'No.'

'Is that all, Con? Just *no*?'

'You know that this is not *just* anything.'

'I do. You're right. You've got more guts than I have. Listen: remember what I told you.'

Bill had told her many things, but what he meant was *I love you*.

'Me too,' Connie breathed. She reached out and put the receiver back in its cradle.

Jeanette and Hilda formed an alliance of two. Bill was to be forgiven, eventually, once he had endured enough reproach. But Connie was never to be properly rehabilitated. She tried to forget Bill by immersing herself in work, by travelling to wherever she could reach that was a long way from London, by constructing all the appearances of a happy and productive life.

Over time, the absolute exclusion from the family softened a little. She was invited to set-piece events like Jeanette's fortieth birthday and Noah's eighteenth, but by then she was with Seb Bourret and this thawing of the ice probably had more to do with his glamor and fame than with Jeanette's or Hilda's reviving affection for herself. But still she went to the parties. The Thornes and the Buntings were the only family she had. And it meant that from time to time she saw Bill, or at least a quiet and correct version of him. They never touched each other, and spoke hardly a word in private. There was, in any case, nothing they could have said that they did not know already.

Then Hilda died, and there was one more terrible argument on the day Connie saw the contents of the old cardboard box.

She and Jeanette did not speak again until Jeanette knew how ill she was.

Connie waded through the water, the soaked hem of her skirt clinging to her legs. At last she saw the dot that was Bill's head dip as he swam in a circle and headed back to the beach.

She waved her arm over her head and pointed to her watch.

Jeanette was lying on her side, but her eyes were open.

'Did you sleep?' Connie asked.

– *No. I just wanted to lie here.*

Connie helped her to sit up. Jeanette rubbed the sand out of her hair and her face twisted because the movement hurt her. Connie put her wrap around her sister's shoulders, and chafed her hands as if she could massage some more life back into them.

Bill sprinted the short distance up the beach. He hopped on one leg as he dragged on his trousers.

'Let's get going.' He took Jeanette's hand to lead her.

Connie picked up the folded blanket and the picnic box and they began the slow walk back. The sand was hot under their feet.

Their taxi was parked in the shade of some scrubby bushes, with all four doors open to catch a breeze. The driver had been asleep on the back seat, but he leapt up as soon as they approached.

'*Lapangan terbang*. Airport, quick, quick,' he beamed, and they settled Jeanette into her seat.

They had spent longer at the beach than they intended, and the check-in queue had shortened to a handful of people. Connie could see from the sign that the Singapore flight was already boarding. Jeanette stood with her hand tucked under Connie's and her slight weight resting against Connie's arm while Bill checked them in.

– *I wish you were coming home.*

'I'll be there in a couple of weeks,' Connie said with an easiness she didn't feel. She had deliberately chosen not to return with Bill and Jeanette because she thought it would be right for them and Noah to have a few days alone together, without having to work out whether or not she should be with them. After that she would fly back to London for what they all knew was likely to be the beginning of the end.

'We'd better go through,' Bill said.

At the barrier Jeanette turned and held up her arms, like a child.

Connie kissed her, and closed her arms around her sister's shoulders. There was almost nothing left of Jeanette's once luscious body.

– *Thank you. It was wonderful*, Jeanette signed.

'It was,' Connie agreed.

A man in a booth held out his hand for passports and boarding passes.

Bill and Connie exchanged the briefest hug. Bill and Jeanette held hands, and walked through the barrier. They turned back just once to wave before they passed out of sight. The last thing that Connie noticed was that the backs of Jeanette's legs were still lightly powdered with sand.

The taxi driver was waiting for her in the line outside Arrivals. Connie waved and he pulled over. 'Back to the village,' she told him.

Noah was driving home from Surrey. He stared at the lines of rush-hour traffic but he couldn't get his mother's changed face out of his mind. In the two weeks since he had last seen her, she had faded and shrunk. Her skin was like stretched tissue paper over knobs of bone. Instead of firing questions at him and demanding to be told the latest details of his life, she was content to sit quietly and hold his hand.

'Mum? Tell me all about Bali. What was it like?'

– *Beautiful*, she smiled.

'Do you feel rested?'

– *Yes*, she agreed, but he knew that she said it only to please him.

'Okay,' Noah murmured. He squeezed her brittle fingers.

– *How is Roxana?*

'She's fine. Very good. She's still working for Auntie Connie's friend, in the film business.'

Jeanette didn't ask any more, whereas once she would have wanted to know all about it.

'Dad? She looks terrible,' Noah burst out when they were alone together.

'The flights were very hard for her,' Bill said.

'She's . . .' Noah began, then stopped. He had been about to exclaim, *She's going to die*. It was stupid; he had known for months. But it was not until now, this minute, that he properly understood what dying was going to mean.

'I should have come with you to Bali,' he said despairingly. 'I didn't realise.' Instead he had gone to meetings, and played football, and made love to Roxana.

Bill smiled at him. 'Bali was very good, for all three of us. You'd have enjoyed it, but it wasn't essential for you to be there.'

Noah absorbed this. 'Was it all right with Auntie Connie?'

'Yes,' Bill said. 'It was.'

Noah blinked, but he couldn't see properly to drive. He pulled over and called Roxana on her mobile.

'Where are you, Rox?'

'Still at work. How is your mother?'

'She's very weak. Not seeing her for two weeks has made me realise how fast she's going.'

'That's bad, Noah. I'm really sorry.'

'What are you doing? I want to see you.' He needed very much to hold her and let some of her life and strength seep into him.

'I was going back to the apartment. But I'll meet you. We can have a drink and talk.'

He smiled, fastening on to the prospect. 'I'll be there in an hour.'

They went to a pub they both liked. Nowadays Roxana knew all about how to order beers and which ones Noah preferred. She came back to their table and set his drink in front of him.

'There,' she said. 'Cheers.'

'Good health,' Noah said sadly.

They had several drinks. Roxana listened to him talk

about his mother, but she didn't try to offer too much sympathy. She just accepted what was happening, and Noah thought that she did it in just the right way. He knew that he loved her, and looking at the angle of her thigh and the way her forearm lay along the back of an empty seat he was even more strongly aware, *right now*, of how much he wanted to fuck her.

He shifted in his chair.

His mother's hold on life was loosening, and his response was to feel an overwhelming need for sex? Was that shocking, or was it perhaps the normal, selfish response of those who were still healthy?

'Roxana?'

'Yes, Noah?' Her mouth curved in a smile he recognised. She knew what he was thinking.

He leaned forward, caught her by the lapels of her jacket with the big buttons and drew her an inch closer.

'Can we go back to Limbeck House?'

Noah didn't feel particularly easy about using Auntie Connie's place, but Andy was in the flat in Hammersmith and Auntie Connie herself was still out in Bali, so it wouldn't matter that much.

Roxana's forehead touched his.

'Why not?' she teased him.

In the mirrored lift as it rose to the top floor, Noah trapped Roxana in a corner. She pretended to dodge him, then crooked her arms to draw him closer.

'Ha ha, now I have you,' she murmured.

The lift doors parted and they stepped out into the lobby. A slit of window gave a different view of the city from the one inside the apartment. Roxana lingered to gaze at the chains of lights separated by mysterious wells of darkness.

'Look, it's so beautiful.'

'I've seen it.' Noah's mind was on other matters.

'Hey. Wait a minute. Let's go inside.'

Roxana searched her bag for the keys, found them, and singled out the heavy Chubb. She fitted it into the lock, laughing a little because she had drunk enough to find the process a challenge. She turned the key to the left, expecting the familiar resistance and then a click, but instead the key refused to turn at all. The door was already unlocked.

Frowning now, she let her shoulder fall against it. The very slight give indicated that the Yale latch was in place.

When she went out to work she must have forgotten to secure the Chubb.

She fitted the Yale without difficulty and the door smoothly opened. She turned on the lights and the white walls were flooded with brightness.

She knew that she hadn't forgotten to lock up properly, that was just the explanation she allowed herself to reach for, but at first glance everything seemed as it always did. Relieved, Roxana took a few steps forward into the big room. Noah turned towards the bathroom and she continued down the corridor towards Connie's music room and bedroom.

And then she saw the open doors and she knew that the worst had actually happened.

The tidy work area had been turned upside down. The computer and the keyboard had gone. File cabinets and drawers stood open and the floor was a drift of music manuscripts and papers and strewn debris. She had no idea what else might have been taken.

A tide of horror swept through Roxana. She wanted to run and bury her head, but she made herself walk on into Connie's bedroom.

Every drawer and cupboard stood open. The mattress had been pulled off the bed. Clothing and lingerie and photographs and emptied boxes had been flung everywhere.

She pressed the heels of her hands into her stinging eyes, then looked again.

The devastation was still there.

She walked back to the big room, although her legs were shaking.

Noah was standing by the window.

'What?' he demanded as soon as he saw her face. 'What's happened?'

Roxana's hands were at her mouth.

'A bad thing.' In her anguish, language escaped her. She couldn't remember the English words for burglar or break-in.

In her room, the mess was the same as in Connie's but Roxana had nothing worth stealing. Her savings were in the bank, thanks to Connie's intervention. Even her beach postcard was still on the wall beside her bed.

Noah was at her shoulder. 'Shit, look at this place,' he breathed.

Cold shockwaves were breaking over Roxana, and the breath was torn out of her as if she were fighting the Suffolk sea all over again.

'It is my fault, it is my fault,' she kept repeating. The whole picture now played itself out in her mind.

Noah put his hands on her arms. 'You've been burgled. How did they get in?'

Roxana could see it all. She was standing over there by

the kitchen counter, where she had made unwanted tea for Cesare, and then tried to kick Philip in the balls. The evening's silly golden glow of champagne and sumptuous food had already faded into the dull reality of stale old bargains and men wanting sex from her. Philip had muttered that he would use the bathroom before Roxana threw them out, and she had let him go.

She had stood there and allowed Cesare to soft-soap her with apologies.

Philip must have crept down the corridor and gone swiftly through Connie's belongings. And somewhere in a drawer he must have discovered a set of keys. How perfectly delighted he would have been with that.

Roxana screwed her eyes shut. If only she and Noah could be coming up in the lift again, with everything still fine, before she had betrayed Connie's trust in her.

'How can it be your fault?' Noah insisted. When she looked again he was picking up clothes from the floor, laying them on the overturned mattress.

'Come and see in Connie's rooms.'

He followed her.

'Shit,' he said again. 'Look, we shouldn't be touching anything. How did they get in? The front door was locked, wasn't it?'

'Yes,' Roxana said miserably. 'I mean, no. I'm sure it was the men who did it.'

'*What* men?'

'I asked them up here.' She could easily have cried, but she kept her neck and mouth frozen. She could have tried to tell a lie, but honesty seemed the last thing she had left to offer.

Noah gazed at her. 'Go on.'

'Mr Cesare Antonelli,' she whispered.

'Who is he?'

'A film director.'

Disjointedly, while Noah still stared at her, Roxana told him about the evening.

'Nothing happened, Noah. I know I was foolish. I was thinking about movies, about maybe being a model. They said I could be.'

'I thought you were pretty streetwise, Rox, but you still brought them up here, to Auntie Con's place? What were you thinking?'

'Nothing. I got rid of them. But one of them, the bad one, I let him go to the bathroom.' She pointed.

Noah let out a long sigh.

'Noah, I am so sorry. I . . . wanted to seem like a London girl. I let them think that this was my place. I wanted to be like your Auntie Con.'

'Well, you aren't, are you?' His voice sounded hard. 'Right. Let's think. We've got to start by calling the police. You'll have to tell them everything.'

Roxana sank down onto a chair. She was afraid of the police. At home, they were not the people you looked to for any help.

'And then we'll have to telephone Auntie Con. What's the time in Bali?'

'I don't know,' she whispered.

'We'll have to deal with everything. I don't want to tell my parents. I don't want Dad to have to think about anything except Mum.'

'I am sorry,' she said again.

Noah took out his mobile, frowned at it, then tapped out 999.

FIFTEEN

Bill stood at his kitchen window and watched the sun rise. The branches of the beech trees formed a dark lattice against the dishwater sky, but then a shaft of light suddenly caught them and they glimmered with rainwater. He was holding a mug of tea; when he looked down it was with surprise because he couldn't remember how it had got there.

The tea was stone cold, and his bare feet were cold on the tiled floor.

He listened, straining his ears. The house was silent, and the silence had a massive quality as if the pressure it exerted on the doors and windows might cause them to fly open.

Upstairs, Jeanette lay seeming to sleep, in the bed where he had finally left her.

The gorge was a ripple of leaves, and from her chair on the veranda Connie could hear the crisp, leathery rustle as a quick breeze sprang up.

In the house the telephone began to ring.

She put down her book and padded inside to answer it. The floorboards were striped with afternoon sunshine.

'Connie.' His voice with a break in it.

'I'm here.'

'Jeanette died about three hours ago. I lay there and held her for an hour or so. I didn't want to come down and leave her all alone, Con, but she's dead, you know?'

Connie took in the words.

'Oh, my darling.'

It wasn't clear to her whether she meant Bill or her sister.

'Last night she was restless and she couldn't find any way to lie that didn't hurt her poor bones. I brought up all the pillows in the house and put them underneath her to make the bed softer. I held her hands, and she smiled at me and signed *good night*. Then in the middle of the night I knew she was dying.'

'It's too soon.'

He raised his head at that. 'No. She's been ill for a long time.'

'I wish I had been there.'

Bill said, 'I think she would have preferred it this way. It's as if she left you straight from Bali. She wanted it to come, you know. She probably willed it. That will of hers was still strong, even at the end.'

'Yes.'

'I've got to go now, Connie.'

'Is Noah with you?'

'It's still early. I thought I'd let him finish his night's sleep.'

'I don't want you to be on your own.'

'I'll call him now. Jeanette's nurse will be here in an hour.'

'All right. I'll be there as soon as I can.'

'Connie, she's gone. She's dead,' he repeated, trying to familiarise himself with the words. 'There is no reason to hurry over here. I don't think the funeral can be for a week or so.'

'No,' Connie agreed.

'I'm sorry,' he said. 'You've lost her too. I'm not thinking properly. It's strange in this house. It's so quiet. The silence makes me think of her silence.'

Behind her eyes, Connie felt the first tears gathering.

After Bill had said goodbye, she went to sit down at her keyboard.

An unexpected phrase of music was running in her head and she picked out the sequence of notes, then repeated them. There was some of the deep humming of the gongs from the village cremation, overlaid by a shimmer of metal, and she frowned in the effort to harness her imagination to a lyrical line. The fingers of her left hand spanned the keys as she reached with her right for a sheet of manuscript paper and scribbled *For Jeanette*.

The music seemed to be caught like floodwater behind a dam. As she struggled to release it Connie lost track of the time. She reached out once to switch on the lamp, but she was surprised when she looked up for the second time to see that it was now pitch dark outside. The night was noisy, as it always was, with dogs barking and the conversation of frogs.

When the telephone rang beside her she thought it was Bill again.

'I'm here,' she said.

'Ms Thorne?' an unfamiliar voice asked.

'Who is this?'

'This is Lloyds Bank.'

She listened in bewilderment. A bank official who might have been in Scotland or Cornwall was telling her about some unusual spending patterns relating to her credit cards.

'*Hi-fi equipment?*' she repeated. 'No, I haven't. No, nor leather goods. What is this about?'

She listened.

'That can't be right. These purchases were made in the UK and I have been out here in Bali for more than three weeks.'

Connie wondered whether this could be to do with Roxana, and then decided that that was impossible.

'Yes, put a stop on the card, please. I will, yes. Yes, thank you.'

Jeanette and the music were filling her mind. Credit-card fraud was profoundly unimportant and she easily dismissed the thought of it. She returned to the keyboard, but only half an hour later the phone rang again.

'Bill?'

'Connie, this is Roxana. I am calling from London on your telephone, I am very sorry, but my mobile will not . . .'

'That's all right, Roxana. What's the matter?'

'I have bad news to tell you and Noah said for me to call you at once about it. He has gone home now to his father because, you know . . .'

'Yes,' Connie interrupted gently. 'Just tell me what has happened, please.'

Roxana's fractured English, breaking up as she tried to explain the news, was eloquent of her distress.

'You know, we are broken into, the things gone, beautiful things belonging to you and all of this because I am stupid and I believe what a man says to me when all my life I am knowing better than to think such words are true. You have been so kind to me and I have paid you like this, Connie, and I don't ask that you forgive me but you will let me pay back everything over some time, I will do this I promise . . .'

Even as she listened, she could not believe that the girl was culpable.

'Roxana, be *quiet*, stop talking for one minute. The flat has been burgled, is that right?'

'Yes. I'm trying now to find out all what has gone because the police are here making questions and I don't know . . .'

'Listen. If the police are there I'll speak to them in a moment. Just tell me how the burglars got into the flat.'

'It was because of me, and I am so sorry for it.'

'How is that?'

Roxana said that she had met some men and she had been a fool to trust them, such a big fool, and she had let them into the apartment and this had happened . . .

'I see,' Connie sighed. 'What have they taken?'

'I am afraid to tell you. Your music machines and the computer.'

'Oh dear.'

Connie couldn't work out yet what the extent of the damage might be. Nor, at this moment, did she care very much.

'And in your bedroom, clothes and such and your little boxes, you know, where jewellery is kept, I think, these are empty now.'

Among her jewellery there were pieces that Seb had given her, and the circle of polished stones in a vaguely art nouveau setting that she had chosen from Hilda's small collection.

From the strangled sound of her voice, Roxana was now in tears.

As calmly as she could, Connie said, 'All right. Let me talk to the police now.'

She discussed with the officer the probability that the thieves had found a spare set of keys in her bureau drawer, and had chosen a convenient time to let themselves in and go through her possessions.

'I understand from your young lady lodger here that she met one of the men through her place of work.'

'Did she? The lap-dancing club?'

'That she didn't mention. No, in her statement she said it was . . .' there was a pause while he seemed to consult his notes '. . . Oyster Films.'

Connie put her hand to her head and pinched the bridge of her nose between her fingers. Now Angela would be involved. She felt rather as if she were in a novel with a very convoluted plot that wasn't holding her attention.

'Officers will be pursuing that line of investigation,' the policeman droned.

'Thank you.'

'I understand they have taken your computer.'

He advised her to put a stop on all her cards and to change her PIN numbers and passwords immediately.

Connie thanked him once more, and asked him to put Roxana on again.

'You see, Connie? It is very bad.'

'It's not very good, but we'll deal with it. The first thing you must do is get in an emergency locksmith to change the locks and make the place secure again.'

'But . . .'

'Just do it, Roxana. Ask the police to help you. One thing I do not want you to do is to trouble Noah or Mr Bunting with any of this.'

'You do not have to tell me such a thing,' Roxana shot back. 'I also have had my family dead. Do you think I do not know what this feels like?'

'Of course you do. I'm sorry.'

'Please. I will make the locks good.'

'Thank you. I'll be home in a day or so, I don't know exactly when. You'll have to be there to let me in.'

'Of course. I dread to see you, Connie, but I will be glad as well.'

Connie smiled, in spite of everything. 'Listen. Whatever the burglars have taken, it's only things. Just stuff. A computer, a few rings and necklaces. No one can break in and steal from us what really matters.'

'I hope so,' Roxana said bleakly. 'And I am very sorry indeed that you have lost your sister.'

Connie booked and paid for a ticket to London. After making sure she had enough cash in dollars to see her home, she made a series of calls to cancel her cards, as the policeman had advised. She found that it was helpful to concentrate on these practical matters. The pressure of grief was steadily gathering inside her skull.

At length, she decided there was nothing more she could do until she reached London again.

In Bali it was just coming up to midnight on the day of Jeanette's death.

The fragments of music that she had been working on meant almost nothing to her when she glanced at them again. She shuffled the jottings into a pile and put them aside. When she stood up her back and legs ached from having sat so long in the same position.

In her bedroom, the bed was neatly made under its white cover. She sat down where Jeanette had slept, and gently touched the pillow.

Beside the bed stood a small wooden cabinet, locally made, with a single drawer. Connie slid the drawer all the way out, unhooked a latch and lifted it out of the way. At the back of the recess was a hidden compartment.

The only item in the secret place was a small box.

She opened the box with a practised twist of her fingers, and tipped the marcasite earring with an old-fashioned screw fastening into the palm of her hand. It glinted in the light of her bedside lamp.

A gecko ran up the white wall behind the bed, briefly startling her.

The burglars hadn't got her earring. It was always with her, her talisman.

She closed her fist on it now. The post dug into the palm of her hand as she clenched her fingers more tightly, and began to cry for Jeanette.

Connie's affair with Bill lasted for fourteen months, and in that time they spent a total of perhaps three hundred hours together.

It was such a brief interval within the drawn-out stretch of the rest of her life that Connie was surprised, once it was all over, by the abject loneliness that descended on her. She responded by parcelling up her days with mechanical attention, immersing herself in mere existence.

She ached for Bill, even to hear the sound of his voice, but she didn't see or speak to him.

There was an instinct for survival buried deep in her.

She had work to do, and plenty of friends who were loosely connected with work. Six months after everything ended, she won an industry award. A piece appeared in *Campaign* titled 'Boom Girl Booming'. More commissions come in, and she wrote the theme music for a hit television serial. Money accumulated in blocks and wedges, but it seemed to hem her in rather than offer greater freedom.

She began to travel, to India and the Far East and South America, with friends or more often alone. She visited temples and archaeological sites, made notes and searched for inspiration and wrote music, and all the time she felt as if she was drifting without an anchor.

One day, drinking Thai beer beside the slow brown river in Bangkok and watching the crowds flooding onto an upriver ferry, she realised with a jolt that in this distant place she was searching the faces for any features that bore a resemblance to her own.

Her companion was a dry Australian woman whom she had met on a plane a few days earlier.

'What's up?' the woman asked.

'I don't think I know what I'm doing here,' Connie responded with deliberate vagueness.

The woman raised her eyebrows. 'What you're doing here is what you're doing, having a beer with me and wondering about heading north. What else is there? What do you want to know?'

'All right. I want to know who I am.'

Connie had told her a little about her history. It was easy to confide in a stranger.

The Australian woman rolled her lower lip over the upper, removing a tideline of beer.

'Why don't you try to find out about your real mother, if it's biting you so hard?'

Connie smiled at the over-simplification of this. But once she was back in England she extracted her short birth certificate from a file of papers and studied it. The baldness of the two shreds of information she possessed reminded her of how difficult the search would be.

On or about 17 June 1963. Found in garden at 14 Constance Crescent, London E8.

Foundling. Such a Victorian word. It seemed to have nothing to do with the 1990s but it was at the heart of her, even as much as Bill was.

She prickled with renewed desire to trace her real mother and as the days passed the need increased, occupying more and more of her thoughts. It was not just in order to experience that maternal tie, blood to blood, that she would never know with Hilda. If she only knew her mother's story, however sad it might be, she could then continue her own, like adding chapters to a serial novel. It was having no beginning, Connie thought, that made it hard to develop a coherent narrative.

She began to read books and memoirs about other foundlings. She felt no less lonely, but to compare her experiences with those of other people provided a kind of comfort.

Fresh determination galvanised her.

She made an appointment, and went back to discuss the circumstances of her adoption with a different social worker. Mrs Palmer had retired. She learned that the social-work file that she had not been allowed even to see would have been kept in a safe place until twenty-five years after her birth, but now it had been removed and destroyed.

'It's a shame, that,' sighed the young woman who interviewed her. 'It's quite a small window, really, for people to apply for the facts. Can't you ask your adoptive mother about the details?'

'Not really,' Connie said.

She refused to be disheartened. She wrote an advertisement giving the date of her birth and the circumstances of her discovery, asking for anyone who might know any more to contact her, and placed it in a series of newspapers and magazines. When the ads appeared in print she sat and gazed at them. She fantasised about how her mother might at that moment be reading the same words, and realising with a flash of joy that this was a message from her lost daughter.

The only response came from a journalist.

A famous actor much older than Connie had published a popular memoir revealing that he had been a foundling, and so it briefly became a hot topic.

Connie agreed to be interviewed by the journalist for a colour supplement article, which appeared alongside a full-page colour picture of herself looking wistfully out of the window of the Belsize Park flat. The introduction read, '*Connie Thorne is a successful musician and composer. But there is a hollow at the centre of her life.*'

Although it was a mass-circulation paper, the article produced no response except a sharp note from Jeanette to say that its appearance had really upset Hilda, and did Connie never think about the consequences of her actions?

After the interview, the journalist asked Connie if she had searched the national newspaper archive for any press coverage following her rescue. It was quite likely that there would have been several local news items about Baby Constance. If it had been a slack news day, the writer pointed out, the story might even have made the national news.

A few days later at a desk in a utilitarian library reading room in a North London suburb, Connie opened up a bound volume of the *Hackney Gazette* for June 1963.

She found herself staring in amazement at a picture of herself as a two-day-old baby.

She was loosely swaddled in a blanket, and her tiny, crunched-up face looked surprisingly serene.

'Baby Constance is being cared for by nurses at the Royal London Hospital who have named her after the street in East London where she was discovered in the front garden of a house. Two-day-old Constance was tucked inside a shopping bag that had been left under the hedge. Police and medical staff are anxious to trace the baby's mother, who may be in urgent need of medical treatment.'

Connie studied the picture for a long time. A hedge and a shopping bag, she thought. They were antecedents of a kind. Better than knowing nothing at all.

Later, she contacted the records department of the newspaper. They provided her with a photographic print of the baby picture. She framed it, and it stood on a shelf in her flat.

Hunched over the newspaper volumes in the dry library atmosphere, greedily absorbing the smallest details of her history, Connie first read the name Kathleen Merriwether. The *Gazette* journalist had even interviewed the girl.

'"My boyfriend Mike thought it was a cat," Kathleen reported, "but I knew straight away it was a baby . . ."'

Connie sat back, staring at the name as it jumped out at her from the grey mass of newsprint.

Kathleen Merriwether had found her, surely only a matter of minutes or a bare hour after her mother had crept along the hedge like a shadow and left her there. If she could find Kathleen, maybe she could cajole her into remembering some tiny scrap of a fact or impression that had been overlooked until now, a detail that would bring her mother closer. Perhaps even close enough to reach.

In her desire not to think about losing Bill, the search began to obsess Connie.

She was having vivid dreams of meeting her mother in strange places – in a laundry, in a flat-bottomed boat in a mangrove swamp – and then having disjointed conversations with her about gardening, or shoes. A sense of urgency grew in her heart, filling some of the space left by Bill's absence. She wanted a real connection, not these phantoms dredged out of her subconscious. She felt her roots like vestigial fibres, coiled up, waiting to reach down into the ground and anchor her at last.

How, she wondered, did you go about tracing someone when all you had was their maiden name and their age? She thought of birth records, but that wouldn't give much of a clue to Kathleen's present whereabouts, and of electoral rolls, but that might well mean searching the whole country for someone who in all probability would now be known by her husband's name.

Connie decided she might as well begin close to home. She took down the London telephone directory and counted the listed Merriwethers. There were only a handful with exactly that spelling, always assuming that the newspapers in 1963 had spelled the name correctly in the first place. With luck, she thought, she might end up speaking to Kathleen's brother or a cousin.

It took her a few days to find the right frame of mind. Then one early evening, alone in her flat after a day in a studio, she began making the calls.

The first four led nowhere. Two were picked up by answering machines and Connie immediately hung up, not wanting or knowing how to leave an appropriate message. Another call was answered by a foreign au pair with small children clamouring in the background, who advised her in a strong Spanish accent to call back when Mrs Merriwether was at home. A very old man

in response to the fourth call said that he had no relatives by the name of Kathleen, but told her a very long
anecdote anyway about his daughter who was now living in Western Australia. Connie listened, hearing the
note of loneliness in his voice.

A woman answered the fifth call.

Connie's speech was well-rehearsed by this time.
'Good evening, I'm sorry to trouble you, I'm trying to
contact a Kathleen Merriwether.'

'This is Kathy Merriwether,' the brisk, pleasant voice
said. 'How can I help you?'

Surprise almost took her breath away. It took her a
moment before she could say, 'My name is Constance
Thorne.'

'It's baby Constance, isn't it?' the woman replied at
once. 'You know, I've always wondered if I'd hear
from you.'

To have found her so easily was such a stroke of good
luck that it seemed almost inevitable to learn that Kathy
Merriwether lived in Kentish Town, only two miles
from Connie's flat.

It was a warm spring evening when Connie walked up
the street. The plane trees were putting out sprays of tender leaves, and music and voices floated out of open
windows. Kathy's house had stone steps leading up to
the front door, net-curtained bay windows, and three
doorbells mounted one above the other.

Connie rang the one marked Merriwether and as
she waited she heard the whistling rush and then the
buried thud-thud of a fast train in a deep cutting, very
close at hand. Echo Street might have been just round
the next corner.

The woman who opened the door was in her late forties. She was broad, with heavy shoulders and pretty plump arms exposed by a pale-blue T-shirt. She was wearing loose trousers and house slippers.

'So you are Constance,' she smiled. 'Baby Constance, after all this time.'

Connie held out the flowers she had brought.

Everything was as she expected yet she felt awkward, and dull with the sudden certainty that this meeting that she had set up with so much eagerness wasn't going to deliver any of the clues she longed for.

Kathy Merriwether's path had briefly intersected with hers more than thirty years ago, that was all. It was difficult not to feel a sense of anticlimax when confronted with this ordinary, heavy-set stranger.

Kathy accepted the flowers and sniffed them appreciatively.

'How lovely. You didn't have to do that.' She shook Connie's hand. 'Come on up. It's the top floor, I'm afraid.'

Kathy puffed slightly as they climbed the steep stairs.

'Dear me. Here we are, then. Make yourself at home.'

The sitting room was over-full with a squashy sofa and a pair of armchairs. China ornaments were lined up on the plain wooden mantelpiece over a gas log fire. The window looked down into a garden that sloped to a high wall, and just as Connie was registering that beyond this was the railway cutting another train whistled through. Vibrations set the window glass rattling in its frame.

'You get so used to them, you don't even hear them go by,' Kathy said.

'I know. The house I grew up in was the same.'

Kathy smiled. 'Was it? Where was that?'

Connie accepted the offer of tea rather than a glass of wine. She sat down in one of the armchairs and called out her answers to questions while Kathy clattered in the kitchen, coming back first of all with the flowers arranged in a jug that she placed on the coffee table, then with a tray. She poured tea into cups patterned with rosebuds and handed one to Connie.

'Echo Street? East London, is that? You know, I've thought about you so often over the years. I wondered how life had turned out for you.'

She glanced at Connie's shoes and the soft leather bag in which she carried her papers. 'It turned out all right, by the look of it. That's very good.'

She offered a plate of foil-wrapped chocolate biscuits. Connie shook her head and Kathy unwrapped one for herself and laid it ready in her saucer.

'Now. What can I tell you?' she began.

Connie hesitated. Now that the moment had come the only question that properly formed itself in her mind was, *Who am I?*

She put it as neutrally as she could. 'What happened when you found me?'

Kathy's laugh turned into a sigh.

'Well. I was sixteen, and out with my boyfriend. I was supposed to be back home by ten o'clock at the very latest. My dad was quite strict.'

Connie put down her cup. Every word was important, and she didn't want to miss a syllable.

Kathy Merriwether told her about the empty street, the way the arched plane trees made a dark tunnel of the pavement. In her mind's eye Connie saw Constance Crescent as it had been on the day she went there with Bill.

'We were behind a hedge in one of the gardens. There was a smell of privet, dustbins and cats. Mike was trying it on, and maybe I was leading him on a bit. Then I heard a cry. It was a baby, I knew that straight away.'

'What did you do?'

'It was there, under the hedge. I picked it up. Brown plastic shopping bag, with handles. And you were inside.'

'Was there anyone else there? Could someone have been watching?'

'I don't think so,' Kathy said. 'There wasn't so much as a shadow moving anywhere.'

Another train plunged through the cutting.

'Perhaps . . .' Connie said ' . . . perhaps she hid nearby, to make sure someone found me?'

The thought that her mother might have fixed her eyes on the woman she was now looking at seemed to create two spans of a bridge, airy yet almost solid enough to dash across.

'Perhaps,' Kathy said doubtfully.

The noise of the train faded and the flat was silent for a moment. Then Kathy went on, and from the way she talked Connie could tell that she was used to retelling the story.

'Mike went to the house next door and rang the bell, and the woman who lived there ran out in her dressing gown. We took you inside and the woman's husband rang for the police and ambulance. While we waited, I held you inside my cardigan. Trying to keep you warm against my skin.'

Even though the story was so well-rehearsed, Kathy's voice caught a little. Connie kept her eyes on the patch of sky outside the window.

'And there was the earring.'

'What? What's that?'

'It was a single earring, I can see it now, fastened to the blanket you were wrapped in. One little glittering droplet. The mother, *your* mother, must have kept the other one. A keepsake, one for each of you. Maybe it was all she had to leave. I thought it was the saddest thing I had ever seen. It still makes me cry, thinking of it.'

Kathy reached into the pocket of her loose trousers and extricated a tissue. Connie kept on looking at the sky.

Kathy blew her nose. 'What could have happened to that poor girl? What circumstances was she in, that made her abandon you?'

'I don't know,' Connie managed to say. 'I'd like to find out.'

'Of course you would. That's only natural,' Kathy was saying. 'It's why you're here. I'll tell you what I can, but I'm not sure it will be all that much help.'

She poured more tea and resettled the cosy on the pot.

'I would have loved to keep in touch with you, you know. I felt so responsible for you, after that night. I went three times to visit you, while you were still in the Royal London. It wasn't too far, just a bus ride after I came out of school, and the nurses used to let me pick you up and give you a cuddle or a feed. You were the sweetest little baby.'

Connie risked a glance at her rescuer.

'Did you? Was I?'

'Oh, yes. So pretty and alert. More than any of the other babies on the ward. I didn't have a camera in those days, not like everyone does now, but I'd have loved a picture of me holding you. Myra, she's the nurse I made friends with, she'd have taken a photo of the two of us. She used to say that I should have been your mother, I'd have taken better care of you. I'm sorry, that sounds a bit harsh. We don't know what made your real mother do it, do we?'

'It's all right,' Connie whispered.

She was moved to hear the words *us* and *we*.

There was a new story involving Kathy, and a nurse with a name, and a ward with other babies on it who would all now be adults, and it affected her to realise that this was her story and theirs, before Hilda and Tony and Jeanette. Along with the photograph this was her own small fragment of a history, tiny but significant.

'Then they took you off to the LCC children's home, didn't they? That was over this side of town so it wasn't on the cards for me to carry on visiting you. I felt very sad about it. I'd even asked my mum if we could try to adopt you but she said she wasn't about to start all over again thank you very much now she'd finally got me and Mark to the age we were.'

Kathy hesitated.

'There was another question too, about you maybe being a bit of a mixture. No one even thinks about that sort of thing nowadays, do they? But it was a lot different back then and my mum and dad were very old-fashioned, Dad especially.'

Kathy bit into another chocolate biscuit as Connie met her eyes.

'You just look very elegant now. Hard to place, that's what I'd think if I met you and I didn't know anything about you.'

Hard to place. That's true enough, Connie thought.

'Go on,' she smiled.

'One day I rang up the home to get news of you, and the clerk there told me that a family had come forward for you, a very nice family, and the adoption procedure was now complete. I asked, but they wouldn't give me any details. It was confidential. So I never heard any more and it's been in my mind ever since then. Do you know, at the hospital they gave you my name? Babies have to have names. Constance Merriwether, that's who you were.'

Connie looked at her again. Constance *Merriwether*. There was a bond between her and Kathy after all: she could feel it tightening, pulling at her.

'I didn't know that,' she said in surprise. 'I never saw the adoption papers.'

'The family who adopted you were called Thorne?'

'Yes.'

'This is like when you're doing a jigsaw, isn't it, and two big pieces suddenly fit together. Tell me some more.'

Connie told her about the Thornes. She realised that Kathy was a good listener.

'So it was a successful adoption,' the other woman concluded, but with a question in her voice.

'Yes, I think so,' was all Connie would say.

'And now? What do you do now?'

Connie told her, briefly. Kathy clapped her hands in delight.

'Really? You wrote that? *Boom, boom, baboom, ba ba . . .*'

'Yes, and the theme music for . . .'

'. . . *bababa ba.*'

'What do you do, Kathy?'

'Do you want to know about all that?'

'Yes, I do. You found me, and you gave me a name.' Nowhere near a mother or even a sister, but a significant connection just the same.

Kathy looked pleased. 'I'll need a glass of wine,' she said.

She went into the kitchen, came back with a bottle and poured two generous glasses.

'Well now. I went into nursing. Because of you, you could say. That night changed things for me.' Kathy's broad face turned solemn.

'Up until then, I was a silly girl. You know . . . boyfriend, clothes, trying not to let my dad find out the half of what I got up to. Then I saw you, dressed in nothing but a little cardigan and a blanket, and left in a bag under a hedge. Once I'd held you, like this, in my arms, I knew I'd never forget you. I was playing about with Mike, and this was before the pill, remember, and I realised all of a sudden that what all that would inevitably lead to was you – not *you*, of course, but a baby who was a scrap of humanity, full of the potential to be someone and to love and be loved, not just me getting pregnant and having to leave school. It was a big, serious world. I looked at poor Mike a bit differently after that, I can tell you.'

'I can imagine,' Connie said. She was gazing at Kathy's plump, pretty arms that had once held her.

'All the boys, they just wanted what they wanted. But when I thought about it, I could just about guess at the mistakes and the bad luck that might have driven your mother to do what she did. She was probably only a girl herself. In the hospital when I visited you, Myra and the other nurses talked to me about their work. I was impressed because it seemed really important and valuable.

My mum and dad were quite pleased when I decided to go for nursing training. I finished with Mike and they didn't mind that, either.'

'Did you marry someone else in the end?' Connie asked. There were no rings on Kathy's fingers.

'I did. It lasted ten years. I was a staff nurse on a paediatric ward, and I did quite a lot of night shifts. What happened was just about what you'd expect.'

'Children?'

'No. I've looked after plenty, though. You were the first, and there must have been hundreds since then.' Kathy sniffed. 'I'm a health visitor now. Hospitals are more about management than nursing these days.'

She drained her glass of wine.

'Are you married, Constance?'

'No,' Connie said.

Kathy didn't miss much. 'I see,' she said gently. 'And are you in love?'

'No. Yes. Or I *was*.'

'Do you want to tell me any more?'

Connie lifted her head. She found that she did want to talk to Kathy Merriwether. She liked her for her warmth and matter-of-factness.

'There's not much to tell. Not now, because it's over. A married man. It's painful, but I've been lucky in many other ways. That's what my life feels like. Luck. A lottery.'

'And you'd rather have facts and tidy explanations?'

Connie thought for a moment. Except with Bill, and the woman she had met on the plane, she wasn't used to discussing these matters.

'I think if you don't have a history, the randomness of life strikes you harder. I also feel that if I knew my real mother, if I could find out what has happened to her, even if it was just enough to know that it wasn't all tragedy, I wouldn't always have this sense of another parallel existence that's waiting for me to step into it. It's partly a sense of foreboding, and partly of something very precious that I lost and need to find again.'

Connie suddenly leaned forward in the velour arm-chair, fierce with urgency.

'Can you remember anything else about that night, Kathy? Any small thing that might be a clue?'

Sadly, Kathy shook her head.

Connie realised that she hadn't heard a train go by for quite a long while. The city's commuters would all be home by now, and it was time she went home herself.

Kathy offered, 'You could speak to Myra, my nurse friend. I still write to her. She retired a few years ago and went back up to Aberdeen with her husband. He works on the rigs. Maybe she can think of something else. I'll jot down the address for you.'

They both stood up. Connie waited as she searched for her handbag, found a little address book and scribbled on a torn-off scrap of paper. Connie knew that she would contact Myra, who would probably tell her a few more details about a foundling infant who had long ago spent a couple of weeks on her ward. She could try through the Royal London nurses' association to trace the other nurses who had worked on the same ward, and they might remember more tiny details, but none of them was likely to lead her to her vanished mother.

Kathy saw her expression.

'Here,' she said. She held out her arms. For a moment, held in a weighty hug and breathing in another woman's smell of cosmetics with the faint trace of sweat caught in folds of flesh, a memory of babyhood and the knowledge of a mother passed over Connie like a shadow from a bird's wing.

'Thank you,' Connie whispered.

Kathy came back down the steep stairs with her. She stood in her slippers on the top stone step, looking up and down the street. It was almost dark.

'You keep in touch, Constance Merriwether.'

'I will,' Connie promised, and she kept the promise.

But her premonition had been correct. None of the investigations she made yielded a trace of her mother.

Connie locked up the Bali house and gave the key to her neighbour Wayan Tupereme. The little man bowed his forehead to the tips of his folded hands and she returned the salute.

'May the *pengabenan* of your sister be blessed, and may her spirit ascend to *suarga*.'

'Thank you, Wayan. You know, funerals in England are not very like Balinese ones.'

'This I have heard.' Wayan sighed in sympathy. 'However, when the rituals are complete, please come back to the village and to your friends. Dewi and my grandson will miss you, and so will I.'

Connie felt the loss of Jeanette like a solid thing, a heavy oak door or a stone pillar that she might batter with her fists until they bled raw, but which would not yield an inch. She had made no plans beyond flying to England for the burial.

'I hope to,' she said.

A taxi driven by Kadek Daging's wife's brother was waiting to take her to the airport. Connie put her suitcase inside and climbed in. Wayan stood in the lane, his hand raised, until the car overtook the stream of scooters and a bullock cart and passed out of sight.

Connie flew up to Singapore and took an overnight flight onwards to Gatwick. It was just getting light as she boarded the train for Victoria, and the day revealed itself as a sullen midwinter apology with the trees shawled in grey mist. The carriages were overheated and crowded with bewildered new arrivals, but Connie shivered after the heat and brilliance of Bali. She shrank into her seat, breathing in grime and watching the backs of the houses, sliced gardens and curtained windows and occasional yellow eyes of light as they swept past her and dropped back into the grey vacuum.

In the apartment at Limbeck House, Roxana was remorsefully waiting for her.

SIXTEEN

'Let us pray.'

Connie bowed her head.

She could see a double row of black-shod feet: opposite her were Bill's shiny Oxfords, Noah's less well polished boots revealed beneath the hems of black trousers that were too short for him and therefore probably belonged to his father, and some improbable Italian loafers sported by a cream-haired, red-faced old man with a wheezy chest who had turned out to be Uncle Geoff, whom Connie had not seen for twenty years.

On Connie's side was a pair of matronly heels, sturdily planted but even so seeming to shudder with the force of Sadie's weeping. Next to those were two sets of black knee-boots, Jackie's and Elaine's, and a shuffled-up line belonging to the cousins' children. When Connie raised her chin she saw out of the corner of her eye the fluttering hem of the vicar's surplice as he read the short prayer. The vicar was wearing wellingtons beneath his cassock.

Between the two rows of shoes lay Jeanette's open grave.

The cemetery path a few yards away was grey, the dolorous marble headstones were grey, and also the squat tower of the church and the bare trees and the swollen sky, and what colour there remained in the thin grass seemed leached away by the murk. At three in the afternoon the daylight was almost gone, and apart from the white flag of the surplice there was not a shiver of movement anywhere. Even the morning's rain had stopped, and although the branches and monumental masonry dripped steadily the undertakers' discreetly fielded black umbrellas had not been called for. Sadie caught her breath, and there was a short break in her sobbing.

Funerals in England are not much like Balinese ones, Connie had told Wayan Tupereme. She thought briefly of the *wadah* and the single swoop of the paper dragon's wings before they were consumed by a sheet of fire, the stench of kerosene and flakes of soot gently drifting in the twilight, and Jeanette's observant admiration of the ceremonies.

Today's event could not have been more different, or more mutedly English and monochromatic by comparison, and yet it was also fitting. Jeanette had expended so much of her formidable energy on living a normal life, and to be conventional in her taste and behaviour – to have chosen a traditional funeral – was all of a piece with that.

At the short church service that had preceded the committal there had been familiar hymns and Psalm 23, and Bill had spoken briefly and movingly about Jeanette's life. Noah had recited from memory – rather well – 'The Lake Isle of Innisfree', which he described as Jeanette's favourite poem.

Connie could read nothing of Bill himself in any of this. He and Jeanette would have discussed the arrangements, and these choices must all have been hers. As she had done often enough before, she thought how remarkable it was that a man as imposing as Bill could be so self-effacing.

Now his black shoes took a step forward out of the opposite line. The toes were almost at the edge of the grave, where the raw earth walls had been masked with a roll of fake turf. Connie lifted her eyes from the ground but she did not venture a glance at him. Instead she looked at Noah. He was red-eyed, and he seemed painfully young.

Bill had been holding a tiny bunch of flowers. There were some twigs of rosemary and three frail white roses, the margins of the tissue petals browned by frost, picked that morning in Jeanette's garden and tied with a piece of thin white ribbon. He kissed the blooms and then let them fall onto the coffin lid.

But that was you, Connie silently said to him, and the blood in her veins seemed to make a complicated double surge.

Sadie choked into her handkerchief, and one of her daughters placed an arm around her shoulders.

Almost briskly now, Bill took the very clean spade that one of the undertaker's men handed to him. He dug one spadeful of earth from an uncovered corner of the mound piled on boards next to the grave and scattered it over the flowers, then Noah took the spade and did the same thing. Cut off by the grave from his ex-wife and daughters, Uncle Geoff seized the spade from Noah and contributed his own few clods of earth. Connie couldn't see beneath the brim of Auntie Sadie's big black hat, but she sensed a glare that smouldered hot enough to dry the flood of tears.

The vicar closed his prayer book. There was a moment's silence as they each attended to their own thoughts. Then he turned and led the family procession away from the grave. Bill and Noah walked side by side, straight-backed, and the rest of them closed into a black phalanx. The heels of their various shoes clicked on the cemetery asphalt path.

Behind them, Connie supposed, the undertakers

would remove their trappings and roll up the turf, and then the gravediggers would come and fill in the earth.

The word *gravedigger* was just about as archaic as *foundling*, she thought irrelevantly. Irrelevance was hardly a sin, though. All this black clothing and the line of waiting black cars beyond the Victorian lych-gate, the polished coffin and the artificial grass and *we are gathered here to remember our dear sister Jeanette* seemed in that moment supremely irrelevant.

– *Bones*, Jeanette had said. – *They don't mean anything. Just dry bones . . . and the spirit set free. I like that.*

Connie was only walking away from bones. She was dry-eyed in front of other people, and she hoped that her back was as straight as Bill's.

'You know,' her own voice ran in her head, words as clearly enunciated as if she were speaking for Jeanette to lip-read, 'you know I love you, don't you?'

The answer was loud, shapeless, formed with effort and with determination that had its roots in the stony subsoil of Jeanette as she had always been.

– *Yes. I know that.*

Minus the hearse, the cortege took the reverse of the two-mile route back to the house that it had followed on the way out. The lead car, carrying Bill in the front and with Connie between Noah and Auntie Sadie in the back, made just one three-quarter circuit of the roundabout, exactly as on the outward journey.

Connie realised that she was smiling quite broadly at the memory of Jeanette's order – *twice round the roundabout on the way to the cemetery for me.* She adjusted her expression before Auntie Sadie could see her.

There were already cars parked up and down the lane outside the house when the cortege drew up, and the caterers were opening the front door to muted couples and groups. The African violets in the big brass bowl in the hallway looked lush and well watered, and the finger of the long-case barometer indicated *Rain*.

On the parquet stood a pinboard on which Noah had put up a series of photographs of his mother. Connie briefly paused to look at them. There was the picture of Jeanette as a baby and the one of her wearing a little kilt and holding Connie on her lap that had stood on the top of the piano in Echo Street. Her graduation picture, in mortarboard and BSc gown and hood, smiled out from among the holiday snaps and Christmas party groups and proud events with Noah. The wedding picture took pride of place. Jeanette had looked so beautiful that day, her arm linked through Bill's and her face bright as a beacon. Off to one side Connie noted herself, scowling in her tight, shiny bridesmaid's dress.

The most recent picture had been taken by Bill. Jeanette sat in the rocker on the veranda, smiling into the lens with the green wave deep behind her. Connie met her eyes and returned her smile.

She moved on into the drawing room that was filling up with dark suits. There were neighbours to meet, and the colleagues Jeanette had introduced her to were waiting to shake her hand and murmur appropriately, and Uncle Geoff was wedged in the corner beside the fireplace.

'I thought the world of her,' he told Connie, sticking out his chin and squaring his shoulders in a double-breasted suit now much too big for him. 'There was no way I was not going to be here. Whatever *she* might think, or say.' He jutted his chin further, at Auntie Sadie's turned back.

'Of course you did, of course you had to be here,' Connie agreed.

Later, when people were beginning to leave, she took some empty glasses out to the kitchen and found Elaine propped against the sink. Connie put down her tray, remembering three empty sticky sherry glasses on Jeanette's dresser on the day of that other funeral, Tony's.

Elaine stubbed out a cigarette and moved aside to let Connie reach into the dishwasher. Two caterers were drying knives and replacing them in a drawer. All these knobs and handles, Connie was thinking again, finger-printed by the years of Bill and Jeanette's marriage, and the invisible paths between the table and the larder, worn by their passing feet.

'How are you, Connie?'

'I'm all right, thanks.' A colourless answer, but it was difficult to be any more expressive to cousin Elaine.

'I still can't believe it,' Elaine sighed. Like Jackie she was divorced. Her two non-committal boys were now in their twenties. They came briefly back to the house to escort their mother, but had already left.

Elaine was reaching for another cigarette. She exhaled smoke and crossed her leather-booted ankles, ready for a talk, while Connie wondered vaguely how to make an escape.

'It was nice, that music of yours,' Elaine offered.

'Was it? Thank you.'

Bill asked Connie if she would play some of her music during the funeral service. 'Jeanette would have wanted this,' he said.

They had decided on a version of the tune she had

been working on the day of Jeanette's death, a simple melody into which she had attempted to weave some of the Balinese gong notes and sinuous drumbeats. In the end, however, the piece had sounded to Connie like an awkward hybrid, without proper roots in either tradition, when she would have wished it to be the best music she had ever composed.

Even worse, as she played it with the polite audience ranged in their pews, she had felt an incongruous resemblance to Elton John.

Funerals were like this, she knew. You tried to concentrate on the person who was no longer there, and tides of inapt reminders of the busy, clamorous, still-living world swept in and eddied distractingly around you.

Connie tried to listen to what Elaine was saying. She felt all her perceptions distorted and her responses headed off into dead ends and irrelevances by the bulky interposition of grief. Elaine was waiting for an answer to a question, her mascara-ed eyes fixed on Connie's face.

'Yes, still doing the composing. Commercials, some film work when I can get it,' Connie managed to say.

'That's nice. It sounds glamorous, anyway,' Elaine sighed.

'What about you?'

'Oh, you know. I work in admin, NHS.'

Connie couldn't even remember the last time she had spoken to Elaine or Jackie. Not at Hilda's funeral, certainly, since that had taken place before she could get home from Tasmania.

Weddings and funerals, when families that were not familial briefly and painfully got together.

Elaine's thoughts must have been following the same path. 'I was thinking about when Uncle Tony died.'

'*He wasn't your dad.*'

'*What do you mean?*'

'*You're adopted, aren't you?*'

'We weren't very nice to you in those days, Jackie and I, and we deliberately got Jeanette on our side as well. I've been meaning to say this for years, and now I'm going to. I shouldn't have told you about being adopted, that was wrong of me.'

'I suppose it was, yes. But I would have had to find out somehow, in the end. Perhaps you did me a good turn.'

Connie tried to imagine how Hilda might have told her, but couldn't envisage it. Maybe Tony would have done it, if he had lived.

Elaine clearly wanted to say more and Connie waited. The caterers had moved away and were stacking up the serving trays that had been used to hand round sandwiches cut into pale triangles and small pieces of sombre cake.

'We were so against anything that was different, back then. So suspicious. You were only such a little bit different, weren't you, really? But it seemed an immense secret, that you weren't born into the family. Whereas nowadays . . .' Elaine sighed again, looking through the door of the kitchen and out into the hall where people were passing on their way to the front door. Bill and Noah were out there, quietly thanking people for coming. '. . . nowadays, we're all alike, everyone. Community, that's the word, isn't it? Ours is the *middle-class* community, the one that Mum and Auntie Hilda were so dead-set on belonging to. Now we find ourselves stuck in it, a bit of difference would be quite welcome, funnily enough.'

Connie realised that Elaine was slightly drunk and that she was talking about her own life, or some choice she had made that Connie would probably never know about. At the same time she reflected that it was Jeanette who had been truly, dramatically different from all of them.

That was why Bill had loved her. She was a series of contradictions: her luscious appearance against her puritanical spirit, her cloak of conventional behaviour adopted as a protection for her deafness, and her constant denial of deafness itself.

The past reared up within the Buntings' kitchen. The whole of Connie's life seemed now to have been lived by and against her sister. The sea of Jeanette's absence swelled and pushed the continents of normality towards the horizon and almost out of sight.

'Do you mind me saying this?' Elaine was asking glassily. 'Do you? I wouldn't be surprised if you did.'

Connie wasn't sure whether she meant the apology or the reference to her perceived difference from Hilda and Sadie and their three daughters.

'No, of course I don't mind,' Connie smiled. She had warmed to Elaine. The other woman immediately grasped Connie's wrists. Her nails were manicured ovals, painted red. She tilted herself forwards until their foreheads almost touched.

'Friends, then,' she murmured dramatically. 'It's taken long enough, hasn't it?'

This was how Jackie and Sadie found them. Sadie's arm was tucked under Jackie's. She looked older than seventy-five and her face was grained and puffy after all the crying.

'I've been saying to Connie that I'm really sorry,' Elaine told them, and Jackie nodded wisely.

'That's what Jeanette would have wanted.'

Quite a number of things have been grouped under that umbrella today, Connie thought.

'It's been a sad day,' Sadie said, in a voice that startlingly resembled Hilda's. Uncle Geoff had already gone, sunk into his black overcoat, coughing with the onset of a chill from wearing thin shoes in the wet cemetery. Sadie hadn't spoken a word to her ex-husband. Her ability to bear a grudge was as developed as Hilda's.

Connie said goodbye, kissing all three of them. She watched them go, out into the night, with Jackie and Elaine supporting their mother on either side.

The last of the friends and neighbours also filtered away and the caterers ferried their equipment out to a waiting van.

Connie emptied ashtrays and put the remaining glasses into the dishwasher. Bill closed the front door.

The house was finally empty, except for the three of them.

'Thank you for doing so much to help,' Bill said to her. He spoke with an odd formality. His face was drained of colour; even his mouth looked bloodless. Connie ached to put out her arms and hold him.

Noah had undone his black tie and it hung loose from his collar. He said, 'I'm going upstairs to phone Rox, then I'm just going to chill for a bit. Is that okay, Dad?'

Roxana had insisted that she would not come to the funeral.

'I didn't know Mrs Bunting so much, and all the family and friends will be there, I don't feel it is quite right. And now, after all this that has happened because of me, I would prefer not.'

Bill answered now, 'Of course, that's fine. Are you all right?'

'Yeah, Dad.'

Bill and Connie watched him walk up the stairs. His

shoulder dragged slightly against the wall and he corrected himself before taking the last steps at a gallop.

Connie followed Bill into the drawing room, past the pinboard with the photographs. Bill poured himself a whisky and Connie shook her head to decline one. They sat down facing each other and silence crept round them.

'Do you think that went the way Jeanette would have wanted?' Bill asked abruptly.

'Yes, I do.'

He let his head fall back against the cushions and gave a congested sound that was more a cough than a laugh. Silence fell again, in the muffled depth of which Connie thought she could hear a door closing upstairs, the creak of polished parquet, maybe even a whisper of the barometer's metal finger creeping from *Rain* to *Storm*.

It's here, Connie thought. Afterwards is now.

And then, *I have to get out of this house.*

'I'm sorry,' Bill said, even more abruptly. He sat up and drained the whisky and then rotated the glass on the sofa arm.

'What for?'

'Let's see. For everything I have done, and also failed to do.'

'Bill, don't *talk*. There's nothing to be said at this minute. It's the day of Jeanette's funeral.'

'So it is,' he said, with a hollowness she had not heard before.

For so many years, even when they hadn't seen each other for months, whenever they spoke the words had been ready and fluent, seeming to spring straight from their hearts. Yet now they found themselves stiffly talking like two actors under a spotlight.

Connie would have gone to him, warmed his hands

between hers and tried to offer what comfort she could, but even the way that Bill was sitting told her that he didn't want – could not bear – to be touched. She sat in her place, her ankles together and her hands folded, and let the silence lengthen. After a moment Bill got up again, with the restlessness of exhaustion, and poured himself more whisky.

'What were you talking to Elaine about?'

'She wanted to say she was sorry for telling me I was adopted.'

'Ah.'

'Funerals are when people feel the need to confess that sort of thing. And weddings.'

'Yes.'

This time the silence seemed to go deeper, into the core of both of them. It seemed that unlike other people on this day, they did not have anything to acknowledge or to confess to each other. Bill was staring out of the window into the dark garden. He knocked back another mouthful of whisky and Connie felt the shudder of it chasing through her own system.

'I think', she said carefully, 'I should head back home now.'

'I miss her.' Bill's words cut across hers and they jumped, because this dissonance was new to them.

'I know you do. So do I. I wish it had been me, not Jeanette.' She spoke impulsively, out of the whirl of her thoughts, not thinking she should measure what she said. To Bill, she had always spoken what she felt.

His eyes moved from the window and settled on her face. 'I don't think you do wish that,' he answered. There was a thin metal edge in the words.

Connie was lost for a response.

'I'm sorry,' he said again, after a moment.

She got up from her seat and went to stand beside him. The black glass of the window reflected their faces.

'What are you going to do?' she asked.

'This week, I am going to look after Noah, do paperwork, write letters. Next week, go back to work. Next month, probably also work. Next year? The year after that? I don't know, Connie. That's the truth.'

'You're wise not to make too many plans. Or to place yourself under any obligations.'

She saw his reflection incline its head. He was so sad that her heart knocked in her chest with pity.

Connie half-turned from the window. She touched her hand to Bill's arm, then withdrew it.

'I'll be at the flat if you need me.'

He came out into the hall, handed her her bag and helped her on with her coat.

'If there's anything I can do,' she began again.

'Thanks, Connie.' He leaned forward and kissed her on the forehead, cold-lipped, as if she were one of the neighbours. He stood in the doorway, his hands at his sides, watching her cross the gravel to her parked car. As she drove out of the gate the door closed behind him and the porch light blinked off.

She navigated the country lanes with furious concentration.

Grief. Everything that was happening to them was a manifestation of grief and it did not have an expiry date, or a set term to run. She was only just beginning to comprehend the pervasiveness of it, but one certainty was growing in her. Jeanette's death was as much of a barrier between Bill and herself as their marriage had ever been. (Connie made herself articulate these thoughts with cold precision.) And that was as it should be. She had made her own pledge to Jeanette, back in the garden of the Surrey house. The separation that she and Bill thought they had endured for so many years was, in reality, only just beginning.

It was still only the middle of the evening, although it felt to Connie somewhere closer to the dead of night. As she came to the outskirts of London she saw the blue-and-green neon lights of a bar/café that she had often noticed on her route out to Surrey. She was very thirsty, and also hungry.

In a booth in the corner of the bar she ordered a drink and food. While she was waiting to be served she reluctantly turned on her mobile. Immediately it started to ring, and the text-message envelope simultaneously blinked at her.

The first voicemail message was from Angela.

'Con, I got your email. I'm really worried. Of course you can count on me, whatever you need. Call me when you get this.'

There were three or four others, on similar lines. The last one was from *Seb*.

'Connie? What's happening? I'm in Chicago but you can reach me on this number any time.'

She read through the text messages, and found more of the same. She realised that she had more friends and supporters than she would have estimated, and that was a happy discovery. She didn't know what was in the email all these people were referring to, but she could make an informed guess.

Blindly, she had put off doing anything about the escalating crisis in her affairs until the funeral was over.

She had not been able to find the necessary reserves of energy and application even to think logically about it. But now, plainly, she was going to have to deal with the situation.

A waitress wearing a plastic name badge that read *Olga* put a bottle of water and a bowl of noodles in front of her. Connie drank all the water and attacked the food. It was, she thought, quite a long time since she had eaten a meal. The hot noodles quickly disappeared. As she ate she was working out what needed to be done.

The text message she sent to Angela read: *Didn't send email. Laptop stolen. My sister's funeral today. I'll call you.* She dealt with the others in similar fashion. Restored by hot food she drank a cup of coffee, paid her bill with a generous tip for Olga, and headed back to her car.

The apartment was in darkness. Connie glanced out at the diamond grid of the city, then clicked on the lights.

'Roxana?' she called.

Roxana wasn't at home. They had had one difficult encounter on Connie's return from Bali, when Roxana had handed over keys for the new locks and blurted out apologies that Connie was too distracted to process, but since then she had made herself invisible.

Connie went down the corridor to Roxana's room and looked in. The bed was made, the beach postcard was in its usual place and Connie was reassured by the sight, but she would have liked it even better if Roxana had been there in person. In spite of the mushrooming chaos the girl had caused, Connie found herself wishing for her company. She didn't work at The Cosmos Club any longer, and she wasn't with Noah because he was with Bill in Surrey. She hoped that wherever she actually was, she was safe.

In the room that before the burglary had been her office and studio, she studied the place on the desk once occupied by her laptop. The drawers of her cabinets were closed on the ransacked files; she had done that much after the police concluded their cursory investigations.

The red numerals on her landline's answering function indicated that she had eleven messages.

Connie sighed. She looked at her watch. It was only ten forty.

'Ange? You're not in bed, are you?'

'What? It's only just past teatime.' Connie could almost see her I'm-hardcore-me-I-am face, and it made her laugh. Angela was launching into rapid questions and assurances, cutting across Connie's incongruous giggle.

'I hope the funeral went all right.'

'Yes. It was done as these things have to be done.'

'That's good, at least. Con, I'm so sorry you've got all this shit to deal with as well. I just wanted to say, money's no problem, I can lend you a couple of grand straight off and if you need more we can work a commission of some sort through the company, I've got a commercial coming up that you could . . .'

'Angie, Angie, hang on. What are you talking about? Money's gone out of a couple of my accounts and it seems my credit cards are maxed out, but I'm not quite destitute. Thanks for the offer, but I don't need a loan . . .'

'So what did you mean in that email? You said you were in trouble with money, just cash flow, because you'd been the victim of some fraud, and could I help out for a week or so? You gave the details of a new safe account that you'd set up. Remember?'

Connie sat down.

'You didn't transfer any money to it, did you? Please tell me you didn't.'

'No. I thought I'd speak to you first. But the money's yours as soon . . .'

'It's another scam. It's from them. I think that message has probably gone out to every single person in my email address book.'

'But the new account's yours, it's in your name.'

'They've used my details to set it up, yes, but the access to it will be theirs. As soon as money comes in from anyone I know who falls for it, the account will be emptied and they'll be off.'

'You can't set up an account just like that. Money-laundering regulations.'

'Angie, I know. But they've hacked into my laptop. They've got all my account details, all my personal information. They went through my office. They took my UK driving licence with photo ID, they even took my file of utility bills. Of course they can set up another account, that's the least of it. They'll probably be in the office tomorrow, trying to sell you the music I was working on. And now it seems they've got all my friends and business contacts thinking I'm out on the street, and transferring money so I don't have to sit on a sheet of cardboard next to the cash machine with a sign reading *homeless and hungry*. Even Seb got the touch from them.'

'Shit,' Angie said.

'What did the email actually say?'

'I'd have to go and look, to tell you the precise words. But it sounded just like you.'

'Clever.'

'I feel responsible. If Roxana hadn't met that man in our office . . .'

'You aren't responsible, Ange. Not even Roxana is, really. Any word on Signor Antonelli?'

'The police interviewed Max. Antonelli was just cold-calling, blagged his way to a meeting, came back a second time on a pretext, and met Roxana in reception. He's disappeared. No one in Rome knows him, it turns out.'

'What a surprise. Was Roxana working today?'

'Yep, she was here. Are you unhappy about that? Because . . .'

'No. I'm glad. I'm worried about her. Look, Angie, I've got to try to contact people before they deposit money in that account.'

'How, if they've got your laptop and the address book?'

Connie thought rapidly. 'That's no problem, I've got all my files backed up. I'll go out first thing, buy a new laptop . . .'

'Er, I thought your cards were all duff?'

I have no *being*, Connie suddenly realised. No ready money, no credit, no way of buying what I need to set myself back on track. As panic seized her she remembered how, when they first met, Roxana had owned no bank account, had no security, and no one to turn to for help except the Buntings and herself.

Angela said, 'Listen, bring your disks or whatever you've got into the office first thing. I've got a spare laptop and Jez from IT will do the business on it for you.'

She did have a being. Of course the theft of her credit cards and a few personal details couldn't undermine it.

'Thanks, Ange. You're a real friend.'

'I'll see you in the morning, then.'

Connie lay awake until she heard the sound of Roxana's key in the lock, and her soft footsteps on the way to her own bed. Then she turned over and fell asleep.

'I'll come in with you,' Connie said to her in the morning. Roxana spun round from the sink where she was rinsing her plate and mug.

'What? Where to?'

'To Oyster Films. That's where you're going, isn't it?'

'Yes. I still have some work for them, I do not know how long it will last.'

Roxana's mouth turned down at the corners. Connie noticed that she had discarded her big-buttoned jacket in favour of her old Soviet-style denims, and her crest of blonde hair was showing dark at the roots. All the gleam and bounce had gone out of her. She looked smaller, with the doughy softness of vulnerability about her.

'Come on then,' Connie said gently. 'We'll get the bus together.'

They found adjacent seats. Roxana stared past Connie at the rush-hour streets and the bobbing heads of people bearing newspapers and Starbucks lattes and shoulder-bags weighted with work towards their desks. To Roxana, the city tide seemed to be streaming away from her and leaving her on an uncomfortable shore.

Connie sent another batch of text messages.

Please DO NOT deposit any money. All a hoax. I will explain today.

Then she stowed her phone away. Roxana's face was turned aside.

'Roxana?'

'Yes.' The syllable slid out between frozen lips.

Connie told her, 'No one's blaming you for anything. I can imagine exactly how it happened. It was a mistake, and you won't make it again.'

Roxana's shoulders twitched. 'I don't know. There are too many things I do not understand. At first it seems a simple business, that you can step into another country and work hard and make yourself what you want. But that is only what you see at first look, because when you look again there are so many things you cannot see. How can you learn them? Not at English language classes. These do not teach you how to be English, do they? You and Angela, even that Zoe, you would know at once that Mr Antonelli is not a person to trust. But all I see is a man with a fine watch, and charming behaviour and a card that tells me he is in the movie business. So I believe what he says to me, and I take him and his friend as guests up to your apartment because I want to make them think I am someone who matters in this world. Then it turns out that he is not what he says, much more than I am not.'

Her lovely mouth twisted. 'All I am is a stupid girl with stupid ideas about being an English girl. And this is the way I repay you for your kindness and for pulling me out of the sea. How much money have these men stolen from you, Connie? Because I will pay it back to you. I will do it if it takes me my whole life.'

Connie's mobile rang in her bag. She thumbed it into silence without a glance.

'I'm going to show you something, Roxana.'

She reached inside the collar of her coat, searching for where the thin cord lay next to her skin. She drew out a tiny silk pouch that hung from the loop of cord and eased it open, then withdrew the marcasite earring. Since the news of the burglary, she had taken to carrying it everywhere with her. She held it cupped in the palm of her hand for Roxana to examine.

'Money, credit cards? None of that matters in the least. The bank and the card issuers will be responsible for most of it anyway. What else? Laptop, musical and studio equipment, a few rings and necklaces, a camera, some clothes? All of those I can easily replace. I am insured. Putting my affairs to rights again? That will take some time and a bit of effort, but I've got time to spare. This earring is the only thing, the one and *only* inanimate object I possess, that I truly value and could never replace. And I've still got it. It's safe here, in my hand.'

Connie closed her fist over it, and smiled.

A spark had rekindled in Roxana's eyes.

'It is pretty, yes, but you have only one?'

Connie craned to see the bus's whereabouts. They would reach their stop in not more than five minutes.

'Long story. I'll tell you quickly.'

Roxana listened. After a minute she kept her eyes on Connie's clenched fist, as if the bus might give a more than usually brutal jolt and shake the earring out of her grasp.

At the end of the brief recounting, Roxana breathed out through parted lips.

'If those men had stolen your mother's earring away from you, I think I would have died,' she said.

Connie was going to laugh with her, but then she saw that Roxana was serious.

They reached their stop. Connie slipped the earring back into its pouch and buried it beneath the layers of her clothes.

At Oyster Films, Roxana made her way, head down, to her desk where her pre-production legwork for the St Petersburg shoot was waiting. Angela was in her office, on the telephone, with the door shut. Connie collected the spare laptop from the receptionist and carried it off to Jez. He was frowning and clicking at the keys when her mobile rang yet again. *Sorry*, she mouthed at him, and retreated to a quiet corner.

'Hello, is that Ms Thorne?'

'Speaking.'

'Hello there, this is Annette from Harrods' fine jewellery department? Just a courtesy call to make sure you're happy with those adjustments to your necklace, Ms Thorne?'

A few questions established that Ms Constance Thorne had purchased a diamond and pearl necklace, had requested that two links be removed to ensure a better fit around her slim neck – urgently, because she was going abroad and wanted to take the lovely necklace with her – and had paid for the item (more money than Connie had ever spent on a single purchase in her life) with her new store card.

The statement and the first payment demand, Connie estimated, would drop through her letterbox in the next two or three weeks. And this was probably only the beginning. There would be statements and demands for purchases made on whichever other major store cards the thieves had also taken out, probably using her existing credit cards as collateral and her driving licence and utility bills as proof of identity. Somewhere out there, Connie thought, was a woman who was not Constance Thorne but who looked like her or was made up to look enough like her (Wig? Coloured contact lenses? How

459

far did they bother to go?) to convince busy bank-counter staff and shop assistants that she actually was herself, or at least as she appeared in the tiny photograph on her driving licence.

'You okay?' Jez wanted to know.

'Yeah. Fine.' She meant it. This, at least, was a set of circumstances she could deal with.

She picked up her mobile again. A moment later she was speaking to a credit reference officer about the startling debts that were being run up in her name.

'I am afraid we see a lot of this. You are a victim of what we call . . .' the woman solemnly paused '. . . identity theft.'

Connie concluded the call, and then stared at the long list of authorities to be contacted and steps that would have to be taken to restore the credit ratings and various degrees of purchasing power that seemed to constitute her identity, as far as the outside world was concerned.

The more she thought about it, the more absurd and perfectly ironic the situation seemed. She sat back in her chair and began to laugh.

Jez flicked her a nervous glance, then hunched attentively over the laptop once more. Clearly, he was keen to get shot of the madwoman as soon as possible.

Connie went across to Angela's office, intending to share with her the comedy of Mr Antonelli and his associates making off so successfully with an identity that she had spent most of her adult life trying to define.

Can I replace it with a nice, plain, utilitarian one? she was going to ask. No problems, no missing history, no racial or social ambiguities? Will my insurance cover that?

But through the glass panel in the door she could see

that Angie was still on the phone. Her shoulder was turned away, and she was shading her eyes with her free hand. Connie backed away.

In a windowless cubicle behind the reception area Roxana was also on the phone, speaking Russian very quickly in a wheedling tone of voice.

Connie looked around her. These were the offices of a busy film production company. A motorbike courier in leathers and a Darth Vader helmet was collecting a package from reception and two ad-agency account executives were sitting over a set of A3 storyboards while they waited for a meeting. She had no place here. She picked up her coat and bag, told Jez that she would be back in half an hour, and went down the street to a coffee shop.

Sitting on a tall stool, she gazed out through the faintly fogged plate-glass window into the street. Crowds passed by, but today their faces leapt out as if they were known to her. She saw how each individual had a different gait, a different path, and the ability to follow it without colliding with anyone else; each one had a set of unique motives that was propelling them past this window at just this hour. The variety of humanity within a few yards of inner-city pavement on an ordinary mid-morning suddenly took her breath away. She was warmed by the sight, and her feeling of separation melted like ice in the sun.

Connie realised how much she would have liked to talk to Bill about this, and about many other things – all the random coincidences and dislocations that made up a life. It took a great effort of will not to reach for her mobile, but she didn't do it. She wouldn't discuss the repercussions of the burglary with him, nor would they laugh about the definitions of identity.

Bill had the broad dimensions of grief to map, and then learn to inhabit.

As she did herself.

The split-second impulse to tell Jeanette about the theft flickered and then snuffed itself out when she recalled – with the same stab of pain that came a hundred times a day – that she couldn't tell Jeanette anything.

Roxana finished her work. It was the end of the day, at last.

Angela had given her some notes but then had hurriedly left for home more than an hour ago, without speaking to anyone. Connie had picked up the laptop computer that Jez had prepared for her and had gone again before it was even lunchtime. For Roxana in her cubicle it had been a very long day. Film pre-production work seemed mostly to consist of trying to persuade local suppliers to offer more of their services for less money, and this was not a system that the Russians were very amenable to.

As she was putting on her coat, Noah called her.

'Where are you?' he wanted to know. When he was at the house in Surrey he was always asking her this, as if he felt trapped there, and feared that she might slip away from him.

'I am still at work,' she said. 'How is your father today?'

'He's quiet. Just – very quiet. Are you going back to the apartment?'

'Yes, in a bit,' Roxana admitted.

She didn't want to go back there yet, because she felt she didn't deserve the privilege. When Noah was with his father, she had taken to staying out on her own until it was late enough for her to slip into Limbeck House and go straight to bed. London was losing the warmth it had briefly acquired and once again beginning to gape around her, a chilly place full of strangers' faces and eyes that never met hers – unless they were men's eyes, with the usual speculation in them.

'Call me, then, when you get there?'

She didn't want to hear the insistent note in Noah's voice. It told her that his mother's death and her mistake with Mr Antonelli had changed matters between them, and they were not as innocent or as easy as they had been.

'If . . .' she began, and then thought that whatever she said it was unlikely to satisfy either of them. 'All right,' she said.

Some evenings, Roxana went to the cinema. It was expensive, though, in the West End. She didn't like sitting alone in pubs or bars, not because that in itself was particularly lonely, but because she was obliged to defend herself. So she went back to the Best Little Internet Café on the Planet. When he saw her, the owner called out that he thought she had deserted them.

'No,' Roxana smiled. 'I have been working very hard, that's all.'

'Good. Work is very good. What will you eat? Souvlaki salad?'

Roxana ate her solitary dinner, saving for later the possibility that there might be an email from Fatima. Afterwards she took her cup of thick sweet coffee back with her to the internet section, even though there was a notice saying that drinks were forbidden near the keyboards. The café man winked at her.

Roxana logged on, and went automatically to the

Uzbek language portal. Up came the picture of the blue domes against the desert-blue sky.

Until this moment Roxana would have denied that she ever felt a moment's homesickness, but now she felt an unwieldy longing to be in this place again.

The news that scrolled underneath the picture was the usual bland propaganda put out by the government. Everything that she had left behind was no doubt still the same – corruption, intimidation, religious hostility. But her gaze kept returning to the picture of Chor Minor. The sights and smells and memories of home rose up, thicker and heavier and more real to her than the damp London street outside the café.

Roxana sat forward in her chair. Abruptly she clicked at the keyboard and the picture of Bokhara disappeared. She opened her email inbox, and saw that there was a message from Fatima.

It was very short, without any of the usual stories about her *biznez* men. It said simply that she had been talking to people, friends from home, and she had heard from them that Yakov wanted to speak to Roxana. It was very urgent, and if it was possible she should telephone him right away.

Fatima gave her a number to ring, but Roxana already knew it. She stood up, pushing back her chair so hard that it almost tipped over.

'You want another coffee?' the owner called to her.

She left the terminal and the usual row of hunched Asian students.

'Not tonight,' she said.

'See you tomorrow, maybe,' echoed after her as she went out into the rain.

There was another shop a few yards away. Peeling

signs read *Cheap Calls/China/Russia/Asia*. It was late, too late really to be making this call, but Roxana could not possibly wait until the morning. Yakov didn't sleep much anyway.

He answered within a few seconds, so she knew he had been awake.

She could see him clearly, a shapeless dome of flesh topped with a bald bean of a head, a man grown so fat that he rarely left his shuttered apartment. Her mother's old friend, the one-time scholar.

'My daughter. I have some news to tell you,' Yakov gasped.

'Roxana?'

Connie had been sitting in the semi-darkness, watching the lights beneath her and the planes on their winking descent.

'Yes.'

'Noah called. He's been trying your mobile. Can you . . . Roxana? What's happened?'

Roxana let her bag and her coat fall to the floor.

'My brother.' She had held herself together all the way home but now her face was beginning to work out of control.

'My brother. He did not die in Andijan. He is in prison, but he is not dead.'

It was the same golden-lit bar that had so impressed Roxana when Cesare Antonelli took her there. Connie and Angela strolled in, choosing one of the leather-circled booths as if the place belonged to them. They scanned the drinks menu and told each other that tonight was definitely the night to have the cachaça and absinthe mint cocktail, and when the drinks came they clinked glasses with each other. They told Roxana to remember that friends were what mattered.

'They are *all* that matters,' Angela said. Deliberately she made a face like someone trying to be tragic in a TV comedy show.

Angela smoked constantly and kept taking off her tinted glasses and then putting them on again, but she and Connie both laughed a lot as well, and teased each other and Roxana, and even after all that had happened they made her feel as if she was one of them, one of the confident women who were at home in places like this.

When the second round of cocktails arrived Connie became serious. She raised her glass again.

'Here's to you, Roxana. I'm so happy for you and your brother, and I hope you'll be able to see him soon. I hope he'll be out of prison before too long, and I know you've got to go back right away to do whatever you can to help him. But I'm really going to miss you.' She took a big gulp of her drink. 'Good luck. *Bon voyage*,' she added.

'You'll miss me, even though I let those men into your home?'

'Those men took the things that don't matter and I've still got everything that does.'

Roxana's eyes went to the thread that held the pouch, just visible in the V of Connie's top.

'Nobody can steal who you are. I'm glad to have found that out,' Connie said. 'I owe the discovery to you, in a way, don't I?'

Connie had even said that she would pay for Roxana's flight home, but Roxana had money saved and wouldn't let her. There had been a joke about how Connie didn't have money or cards anyway.

'Good luck, Roxana,' Angie added. 'Now, are we going to have another of these?'

They went on to dinner in a restaurant. In the taxi on the way there, Roxana looked out of the window at the shiny shop windows and the neon signs in Piccadilly Circus, the strings of blue twinkling lights strung in the bare branches of trees along the river, and all the big, imposing old buildings. She wasn't seeing them as a stranger any longer, but still, London was slipping away, receding from her, already turning from what was real into what was only recollected, or imagined, a trick of the light, like a mirage in the desert. Her moment of longing for Bokhara now felt like a premonition.

It was not the same restaurant as the one Cesare Antonelli took her to, but it looked quite similar. Angela knew the man at the desk inside the door, and he said good evening and led them to a table in the corner with a view of all the other tables. Roxana noticed that none of the other diners glanced at her this time, and she didn't feel the need to watch them either, or to compare her clothes with theirs. Instead of having to say and be what sounded right for the two men, she could speak as a friend to her two friends.

The day after tomorrow she would be in Tashkent.

To have Niki given back to her, even Niki imprisoned on such serious charges without trial and without a release date, was the best thing that could and would ever happen.

Caught on the cusp between two worlds, this night made her glow with a rare happiness.

They were all a bit drunk by now.

They were still talking and laughing when, without any warning, Angela's eyes filled up with tears. She gave a sob and then tried to cover it up, and Connie gently grasped her wrist.

'Bugger it,' Angela sniffed. 'Sorry.'

Roxana knew that Angela had just split up with her boyfriend. She guessed it was the man who had been with her in Suffolk, after the night of the storm, although she couldn't be sure.

Angela said, 'I am going to give you some advice, Roxy. Don't ever get involved with a married man. Conmen, nightclub owners, even ad men if you must. But never ever, take it from me, lose your heart or give your life to a man with a wife and children.'

Roxana felt awkward, because of Connie and Mr Bunting. It came to her that even Angela did not know about this piece of Connie's life, and when she met Connie's dark eyes she saw that this was the case.

'I will remember,' she said carefully.

Connie squeezed Angela's hand. 'Have some coffee.'

Roxana tried to pay for the dinner, but they wouldn't let her. Angela took one of about a dozen cards out of her wallet.

'It's on expenses. Pre-production meeting, St Petersburg shoot.' The tears had dried up and she was smiling again.

Connie and Roxana saw her into a taxi, and then took another back to Limbeck House.

Roxana's bag was packed, ready to go, and her room was bare except for the postcard.

Connie went into her bedroom and came out with something draped over her arm.

'Would you like to have this, as a goodbye present? The burglars didn't take it. Probably too last season for them. I know it won't be that much use in the desert heat, but as a souvenir?'

It was the Chloé suede jacket that Roxana had once borrowed without Connie's permission. She took it now and eased her arms into the sleeves. She couldn't help stroking the soft lapels, and then giving a dancer's pirouette.

'Yes, I would love so much to have this,' she said.

She saw the direction of Connie's glance, and laughed, because she had already thought of it. She eased the postcard off the wall, and gave it to her.

Connie held out her arms and they hugged each other. It was a motherly and sisterly embrace, and it acknowledged that they were more equal than either of them had thought.

'Maybe some day you will come to visit me and Niki in Uzbekistan,' Roxana said.

Noah took her to the airport.

He didn't want her to go, but there was no hope of her staying. Her brother had been delivered back from the dead, and there wasn't a single card in the pack that he could play to trump that. He was happy for her, and bereft for himself.

'Are you sure you will be able to get on the flight? And back into Uzbekistan, on an expired holiday visa?'

She reassured him. The confidence and determination that had temporarily seeped away were back again.

'At Tashkent I will have to pay some fine, for an expired visa, I think. Your people, the British, will be happy to see the back of me.'

'I have never so not wanted to see anyone's back.'

He grasped the lapels of her denim jacket as if he could physically prevent her from leaving. Noah had always hated goodbyes.

She was so beautiful. He stared down into her eyes,

then outlined her mouth with the tip of his finger, like some romantic loser in a date movie. He acknowledged to himself that that was quite close to what he was. He was losing her to Uzbekistan and history.

'Roxana, you have to promise that you'll call me, and email. I want to know about Niki. I want to know you're safe and well.'

'Yes.' She pressed her warm mouth to his. 'Noah?'

'I'm here.'

'Thank you for all the times we have had. You have been kinder to me than anyone else in my whole life. You and Connie.'

If only we could leave Auntie Con out of this, Noah thought in despair.

They were at the Departures line.

'Tell your father I send him my best wishes,' Roxana said.

'I'll do that.'

'It's time for me to go,' she whispered.

'Roxana, wait. What about us?'

For a second, he was going to ask her to marry him. That would solve everything.

Gravely, she shook her head. 'I am from Uzbekistan,' she said.

'*Fuck* that. I love you. I . . .'

'Shhh.' She placed her finger on his lips. 'Don't say any more.'

They kissed each other, and then very firmly she put her hands on his arms and turned him to face away from the line. She gave him a gentle but definite push.

'Are you coming back?' Noah insisted.

'Maybe one day I will come back,' Roxana grinned. Then she shrugged, a fatalistic, comical gesture that was more eloquent than any words. 'But . . . I never was an English girl, was I? I don't think I ever will be.'

She stepped back and blew him a kiss. Then she walked towards the departure gate and out of his sight.

SEVENTEEN

Connie had been travelling for almost a year.

She had been working, writing music, and watching the constant flow of the crowds in a series of cities from Berlin to New York and Mumbai. She hadn't been alone all the time: in New York she went to a Beethoven concert given by Sung Mae Lin, with the New York Philharmonic conducted by Sébastian Bourret. The three of them had dinner afterwards, and she was even on the point of accepting their invitation to spend a weekend with them and their twin girls at their Long Island home. Seb confided that he had always believed they would be good friends, given time. But then Connie had a call to do some urgent rescue work on the musical score for a Bollywood/Pinewood joint film production, and she had flown out to Mumbai instead. There had followed a month of intense collaboration with people she didn't know well, which had been stimulating but also very hard work. Afterwards she felt tired and full of a kind of shapeless desperation, so she thought a holiday might be a good idea. She went to China and travelled overland to Kashgar, a remote trading city in the far west that she had always wanted to visit.

It was an interesting trip, although as soon as it was over Connie realised that since Jeanette's death she had been moving constantly from place to place, meeting people, listening and responding with only a part of herself, all the while telling herself that everything was fine and that this was the way her life was lived.

But she felt more rootless than she had ever done, and now she was bone-weary as well.

After China, while staying with friends in Singapore, she had a sharp urge to go back to Bali and look at her green wave. She flew down to Denpasar, and took the public *bemo* up to the village.

'Long time, my friend,' Wayan Tupereme said to her.

'Long time,' Connie agreed, bowing over her folded hands to return his greeting.

Dewi had just given birth to another baby, a second boy. Connie went to visit them with gifts of flowers and rice, as she had done the first time.

The view from her veranda pleased Connie as much as it had ever done. But as she had guessed she might do, she kept seeing Bill sitting in the old rattan chair or opening the drawers in her simple kitchen. This almost-presence only highlighted the real absence.

She could see Jeanette just as clearly, but Jeanette was a more peaceful memory now.

Then an email arrived from Roxana.

Hello Connie! How are you? I am well. I have been visiting my brother in jail in Tashkent. It is a bad place, but at least I can see him. I miss you and London and Noah, but this is where I must be and where I want to be because Niki is my brother and to me that is the most important thing in this world.

So this is to ask, when can you come to Uzbekistan to visit me, my friend?

Connie walked out onto her veranda again and studied the silver loops of the river far beneath her. A breeze laden with moisture shivered the leaves. The little house and the village and the view all soothed her, but there was nothing tangible to hold her here. It would be good to see and talk to Roxana.

Travelling on was more than a habit, she reflected. It was becoming a way of life. She wrote back:

I'll look into flights and mail you in a day or so.

Less than a week later she found herself in Bokhara, waiting for Roxana in the shade of the mulberry trees that fringed an ancient pool.

After the mists of her fecund Balinese valley and the air-conditioned voids of Singapore, she was finding it hard to adjust to the desert furnace of Central Asia. She felt not unlike one of the dogs that lay panting in the dust beside the outer wall of the mosque, or perhaps a camel taking advantage of a lone palm tree. A yellow-and-brown hornet the size of a cockroach was hovering over her *chai* glass. With an effort, she lifted her hand and batted it away.

Connie blinked to clear her eyes of dust and the harsh dazzle of the sun, and saw Roxana striding towards her.

They had met briefly the night before when Connie flew in. Today Roxana had been at her job. She was still wearing her work clothes – a hotel receptionist's frumpy skirt-suit and open-necked blouse, with a pair of mid-heeled court shoes, clunky, probably manufactured in China. She was bare-headed even in the baking mid-afternoon, and she carried bulging string bags that swung and bumped with the rhythm of her stride.

'You are here already,' Roxana exclaimed as she reached Connie's table. 'I hope I am not late?'

Connie edged along the bench, making room for her in the mulberry shade.

'I was early,' she smiled. 'It's very warm.'

It was almost forty degrees. The light was blinding, flat out of a white sky, striking into the crucible of baked mud walls and dust-coated streets and further concentrating the heat. Roxana sat down and spoke quickly to the waiter, then turned back to Connie.

'And so, tell me, what sights of Bokhara have you seen so far?'

Roxana was taking her role as hostess and tour guide quite seriously.

'Let's see. I went up the minaret.'

From one hundred and fifty feet up a slim brown tower there had been a wide view over turquoise-blue domes and tiled archways, and a jumble of smaller brown domes and arches cracked by dog-leg alleyways, away to the city's flat outskirts marked out in Soviet-built apartment blocks, and beyond that to the limitless, colourless extent of the desert that faded into a purple-grey haze on the horizon. At that height a breeze had been stirring, but it was as hot and abrasive as the lick of an animal's tongue.

'And then I went to the Ark.'

'First built here, you know, over one thousand years ago.'

The ancient fortress and home to the Emirs of Bokhara, massive in shimmering brick, was now mostly given over to a series of museums. It had been slightly cooler within the thick walls. Connie trod her way past the various exhibits along with a trickle of Dutch and German couples.

Outside, strings of entrepreneurial small girls chased after the tourists. They tugged at the pockets of Connie's khakis and the hem of her shirt. The biggest skipped in front of her, blocking her path.

'What's your name? What's your name?'

'Connie. I'm from England. What's yours?'

'Samida. Come, see my pottery. I give you best price.'

'Maybe later.'

The child snatched a handshake and offered her a wide, mirthless, professional smile. 'Okay, we are friends. You come back. I saw you first, you come to me.'

'It sounds like a deal, Samida.'

Connie had walked on past the carpet bazaars and postcard sellers, and the one-time *madrassah* niches where men wearing traditional four-cornered hats now sat amid heaps of decorative wrought-iron, and rows of scissors, and wickedly curved knife blades. She made her way to the ancient tree-shaded tank in the middle of the old town and chose a seat at one of the *chaikhanas* that lined it. The scummy water was as thick and green as pea soup and the huge yellow-and-brown hornets skimmed across the surface, but the reflections of twisted branches gave the illusion of coolness.

She was thinking about Roxana at Samida's age, growing up in this place, scurrying and fistfighting her way towards the top of a heap that was about as stable as a sand dune.

Roxana quickly drained her Coke. She was eager to show Connie something new.

'And now, are you ready for the women's *hammam*?'

'I'm ready,' Connie said equably. She had no idea what to expect. Roxana had told her only that this was a proper Bokharan tradition, for women of the city, not tourists.

Roxana set off, heading at an angle away from the central pool, with Connie walking quickly to keep up. Within ten steps sweat glued her shirt to her back.

They ducked beneath the domes and multiple arches of a covered bazaar, where the carpet hucksters and the hordes of children ignored their passing because Roxana was one of them. They came out again into a warren of streets, barely wide enough for the two of them to walk side by side. The mud walls were broken by wooden doors, painted flat blue or green, peeling and blistered by the sun, all of them tightly closed. Black or blue numerals marched haphazardly on the doorposts, 67 next to 17 and also to 93. Power lines drooped and knitted from brackets on every corner, and the only sign of life was the scabbed dogs keeping pace with them in the thin ribbons of shade.

'It is not so far,' Roxana called over her shoulder.

The low, domed building was buried deep in a maze of unmarked streets in the old town. Connie knew that she could never have found it on her own. Above the brown doorway, in both Arabic and Cyrillic scripts, the single word *Hammam* was carved in stone.

Inside the doors was a dim, cool passage. Thick walls closed out the sounds of the street. There was the steady drip of water, a faint sulphurous whiff, and the sunless scent of old stone. Connie followed Roxana into a room lit from above by skylights.

The first impression was of a mass of female bodies, which resolved itself into a group of women undressing and stowing their clothes in rickety lockers. Copying Roxana and the others, Connie stripped off too. Naked except for the silk pouch containing her earring, she felt ridged and bony, and conspicuously hairy among such lush expanses of billowy, smooth flesh. All the other women were fully depilated, even the oldest ones. Feeling like Effie Ruskin on her wedding night, Connie suppressed a snort of laughter.

Slowly, she undid the strings of the pouch. Roxana briskly took it from her, extracted the earring and fixed it to Connie's ear lobe. She studied the effect with her head on one side.

'Nice,' she said. She tossed the pouch in after the rest of their clothes and shut the tin locker, then gathered up the soap and shampoo and towels that she had brought in one of her bags.

'Now, come.'

Connie hooked her hair behind her ears and meekly followed Roxana down a spiral of hollowed stone steps. The drip of water grew louder, and a thin veil of steam rose to meet them.

There was a circular stone room under the dome, insulated because except for the dome itself the building was all underground. Water splashed from ancient piping and ran over the stone slabs. The walls and the stone benches dripped and steam curled lazily through metal grilles. The room was full of pairs of women, coils of hair wound on their heads, their broad backs and buttocks and thighs shining. They were talking and laughing and scrubbing each other.

Connie gazed around her.

A series of smaller, domed alcoves led off the central space. Roxana beckoned. The first was the hot chamber. Steam hissed from the gratings and swirled in dense clouds, and the women lay like basking seals on tiers of stone slabs. Their talk subsided to a low murmur as they gave themselves up to the heat.

As they progressed through the sequence of *hammam* chambers, Connie was thinking of the thousands of women, Bokharans and travellers alike, who had preceded her through these stone arches. The *hammam* itself had stood here, at the heart of its Silk Road oasis, for more than four hundred years.

She felt herself slipping and sliding, out of her present self, into a place of unexpected comfort. She didn't any longer feel conspicuous among the languid, smooth, fleshy women of the city. Roxana was one of them too, even with her bleach-blonde hair and her dancer's body. They moved slowly, all of them, through the steam and through curtains of tepid water, over the corroded gratings where the water ran away through subterranean channels, and into cooler rooms where the talk and laughter broke out afresh.

Roxana reached for the soap and shampoo, and like the other pairs of women they took turns at rubbing each other's skin with a coarse mitt, shampooing one another's hair and bringing buckets of water to sluice over their heads.

Connie scrubbed Roxana's long shins and the curved wings of her shoulder blades. With a swell of affection, she noted the hollows on either side of her heels, the undulations of her ribs and the enviably taut span between the crests of her hipbones. She submitted to the same attentions from Roxana, without trying to shrink away or to hunch inwards to protect herself.

Afterwards, with their skin tingling, they sat in a tepid room to rest. Connie fingered her rakish earring.

'It is still there,' Roxana assured her. She leaned back against the stone seat and sighed with satisfaction, ready for a talk. 'Tell me, how is Angela?'

'It's taken time, but I think she's forgetting about Rayner.'

'She has fallen in love again?'

'Not that. Not yet.'

'Have you heard any news from Noah?'

'Hardly anything. His father told me he is fine, more or less, although he misses his mother a good deal.'

Roxana waited attentively.

Connie's communications with Bill over the past months had been brief and businesslike, mostly concerned with Jeanette's estate. They were respectful of each other, and concerned not to intrude on one another's private mourning. Or to intrude in any way, Connie thought with a touch of bleakness.

When Connie didn't expand further, Roxana remarked, 'I have had some emails from Noah, you know.'

'What does he say?'

'One of the things he said is that he would like me to go back to London.'

'And what do you feel about that?'

'What do I feel about London, or Noah?'

'Okay. Noah first.'

Roxana drew up her legs and rested her chin on her knees.

'He is the best person I ever met.' Then she laughingly rolled her head to look at Connie. 'I don't mean that! You are the best person, of course. Noah is only the best *boy* I know, but that is by a very long way, believe me. But he is in London and I am here. I want to be in Uzbekistan to be near to Niki, and to work with Yakov and Niki's friends to get him out of prison. So that is also the answer to the other half of your question, about London, isn't it? I dreamed of it, yes, and of being an English girl, and I tried very hard to – what is the word? – integrate myself. I thought that by making myself similar to you, and being a part of Noah's beautiful English family, I could belong even more in England.' She sighed, and her expression was eloquent. 'But as you know, that was not such a success because if I was truly English I would not have been taken in for one moment by Mr Antonelli.'

Connie patted her shoulder. 'That's all in the past. It's dealt with, finished.'

It had taken some time, and it had been complicated, but her formal identity was her own once more.

'I'm so glad of that. I learned a very big lesson. You know, Connie, what truly matters is your family. Niki is my family and Noah is not, even though I like him so much. It was all very well when I believed I had only myself to consider, I could decide to make myself like that because like this was not good enough. But now my brother is alive again. The first time I went to the prison I was – oh – so happy to see him. Can you imagine what that was like? He had come back from the dead. He is very thin and he had been beaten, and he had spent many days locked up alone, but still he was there, the same smile, the same person. My brother. Now I know what is important. Here I am. In Uzbekistan. This must be my place.'

The passion in her words touched Connie. Her admiration for Roxana renewed itself.

'I understand,' she murmured. 'And you are quite right.'

There was a burst of laughter from the main chamber. The pairs of glistening, wobbling women passed from the heat to the cooler rooms, gasped as they were deluged with water, or sat and gossiped on the old stone benches.

Roxana beamed. 'You see? You come here with your

mother or your sister, and if you are not lucky to have them you are like us, with your good friend, and you talk and talk. You are scrubbed clean and you have opened your heart, and then you go out into the world again. Look, over there.'

Roxana pointed at a larger group of women. There were two elderly ones, one fat, and the other tiny with breasts like two dead leaves. They were issuing orders to a circle of laughing girls with one at the centre. The whole group was busy with white towels and jars of cream and lotion, and they set about scrubbing and massaging the girl's skin and teasing out the thick coils of her black hair.

'What's happening?'

'That one in the middle, she is a bride. These are her sisters and friends and those two, they are her grandmother and her fiancé's grandmother. It is our custom. They are making sure that she is prepared for her wedding night. She will be beautiful for her husband, the grandmothers must see to that. And the bridegroom's family, they must pay for all the cosmetics to make her ready. Combs and towels and soap, everything.'

The fat grandmother slapped a paste like thick red mud into the roots of the laughing bride's hair.

'Would you like to get married?' Connie asked.

'Ha. I have other things to attend to first. And I will wait my turn, after you.'

'That might be a little *too* long to wait,' Connie smiled.

Roxana sniffed. 'We shall see. We will have another turn in the hot room now. And after that, the massage.'

Later they went back up the spiral stone steps. Off the upper corridor was another, much grander salon with a marble floor and lamp sconces made of wrought-iron. There were towel-covered divans against the wall and rugs and cushions on the floor. After their *hammam*, the women lounged and drank tea. Their hair was tied up in coloured turbans, naked fat babies lay on blankets and brown-skinned toddlers ran between them. Connie thought it was like walking into a Victorian academician's painting of a *seraglio*. Roxana delivered her to an enormous, towelled Russian woman with a wide slash of gold tombstone teeth.

'Massage, *da*?'

'Um, yes. Thank you,' Connie murmured, as she was stretched out like a sacrifice on one of the divans.

The Russian masseuse was strong as well as big. Under her vigorous hands Connie's joints creaked and snapped and the women within earshot all laughed appreciatively. At the end, when her muscles were unknotted and her limbs felt like jelly, the woman scooped her up like a rag doll and cradled Connie's head against her immense bosom.

It was like being held by Mother Earth herself.

Fingers massaged Connie's scalp and her neck, even her ears, with as much love and tenderness as if she were a baby.

And without the slightest warning, without the accompaniment of pain in her chest or a clutch to her heart, Connie began to cry.

The tears poured out of her eyes. She wept like a baby in its mother's arms, hiding her face against the massive breasts as the woman hummed and crooned to her. She stroked Connie's hair and patted her hands, waiting until she was done with crying and began to regain possession of herself. When the flood finally stopped the woman dried her face for her, and gently set her upright once more.

'Oh dear. I am so sorry,' Connie gulped.

She pressed her hands to her eyes. The women in their turbans – daughters, sisters, mothers and grandmothers – were still drinking tea and playing with the babies.

Then she realised that she didn't feel sorry at all.

She felt light, and calm, and peaceful. A small, hard knob of anger that she had carried within her for too long had detached itself from the place beneath her breastbone, and it had floated clean away.

She wasn't going to know the woman who had given birth to her, and she would never learn why – in all the years since then – she hadn't tried to find her lost daughter.

She would have her reasons, whatever they were, whoever she was.

That was all there was to know. The difference was that now, among all these women in this strangest of places, Connie thought truthfully, for the first time, that she could forgive her.

The masseuse leaned forward and pointed with a sausage finger at Connie's marcasite droplet. She asked a question in Russian.

Roxana had retreated to have her eyebrows threaded, but now she came back.

'What's she saying?' Connie asked.

'She is worried that you have perhaps lost your ear-ring in here.'

'Tell her I only have one. My mother –' the word unfamiliar on her tongue, but also satisfying '– has always kept the pair to it.'

Roxana relayed the information. The masseuse was folding towels. Her huge arms swallowed up the pile.

'Mother. Very good,' she said in English, and beamed at Connie.

Outside the *hammam* it was stiflingly hot, and growing dark. They walked slowly, scuffing up the dust, and Connie's feet and head felt light with happiness.

'Where are we going?' she murmured to Roxana.

There was no one to be seen in the narrow streets of the old city, but from one window came the blare of a televised football game and from another a steamy waft of cooking. Doors stood ajar to admit the suggestion of a breeze, and from a third house came the sound of a baby crying.

Roxana hesitated. 'I am going home to Yakov, to take this shopping.' She held up her string bags. 'Maybe you would like to come with me?'

Connie interpreted that Roxana would like her to meet Yakov and see where she lived but wasn't sure what she would make of it.

Without placing undue emphasis she answered lightly, 'Yes, I'll come. I'd like to meet him.'

A sequence of alleys and squares guarded by closed mosques brought them into a slightly more modern quarter. They passed a butcher's shop with muslin-wrapped animal shanks hanging in the opening. The shop's sign was a stuffed cow's head, complete with horns and whiskered muzzle. The animal's sceptical glass eye followed Connie as she walked by. Next door was a cavern heaped with hundreds of onyx-green watermelons. Roxana stopped her march to buy one and drop it into another string bag. Connie offered to carry it for her, but Roxana wouldn't permit it.

They came to a brown door in a blank wall, as anonymous as each of its neighbours.

Roxana unlatched the door and they stepped over a wooden sill into a courtyard.

There was silence, broken by the scratch of music and a sudden flutter of wings. One entire wall of the courtyard was taken up by a cage full of green finches. Roxana put down her bags and called out, 'Yakov! We are here.'

She held aside a curtain of beads. Connie blinked in the light. The whole room was taken up with crowded bookshelves, and there were stacks and pyramids of books on the tiled floor and on the table in the centre.

In an armchair sat one of the fattest men she had ever seen. He had an oval, bald head, and a neck that seemed to slide downwards into unconfined billows of flesh. Even his feet in leather slippers were monstrously fat, and his bruise-purple ankles seemed as thick as a man's thigh. He looked up at them and shuffled his bulk to the edge of his seat.

'You are here, that's good. Please. Please come and be comfortable.'

'Yakov, this is my good friend Connie.'

Connie held out her hand and he grasped it. His skin was smooth and very soft, almost liquid, as if it was close to dissolving point.

Roxana was moving books and papers off a straight-backed sofa draped with worn throws. 'Sit here, Connie. Yakov, would you like *chai*? Some fruit? Connie and I were at the *hammam*.'

He nodded, and Roxana ducked out of the room.

'So,' Yakov breathed.

His glance was very sharp. He might have been immobilised by his bulk, but Connie did not think that he would miss very much. Her eyes slid over the books.

The titles were in English, Russian, Arabic, and other languages that she couldn't even identify.

Yakov said, 'You have been very kind to the child. I want to thank you.'

Connie smiled. 'I don't know about kind. I loved her company. You taught her to speak English, didn't you?'

He nodded. The small movement set up a ripple under his loose grey pyjama suit. There were dark rings under his arms and another patch over his chest. Connie speculated about the precise arrangement between Yakov and Roxana. He had been a friend of her mother's, maybe at one time her protector, and then he had extended that protection in some way to Roxana when Leonid, the stepfather, had mistreated her.

Whatever had happened, Roxana never spoke of such things. She just did what it was necessary for her to do, crimping the corners of her mouth and setting her shoulders with renewed determination.

'She was an apt pupil. I did not have to repeat myself very many times. What brings you to Bokhara, Connie?'

'I have been travelling, and when Roxana left London I promised I would visit her. Will her brother be released, do you think?'

'When you come to know this country, Connie, you will understand that that is a question that does not have a simple answer. It depends on many things.'

There was a clink of glass as Roxana nudged the beads aside and came in with a beaten-metal tray. She had taken off her shoes, and replaced them with leather slippers like Yakov's. The effect was to shorten her legs and broaden her hips, as if she was edging out of girlhood. She poured tea into three glasses and held out a dish of sliced watermelon. Yakov took a piece and gobbled it, catching the juice with his hand as it ran down his chin and then lick-ing each of his fingers. He belched loudly. Roxana glanced to see Connie's reaction as Yakov tossed the melon rind back into the dish.

'I am an old man,' he snapped, and crooked his finger to indicate that he wanted another piece. 'Now. We are talking about Niki.'

Niki was allowed one visit a month. It took a ten-hour bus journey to reach the prison where he was held, and the same for the return trip. Roxana had told Connie that in order to be nearer to him she could try to find work in Tashkent – 'like my friend Fatima' – but she had stayed here in Bokhara because she could live with Yakov without paying any rent, and thanks to her expe-rience in London she had been able to get a very good job at the old Intourist Hotel.

'The fact is, Connie, that Niki will not choose to say or do what will help himself,' Yakov added. 'So his release is not likely to come soon.'

Roxana jumped to her feet. She stood in front of Yakov, hands on her hips.

'Niki has a belief. *I* do not want him to change his belief or pretend that he does not have it, because then he will not any longer be Niki and he might as well have died in the square at Andijan with his friends.'

Yakov shrugged and wiped his mouth with the back of his hand.

He spoke quickly, dismissively, in Russian.

Roxana ran at him and drummed her fists on his chest and shoulders, shouting into his face. Moving with sur-prising speed Yakov caught her wrists and held her off to one side. Connie was going to intervene, but Yakov only laughed.

'You see, Roxana always has a temper.'

'When you are speaking about my *brother*, yes,' Roxana spat back at him. But she detached herself and flopped back into her chair. She said to Connie,

'Niki is a Muslim. He is gentle and his beliefs are peaceful but our government does not like independent practices, and religious men are called by this label of fundamentalists. This is what *Comrade* Yakov here is saying.'

Her face went tight and dark. 'I have seen what it is like for Niki and all religious prisoners. They try to make him renounce his faith, confess to terrorism, beg our President for forgiveness. Niki will not do it, and so he is beaten and put in punishment cells. But if he does confess, he will be sentenced for many years for crimes that are not his. There is no point, because now at least he is true to himself. He is a brave man. It is terrible, what happens, but I am so proud of him.'

'He is an idealist, and therefore a fool,' Yakov snapped.

Roxana rounded on him. 'And you? What are you? Who is proud of you, I might say?' She waved her hand. 'Look at all this, all that you have read and everything you know. But still you will say any lie, pretend anything people want to hear, just to be comfortable.'

'I am a realist. And therefore I am not only alive, but also a free man.'

Roxana's laugh was like a splash of acid. She waved her hand again, at the shuttered room and at Yakov's beached body.

'Free? You call this *freedom*?'

He slumped slightly, and then nodded as if to say *touché*.

'Two idealists, you and your brother.'

He turned his gaze to Connie. He held up a finger and pointed at her, then to the shuttered window. 'This is one of the first things you will learn about our precious Uzbekistan. Always, we will be caught between Marx and Mohammed. And me, I care little for either.'

Connie shivered, in spite of the heat. She was only glimpsing a corner of Roxana's world and a fragment of the history of this ancient oasis city, but she began to understand the obstacles her friend had negotiated in order to escape. That she had come back again for her family made her love Roxana and admire her even more.

Yakov was bored by the argument.

'Tell me now, is Roxana showing you the famous remains of Bokhara?'

'Yes, she is,' Connie said.

'Good. You will not want to miss anything. There are some fine sights in this city of ours.'

'I will show her. I am proud of Bokhara, even if am not proud of what our country has become.' Roxana was on her feet, gathering up melon rinds and the empty *chai* glasses.

'Ha.' Yakov laced his fingers over his belly. 'Now, please, let me have some peace.'

Roxana led the way out, and Connie hung back to say goodbye. Yakov pushed out his lower lip and studied her face for a moment.

'I have not given up hope for Niki, you know. There are ways, and there are some people who can help him,' he murmured. 'Roxana sees only one way. But she is young.'

'Is there anything I could do, perhaps?' Connie asked. He laughed at her naiveté.

'Thank you. But you do not know Uzbekistan. Enjoy your visit.' Then he raised his hand, dismissing her.

Connie followed Roxana up the shallow outside steps to the upper floor. There were herbs and scented plants in pots against the wall, and the caged finches fluttered between their perches.

Roxana's room was small and bare. Her work shoes were neatly placed against the wall, a rail across one corner held her clothes – including the Chloé jacket – on a few hangers. Two narrow windows looked out on starry sky and a series of flat roofs, and there were no pictures. Connie wished that she hadn't kept the beach postcard.

Roxana's face was more shadowed than it had been, and there were faint lines just beginning to show at the sides of her mouth. Her beauty was only increased by this intimation of maturity.

'Is it . . . comfortable, living here?' Connie asked her. She didn't mean in the physical sense, exactly.

'Yakov reads books, and listens to his music. I go to the market for food, and make some meals for him. It's not such a bad arrangement, you know. I have work, and I save a little money. I am only a bus journey from Niki. Yakov is . . . you saw, like he is. Not very similar to Mr Bunting, or any of your English men. But he is kind to me. In his way.' She lifted her chin and stared straight at Connie. 'I would not stay here if it did not suit me and Niki, as well as Yakov.'

'Good. Forgive me for asking, then.'

Roxana looked round the confined space. 'Do you remember, when we were in Suffolk?'

'Yes. I remember everything about it.'

'We talked, in that bedroom, in the storm. And now

it is the other way round for us, because your sister is dead and my brother is alive. That is very strange.'

'It is,' Connie agreed.

Roxana turned her head again, to look full at her. 'I would rather be in this country, and have my brother still alive and with some hope in the future, than be in England for ever without him. To be a sister comes from in here.'

Roxana pressed her fist against her breastbone.

Connie knew what it meant. 'Yes. Niki is lucky to have you for his sister.'

'Mrs Bunting was lucky to have you.'

Connie said quietly, 'Actually, I think it was the other way round.'

After a moment Roxana's face brightened again. 'At least I saw the sea. I am so pleased I saw the sea, even that I fell in it. And you saved me from drowning. You remember what you said afterwards, *You know that life is precious, if you can't bear to lose it?* It's true. That beach, those waves, that was amazing.'

Connie nodded, but she was wondering whether her own life meant so much, whether it meant anything at all, without Bill in it.

'You'll be able to come back to London some day,' she said. 'And you'll see plenty of other beaches. Maybe the very one on your postcard. We could plan to meet there.'

Roxana pursed her lips. 'Maybe. But I prefer Suffolk.'

They both laughed.

'It's late,' Roxana said. 'Come on, I'll walk you back to your hotel.'

'I think you'd better. I don't stand a chance of finding the place on my own.'

There was another session of sightseeing.

It was Roxana's half-day and following in her energetic wake Connie toured the Mosque of Forty Pillars, and the Chor Minor, a tiny architectural jewel of a *madrassah* with four towers topped with azure tiles. Roxana stood with her feet planted in the dust, gazing up at the intricate brick facade.

'You know, Connie, this place is the picture I saw inside my head when I was in England and I thought of home. And what is it? Just an old building. History is only what has gone, religion I don't care about, and still this is what appears to me. I don't see the places that are real Uzbekistan, the cement works or the bus station, or even the *hammam*. That's funny, isn't it?'

Connie leaned in the shade against a wall and fanned herself.

'It's very beautiful,' she said. Roxana's appreciation of it didn't surprise her at all. If only it wasn't so hot.

Roxana looked at her. 'You are tired,' she said.

'A little,' Connie admitted.

'Come. We will go and have a cold drink. There is a place near here.'

They were threading their way through the old centre when Samida and her cohorts dashed out in front of them.

'Hello, Connie from England. You look at my pottery now.'

It was not a question. Insistent fingers tugged at her clothes.

Roxana tried to dismiss the children with a few sharp words, but Connie looked down at the circle of narrow brown faces.

'Show me,' she said. At once she was propelled towards a cloth laid out in the shade of a wall.

'Don't buy these dishes. This is machine-made, just rubbish for tourists,' Roxana cried. But Connie filled a bag with painted earthenware plates and bargained energetically to reduce Samida's price.

The children giggled as they pocketed her money, and scampered off in search of the next target.

'Why did you buy these?' Roxana demanded. 'If you want dishes you should tell me, I will take you to the best place.'

Connie grinned at her dismay. 'I don't care about the plates, it was the children. They made me think of you when you were small.'

Roxana only glared. 'Of me? Let me tell you that compared to my friend Fatima and me, in our day, those children are *amateurs*.'

Laughing, they reached a low concrete cube of a building with faded awnings offering some shade from the sun.

'Here,' Roxana said. They passed inside to a line of metal-topped café tables beside a tall counter. Connie glanced to the back of the room and saw three computer terminals with keyboards cased in plastic to protect them from the all-pervading dust. 'Maybe I will check my mail while we are here,' Roxana casually added.

'This is the Bokhara internet café?'

'Why not?' Roxana countered. 'I used to go in London, when I lived there, to somewhere calling itself The Best Little Internet Café on the Planet, which is quite funny, but I think personally this place is better. Of course if I was lazy I could do the same thing at my work, but . . .' she glanced round at the bare walls, the dog panting on the threshold, the chest freezer humming and shuddering in the corner ' . . . from here for a few *som*, I am free to surf the net, to chat to Fatima and my other friends, whatever I wish.'

'Of course,' Connie agreed.

A boy of about ten brought their drinks and they settled at one of the terminals. Roxana peered and tapped at the plastic-shrouded keyboard.

'And here is an email, for example, from Noah. Hm. Hm. Would you like to read it, Connie?'

'Isn't it private?' Connie asked curiously.

'Not so much that you should not see it.'

Connie changed the angle of her chair so that she could see the screen more clearly. Roxana took a long gulp of her drink. Connie read,

Hi Roxy, how's it going?

I miss you, babe, same as always. Life still seems so quiet without you. I've been working hard – ☹ – no, it's okay really, just got a pay hike which helps.

Strange to think it's nearly a whole year since my mum died. I think of her every day, and sometimes I still go, 'must tell her about this or that', and then remember that I can't – but I don't have to tell you what that feels like, do I? But time is doing its thing. She was such a great mother and such a good person to know, and I feel lucky to have had all that.

Been spending quite a lot of time with my dad. He's pretty good, considering. Time's doing its thing for him as well. He's lonely, though. I asked him this weekend if he could imagine being with someone else some day and he gave a smile and said yes, he imagined it regularly.

Have you heard from Connie? I know Dad hasn't,

*and neither have I. Did anything come of that plan
for her to come and visit you?*

What's the latest news on Niki?

Connie read on down to the end of the message.
There was a PS.

*My sort-of ex Lauren is back in town. I had a cou-
ple of emails and texts from her, wanting to hook
up. I'm going to give her a call, Roxy, but just wanted you to know that if you were in London there'd
be no question, no contest. Nxxxxxx*

Then Connie looked at the date. The message was several days old. Of course Roxana had been intending all
along for her to read it.

Roxana got up and strolled to the entrance. She gazed
out into the baking street, standing half in and half out
of the doorway as if the rest of the world pulled at her
in one direction via the computer terminal, and Niki and
Bokhara and Uzbekistan pinned her in the other. Then
she looked back at the café interior, to where Connie
was still sitting, and gave her a brilliant smile of expectation and encouragement.

Connie's mind was spinning.

She had been running away: constructing defences
and then racing behind them whenever a breach was
threatened.

She had started to put up the barriers long ago, years
before she met Bill, even before the day of Tony's funeral
and Elaine's blurted truth, *he wasn't your dad . . . you're
adopted, aren't you?* That had only been putting into

words what troubled her already and the trouble had started before she could even articulate the word *different*.

Connie thought, I rejected *them*, Hilda and Jeanette, just as much as the other way round.

That one word – adopted – and all the longing, and mystery, and opportunities for disappointment and betrayal that crowded with it, had always stood between them.

What chance did we have, in the face of that? she asked herself.

As the realisation dawned on her, she braced herself for the sadness and regret that might have followed it.

But all that happened was the joy and lightness that had been with her since the *hammam* lifted her to her feet. She floated to the door where Roxana was waiting for her.

'Thank you for letting me see Noah's email. You wanted me to read about his dad being lonely and the implication that I could change that, didn't you?'

'I am not so cut off from my friends that I cannot help out here and there, you see.'

Connie touched her hand. 'What about you and Noah? And Lauren?'

Roxana sighed. 'I am jealous, of course. But I am Niki's sister first and always, before I can be girlfriend to an English boy. And I don't want Noah to be waiting for me for ever. Nobody waits for ever, do they?'

A lick of a breeze chased down the street, raising plumes of dust and stirring the coarse hair on the dog's back.

'No, they don't,' Connie agreed.

Roxana said softly, 'Do you want to know what I think?'

'Go on.'

'I think you should go back to England. I think you should go to see Mr Bunting, and tell him that you love him.'

'Do you? Why?'

'Because it is the *truth*.'

Roxana's smile flashed at her. She made a loose fist and tapped at the air six inches from Connie's shoulder.

'Knock, knock. Open the door in this wall, Connie. Walls keep out bad things, yes, but they trap you inside in the dark.'

Slowly, Connie raised her hands, palms outstretched. She pushed outwards until her arms were fully extended, and there was nothing to block her way. There was nothing but the air and the light on the old walls.

By the time Connie reached England, it was almost summer again.

The trees in the parks were in leaf and at lunchtimes girls with bare arms poured into the streets. From her apartment, which seemed empty without Roxana, she telephoned Bill.

'It's Connie,' she said.

'Connie. Are you in London?'

Bill's warm voice was very close, as if it came from somewhere within her own head.

'Yes. How are you? You sound different.'

There was a silence while they listened to each other.

'It's you who sounds different,' he said at length.

Connie took a breath. 'I've been bouncing round the world like a ping-pong ball. I want to stop now.'

'That's good.'

'Can I see you? I want to so much, but maybe it's too early, or you may feel that it wouldn't be right?'

'I want to see you too,' Bill answered. 'Just lately, it seems that you're in my head more than ever. I wasn't even surprised to hear your voice just now.'

Connie looked out at the cranes angled over the city's building sites. Skeletons of towers had risen in her absence.

'Shall I come up to London?' Bill asked.

Connie thought quickly. London's streets were mapped out by the past. Nowhere came to mind that was not touched in some way either by the years of being painfully apart from him, or by the snatched intervals of their love affair.

'No, not London,' she said hastily. 'Somewhere else.'

She didn't know what was going to happen next, and she was so used to defending herself that this degree of exposure left her feeling like a vertigo sufferer on the lip of a precipice. All she did know was that whatever was to be written, she wanted this new chapter to begin on a fresh page – not in London, or Surrey, or even in Bali.

'Where?'

She knew why he sounded different. The ripple in his voice that had faded years ago was there again.

'I know. Let's go to the seaside.' The wind and the tides would do their scouring work.

'That's a good idea. Do you want to go a long way from home? Abroad?'

'No more planes and airports. Let's go to . . . Devon.'

Connie couldn't recall ever having been there. They would have to take the opposite direction out of London, away from the route they had followed on the day of the picnic and the way she had taken Roxana on their trip to the sea. And an English shingle beach with mild, greyish breakers would be far enough removed from the last beach they had visited, back in Bali.

'Devon?'

Bill was laughing openly now. But he understood what she was thinking, and he entered into the idea with her. There would be an unmarked page for both of them, without even a shared journey to preface it. 'I will meet you in Devon in . . . let's see. Forty-eight hours from now. Look at your watch. It's three o'clock. Take your mobile with you. I'll call you at eleven a.m. the day after tomorrow, and tell you where.'

Connie laughed too, although her heart was thumping.

'Forty-eight hours,' she repeated.

The spell of early summer fine weather continued. In the morning sunshine before she set out to meet Bill, Connie put on a bright red cotton dress and stared at herself in the mirror. There were deep lines bracketing her mouth and at the corners of her eyes, but at the same time she felt stripped of all the armour of experience, as if inside her skin she was sixteen again.

She drove out of London and at eleven a.m. precisely, her mobile rang. His voice in her ear stilled the roar of motorway traffic.

'Where are you now?'

'I am at the service station just before the M5 junction.'

He gave her the exact details of where he was waiting.

'I'll be there,' she promised. She drove carefully, like the mature woman she was, but at the same time she was thinking that this was the most erotically charged moment of her life.

It was a weekday, but the car park of the little seaside town was almost full. As Connie searched for a space, men with bare, sun-reddened chests padded towards the sea front laden with body boards and heavy cold-boxes, and children chased between the cars. It was a few minutes before three o'clock. She parked at the end of a row and sat with her hands still resting on the steering wheel. The hot smell of the car merged with salt and sun-cream and frying fish, and a pair of kites tugged towards freedom in the blue space between earth and sea. All her senses were sharpened.

I am alive.

A swell of amazed gratitude and happiness lifted her.

Before she went to meet Bill, there was one more conversation she must have.

I am alive, she repeated. *And I wish you were alive and here with me. With us. I miss you, Jeanette, every day.*

Connie let her hands slip into her lap.

Afterwards was now.

She loved Bill and had always loved him, and whereas that had once been wrong she didn't believe it was wrong any longer.

I love you just as much, she added to Jeanette. *Forgive me now, if there is anything still to forgive.*

A man carrying a deckchair glanced through the windscreen at the woman talking to herself in her car. It was two minutes to three.

Connie walked across the road to the sea front. Outlined against the glitter of the water a man was standing against the railings with his back turned, his arms spread and his hands resting on the top rail. He was the only person in the world.

She ran forwards and put her hands over his, fitting her body against him.

They hung there for a moment, their faces hidden from each other, waiting for the future.

Then Bill spun round and caught her face between his hands. He kissed her, blotting out the sun-dazzle and the twirling kites. Without lifting his mouth from hers he murmured, 'It felt like making an assignation with a stranger. Driving down here, waiting for you to arrive. It was extremely exciting.'

'I know. I felt that too.'

'But now I see you and touch you, you're the opposite of a stranger. You fit me, Connie.' His voice was very low. As he had done many times before, he drew her closer to him so that her head rested at the angle of his jaw. She let herself melt against him and the easiness of it surprised her. There had always been a thin layer separating them, she realised now. It had been her own guilt interleaved with his, and her old, wary defensiveness. The barriers felt stale and constricting and she wriggled to free herself like a snake shedding its skin. His body felt very warm and solid.

'Is it less exciting, me turning out not to be a stranger?'

'No,' he said roughly. 'I want you to know straight away that I have booked a room. I want you to come back there with me. Will you do that?'

'I will,' she said.

Her composure suddenly struck both of them as funny. They laughed, and a teenaged couple glanced back at them as if they were wondering what two middle-aged people could find so comical.

They linked hands and began to walk along the sea front. A wall projected out into the waves, enclosing a little harbour where fishing boats and sailing dinghies were moored.

'How have you been, Bill?'

He said, 'Grief is a strange commodity, don't you think? I thought it was something you dealt with. I thought you either coped well or not, depending on who you were and the particular circumstances, but that you handled it in some way. But I have found that it doesn't make much difference what you do. You can go out and be with friends or strangers, or you can go to a film or look at art. You can stay in with a book or a bottle of whisky, or just yourself and silence. You can square up to it, saying, "Come on, wash right over me, do your worst because I'm ready for you." Or you can try to ignore it. Whatever you do doesn't matter, because grief is still just *there*. What happens, of course, is that as time passes the presence becomes less constant. Now I can see how its absence begins to take shape.' He looked down at her, his mouth curling in the way it always did. 'That's how I've been. What about you?'

Connie nodded. 'Similar, only I didn't handle it as well as you. I miss her so much, so I tried to escape the loss by running away. True to form, you might say. It wasn't until Roxana took me to the *hammam* in Bokhara that I broke up and cried properly, from right inside myself.'

Bill gazed at her. 'Noah's Roxana, is that? *Bokhara?*'

'I have been bouncing around the world . . .'

'Are you ready to stop now, or are you still my wild, wandering girl?'

'I am ready to stop,' Connie said soberly. 'I've been thinking a lot. About Jeanette and me when we were girls, about Echo Street, and when Noah was born and when Hilda died. All those years.' With the hand that wasn't linked in Bill's she lightly touched the silk pouch that still hung at her throat. 'And I have been making peace, with Jeanette and my real mother and with myself.'

They were walking out along the harbour wall now, where waves slapped against slippery stone steps. They reached a line of bollards at the far end, and a stone bench set into an angle of the wall that reminded Connie of her perch in the *hammam* with Roxana. They sat down and Bill's arm circled her shoulders while they watched the strutting gulls at their feet and the kite-fly-ers out on the beach. Connie told him about Roxana and the email from Noah, and Roxana's words of advice.

'And what exactly was her advice?' Bill murmured.

Connie turned to face him. 'She said that I should come back to England, see Mr Bunting, and tell him that I love him.'

'I see. You know what? Despite what I know about Roxana, I'd say that was very, *very* sound advice.'

Their mouths were almost touching now.

'Yes,' Connie agreed. 'And so I am acting on it.'

Arm in arm, as if they had been together for ever, they retraced their steps along the harbour wall. The wind had strengthened and the rigging of the dinghies tapped out a metallic rhythm. There were families picnicking on the shingle, light glinting off the cars crawling along the sea-front road, the distant tinkle of music from a child's fair-ground ride. To both of them, the world looked new and fresh and completely enticing.

Bill said suddenly, 'I'd like an ice cream, wouldn't you?'